continued ...

Magic at the Gate

"The action-packed fifth Allie Beckstrom novel amps up the magical mayhem. . . . Allie's adventures are gripping and engrossing, with an even, clever mix of humor, love, and brutality."
— *Publishers Weekly*

"Devon Monk takes her story to places I couldn't have dreamed of. Each twist and turn was completely surprising for me. *Magic at the Gate* truly stands out."
— Reading on the Dark Side

"A spellbinding story that will keep readers on the edge of their seats." — Romance Reviews Today

"Suspense is the name of the game. . . . I'm really enjoying this series. . . . Each book brings you a little bit further in to it and leaves you wanting more." — Night Owl Reviews

Magic on the Storm

"The latest Allie Beckstrom urban fantasy is a terrific entry. . . . This is a strong tale." — Genre Go Round Reviews

"First-rate urban fantasy entertainment." — Lurv a la Mode

Magic in the Shadows

"Snappy dialogue, a brisk pace, and plenty of magic keep the pages turning to the end. . . . This gritty, original urban fantasy packs a punch." — Monsters and Critics

"This is a wonderful read full of different types of magic, fascinating characters, an intriguing plot. . . . Devon Monk is an excellent storyteller." — Fresh Fiction

"Monk sweeps readers up in the drama and dangers of the heroine's life as it steadily changes and grows . . . an intriguing read with fascinating characters and new magical elements introduced to the mix." — Darque Reviews

"The writing moves at a fast pace with plenty of exciting action. . . . This series just gets better and better with each new book." — Night Owl Reviews

HELL BENT

A BROKEN MAGIC NOVEL

Devon Monk

A ROC BOOK

ROC
Published by the Penguin Group
Penguin Group (USA) LLC, 375 Hudson Street,
New York, New York 10014

USA | Canada | UK | Ireland | Australia | New Zealand | India | South Africa | China
penguin.com
A Penguin Random House Company

First published by Roc, an imprint of New American Library,
a division of Penguin Group (USA) LLC

First Printing, November 2013

ROC REGISTERED TRADEMARK—MARCA REGISTRADA

ISBN 978-0-451-41792-3

Printed in the United States of America
10 9 8 7 6 5 4 3 2 1

For my family

ACKNOWLEDGMENTS

This book might never have seen the light of day if readers hadn't asked me to share Shame and Terric's story with them. Yes, I'm looking at you, John DeBudge. Thank you all for wanting to spend a little more time with these troublemakers.

Deepest thanks also to my agent, Miriam Kriss, and my editor, Anne Sowards, who has an amazing knack for making each book better. A huge thank-you also to the wonderful artist, Mike Heath, and to the many people within Penguin who have gone above and beyond to make this baby shine.

To my first readers extraordinaire, Dean Woods and Dejsha Knight: your unflagging enthusiasm, support, and red-eye reads are things of legend. Thank you. I could not have done this without you. A big, big thanks to my family, one and all, for being there for me, offering encouragement, and sharing in the joy. To my husband, Russ, and sons, Kameron and Konner: thanks for all your love and support. You are the very best part of my life and I love you.

So here we are, dear readers. Thank you for the chance to share these people, this world, and this journey with you.

Chapter 1

I'm the kind of guy who, given the chance, can break anything: hearts, dreams, lives, and yes, magic. Death magic user here. Everything I touch dies.

It's not as much fun as it sounds.

Ever since the magical apocalypse that those of us in the great city of Portland, Oregon, like to call "just another Thursday" slapped the crap out of our city and made balloon animals out of the rules of magic, my life has gone from handbasket to hell.

And today wasn't looking up.

"Don't make me throw water over your head, Shamus Flynn," Terric Conley said from where he'd settled down on the crappy chair next to my bed.

I don't like Terric. This is a problem because Terric and I not only have to work the same damn office job together, but are also tied by the only magic I can't break.

Ironic, right?

About an hour ago, I'd stumbled into my room here at my mum's inn and managed to unbutton my pants and belt and throw my jacket somewhere on the floor. From the sweaty weight on my feet, I hadn't gotten my boots off yet.

About fifteen minutes ago Terric had shown up, cheerfully yelling over the top of my hangover and pulling back curtains to let the light in.

Daylight, for shit's sake.

"Get out of my room," I mumbled into the pillow on top of my face.

"It's Wednesday."

"Fuck-de-doo."

"You said you'd come to work today, Shame. The meeting's today. No option. Not this time."

"No option?" I pushed the pillow off my face. Oh God, the light. It was blinding, even through my eyelids. "I'm the boss—remember, mate? I work when I say I work."

"No, *we* are the boss. We, Shame, not you. Not you alone. Which is good because you haven't worked for a year and a half."

Gut punch. Not that he was wrong. I'd put in a solid year of civic-mindedness before deciding I am not a people person and am more suited for darkness, destruction, and the slow madness of trying not to give a damn.

Plus, there was the whole death-touch thing, the constant hunger to kill, to consume, that made me count the pulse beat of every living thing around me. After a year, that had gotten so bad I salivated whenever I was in a closed room with people, plants, or combustibles.

I needed life. Needed to drink it down, lap it up. Food helped, so did smoking, drinking, and other unsavory recreations. But none of it pushed the hunger away for long. I needed life, to consume it, burn it out, extinguish it.

Grim-damn-Reaper style.

So of course someone thought it would be funny to put me in charge of a city full of angry magic users. A desk job, people. Customer service. Paperwork and complaints about every magical glitch that happened in the entire damn city.

A lot of people were alive right now because I'd had the brains to stop punching the time clock. Not that I'd told Terric about it. Not that I had to. He knew me better than almost anyone. That came from half our lives spent together growing up in the Authority, which used to be the, well, authority on magic, chasing down illegal magic and deadly creatures like it was all one big game.

Until I almost killed him. And he repaid the favor.

We have what is known as a difficult relationship.

"Shame." This time he shook the bed with his foot.

"Have I said fuck off yet?"

"I'll drag you out of here."

I huffed out a laugh. Terric had spent the better part of a year going out of his way to keep his hands to himself. Well, to himself and his boyfriend of the month.

"I'd like to see you tr—"

Terric was up out of that chair, his hands around my ankles so quick I didn't even hear him move. He yanked on my boots and dragged me half down my bed before I could finish insulting him.

Eyes snapped open: Jesus, the light! Every damn window poured full-watt sunlight into the room. It was daymageddon in here.

I glared up at him.

Terric was nearly my opposite. I had dark hair, eyes that were sometimes black and sometimes dark green, rarely bothered to shave, and lately, I'd been running a good twenty pounds under my fighting weight.

Terric was taller than me, which I hated, and built like a guy who might need to jump on a jet and hit the catwalk at any moment. His hair was white-silver even though he was on one side or the other of thirty and his eyes were blue and set in a face that could knock Hollywood's leading man off the marquee. We used to be best friends before I'd almost destroyed his ability to use magic.

After that he'd moved to Seattle and become a graphic designer and gay, although he insisted he'd actually always been into both those things, I just never noticed.

"Shame," he said, almost gently. His hands were at his sides, fingers stretched out wide as if he'd just touched something filthy. "You can't keep doing this. Not this way."

"What? Get some sleep? No, apparently I can't. Because you won't leave me the hell alone."

I knew what he really meant. With that one small contact, he'd realized I was starving for life. The Death magic inside me demanded to be fed life. Any life. Mine, if there was nothing else to devour. It grew stronger, more uncontrolled, the more I denied it.

I hadn't killed anyone for more than a year, and that had been an accident—I'd passed out in an alley and woken up next to a dead bum. I hadn't destroyed, drained, demolished a living thing since. Sure, I consumed. Some. A little. Enough. Just enough. Maybe a plant withered and died, maybe a bird fell out of the sky. But not as much life as I wanted. Not what death craved.

I'd always wanted to be a superhero, well, maybe a superneutral. But Reaperman? No.

It was a fucked-up and damn slow death, staying as far away from the living world as I could. To starve myself and offer up my life to the Death inside me. But it was my death, not someone else's. And it was under my control.

Terric opened his mouth, then shut it on whatever lecture he'd been about to launch into. He tipped his head and there was, briefly, sorrow and desperation in his eyes that made my heart stop beating.

I hated when he looked at me like that. I hated that I could make him look like that.

Even though I don't like Terric, it's not because *he's* a bad man. Quite the opposite: I am.

"Why don't you take a shower?" Terric said in that calm and easy tone he always used when he didn't want to let on how he was really feeling. "We have time."

"You're not my boss." I shoved up on my feet. "Not even my friend."

"I'm not leaving."

"Then close the blinds." I crossed the floor to the bathroom and shut the door behind me. "And don't touch my stuff."

I stripped, pissed, then got in the shower. Turned the water on as hot as my skin could stand it. I let it pound down over my back while I washed my hair. The inside of my mouth tasted like gutter runoff, so I stepped out of the shower and dripped on the floor while I grabbed my toothbrush and toothpaste.

Took those with me into the shower and scrubbed until I could feel my teeth. Then I applied soap and a washrag. Got that done, got out, even though both me and my headache wanted to linger awhile.

I didn't bother to shave.

Took all of three minutes from start to finish; then I wrapped a towel around my hips and barefooted it to the bedroom.

Terric was standing there, a mug from the restaurant downstairs in one hand. "Coffee."

"Apology coffee?" I asked as I stepped over a week's worth of dirty clothes on the way to my dresser.

"No, just coffee."

I pulled on boxers, blue jeans, black T-shirt. Then I added a black sweater and dug for socks of similar color.

"Have you eaten at all this week?" Terric asked. I could practically feel his gaze scraping over my ribs, spine, and shoulder blades.

"Yes. Also? None of your business."

There were four heavy rings on my dresser. Made of metal and Void stones, they looked like brushed steel with stones inset in their flat, square surfaces. I slipped them on each finger of my right hand, the red stone, the black stone, the amber, and the white, and shivered at the slight ease from the push of Death magic they gave me.

I curled my fingers into a fist, the rings lining up like brass knuckles.

"How about you drink this?" Terric said.

I turned. He held the coffee out.

"Why? Did you poison it?"

That, finally, got a dazzler of a smile out of him. Yep. Leading man material. "And ruin a good dark roast? Please."

I took the cup, which meant he and I were standing pretty close together. I could feel the Life magic coiled around him like a second skin. Just as Death magic had changed me, Life magic had changed him. He carried it inside his body, just like I carried Death. This close, I could feel Life magic reaching out to me like a cool breeze. It made my mouth water.

I took the cup. We both ignored how bad my hand was shaking.

"We could solve this," Terric said. "Use magic together, you and I. Cast a spell. Life, Shame."

"No."

"I don't understand why you won't." He lifted a hand but didn't touch me. "I've respected that you want space and time. An entire year and a half. We're still Soul Complements. We can use magic like no one else, break it so that it's just as strong as it used to be. Why fight that?"

He was right about magic. It didn't have the delightfully dangerous "use it hard and it will use you back harder" kick like the days before the apocalypse. We'd forced dark and light magic to join and mingle together, diluting the strength of both. Magic had gone soft. Limp. Light spells were a dim glow, Illusions were thin as glass, and a knock-you-senseless Impact spell was no worse than a polite pat. The price to pay for those spells had lessened too. No more weeks of pain and agony in exchange for powerful spells. The best you could hope for was a barely discernible spell that might give you a case of gas.

And while I found it hilarious that people who used to do very bad things with magic were now raging to find the magical equivalent to Viagra, I was simultaneously just a little terrified about what magic could do in my hands.

Well, in my hands and Terric's hands. Magic might be

neutered, or "healed" as Terric likes to remind me, for other magic users . . . but not for us. Soul Complements, or Breakers, as some people like to call us, could make magic do all those powerful things.

As long as we used it together.

I could have told him all that. But he had heard it before. He knew why I didn't want to cast magic with him.

I took a drink of the coffee. Whatever snappy comeback I was working out died on my lips at about the same moment the coffee came alive on my taste buds. I didn't care that it was hot enough to scorch. I gulped it down all in one go.

"You know you need it," Terric said. "Need me. Need Life magic. Just like that coffee."

I tipped the cup down. Was going to ask what the hell he was talking about. But then I got it. He'd put something, a spell of some kind, in the coffee.

"You spiked my coffee."

"I spelled your coffee."

"With what?"

"Health. A little Life will do you good, Shame. Nothing you say will change my opinion on that."

I dragged my tongue over the roof of my mouth a couple times. "Gritty." Truth was, I felt a hell of a lot better. Sure, I was still hungry, sure, I was still hungover, but at least there was something—coffee and magic—in my belly. Something to stave off the death growing in me.

I hated to admit that Terric could do something to make my hunger and need go away.

Because every time he cast magic with me, every time I admitted I needed him, magic tied us closer together. I'd watched it happen with other people like us, other Soul Complements.

I knew what my future held. Either I would become a killing monstrosity like Jingo Jingo and other Death magic users before me, or I would die, consumed by my own hunger. Since the whole monstrosity thing was just too cliché and would make my mum cry, I'd made my choice.

There was no need to drag Terric down with me.

"There's a meeting today?" I asked.

He nodded slowly. "The Overseer called. He's flying into Portland. Says it's urgent?"

"I knew this?" I kicked pants, shirts, and half a dozen random cheeseburger wrappers out of the way, looking for my shoes. My room was a mess of clothes and broken things—a pile of burnt matches on the dresser, the phone book I'd compulsively shredded page by page for six hours straight that overflowed the wastebasket, and six dead potted plants that had been alive the day before yesterday.

I could draw life out of almost anything. And I did. The furniture in my room wasn't antique; it had gone frail beneath the incessant picking of Death magic. My jeans weren't faded and shredded at the edges for fashion's sake.

"Yes," I realized Terric was saying, "I told you on the phone yesterday. I told you at the bar the day before. And I told you by e-mail the day before that. You're not listening to me, are you?"

"What?"

He sighed. "Your boots are in the bathroom."

"Right." I pulled my coat off the bottom of the bed and shrugged into it. "Where's the meeting?"

"St. Johns."

"Again?"

I walked into the bathroom and sat on the edge of the bathtub to tie my boots. Ever since the four wells of magic under Portland had turned out to be five—the hidden fifth well crystallized beneath St. Johns—a lot of magic users saw it as some kind of sacred ground. Neutral territory, peaceful land of blessed magic users mumbo-in-the-jumbo.

Not that magic users had much in the way of fighting one another anymore, other than traditional guns and violence. Which, sure, could be handy, but lacked the particularly satisfying backstab–double-cross–kill-you-dead-without-anyone-knowing that magic used to offer.

Since healing magic had included restoring people's memories that those of us in the magic-oversight business had worked hard to take away, well, both the government and law enforcement agencies and the magic-ruling Authority were pretty twitchy about the role magic played on all levels now.

Or at least that's how it had been the last time I was paying attention a year ago.

". . . be there," Terric was saying. "Are you listening?"

"Yes," I lied. I walked out of the bathroom.

Terric lounged by the front door, staring at his nails. "Liar."

I grinned. "Only when I'm conscious. Ready?"

"Waiting on you."

But I wasn't talking to Terric. I was talking to the ghost who was hovering near my half-filled bookshelf.

Eleanor Roth. She had long light hair, an athletic twentysomething body, and a smile that transformed her from pretty to pretty please. She had wanted to date me once.

But now she was a ghost, tied to me and the magic I wielded. She was a constant reminder of what happens when I lose control over the Death magic inside me. I had consumed her. Put my hands on her and drunk her down.

I'd taken her life, but somehow she hadn't quite gotten death out of it either.

Like I said, I can break anything.

And I regretted what I did to her more than anyone would know.

She pointed to a book on the shelf. I strode over, pulled it out, glanced at the front cover. *The Eyre Affair* by Jasper Fforde. It was probably a gift from my mum. I didn't remember reading it.

"I don't think you'll need reading material at the meeting," Terric said. "It won't be that boring."

He couldn't see Eleanor. Not without working magic specifically to look for her. I made it a point not to mention her. Ever.

Over the last three years of being haunted, I'd found out Eleanor liked to read. So I helped out with that, tried to get to the bookstore once a month so she could pick out new books, turned the pages so she could read.

It was the least I could do for what I'd done to her.

I pocketed the book. Eleanor smiled and floated along beside me.

"Everything about this job bores me," I said to Terric.

He just shook his head. He didn't believe me.

Who could blame him?

Chapter 2

Terric did the driving. I did what I did best: nothing. Just slouched in the front seat, eyes closed behind dark sunglasses, coat collar flipped up to my cheekbones, head pounding. It took a lot to get me drunk, double that to push me into hangover land. Three days and nights in a bar just about did it every time.

Except I usually got a day or so of sleep afterward. The half hour of shut-eye I'd managed only sharpened my headache.

"Shit," Terric said, slowing the car. "That's Hamilton. Stay here. I'll be right back." He parked the car, opened the door, and was out of it in the same amount of time it took me to open my eyes.

Narrow street, old warehouses, MLK Boulevard. Whatever, whoever Hamilton was, it must be serious. Not only was Terric running down the street all long-legged and action-heroed, but he had also double-parked on the wrong side of the street.

I thought about calling the cops to ticket him for it. Imagined how angry he would be. Smiled. Closed my eyes again.

Eleanor poked me in the shoulder.

Thing about ghosts—they are dead cold. And stubborn. She poked my arm a second time, gentle as a dull ice pick chipping at my bones.

"What?" I said. "He's fine."

Poke.

Opened my eyes. Again. "I am not running out there after him."

She pointed at my heart.

"Nothing there, love," I said. "Empty as a shadow."

A man slipped out one of the warehouse doors and walked quickly in the opposite direction that Terric had gone. He looked over his shoulder, then caught sight of me sitting in the car. Light hair cut short and clean, thin, tanned face with eyes set just too wide on either side of his nose. He wore black boots, dark jeans, and a button-down short-sleeve shirt he'd rolled the sleeves up on to show the tattoo of a stylized black feather.

He pulled one hand up, stuck his finger at me, thumb cocked like a gun. Even from this distance I could read his lips as he jerked his hand in a shooting motion: "dead."

There was no spell attached to that action, and I'd never seen this joker before in my life. I flipped him off and mouthed, *Bite me.*

He scowled and moved off at a jog. Sure was in a hurry to be somewhere.

Then the back-of-the-head slap of magic being used, bent, and manhandled hit me hard enough I hissed. Terric was casting magic. More than that, Terric was trying to break magic.

Without me.

"Balls. What does he think he's doing?"

Eleanor poked right in the middle of my forehead this time, the pain and cold of her finger mixing with all the rest of the hurt in me.

"Damn it, woman, stop touching me."

She held up a finger and aimed it at my eye.

"Fine!" I shoved the door open and groaned. It was too damn sunny, too damn cold, and too damn early for me to be walking this damn street to save Terric's damn magic-wielding skin.

New plan: find Terric, knock him out, no magic required. Then drive back to my room where I could sleep off the knife-wielding banshees screaming in my head.

I stormed down the street clenching and unclenching my fists, the rings scraping between my fingers. I hoped to hell there was going to be someone I could punch at the end of this.

Unfortunately, someone else had the same idea.

Just as I reached the corner of the alley, I saw a guy move out of the shadow. I ducked the fist aimed at my face. Took a shot at the guy's ribs. Since the man was built like an ox, the only bones that cracked were my knuckles.

"Bloody hell!"

"Don't kill him, Shame," Terric said from somewhere farther down the alley where he was, apparently, holding his own against three guys.

"If I'd wanted him dead . . ." I jumped back out of the man's reach. "I'd have already . . ." The heel of my boot hit something slick.

Fuck.

I went down hard, knocking the back of my head against the moss-covered brick wall.

I'll take "concussion" for four hundred, Alex.

While I reacquainted myself with the inside of my eyelids, Terric got busy with the swearwords he saved for injuries, breakups, and soccer—excuse me—*football*. Since I didn't hear any vuvuzelas, I didn't know why he was cussing.

Sure, Terric was my partner—work, not bed—but half the time I had no idea what was going on in that head of his.

I opened my eyes just in time to see the ox swing a steel-toed boot the size of a Hummer at my gut. I rolled.

Not fast enough.

The boot clipped me in the low back. White, ragged pain shot down my butt and leg. It didn't do a damn thing to improve my mood.

It did, however, shake loose my hunger.

Hunger to kill. Hunger to consume.

Death magic is never more than a thought away for me. I've been told that I look like the Grim Reaper himself when I spend too much time away from Terric, who has the same screwed-up overpowerful thing going with Life magic and therefore sort of cancels my Death magic thing. Yes, it's more involved than that. No, I don't like to go into the details.

But my point: Grim Reaper—with a hangover.

Bad news for the bastard beating me up.

"Changed my mind about the whole not-killing thing," I said. "Too bad for you, mate."

"Shame," Terric warned. I heard footsteps running away. Was he letting those men go?

Didn't have time to look.

I flicked my fingers, rings sparking as I carved a glyph in the air between me and the ox. Binding spell, not death. I wanted him to hurt before I snapped his neck.

The Binding, a net of black and silver magic sharp as razor blades, lashed out to hover in the air in front of me.

Magic might be kinder and gentler for most people. But it wasn't kinder or gentler for me. Nor was it was invisible.

The ox held up his hands, maybe to cast a Block spell or maybe just surprised to see such a huge, violent spell snarling inches in front of his flattened nose.

Only a handful of people can temporarily break magic into light and dark. Like splitting an atom, when you break magic, it is a power untamed. The only Breakers I knew of were Soul Complements, and there weren't many in the world.

You want to know how I know God has a twisted sense of humor? I'm one of the people who can break magic. Power at the snap of my fingers. Well, if Terric and I snap our fingers at the same time.

Casting magic on my own delivered a harder hit than a non-Breaker could ever hope for. After all, Death magic coiled inside me and raged through any spell I cast.

But casting magic didn't come without a bit of a price to

pay. That headache of mine was ramping up to ride me for a day at least.

"Shamus Flynn, do not. Do. Not," Terric was saying.

Another price I paid for casting magic? Terric's nagging.

"Bind," I said, using that word to push the spell at the ox. The spell wrapped him from knee to throat and squeezed tight, dipping razor tips into his skin just deep enough to draw blood.

The ox yelled.

Now for a little Shamus happy fun time.

"This is how it's going to work, my friend." I braced my hand on the wall and tested my vertical capabilities. Knees held, back straightened, world steady as a drunken hobo.

I hurt from the kick, concussion, whiskey overdose, and magic price. But more than that, the fingers-down-the-pants *need* to consume the man's life and every living thing around me set my heart kicking it junkie-style.

I wanted life. I wanted to drink it down and lap out the bottom of the bottle.

The moss under my fingertips was wet, spongy, and very, very alive. A tip-of-the-tongue honey-sweet burn of life filled my mouth as the moss turned brown and died. Consumed. Dead.

And I was just getting started.

I glanced over at Eleanor, who stood at the opening of the alley. She looked afraid.

"If you touch him." Terric strode my way, his pace hampered by a slight limp. "I will kick your scrawny Irish ass. And then I will tell your mother what you did."

"You're going to tell on me to my mum? What are you, six?"

That got half a smile out of him. But it did not soften the look in his eyes. The one that said Shame's happy fun time was over.

"I called Detective Stotts." Terric held up his phone like I'd be impressed he had a cop on speed dial.

"Why Stotts?" Hungry now. Done talking now. Not paying attention.

"Because the police handle murder cases. We just handle magic users."

"Paperwork. All we handle is paperwork."

"*You* don't even do that. Why did you follow me? I told you to stay in the car. Do you enjoy getting the crap beat out of you? Don't you know how dangerous . . ."

That's when I completely tuned him out because I'd heard this lecture so many times I could sing along without the bouncing ball.

Also, the need for life and the consuming of it wasn't getting any less. The ox was still standing there, wrapped in that Binding spell I'd cast. Hurting. Ripe. Alive.

Bleeding.

Since he liked to beat up perfect strangers in dirty alleys, I presumed he was not a nice person. Therefore I would feel less horrible about killing him.

". . . just deal, you idiot." Terric slammed his hand into the middle of my chest. Hard enough both my shoulders hit the bricks behind me.

I blinked, swallowed. Focused on him.

"So, Terric," I said. "When I'm breaking your fingers do you want me to start or finish with your thumbs?"

Terric completely tuned me out and was whispering to himself. So rude.

That's when I noticed he'd pulled off his Void stone necklace and dropped it somewhere at our feet where it would do exactly zip to dampen the magic coursing through him.

Life magic.

"No," I said. "Not happening. Not here. I told you to keep your hands off—"

Terric called on Life magic.

Here's what happens when he does that—he goes all white-light angelic looking, which the chicks, and I guess some of the dudes, really like. Then the magic inside him devours his humanity. His eyes go silver, no pupils, no white. Any shred of heart, soul, or mind of that man is wiped away. Replaced with a cold, alien thing that looks out from behind his eyes. Life magic. It was not human. It was not Terric.

And one of these days when he called on it, Life magic was going to take over for good and Terric wasn't going to come back to being Terric.

Every time he lost control of Life magic, it changed him. Sure, it had been subtle for the first year or so. How he'd forget to laugh or to carry on a conversation without long pauses. How he'd stare out a window and whisper to himself for hours and not remember doing it.

Each time he used Life magic, it took him a little longer to come back to being the Terric I knew and sometimes, such as around repentance holidays, liked.

He'd told me I was just making shit up about him going inhuman.

He was right to think so. I made shit up all the time. But not that shit.

Terric, who still looked mostly human, drew a glyph with his free hand, tracing white magic that glowed green at the edges into the air.

Something brushed my boot.

Plants sprang to life. Vines and flowers and those tropical leafy things that always look plastic in hotel lobbies wriggled up out of the cracks in the concrete and bricks, growing at time-lapse speeds.

"No. Just. Don't," I said.

"Shut up and eat your vegetables," Terric snarled.

Annoying—that was still the Terric I knew.

The plants were elbow high, vibrating with life. Terric showed no sign of backing down.

I hated him for not backing down. I hated him for being right. I needed life. And he could give it to me without it killing him.

Much.

I couldn't endure the hunger a second more. I cussed and threw my hands out to both sides, palms down. I gave in to the hunger and devoured the plants, greedily consuming, killing. Without moving a single inch, I sucked the sweet life out of every stalk and frond he called up out of the world.

I was pulling on the life around me so hard the concrete under my feet cracked and shifted as I dug down looking for more.

As fast as I could consume life, Terric could call upon it faster. Life magic poured out of him in that alien white light, green and growing, smothering me, drowning me in life.

Somewhere in the back of my head a reasonable part of me was counting down from ten. When I hit one, I'd punch Terric in the face if that's what it took to get his hands off me and break his magic spree.

We'd both done stupid things when we lost control of magic. Stupider things when we'd lost it at the same time, together.

I'd sort of made it my life's goal not to use magic with him. Not to let him use magic with me. Because when I did, when *we* did, Terric wasn't Terric anymore. He wasn't human. And one of these days he wasn't going to recover from that.

Five.

Four.

Three.

Two.

Two and a haaalf.

I curled my right hand into a fist. Time to stop this. Time to stop him.

Before I lost him.

"Terric," Detective Stotts said from somewhere to my right, completely blowing my concentration. "What is going on?"

Detective Paul Stotts was a decent human being with

Hispanic heritage and an unflappable moral code. Today, he was wearing a blue scarf tucked into the collar of his jacket, dark slacks, and a frown. They used to say he was cursed, but that wasn't true. An awful lot of cover-ups and deaths in this city were caused by magic people didn't know about, and it was Stotts's job to investigate those deaths.

It had also been the job of the Authority to keep people, and especially detectives like Stotts, from discovering how deadly magic could be back then. The Authority did that by taking away people's memories.

Weird stuff used to happen a lot around Detective Stotts. There had been no explanation for it because we made sure there wouldn't be.

Now everyone had their memories back. Including him. It was a problem.

"About time you got here," I said. I shoved Terric's hand off me and stepped to one side to make sure I was out of his reach. I stuffed my hands in my coat pockets to keep from touching him again.

Terric took a step back, blinking hard like he wasn't quite seeing the real world yet. Not a lot of human in that angelic face of his. Not a lot of my friend.

Had I let it go on too long?

I bent, scooped up the Void stone buried in the plant ashes, and dropped the stone into his hand. He shuddered at the contact of the magic-canceling stone.

"Shamus," Stotts said. "I haven't seen you out of a bar for the last month."

"You've been keeping an eye on me? You're a sweetheart. This"—I pointed at the ox—"is something Terric seemed worried about."

Stotts glanced at the man. His eyebrows went up a bit. That Bind spell I'd cast was standard back in the day, but much rarer to see now.

"Did you do this?" he asked.

"Yes."

"Why?"

"He wasn't using his inside voice."

Stotts slid me a scowl.

I so didn't care.

"Terric?" he asked.

Terric didn't say anything.

His eyes were closed, hands curled around the stone, pressing it against his chest as if hoping it would fill a hole inside him. His lips were moving so slightly I couldn't tell what he might be whispering.

He swallowed hard, then opened his eyes.

A lot of light coming out of those blues. Cold, silver light.

"Terric?" Stotts said in his put-the-gun-down voice.

"We got a lead," Terric said like he was reading someone else's lines from a note card. "This man, Hamilton, Stan Hamilton, has information on the girl who showed up dead out in Forest Park yesterday."

By the end of the sentence, he sounded more like Terric. Looked more like him too. Blue eyes blue, white glow gone. Life magic was pushed back somewhere inside him where most people wouldn't look.

He crossed his arms and made a point of not looking at me. I wasn't most people.

"I called as soon as I saw him," he said. "Then Shame got involved. Started a fight."

"Started? You mean ended a fight," I corrected. "Like usual."

"You should know better," Stotts said.

"Excuse me?"

"There are procedures for using magic on other citizens, Mr. Flynn. Rules that every person in this city must follow now, whether they are Authority or non-Authority."

"Hello? Choir here you're singing to."

"I'm assuming Terric told you to stay out of this matter with Hamilton?"

"Yes, but—"

"Procedure. You will make some effort to follow it from now on."

I bit down on a smile. My bad habit of arguing with police officers had never once worked in my favor. "We called you, didn't we?"

"Terric called me."

"And?"

"This town doesn't need a vigilante," he said.

"Vigilante? You got me wrong, mate. I'm too lazy for that kind of thing. Spent a month in a bar, remember?"

"I've seen the things you've done in the past."

"Yeah, well, that was the past."

Right about then another police car pulled up.

"Let's keep it that way," Stotts said. "Just to be clear, you'll let the police do our job and you'll stay out of it. If you want a fight, do me a favor to take it outside my jurisdiction so I don't have to explain to Allie or Nola why I threw you in jail. Better yet, go on vacation, get a girlfriend."

"I'll get right on that," I said.

Stotts headed to the ox with a pair of handcuffs. Yes, my spell had held. Because I'm that good.

I didn't think he really worried about telling his wife, Nola, or her best friend, Allie, that he'd thrown me in jail. It wouldn't surprise them, anyway. More likely he just didn't want to deal with the paperwork.

I sympathized.

I turned and made for the street.

"Shame?" Stotts said. "The spell?"

I waved my hand over my shoulder and broke the spell. It pattered to the ground and hissed out like wet coals.

Eleanor floated along at my right, keeping her distance. Smart ghost. Not that there was anything more horrible I could do to her. I hoped.

Terric fell into step on my left.

"Are you going to tell me what the hell I just got in the middle of?" I asked.

"A murder. They think. Ten-year-old. Forest Park."

"I thought you said we didn't deal with murderers."

"We don't," he said. "Unless they use magic to do it."

Fuck. That sort of thing wasn't supposed to happen anymore. People weren't supposed to be able to use magic to kill.

I dug in my coat pocket, pulled out a cigarette, and lit up. The ache to consume was satisfied for the moment, thanks to Terric, but I was still twitchy.

"Let's just get to the damn meeting," I said.

"You don't care about any of this, do you?"

"Been saying that for months, mate."

"Shame." He grabbed my arm.

I stopped, turned, and looked at him.

"Someone is murdering people with magic," he said.

"I heard you. Let go of my arm."

"And you don't care."

"I don't *anything.*" I shoved his shoulder. He took half a step back but didn't let go of my sleeve. "I haven't been involved in this shit for a year," I snapped. "Why should I change that now?"

"Because a little girl is dead."

I nodded and sucked on my cigarette, doing what I could to hide how that really made me feel—angry and sick. And, yeah, helpless. The world was a fucked-up place. There was jack all I could do about it.

"And?" I asked with no tone.

"Jesus." He exhaled. "What happened to you, Shame?"

"Not everyone wants to be a hero."

"How about being a decent human being?"

"This is as decent as I get."

He stared at me a little longer. I had nothing left to say. He let go of my coat. Let go of me. Stormed off to the car.

Didn't blame him.

I threw the cig on the ground. It was ashes already. Consumed.

I tipped my head and sunglasses down so I could get a good look at the redheaded chick with the sniper rifle on the roof of the building across the street. She had a hell of a view of the alley from up there, an unobstructed shot, and had been following me since yesterday morning, or maybe the day before that.

I hadn't told Terric about her yet. Thought for sure she'd have taken the shot at him or me when she had the chance, but she hadn't. So, rule out our imminent death by sniper rifle.

That was good, right?

She was also packing up, so that meant the cops weren't her target either, and neither was the ox, Hamilton. Huh.

"Haul it, Flynn," Terric yelled. "We're late."

"Like normal?" I asked.

He didn't answer. Yep. He was angry. How human of him.

"Maybe you should take a vacation," I said as I neared the car.

"Oh, every day's a vacation when I'm around you, Flynn."

"Right. I know. But I'm serious. You could take your boyfriend. Is it still Mike? No. Greg? Wait. That was last year's model. You've traded him in for someone shiny and new, haven't you?"

I ducked into the car and Eleanor passed through the closed door to sit in the backseat.

"Shut up, Shame," he said.

And just because we were sometimes friends, and that redheaded sniper not killing us had oddly put me in a better mood, I did.

Chapter 3

If you ask me, there are about a thousand better places to have a meeting in Portland than the old woolen mill over in St. Johns. For instance, any place that sells beer.

Obviously, no one asked me.

Terric parked a couple blocks away and started walking without so much as a single word. He hadn't said anything on the drive over either. Not that I cared. My headache was pounding spikes into my brain. Sure, he'd used magic to make things grow so I could kill and consume so my hunger for death wasn't back yet. But it wouldn't be gone long.

I got out of the car and lit a cigarette, smoking as I made my way to the front entrance. Terric stormed inside the building before I'd even made it halfway down the street. I took a look around to see if Assassin Chick was up on the roofs or down the dark alleys.

Nope.

I'd be lying if I said I wasn't just a little disappointed.

Ah well. It was, if not fun, at least distracting while it lasted.

Of course a meeting roomful of magic users might be its own little good time.

I threw my cigarette to the ground, then walked into the building. The main meeting room was up a couple flights, and I so wasn't walking those. I took the elevator at the end of the hall, stepped in, pushed the button, and stuffed my hands in my coat pockets while I waited.

The only other person in the elevator with me was Eleanor. She stood near the buttons and bent a little, her hair flowing down around her face in that sort of underwater slo-mo she had going for her.

She pushed a button, but it didn't respond to her, so she quickly pushed all the other buttons.

"Worst. Poltergeist. Ever," I muttered.

She made a face at me.

The door opened and that kind of silence that makes you want to chew gum filled the hall. Mute spell, I'd guess. Couldn't have a secret meeting of secret magic users and make a ruckus.

As soon as I reached the meeting room at the end of the hall, the Mute spell swallowed me up and let in the roll of voices. Sounded like we had a crowd today. Of course, last I knew it had been a while since the Overseer of the Authority had been here in our little, but dangerously quirky, town.

I paused in the doorway and tipped my sunglasses down.

Crowd was right. Fifty people at the least. Lots of familiar faces.

Bring on the good times.

I pushed my glasses back up, spread my hands wide, and called out, "Hello, party people! Drinks are on Terric!"

I grinned as all eyes turned to me. A lot of people had retired out of the secret magic business over the last three years. It made sense—there wasn't much of a secret left about magic's business, and since magic couldn't do the big world-changing explosive sorts of spells anymore, the gig had lost a lot of financial and political influence.

Most of the people in the room I knew either well or well enough.

Zayvion Jones: tall, dark, and deadly. My best friend and a real goody-goody, though I'd never held it against him. Allie Beckstrom: tall, light, and deadly, she was Zay's girlfriend and really, the reason we had all survived the apocalypse.

Next up: Victor Forsythe. Dressed casual, which meant no vest with his jacket today. He was one of my teachers and an old-school magic stick-in-the-mud. Clyde Turner: rocking the NY Giants jersey in extra-extra large. A down-to-earth guy who took over the position of Blood magic when my mum ran off to Alaska with her old crush.

Plenty of other people I knew too. Violet Beckstrom-Cooper, slender, but a little icy for my tastes. She used to be married to Allie's dad and had taken over his magic and tech enterprise. Next to her was Kevin Cooper, a man with an unremarkable face, and a killer's instincts who used to be her bodyguard.

Melba Maide looked as disheveled as always, which I'd long suspected she did to throw people off her litigious brilliance. She was talking to the Beckstrom accountant, Ethan Katz.

It did not escape my devious little mind that there were only old-timey Authority magic users in the room. No police. No Hounds who used to track illegal spells and, yeah, might still do that, but more often worked with the police as informants. No government officials.

No "normals."

This appeared to be a magic-user-only invitation. Naughty. It wasn't like us magic users or the Overseer to sneak around behind the law anymore. We were purely aboveboard open-book saintly types nowadays.

Well, except for when it came to the things we wanted to hide.

My grand entrance got a mixed reaction from the crowd. A little hatred and amusement, but mostly just long-suffering annoyance. Huh, I must be losing my touch. I could usually get at least one or two people riled up enough to tell me to shut up.

"Everyone." Terric was on the other side of the room, his

coat shucked and already draped over the back of a chair. He had found a microphone. Bastard.

"Thank you for coming." He tipped his head down and gave me a look. "Shame, shut the door."

Doorman. Really?

If I cared about the fact that I should be up there at that microphone with him, doing this job with him, I might be angry that he'd pretty much just publically demoted me from Head of the Authority to Guy Who Shuts Doors.

Luckily, I didn't care about any of it. Right?

I turned, shut the door. Then leaned against the wall and glared at Terric through my sunglasses.

He felt the glare. Even across the room. He lifted his chin and pulled his shoulders back. Then he ignored me.

"You two still fighting?" Zayvion asked.

Zay and Allie stopped next to me. They stood there, arm in arm, Allie just an inch or two shorter than Zavyion's six foot something. She wore a tank top that showed off those kick-ass magic-born tattoos down her arm and the bands of dusty black ringing her other wrist and elbow. Now that we weren't on the run for our lives, both Allie and Zay had put on about ten pounds, and lost the dark circles under their eyes.

They smiled more, laughed more, and had that calm, sweet dedication to each other that meant they never walked into a room without holding hands.

I figured kids couldn't be far off now.

Zay's hair was buzzed short, and he had on a gray T-shirt that made his dark skin look even darker and set off the stone in the necklace he insisted on wearing. Apparently, the necklace had been an anniversary gift from Allie. Apparently, they were keeping track of those sorts of things now.

"You know how he is," I said. "Stick up his ass." I leaned toward Zay just a bit and pulled my glasses down. "Which he enjoys."

Allie just rolled her eyes. Green, with a glint of mischief tempered by that lingering sadness that made a man's heart skip a beat or two. Dark hair brushing right at her shoulders, pale skin. And yes, a beauty.

"We haven't seen you around much lately," she said. "What have you been doing?"

"Who. Ask me who I've been doing."

"You have a girlfriend?" Didn't sound like she believed me.

"I have a beautiful, full-bodied flaxen vixen at my side every night."

"So, a bottle of whiskey?" Zay asked.

I grinned. "Ah, now. Do I look like a lad who'd kiss and tell?"

Zay gave me one of those looks of his that could wound a man who still had a heart. "You're in a slump, Shamus. If you don't pull out of it, I'm going to pull you out. By your nostrils."

"I like how you think I'm afraid of you, Jones. What are you going to do? Throw magic at me?"

"Yes," Allie and Zay said at the same time.

I made a tsk-tsk sound. "Listen to you two. Aren't you just the hard-core Soul Complements now? Not only finishing, but also starting each other's sentences. Do you still remember who pees standing up?"

Allie pulled her hand away from where she'd draped it through Zayvion's arm. She took me down a notch with one raised eyebrow. "Don't be an ass, Shame."

It was unfair of me to dig at them about how fucking in sync they'd become with each other since the apocalypse. They'd both, separately, told me they were happy. Allie had given up the life of a Hound so she could restore an old house in St. Johns. She had plans of opening it up as a community center for disadvantaged kids or something. Zayvion had given up being Guardian of the gates so he could do whatever Allie was doing.

I didn't begrudge them their happiness.

Oh, who was I kidding? I hated them for it. Hated that they'd gone through hell and back again for each other and ended up so damn happy. What had I gotten? A round-trip through hell, then a "We're sorry, Mr. Flynn. Your happiness was lost in route through purgatory. Better luck next time."

"By the nostrils," Zay said with enough chill in his words I knew I'd struck a nerve.

It was good to see him rile a bit. To know he'd still threaten to wipe the floor with me — not that he could — if I made Allie frown.

I counted on him standing up and taking me down one of these days. And the way things were going, it would be sooner rather than later.

The first pangs of hunger, of the need to consume life, scraped through my belly. And there was a hell of a lot of life in this room.

I pushed my sunglasses back into place. I usually didn't regret giving him a hard time, but Allie was right — that had been an ass move. I might hate that they had found happiness, but I didn't hate them. They were the closest damn thing I had to a brother and sister. I thought very highly of those two crazy kids.

"Duly noted, mate."

Zay was classy enough to take it as the apology I meant it as.

"Shh." Allie pointed to the stage.

I tuned the world back in. Roomful of people who thought they were important, magically speaking. Terric up onstage glowing like he'd been dipped in angel shit.

Yes, angel shit glows. Never seen proof it doesn't.

". . . welcome the Overseer of the Authority, Salvatore Moretti." Terric stepped away from the mic, and even though a normal crowd would clap, we didn't.

Not so good at the normal, us magic users.

A man stepped up to the stage. He was just under six feet tall, I'd guess, built a little on the thick side with an impressive mop of steel gray hair and mustache to match. I'd guess he was a lady-killer in his day, but was a little heavy in the jowl now. Still, there was a wicked intensity to his dark eyes.

This was the second time I'd ever seen the man. The Overseer position of the Authority used to mean making the hard calls for all members of the Authority in the world, dealing with reports from the regional Watch and Ward, who in turn took reports and complaints from those of us on the street, as it were.

The Overseer position changed hands and countries every four years. He had taken it on right after we'd snipped magic's nads. It had been a chaotic time, an uncomfortable coming-out between the secret organization of magic users and the rest of the world.

A few people had been thrown in jail, still more were up on trial, but the world hadn't gone to war or followed through with those witch-hunt rallies that were all the rage for the first couple years.

Well, not officially.

And the Overseer had handled the entire mess pretty well. We'd held up our side of the bargain too, or at least Terric had. And since Portland was one of the only cities in the world that had five wells of magic beneath it, that meant we had more than our share of crazies, cover-ups, and other dangerous meltdowns to handle.

"Thank you all for coming here, especially those of you from other areas of the United States," he began.

What? Reassess the room, Flynn.

Local faces, local faces. Ah, there. Three sets of couples I hadn't noticed before because they were sitting at a table and the standing crowd obscured them. I didn't recognize the twentysomething guy with the cougar fortysomething woman, nor the milk-skinned yuppie man and woman who were both squarely in their thirties. I did, however, recognize the elderly man and woman.

Doug and Nancy Williams. They were legends when I was a kid, and old then. They had to be pushing their nineties. Seeing two old magic users wasn't all that unusual. The unusual thing was that they were Soul Complements, the oldest known to be living, even though they hadn't found each other until they were in their sixties.

My mum and all my other teachers in the ways of magic made a point of telling us, constantly, that Soul Complements didn't last. Soul Complements burned out, were killed, went crazy, or simply croaked from magical ailments.

No happy endings for those of us who can use magic together stronger than anyone else.

Not even a happy middle.

But every breath old Doug and Nancy took was one more whack with the cane to that shack of lies. Happy endings for Soul Complements, which included growing old and gray together without killing each other like me and Terric, or losing yourself in the other person's mind and personality like Allie and Zay, might just be possible.

Or, you know, Doug and Nancy could be a complete fluke.

I wasn't the only one staring at the couples at the table. Everyone else in the room realized there were an awful lot of Soul Complements gathered in one place. To be specific, there were five sets. The three couples at the table, lovebirds Allie and Zay, and though it made me barf in my mouth a little, Terric and me.

Which meant I got a few stares too. Mostly followed by disgust.

Ain't that just special?

"Shame," Zay said quietly.

I looked over at him. He nodded toward the stage.

". . . of quite a serious nature," the Overseer was saying. "We all know that three years ago, magic was healed: dark and light magic rejoined. We didn't realize just how mild magic would become due to that rejoining. I believe we, and most of the world, have done an admirable job coping with that loss of magic, and the changes it has brought about.

"Soul Complements are in a unique position. When they work magic together, they are able to briefly break magic into its dark and light states, and cast it once again with the full force and effect it once offered."

Not news. Not even worth rehashing. There'd been a hustle back in the early-postapocalypse days to try to find more Soul Complements. To seek the poor suckers out and shove this happy screwed-if-you-do, screwed-if-you-don't life down their craws.

Hadn't worked. One, the system for judging if when two people use magic together they are so in sync they can break it used to involve several dozen experienced magic users and a fine manipulation of magic for both the testees and the testers. With the dulling of magic, that system was simply not viable anymore.

Two, there are a lot of people in this old world. And since everyone can use magic if they want to, tracking down perfect matches was damn near impossible and turned out to be a waste of time, what with all the magic haters out there.

We'd given up, and done our best to keep the whole Soul Complement situation on the down-low.

"We have recent proof that high-ranking government officials in major countries are now aware of Soul Complements and what they can do with magic. They know there aren't many Soul Complements in the world, but we believe they have their names and information. They know that Soul Complements can break magic."

Huh. Maybe the redheaded assassin was government issue. Still didn't explain why she hadn't shot us.

"We believe governments are screening magic users and setting up protocol to search for Soul Complements."

"For real?" I asked. "Why do they give a damn?"

Shut-up glares zinged my way from all corners.

I didn't care. Life was a lot more fun now that magic couldn't do the bigger "shut up, Shame" spells I'd been dealt in the past.

The Overseer didn't seem overly bothered by the question. "We believe, Mr. Flynn, that they intend to use Soul Complements to break magic and use magic either as a resource, or a weapon. They are certainly more interested in finding Soul Complements than makes me comfortable."

"Right, sure," I said. "Who wouldn't want to get their hands on the only people who can use magic to kill, destroy, and yada-yada ultimate destruction. What do you think we can do about it? Go on strike? Sign a petition?"

I wasn't going to lie. I had a bad feeling of exactly what he wanted us to do about it. Probably something heroic like band together and take down the government forces that wanted to use magic for less than savory reasons.

And while some people, like Zay and Allie and Terric, would probably line up like good little soldiers and do just what was expected of them, I wasn't good at doing what I was told.

Ever.

"That is why I am here," he intoned. Yes, intoned.

"We believe you are each in grave danger and may, even now, be targeted. Our intelligence suggests government forces want you alive. But we cannot be one hundred percent sure of that.

"This meeting is both a warning and an offer of assistance. If you want to go into hiding, we in the Authority can make that happen. If you want security guards, we can provide that too. But it is of the highest importance you understand you are in terrible danger before you make the decision of how you want to go forward."

I wondered how the other Soul Comps were taking the news of their sudden popularity.

They looked startled. Even old Doug and Nancy had

gone a whiter shade of white. I'd say they were going to run.
All of them. They were going to hide.

Good on them.

Then I glanced at Allie and Zay. They were staring straight
ahead at Moretti with that odd blank look Zay had once told
me meant they were speaking to each other silently.

Creeped me the hell out that they could do it, but I had
to admit it would be useful.

They were also holding hands, fingers slipped one between the next, pale, dark, pale. I didn't expect them to run.
Hide? Maybe.

No way the old Zavyion would have run, but now that
Allie was in his life, he was all about safer decisions. Being
responsible.

And boring.

Allie, though . . . there was something about her. She had
that tough-as-nails but fragile-as-glass thing going on. I'd
seen her handle some really crappy situations, most of them
while her life was on the line.

So death threats weren't anything she hadn't heard before. She knew how to deal with death. Dying did not scare
that chick. She'd done it too damn many times.

But this threat shook her. Her hand in Zay's was so tight
I could see the bone of her knuckles. And her other hand
was flat across her stomach as if just thinking about someone out to kill her and Zay made her sick.

It was . . . weird.

I frowned, caught Zay's eyes. He gave me a blank stare.

No, that wouldn't do at all.

I slid my gaze to Allie's hand over her stomach, then
right back at him.

Well, mate? What's that all about?

Gold flashed in his eyes like paint hitting ink. Not a
speck of brown left, only violent anger.

Holy shit. Z didn't like me pointing this out to him. I
wondered what the hell I was pointing out to him.

I gave him a sly I-know-what's-going-on-here smile, even though I had no clue what had made him so angry.

He tipped his head down just enough to tell me, he knew I knew, and he'd talk to me about it later.

Good. It was going to be all kinds of fun to find out what he didn't want me to know.

He lifted a finger and pointed at the stage.

Right, there were important people talking about important things.

I'd heard the only thing that really mattered—someone wanted me dead.

Big deal. The line started on the left.

Up onstage, Terric was wide-eyed and still, like a deer caught in rifle sights who'd just heard a stick snap. He was frozen, staring at me. I wasn't sure if he was breathing.

Fuck. Of all the time for him to lose his composure.

I started toward the stage. No need for everyone to be staring at him like that.

"I am sorry, Mr. Flynn," the Overseer was saying.

Hold on. I must have missed something.

"About what?" I asked, still moving toward Terric.

"About relieving you and Terric Conley of your position as Head of the Authority here in Portland."

Chapter 4

"What?" I stopped, twisted on my heel so I could face the guy. I was still on the floor and he was up on the slightly raised stage. "You're *firing* me?"

"I am ending your position and will be reassigning a new Head of the Authority to speak for the magic users in Portland."

My brain was running a beat behind my mouth. "Don't bother. It should be Terric. He should be the Head of the Authority," I said. "Just because I fuck up doesn't mean he has to take the fall."

"Mr. Flynn." He somehow made my name sound like a venereal disease. "I have made my decision. You are *both* relieved of your duties as of today. I expect each of you to turn over your files and offices, clean out your desks, and assist in the transfer of duties to the new Head of the Authority."

I was almost at the stage now. My brain had finally caught up with my mouth and run into anger on the way.

"Who's that unlucky bastard?"

"If you shut your mouth," he snapped, "I will announce his name."

Bet if he could use magic like the old days I would have just earned myself a three-month crotch rash.

"Shame." Terric waved his hand and pointed for me to come stand beside him.

Oh, God no. If Terric had his wits back, then I was not needed up there. I hated smiling and making nice. Especially in front of a crowd.

The Overseer stowed his sneer beneath his mustache and addressed the room. "It is my great pleasure to announce to you the new Head of the Authority in Portland: Clyde Turner. Mr. Turner, please come up to the microphone."

Now I didn't have to make nice. I happened to like Clyde, poor sod.

Clyde was a regular kind of guy who looked like he belonged in a beer commercial. Didn't get in anyone's business and made it clear that people could stay out of his. He was currently the Voice, or representative, of Blood magic here in town—a position my mum had abandoned after the world almost ended.

The crowd got it right this time and clapped while he walked from the side of the room to the stage. He was wearing the same combination that he always wore: baseball cap on backward, flannel shirt over a team jersey—Giants. He shook hands with the Overseer, then stuck his fingers in his jean pockets while he leaned forward toward the microphone.

"Thank you for your applause. But I'd like us all to take a moment to show some appreciation for Terric Conley and all the hard work he's done for this city over the last three years."

Terric smiled and did the hand wave thing again to get me up on the stage. I really didn't think he'd want me up there stealing his sunshine, but hey, who am I to argue?

I walked up the stairs nearest Terric. The applause faltered as I crossed the stage, and was completely silent when I stood next to him.

But now that I was this near, I could see the tension bleed out of him just a fraction. Yeah, the tie between us worked that way for him too. Some things were easier for him when I was around. Still, the majority of things, important things like living, were harder.

He was really wound up over this firing thing. Probably worried it would look bad on his résumé.

". . . and Shamus Flynn did his part too," Clyde finished.

Faint praise, and true. But he didn't mean it to sound derogatory, and I didn't take it that way. When Clyde had a problem with me, he let me know. No bullshit from that guy.

"I will do everything in my power to listen to the concerns of the magical community here in Portland and make sure magic is running smoothly and working efficiently with the nonmagical businesses and communities in the Northwest.

"Now"—he glanced over his shoulder at the Overseer—"is there more that needs to be discussed on the stage, or should we open this up to a full conversation?"

Mr. Moretti strolled over to the microphone. "There is just one last thing. Please, each of you who are a Soul Complement, ask me any questions you have. I will need to know by tomorrow morning what your decisions are: to stay, to retreat. Remember we have places in all the world where you can hide.

"I will hold a second meeting with the Voices tomorrow afternoon, and tomorrow evening we will have a plan in place to accommodate the needs and safety of Soul Complements. Please make your decisions swiftly and carefully."

Decent of him. Didn't think it was going to help much. Unless the Authority had a hell of a lot more guns and technology than I knew about—which I didn't imagine they did seeing as how they'd spent hundreds of years relying on magic to take care of their problems—then it was just a matter of time before the government outpowered whatever the common magic users were doing to try to help the Soul Comps.

Cue the conversation. The rise of voices stroked across my senses and rattled my hunger loose. Sure, Terric's magic had helped push the need to feed away a bit, but this many people in one place, especially all worked up with heartbeats elevated, triggered my need to drink them down. The whole rich, alive stew of them.

But if I started feeding, I'd wipe out the room, then wipe out every living thing in the building and probably a block radius.

I stuck my right hand in my jacket and ran my thumb over the Void stone rings, rubbing them together when what I really wanted was to tear something, anything, apart. Breaking things kept my mind off the need to feed.

Terric's hand landed on my shoulder and I shivered at the rush that shot down my spine and clenched my gut. Life magic right there inside him, easy for the picking.

Jesus.

He leaned in close enough he didn't have to raise his voice over the sound of the crowd. "Be nice, shake hands, make it quick. We're going to the office to take care of things."

"Why would I want to go to the office?"

His hand squeezed until my neck hurt. "Because. I. Need. You. To."

Then he released my shoulder and walked away, calm and smiling, and in control. The bastard.

I strode across the room, making eye contact with anyone who looked at me. They all looked away. Terric played his part. Shook hands, made conversation, appeared concerned for people.

But I was doing them the highest favor of all: getting the hell away from them.

Eleanor drifted along beside me, arms crossed, and frowning.

I stopped halfway down the hall and fumbled for a cigarette. Pulled out the pack and tapped out two. Lit one, which burned to ash in my shaking hand almost too quickly for me to use it to light the other cigarette.

I inhaled, savoring chemicals and tobacco, and more so, savoring the burning, destructive death of plant matter and paper. Got about halfway through it before I noticed Eleanor was pointing at a No Smoking sign.

"Sorry, love," I said. "I'm immune to rules. Followed too many when I was young." I exhaled smoke. "Built up a tolerance."

I leaned on the wall next to the sign, finished off the cigarette, and lit another one. Even at this distance and through the Mute spell, I could feel their heartbeats, could feel the pulse of their lives filling that room like warm, thick water I wanted to drown myself in.

Terric was in there. I could sense him like a clear beam of light in the dark shit hole of my life. Sure, I could consume all those people. Or I could consume him. He'd be better. Far better than the entire population of this city.

Then he'd be dead.

"You know what?" I said, pinching out the smoldering end of the cigarette with my fingers. Ouch. Yeah, even pain could feed my need, if necessary. "I'm done waiting. Let's go."

Eleanor pointed at the closed door to the meeting room, then tapped her wrist like she had a watch there. She didn't, but I got her point.

I hadn't waited very long for Terric.

"I'll leave him a note, all right?" I was already walking toward the elevator and she, of course, followed along.

When I'd first killed her, I could hear her. She had been angry, furious. But as time went on, it was harder and harder to hear her. Either that was how it always was for ghosts, or maybe it just took a hell of a lot of emotion to make words carry between the living and dead.

Charades usually got her point across, and even though it meant I talked out loud to myself like some kind of crazy, it worked.

Plus, it made people avoid me. So, win-win.

Didn't see anyone on the main floor.

Outside. Still too damn sunny and freezing. October sky was blue, but the air was bitch-cold. I flipped up my collar and strode up the block to Terric's car.

Pulled a piece of gum out of my pocket, chewed. Smoothed out the gum wrapper, pulled out a pen. Used the top of his hood to write *See U There* on the gum wrapper, then spit out the chewed gum and stuck it and the note on his windshield, dead square in the middle of his field of vision.

"There," I said to Eleanor. "Note. Let's get moving."

Buses were a bad idea—too many people. Same for the light rail. I had enough money for a cab, but walking was good. The motion, the burning of calories, did a lot to satisfy my need to destroy, consume. But there was no way in hell I was walking clear across town.

I'd probably catch the MAX—light rail—on the other side of the bridge.

Forty, twenty-seven, three, sixteen. I counted the people in the shops I passed, could tell by their heartbeat if they were young, old, or really old.

Hardest to ignore were the young and old, both so close to one side of the grave. Easy pickings.

I shoved my hands harder down in my coat pockets and dug my nails into the weave of my pockets, tearing at the threads.

Could this day tick by any damn slower?

I needed to feed. And if not that, because fuck me if I was going to kill anyone today, I needed a damn drink. Several, actually. Something to take the hard light out of the day, and sand all the edges off the world.

I was about a block away from the bridge when the slick black Corvette rolled up and stopped just in front of me. I probably should have been paying attention, but survival hadn't really been my thing lately.

"Hey, you!"

I pulled my chin up out of my coat collar, and the world snapped down around me with all its clean, hard edges.

Situation: two guys in dark coats stepping out of the car. Driver built like a lumberjack, hair skinhead chic with a shaved lightning bolt, or maybe scar showing skin about three inches into his hairline above his right eyebrow. Unibrow, eyes set too close together, old acne scars.

Other guy was skin over bone. Goat face, long nose, eyes set too wide. Hair shaved up both sides left to fall in a greasy swatch over one eye. Half a hardware store worth of hooks pierced his ears, eyebrows, and down the left side of his neck.

I didn't know these jackasses. I kept walking.

"I'm talking to you," Driver yelled. Driver also started toward me with a swagger that made it look like he was an inch short in one leg.

I flipped him off.

He kept coming, and even though I shouldn't, I stopped. "What is your problem?" I said.

"You know a buddy of ours," Driver said.

"Doubt it. I don't hang out with assholes."

Driver smiled, showing a lot of gold on those teeth.

"Sure you do," he said. "Met him in an alley over on MLK this morning. Called the cops on him."

He must be talking about the ox. I wondered if these were the two men Terric had sent running.

"We don't like people who inconvenience our friends," Goat-face said. He had a slight lisp. He also had a baseball bat.

I held up one finger. "Time out. I didn't call the cops on that jackhole. I don't even know what they took him in for. Also, you really want to put that bat down, mate."

He did not put the bat down.

Eleanor was floating a few yards in front of me. She was shaking her head and waving her hands in very clear "no," "stop" gestures.

Right, like I was going to stand here and let them beat the crap out of me.

Driver stepped all up in my space, breathing garlic and beer over every word. "We are going to fuck you up."

His heart was thumping up in the heart attack levels. He was excited. Revved up. Alive.

"One last chance," I said evenly. "Walk away. I have no quarrel with you. You'll regret having a quarrel with me."

It made him pause. At least he had some sense of self-preservation. I am not joking when I say I look like death. And right now I was doing nothing to hide what I really was. I was trying in no way to look human.

The magic that had changed me was usually enough for people to know there was something terribly wrong with me.

Driver saw what I really was.

I gave him a slow nod. Permission to back away.

He took a step back.

But the other guy? Not so much with the smart. He'd come up on my right and swung the bat at my ribs.

I moved out of the way enough that it just clipped me. Which, yes, hurt like a bitch. Bruises, though I don't think anything cracked.

Unfortunately for the guy swinging the bat, I didn't need weapons in a fight. I am a weapon.

I rushed him and caught hold of his arm with my left, unringed hand. Stepped in close. "This is not your lucky day."

I squeezed his arm, my fingers curled over the veins beneath fabric, beneath skin. Easy to find that pulse, easy to drink that life.

Counted his heartbeat. Fast. Terrified.

Fear made it taste better. I hated it, hated that I wanted it. Hated even more that I liked it that way.

But the man was going beat me with a baseball bat. He had it coming.

I inhaled. Easy as breathing, I drew on his life.

He groaned and tried to pull away.

But I'd only had one little mouthful, barely a taste. I wanted more. Hell, I wanted his life, his buddy's life, and maybe the lives of all the people on this side of the river.

I licked my lips and then gave him a smile. "You will never cross my path again—understand me?"

His eyes went wide and he was sweating hard. He dropped the bat and it clattered against the street. He made a sound that never quite formed a word, but I took it as yes, he understood I'd kill him if he ever bothered me again.

Just to make sure, I drank down a little more of his days.

He slumped to his knees. Passed out.

A slap of ice punched my face. I blinked. I'd gone on my knees next to the guy. Couldn't seem to let go of his arm. Couldn't seem to let go of this meal I hadn't finished.

Like a goddamn brainless leech.

Eleanor was next to me, her hand cocked back in a fist. She was ranting off a list of filthy swearwords I could make out even without sound. Angry ghost.

I owed her for that. For being angry enough she had pulled me back from the brink. Again.

I rocked up onto my feet. Stood. The guy wasn't dead. But he'd feel like shit for a few days.

Okay, probably a few months.

I was feeling much, much better.

"What the hell did you do to him?" Driver yelled.

I bent, picked up the baseball bat. "What you need to know," I said, "is that I could have killed him, and I didn't. Just like I could have killed your friend in the alley this morning, and"—I lifted the bat, adjusted my grip on it— "I could kill you too. But I'm not going to. And you know why?"

I didn't wait for his answer. "Because I want you to scrape that piece of shit off the sidewalk." I pointed the bat at his friend. "And I want you to go back to whoever you work for and explain to them that I am not a person with whom to fuck. Understand?"

He nodded.

"Good. Now give me your keys."

He reached in his coat pocket and tossed them at me.

Huh. I'd expected him to argue over that one.

Cool. Free car.

I caught the keys and stepped over his friend on the way to the Vette. Kept the bat.

Got in, checked the rearview mirror to make sure Driver hadn't suffered a sudden case of bravery. Nope. He was crouched next to his friend, making sure he was breathing.

Me? Doing shit like that did one of two things: threw me into a self-hating bender, or bright-siding it, made me feel pretty damn good about not killing someone.

I was a man with a monster in my bones. And this time the monster had not won.

So, yeah, I felt pretty pleased with myself at the moment.

The car? Damn sweet ride.

I adjusted mirrors and seat and rolled out into traffic.

I'd lost my job, but I hated it anyway. I'd lost my grip on my hunger—twice. But I hadn't killed anyone today yet.

It was a low bar, but it felt good to hit it.

Also, now there was a definite chance I was going to beat Terric to the office. What wasn't to like about that?

Chapter 5

Okay, a small detour.

The Corvette's navigation system was too tempting to ignore. Since it stored locations where those punks had been lately, I decided to give it a look.

I pulled down a side road, parked, and scrolled through the list: a couple out-of-state addresses, a few trips to the east and west side of the state. Then an address I knew very well.

Terric's house.

They knew where he lived. Which meant they either knew him or were keeping an eye on him. I didn't like either idea. A couple other addresses showed up on the list: someplace out in the West Hills, Allie and Zay's house, and the inn.

So those dicks who liked to settle arguments with a baseball bat were keeping an eye on all of us Soul Complements. Who were they working for?

Terric said the ox, Hamilton, might be involved with the girl killed by magic found up in Forest Park. If these guys were his friends, were they magic users? Murderers?

Probably would have been smart of me to ask Terric a few more details about the whole thing. Maybe then I'd understand why they were stalking members of the Authority.

What did they, or their boss, want?

I forwarded the last-visited addresses to my phone,

which was back in my room, and did a quick search of the car for anything else that might tell me something about these guys. Nothing in the glove compartment, nothing in the trunk. I did find a black crow feather tucked beneath the visor. Not exactly useful.

Then I rubbed my fingerprints off the dashboard and everywhere else I'd been snooping. Time to hand this thing over to someone who might get some information out of it.

In under five minutes, I was strolling into the police department and wishing the cool, clean air from outside reached more than three feet into the stale funk of the place. But it didn't. It never did.

Detective Stott's real office was somewhere downstairs, but I didn't want to stay that long or get that cozy. Walked up to the first workstation at the end of the hall, knocked on the top of the desk. Waved at the security camera. Didn't have to wait long for a cop to show up.

"You still breathing, Flynn?" Cop was a huge dude from Hawaii, name of Mackanie Love. We'd met back in my petty crime days. He'd never cut me slack. But then, I hadn't deserved any.

"Once or twice a day, whether I need it or not. I have something for you." I held out my hand, the car keys hanging from my fingers, the baseball bat in the other.

He eased his bulk down into the chair and nodded at the keys. "What's that all about?"

I placed them on the desk. "Car about halfway down the block. Black Vette. It belongs to some people you might want to keep an eye on."

"Did you steal a car?"

"Please." I pressed my fingers against my chest. "You think I'd steal a car and just walk in here to turn myself in? I'd make you work for it, mate. You know that."

"So what's that really?" This time he pointed at the keys.

"Detective Stotts was pretty interested in a guy Terric tipped him off to this morning. Name of Hamilton. And those"—I nodded toward the keys—"belong to two other guys who didn't like Terric and me getting in the middle of their friend's business."

"Tell me you didn't steal a car from the Black Crane Syndicate."

"Okay."

He leaned back just a little, the chair creaking in protest. "You know what Black Crane is, yeah? Blood and drugs. Human trafficking. Dark magic."

Black Crane. A crime syndicate we'd kept under control when magic was strong, and that apparently continued to thrive off the magic and drug trade, even though magic didn't have the kick it used to.

"Sure, I know Black Crane." Oh! Crow feather. Suddenly made sense. "But I only borrowed their car. *Borrowed.* After they stopped me in the street to express their displeasure with me."

"Are they dead?"

"Not stupid enough to come in here if they were."

From the look on his face, he didn't think that was funny.

"Listen, I don't care what you do," I said. "Terric got me involved when he chased down Hamilton this morning. And, I'd like to point out, nobody told *him* to mind his own business. But when two guys get out of their car and tell me they want to beat me senseless because *I'd* gotten their friend arrested, I'm not going to stand there and take it."

"What did you do?"

"Left them reconsidering their manners beside the road. And brought you their car."

"You shouldn't have done that."

"What part?"

"Any of it. Don't you own a phone?"

"Not on me. Would you rather I had brought them here with me? Citizen's arrest?"

"No. I'd rather you stayed out of this, Shamus. From now on."

"That's what I've been trying to say. I am staying out of it. See you around, Detective."

I turned and strolled off, baseball bat over my shoulder.

"Flynn?" he called out. "Go see a doctor. You look like death warmed over."

He had no idea.

I just kept walking.

Fresh air and more sunlight. It wasn't far to the office. Fifteen or twenty minutes. If I walked fast enough, Eleanor might not even notice all the fancy shops we were passing by.

Keep walking. Keep walking. Dodge the man with the dog. Dodge the woman on her phone. Green light. Yellow. Sprint across the intersection. Almost clear of the shops. . . . no luck.

Eleanor went from drifting along to a dead stop. She got one look at a hat shop on the corner and clapped excitedly. I groaned.

"I promised Terric I'd be there," I whined.

She just raised her eyebrows. Yeah, telling her I didn't want to be late for work was not going to fly. She knew I didn't care.

"You can't even wear them."

She drifted toward the hat shop door. Got her max distance from me and waited, arms crossed.

"I don't wanna." I started toward her anyway. Living women: stubborn. Dead women: about a hundred times worse.

I walked to the front window, close enough she could go in the shop. She waved at me to follow her.

"No." I pulled out a cigarette and backed away from the door so the shop owners wouldn't call the cops on me for smoking. I lit up.

Glanced over. Eleanor stuck her tongue out at me, then slipped through the glass door into the hat shop.

I leaned my head against the brick and ignored everyone

around me. Didn't care that they were alive. Didn't care that their pulse echoed in my skull like drums. Didn't care that my cigarette was out before I'd had more than two drags on it. Did. Not. Care.

Pushed the world into dimness, into fog. Away. So I didn't have to feel the life. So I didn't have to feel.

Cold fingers pressed on my fingers. Eleanor. I let the world back in.

Snap, click. Pow. Edges and beating hearts.

She pointed at her head, then at mine. Big grin on her face, all excited. Talking. Too fast for me to figure out what she was saying, not that I could hear any of it.

A few more gestures toward the shop, and finally I got the basic of it.

"No. Hell no. I do not want a hat."

I pushed off the wall and ignored her for the next five blocks.

She finally gave up floating in front of me with her hand in my face—sorry; that doesn't make me trip anymore—and flipped me off before window-shopping along behind me.

Building, up a flight of stairs, office: destination achieved.

Pushed through the second set of doors and past a short lobby that had four potted plants, all growing.

When had the place gotten so damn green? I pushed through the next set of doors, leaving two potted plants still growing.

Tall ceilings, lots of light coming in through windows, hardwood floors, shelves, and several desks. Modern, but unable to shake its past as a grain warehouse, it was expensive real estate the Beckstrom fortune had donated to the Authority back when Allie's dad was moving and shaking the world of magic.

Eleanor floated off and sat outside on the window ledge to pout.

There was exactly one heartbeat in the room besides mine.

"Well, if it isn't Mr. Dashiell Spade," I said to the man walking toward me with a file folder in his hand.

He was younger than me by a few years, about five eleven, dark hair combed back and up with just a bit of muss to it, black-rimmed glasses that didn't hide the fact that he had a face that had probably gotten him all the prom dates he could handle. Trim, dressed in a checkered long sleeve with a light sweater, slacks, and dress shoes. Northwest office chic.

Came in as our assistant three years ago. Looked like the poor guy hadn't found a way to break free. Wondered what kept him here.

"Shame! It's great to see you again. Coffee? Booze?"

"Yes, please."

"The whiskey's where you left it," he said. "I'll pour the coffee."

I pushed off to the desk where I used to sit. Corner of the room where I could see the doors and all the windows.

Everything was pretty much where I'd left it. Phone, computer, knife stabbed into a stack of notes. There were also three potted plants on the desk, two of which were some kind of vine that crawled up the brick wall into the rafters and across the windows.

Those I had not left there.

"So, how's life been treating you, Dash? I thought you'd have moved on by now."

"Things are good, thanks."

I crouched down and pulled the bottle out of the holster that kept it stuck beneath the top of the desk.

"We've missed you around here," he said. "Most people's long weekends don't last for months. Or years."

"Well." I stood, studied the bottle, which was nearly full. "I knew the place was in good hands. Terric, he's all right at what he does, I suppose."

Dash grinned and shook his head. "No one's cared more or worked harder than he has."

"Proving my point. And you are damn near the best secretary . . . administrative assistant?"

He handed me the cup of coffee. "Second. I'm Terric's second."

"So, that's a step up, right?"

He nodded. "I've left you a few messages lately."

"Oh?"

He glanced over at the door and frowned.

"Terric should be here soon," I said. "Out with it, lad."

He seemed to make up his mind. "Come on back to my office."

"You have an office?"

He just pointed toward one end of the large room that had been sectioned off into two with wooden walls and windows. The office on the right took up the majority of the room and lorded over the outer windows. That would probably be Terric's.

I, correctly, took the door to the left into the smaller office.

He stepped in behind me, and shut the door.

"You okay with this?" he asked.

"With what?" I gulped coffee and whiskey and savored the double burn. His heartbeat was steady, calm.

"Close quarters, all these plants, me living. That what."

He sat behind the desk and watched me, waiting. He had hazel eyes that were moss green with bits of brass in them. And those eyes were giving me a very knowing look.

Jesus. He knew. How much I wanted to consume. That I barely held it in check. I hadn't ever talked to him about it.

Well, maybe just that one time when I was really drunk.

"Want me to pinkie-swear I won't kill you, mate? Worried that I'll lose control of Death magic and squeeze the pulse out of your ticker?"

"No. You've got this. Your control is solid. Criminally so."

"Bless you. Talk."

"I try not to get into Terric's personal life. But there's

something that I can't stay quiet about anymore. I"—he looked down at the desktop, suddenly interested in the calendar there that he pushed slightly to one side— "care for him." Eyes up again, steady on me. "As his second. We've worked together for a long time and he is—his health is important to me."

Lie. Well, not lie. More like truth pushing to be heard behind all those careful, yet oddly clumsy words. He cared for Terric as his boss, sure. And he cared for him a hell of a lot more than that.

Huh.

"Right," I said, letting the subtext go. "I know that. But if you're going to give me the lecture about how I should be around more because I make him feel better, Soul Complements, and blah-de-blah, don't bother."

"No." He shook his head. "You already know you should be. You'll change your mind, or you won't. It doesn't matter what I say about that. I'm talking about Jeremy Wilson."

"Who?"

"The man he's dating."

"Do I need to know about this?"

"I think Jeremy is hurting him."

Silence. I drank coffee. Not because I had nothing to say. A hurricane of words and rage ignited in my head, pounding to get out. If I said one thing, I'd be yelling. Incoherent. And then I'd kill.

Dash waited. Didn't make any sudden moves. Didn't breathe faster, didn't elevate his heart rate.

He was a smart man. A good man. He waited me out while I bitch-slapped my demons.

I took one last swallow of the coffee and set the empty cup down on the edge of his desk. The cup crumbled into a dusty pile of ceramic.

And . . . I had my cool back.

Dash's eyebrows ticked up. "Maybe I *should* talk to you about that other thing."

I gave him a smile, shook my head. "I never liked that cup."

"Noted."

"Talk to me about Jeremy."

"He and Terric started dating about four months ago. Terric was . . . discreet about it. He tries to keep personal stuff away from work. But about six weeks ago, I came into the office early. Found Terric coming out of the bathroom without his shirt and shoes. He'd slept here most the night. He had burns down his arms—cigarette burns. His wrists were raw and his ribs were black and blue."

Ticked it off like a laundry list. No emotion. But his pupils dilated. Dash was pissed about this.

"Maybe he and the boyfriend like it rough," I said. "Terric can take care of himself."

"I know he can. And he did. By that afternoon, the burns and wrist scars were gone. He wore a T-shirt just so I'd notice. He has Life magic in his blood. He can use it to heal himself."

I hadn't thought of that. I supposed he could, though.

"I've seen him with a lot of men, and never seen a mark on him," Dash continued. "But every time he's with Jeremy, he comes in bruised or limping."

I shrugged. I just couldn't picture Terric willingly being abused. There must be more to it than that.

Dash leaned back a bit. "Shame, he can heal himself. And he does. I think Jeremy makes sure that no matter how fast he heals himself, he still walks away from their time together injured. And too tired to make himself better."

"Maybe he just—"

"Too tired to make himself better," Dash repeated, "because he's spent his energy, poured his life into Jeremy."

I took a breath, let it out. "Dash, you're a smart guy. But I think you're stretching this a bit."

"So I looked Jeremy up," he went on quietly like I'd never said a word. "Records are easy to get ahold of. He used to be into Blood magic. Ran money for some of the drug lords. Big syndicate."

Bet I could guess which one.

"No recent activity of that on his record now. Not since his diagnosis. Cancer, Shame. Brain. Stage three. He's dying. He's been dying for years. But in the last four months, he's gone into complete remission."

"Because of Terric," I said unnecessarily.

Dash pressed his lips together, then nodded. "I think so, yes."

"Okay. Fine. Listen, maybe it looks like a twisted sort of relationship to you"—I held up one finger at his expression—"and to me, but Terric is a grown man. He's made his choice and lives his life the way he wants. If he didn't like the guy, he'd walk away in a flat second. You've seen him go through boyfriends before."

"That's true. I have. Which is why I'm telling you, this guy is different. He's hurting Terric, and Terric's not doing anything about it. You know him, Shame. Better than I do. Does that sound like Terric?"

"No."

That was all I had time to say, because the exterior door opened.

Dash looked over my shoulder through the window to see who was coming into the office. I didn't have to look. I'd know that heart, that pulse, that life anywhere. Terric.

"You killed my ficus," he called out across the room.

I stood. Strolled out into the main office. "They were ugly."

"They were fragile. And hard to keep alive."

"Took care of that. You're welcome."

He dragged his fingers back through his platinum white hair, grabbing at the back of his head before letting go. "It's coming out of your paycheck."

"Don't bother. I don't work here anymore. Neither," I said, "do you."

"What?" Dash came into the room. "You quit?"

"No," Terric said. "I didn't quit. The Overseer has named a new Head of the Authority. Perfectly normal. The position should change hands every once in a while. Keeps things fresh." He gave Dash a small smile.

Dash swallowed several times, not doing a very good job of hiding that the news had shattered something inside him.

I watched Terric. He didn't seem to notice Dash was devastated that they wouldn't be working together anymore.

"But don't worry about your job," Terric said. "Clyde is taking our position, and he'll need a strong second to keep the continuity of everything flowing. You've always been the heart of this place, Dash. I'll hope you'll stay."

"I . . ." Dash looked down. When he looked back up, he'd pulled it together and didn't look shaken at all. "Of course. Of course I'll stay. Have you thought about what you're going to do next?"

"Pack," Terric said. "Take care of some paperwork. Get drunk."

"Singing my song, mate," I said. "Well, except for the packing and paperwork thing." I offered him the whiskey. He took the bottle, pulled the cork, and then tipped it up for a long, hard drink.

"Good," he said, gesturing toward me with the bottle. "Thanks."

He started off to his office. With my bottle.

"Just give me a minute or two, and I'll be right back out," he said.

Then he walked down the hall. With my bottle.

And shut the door. With my bottle.

Dash exhaled and folded down on a chair, his palms pressed evenly on his thighs. No more calm heart, his pulse was clattering. "Why?" he asked. "Why would the Overseer take this away from him? It meant . . . everything."

"Dash, buddy. It's going to be okay. Mommy and Daddy will still love you. They just can't come to work with you anymore."

"Fuck you, Shame."

Had a little fire behind that. Good. Fire meant I wasn't going to have to deal with tears.

"Honestly? It probably has more to do with me than him. I haven't been pulling my weight lately."

"Not everything is about you." Dash tugged his cuffs, checked the buttons to make sure they were buttoned. They were. Then he got back on his feet. "You want any help packing your desk?"

"Hell, let's just set fire to the thing. Nothing there I want."

"So I can have the knife?"

"No. Fine. Get the boxes, Boy Wonder."

Dash walked out and down the hall to the storeroom. I stood there for a bit, enjoying the aloneness. Except being this close to Terric meant I wasn't really alone. I wandered over to my desk. Then I found myself walking instead down to Terric's office.

I paused just before his door. I could see him through his office window. Sitting with his desk at his back, bottle resting on his thigh, other hand over his eyes, head bent.

I should probably just leave. Let him deal with this loss in private.

Terric lifted the bottle, but instead of drinking, he held it out toward me. Still had his hand over his eyes.

I opened his office door. Leaned there in the doorway.

"I don't want the booze," I said quietly.

"Yes, you do." He took his hand off his eyes and leaned back in his chair.

"Yeah, I do." I walked in, took it from his hand. It was a fair share lighter than it'd been just a few minutes ago.

Tipped it up, took a swallow. Booze went down hot, but the mouthwatering sweet of cinnamon and mint lingered on my lips. Life magic stirred the need in my belly. Terric had been drinking out of the bottle. I should have wiped it off before doing the same.

"I was good at this, Shame," Terric said. He wasn't looking at me.

I sat in the chair against the wall opposite his desk. "You're still good at this."

"We were amazing at it," he said.

"True."

He didn't say anything else. I took another swig of the whiskey. Ignored my disappointment that the taste of life was gone.

A couple minutes ticked by in silence.

"So, if you don't need anything," I started.

"Just." Terric turned, held my gaze. Blue eyes darkened by sorrow. "Would you shut up and sit here for a few minutes?"

I opened my mouth.

"Please."

I closed my mouth. Handed him the bottle. He took another drink and handed it back, swiveling his chair so he could stare out the window.

I watched him for a minute. Thought about things I could say. Thought about things I probably should have said a long time ago.

Decided to just do what he asked and kept quiet. I even remembered to wipe the taste of him off the bottle before I took another gulping swallow.

Chapter 6

I left Terric in his office and took the half-empty bottle with me. Dash was moving around the office like a cleaning lady who wasn't sure what to dust first.

A pile of empty boxes towered next to my desk. Enough to pack away the room, Terric's office, and probably everything else on this floor of the building.

Lord.

"How about you give me a hand?" I said.

Dash walked over. "I wasn't sure how much you wanted to pack."

"I see that."

I gave Dash the whiskey and he turned to place it on a windowsill. Eleanor was back in the room again, and seemed interested in some of the art on the walls.

"No. Drink," I said. "You need to relax a little, mate."

"No, I don't."

"Fine, then *I* need you to relax. A lot." I gave him a drink-up gesture and turned to the pile of boxes, chose one, and dropped it in front of my desk.

Listened for the cork, swish of liquid, then cork before I spoke again. "There was something else brought up at the meeting today."

I opened a drawer. So that's where I left my gun.

"What?" Dash leaned against the windowsill, his shadow stretching out over the boxes.

"Do you know what Soul Complements are?"

"Two people who are a perfect match when casting magic."

"Good. Anything else?"

"They're usually perfect matches in life too. Partners, friends, lovers. But it's incredibly rare to find that kind of match, especially with magic. Since being even a little unmatched can cause spells to destabilize and blow."

"Very good. How many are in Portland?"

"Just Zayvion and Allie." Pause. Quieter, "And you and Terric."

"Gold star." I glanced over my shoulder. He took another drink of the whiskey, then set it down on the far side of the windowsill, out of his easy reach.

"Why?" He crossed his arms over his chest and leaned against the wall.

"The government is suddenly all interested in Soul Complements and what they can do," I said.

"Break magic?"

I nodded. "Overseer is suggesting we get the hell out of town. Out of the country too. Thinks we're in a lot of danger."

He looked over at Terric's office. Worried.

Jesus. He didn't just like Terric. He was harboring much deeper feelings for him.

It was strange to see someone fall in love with a person you were connected to. I found the best way to deal with it was to ignore the hell out of it.

Drinking helped too.

"So you're saying you're leaving? He's leaving?" Dash asked.

"No, I'm saying we're going to make some choices. Or I assume we're going to. Terric is fussy about me making life-and-death decisions when he's involved."

"Is that why you came by today?" Still wasn't looking at me.

"I thought so."

The door to Terric's office opened and closed and then I heard his footsteps. Every plant in the room stirred as if a soft wind brushed over them. The damn things grew, vines snaking out half a foot in just a few seconds.

Someone wasn't keeping very good control of their Life magic. I wondered if Terric was drunk.

"Gentlemen," Terric said with a lift in his voice. "Let's leave the packing for later. I want lunch. Shame, you're coming with me even if I have to knock you out and drag you there. Dash, you're welcome to come if you want."

Not drunk yet. He still had his clothes on. Definitely buzzed, though. The day was looking up.

Dash pushed away from the wall and pressed his fingers down into his front pockets. "No, that's okay. I'll stay here and fill a couple of these boxes. See you later this afternoon?"

Terric nodded. "I should be back."

"Don't count on me," I said. "But don't pack the whiskey either."

"Wait. Terric?" Dash jogged toward his office. "I have a message for you."

He jogged right back with a folder in his hand. "There's been another missing person report that matches the others."

Terric took the folder, opened it. "He looks familiar. Shame?"

I took the folder. Printout of a missing person report. Paper-clipped to that was a photo of an older man, gray beard and hair, eyes nearly lost in the wrinkles from his smile.

"I've seen him," I said. "Don't remember where. And not recently."

"So we can rule out the bars and gutters," Terric said.

"Look who finally found his sense of humor," I said. "I'm thinking a while ago. Couple years. Was he part of the Authority?"

Terric took the folder back and glanced at the name. "Harry Schol. Doesn't ring a bell. Run his history through our records, will you, Dash?"

Dash took the folder. "Already on it. You two have a nice lunch."

"Oh, I'm sure it's going to be swell," Terric said, taking two tries to pluck his coat off the hook as he made his way to the door.

"We still have records the police can't access?" I asked Dash. "I thought there was a total transparency-of-records thing that went down a couple years ago."

"Well, there's transparency," Dash said with a tilt of the folder, "and there's the Authority." He nodded toward Terric.

I grinned. "Maybe things aren't all that different after all." I started off after Terric, caught up to him halfway down the hall.

"I think I should drive," I said.

"I'm fine." He aimed for the elevator button with exaggerated precision.

"Just the same, mate, hand over the keys."

The elevator door opened and we stepped in, Eleanor behind us.

"You've been drinking," he said.

"Sure. Three swallows. You tanked a third of that bottle. I drive, or you're going alone."

"Why is every conversation with you an argument?"

"Seems a waste of time, doesn't it? Especially since I'm always right."

He leaned one shoulder against the elevator wall, half turned toward me. "Like the time you said Victor was going to give up his place as Head of Faith magic? Or the time you bet Allie—Allie of all people—that you knew what Zayvion was thinking better than she did? Or the time when you bet me I could bring that fossil back to life? Or—"

"That," I interrupted, "is why every conversation is an argument. You just can't let things go."

"I *can* let things go." He held my gaze, eyes sober and dark with unveiled pain. I looked away.

"I can't ignore facts," he went on. "Or the truth when it's right in front of me."

I stared at my shoes. "You should practice," I said quietly, ignoring the slow thud of his heartbeat. "It gets easier."

The door split and I couldn't get through it fast enough. I strode down to the front doors. Pulled sunglasses out of my pocket and got them over my eyes. Stepped out into the daylight.

Afternoon was rolling toward evening, the sun giving up the fight to clouds. City was in full swing now, plenty of people on the street.

So many beating hearts.

Enough that it took me a second to realize Terric was walking in the opposite direction than I was facing.

". . . way, Shamus," he called back over his shoulder.

I swore, popped up the collar of my coat, not that it did much to block the living from my notice, but it usually signaled people to stay the hell out of my way.

He'd found street parking just half a block down, and was waiting by the passenger's side, one hand on the roof in both a possessive and steadying grip, keys in his other hand.

"If you scratch it, dent it, or grind one single gear, I will come over to your place every morning at five, steal your curtains, and sing ABBA at the top of my lungs."

"Hey, now," I said, taking the keys from him. "You don't have to be mean."

I unlocked doors and slid behind the driver's wheel. The car was clean as the day it'd been driven out of the factory, with only the scent of Terric's cologne indicating someone living owned the thing.

I wondered, not for the first time, how a person could go through life leaving such a faint mark on the things he possessed.

He folded down into the passenger seat, buckled his seat belt. "Not a scratch," he reminded me.

"Yeah, yeah," I said. "I heard you. Burgers?"

"Sushi."

"Fish and chips."

"Vegan."

"Over your dead body," I said. We were quiet while I eased out into traffic.

"Bar food so neither of us is happy?" I offered.

"That works."

I decided short drive was better than long, so I headed to Paddy's. We didn't say anything else until I parked in a loading zone and Terric had a fit about it. I finally relented and found a place a few blocks away.

Clouds threw gray across the sky, and the wind had picked up. Not as many people on the street here. By the time we reached the bar, I, for one, was glad for the heat of the place.

Terric found a table in the corner where the lighting was low enough I could take off my sunglasses. It was thoughtful of him.

Eleanor got busy checking what the other patrons in the bar were eating and drinking. She finally sat next to a good-looking man who was reading on a screen, and leaned forward just enough to read along with him.

The waitress, a curvy girl with a great smile, came around and took our beer orders. Terric also ordered shepherd's pie.

"Get food," he said.

"Not hungry."

"Yes, you are. He'll have the baby spinach and beet salad."

"Like hell he will."

The waitress raised her eyebrows, then reapplied her smile. "It's a good salad."

"Just bring me a burger. Rare. Lots of cheese. Fries."

"Good choice." She sauntered off.

"So," Terric said. "We're unemployed and being hunted. Got any ideas about that?"

"You're a graphic designer," I said. "So you've that to fall back on. Mum's inn brings in enough I can skim profits, and she doesn't care."

"I was talking about the hunted part. Price on our heads. Wanted by the government?"

I shrugged. "Let them want me. I'm not worried."

He leaned forward, the Void stone necklace swinging outward just a bit before it settled again against his pale gray dress shirt, and regarded me with a look that was too kind for the sort of hell he'd been through in his life. "You won't even consider relocating? There's nothing holding you here, Shame."

"Sure there is."

"What? Name one thing that ties you down to Portland."

Was that a dare? Did he want me to say it was him? Us? Soul Complements and magic?

"I have a better idea," I said, picking apart the side of the wooden table with my thumbnail. "You just tell me what you want to do, since that's why we're really talking, right?"

He inhaled, exhaled, eyes tightening slightly. Annoyed.

"I get that you don't fear death," he said. The waitress showed up, set our beers out for us. Mine: dark. His: dark. Huh. I wondered when he'd switched over from the light brews.

"And I know you don't care if someone tries to kill you," he continued once she had moved on. "But this isn't a street brawl, Shame. This isn't even a magic user after you. This is the government. Bullets are faster than magic. Even our magic. The government has resources and reach you can't escape."

"Who says I want to escape?" I said cheerfully. I picked up my beer, swallowed some down. Damn fine. Set it back on the table. "It does sound like fun, doesn't it? Being chased. Wanted man. Final showdown."

He leaned back and gave me a courtroom stare. No more happy in those eyes. No more kindness. "Ever think that maybe they don't want to kill you, Shame? Ever think that maybe they have ways to force you to stay alive? Ways to force you to do what they want you to do?"

"That someone might want to use me, use this thing inside me? Sure," I said. "I think about it every damn minute. What happens if I lose control. What happens if someone else tries to control this." I lifted my fingers just a bit and the rings across my right knuckles crackled with sparks of red.

"There isn't anything out there that scares me anymore, Terric. Not the big bad government, not the big bad Authority. Not life. Not death."

He took a drink of his beer, set it down, and turned it slowly with just the tips of his fingers clearing away the condensation. Didn't look at me. "Three out of four, anyway."

"How's that?"

Took another drink. Looked at me this time.

"I believe three out of four of those. You might not be afraid of the government or the Authority, or death. But life? I think life scares the crap out of you, Shame Flynn. Why else have you been running and hiding from it for almost two years?"

I just shook my head and drank my beer.

I hated when he was right.

Terric's phone rang. Which was just as well. I was done with this conversation years ago.

The waitress showed up with our plates. I gave her a hey-baby smile and a thank-you.

When I looked back over at Terric he was frowning at his phone and texting.

I took a huge bite of the burger and groaned with joy. I felt like I hadn't eaten in days. Did a quick count in my head.

Yep. Days.

Terric didn't touch his food. He hit SEND on the text, then wrapped his fingers around his beer and stared at the table.

"More bad news?" I asked.

"No." He lifted his fork and dug at his food before putting a bite in his mouth.

I worked my way through half the burger. Watched Terric rearranging the food on his plate.

"What was that text?" I asked.

"Personal."

"And?"

"Do you really want to know what's going on in my personal life?"

"Well, no. Not really. But that text made you stop talking. And I am always interested in ways of accomplishing that."

Faint smile. He sat back, fork left behind in the mashed potatoes. "I'm dating someone."

"Uh-huh." I drank beer to wash down salt and grease.

He was watching me. Waiting.

"Terric, you always have a boyfriend. Don't care." Half the burger down, half to go. I took another bite.

"That was him on the phone." Shrug.

"You like him?" I asked.

His eyes skittered away from mine. "Most of the time." Eyes back on me again. Smile that faded too quickly.

I moved on to the pile of french fries. "And the rest of the time?"

"It's complicated."

I ate for a bit, wiped my fingertips on the napkin, then finished my beer.

Terric still wasn't eating. Wasn't looking at me either.

"Here's what I think," I started.

"Didn't ask for your opinion."

"I think when you date guys you like, you smile a lot.

You talk about them a lot. And when you talk about them, you don't lose your appetite."

"Your point?"

"You haven't even told me his name, and for a guy who insisted I go out to lunch because *you* were hungry . . ." I pointed at his nearly untouched plate, then pointed at mine.

Terric shook his head, then leaned off the back of his chair and took a couple bites.

I flagged the waitress for another round of beers and finished the rest of my lunch. My gut was killing me. I think that was more than I'd eaten in a week.

"Maybe it's time to move on," I said.

"Which subject are we on now?"

"Boyfriend. Maybe you got what you wanted, and it's time to move on."

"He has cancer, Shame."

"That's not your fault."

Terric shook his head again. This time there was some fire in his eyes. "You might not give a damn about people, Shame, but I do."

"No. What I care about doesn't matter," I said. "I'm just telling you what you already know. Guilt is a stupid reason to remain in a bad situation."

"Are you done?"

"Yes."

"Good. So what do you want to do?"

"About your boyfriend?" I asked.

"No. Being hunted."

The waitress showed up with our beers and I took a long pull before answering, "Fuck all if I know. Stay here. Watch things blow up. Or make things blow up. Do you know what Zay and Allie are doing?"

"Staying. For now. But they're making . . . other plans."

"Like?"

He shook his head. "You should talk to them. They should be the ones who tell you."

"Tell me what?"

"Nope. New subject: Who's the redhead following you?"

I sat back a bit. Impressed. I didn't think he'd noticed. "Redhead?"

"You're not blind. You've seen her."

"I have no idea. And you didn't answer me," I said.

"About?"

"If you're staying."

"With Jeremy?"

"Is that his name? Also, no. In Portland."

"It makes more sense for me to leave."

"That's not an answer."

"Yes," he said.

"Yes, it's an answer?"

"Yes, I'm going to stay. Also, yes. It's an answer."

"I forget how much I don't miss this," I said.

"What?"

"Talking with you."

"Nice try," he said. "You love it. Because there's no one who knows you as well as I do."

"Zay knows me."

"I don't see you having lunch with him."

"So you're really staying?"

He tipped his head down just enough that his hair fell over his eyes a bit. He gave me a predatory smile. "Someone has to keep an eye on you."

"Me?" I grinned. "I'm not the one causing trouble in this town."

"No, but you'll be right in the middle of it when it happens. You can't resist."

"Trouble?"

"Danger."

I waved my hand dismissively. "I got no stake in this game, mate."

"Yes, you do."

He was right. I did. For one thing, I cared about what

happened to Zay and Allie. And my other friends like Dash, and Clyde, and some of the people who worked at my mum's inn. But that's not was Terric was getting at.

He meant him.

"You mean you," I said.

"I mean me. You're worried about me."

"Please."

"You asked me about my boyfriend. My *boyfriend*, Shame. You never ask me about my relationships."

I opened my mouth, closed it. Sat back. Scowled. And flagged the waitress.

"Leaving?" he asked.

"Drinking. More than beer. And so are you. Because I am done with the talking. And so are you."

He grinned. "Not even close."

Chapter 7

A thing I don't tell a lot of people: Terric is hilarious drunk.

Mostly because as the drinks go down, his clothes come off. It usually starts with the shoes, then socks, belt, and shirt. Sometimes it goes a lot further than that. I'd bailed him out of jail once for indecent exposure. I've never let him live it down either.

So, yes. I was thinking about seeing how many layers he was going to shed here in a very public pub, but he'd only taken off his shoes and unbuttoned the top button on his shirt before his phone rang. Again.

He'd ignored it twice already.

"You going to get that?" I asked.

The waitress had cleared the food from our table, and now five shot glasses were lined up, neat as socks in a drawer, in front of Terric.

He downed the sixth and carefully set it in place at the back of the line like a good little soldier.

"It's Jeremy."

"Right," I said, toying with my third shot that wasn't even half-empty yet. Another thing I don't tell people: when Terric drinks, I just . . . don't as much. Seems like one of us should be sober in any given situation.

"Your boyfriend wants to talk to you, mate."

Terric looked off over my shoulder, pretending he hadn't

heard what I'd just said. But his heartbeat sped up, and I could see his eyes dilate. Fear? Lust? I sipped my whiskey and waited.

"He's picking me up," he said. "Here."

"Is that a problem?"

He wiped his hand over his eyes. When he took his hand away, his eyes were still closed. He set the fingers of both hands one-at-a-time precisely on the tabletop, as if ready to play a piano.

"I can feel your heartbeat, Shame." He said it almost too quietly for me to hear over the noise in the bar. But his finger was tapping the tabletop. Tapping in exact rhythm to my pulse.

"I can feel all their heartbeats. I can tell who is healthy, who is sick. Who is dying. I can feel their time ticking away under my skin. It burns there with every beat of their heart. And sometimes, some days, I can't keep the magic from spreading out to swallow them. Life magic heals, mends, fixes." He nodded, his fingers tapping, tapping.

"But when I lose control of it, it makes anything grow, accelerate, thrive. Even disease. Even sickness. The living are made stronger, but the dying are accelerated, burned out like old candles. If I refuse to use Life magic, it consumes . . . me. I drown in it, lose my thoughts, my reason. My mind."

He opened his eyes. Maybe realized those words were coming out of his mouth. Maybe realized who he was talking to and where he was.

I wondered if he'd given up trying to explain to people what it was like to die and come back with magic having changed you. Changed your body. Changed your blood. Changed your needs. I'd stopped trying to explain it years ago.

Let them think I was a burnout. A loser. A slacker.

I guess Terric let them believe he was a success. A winner. A hero.

It didn't matter. There wasn't anything to do to fix what we really were. What we both had become: monsters.

Most people did not want to be reminded of how dangerous we were.

But I rarely heard Terric's fight with Life magic. He never spoke to me about it. Just like I didn't talk to him about Death magic. I had no idea what it was like to be driven by Life magic. I had no idea what it demanded of him. What it made him do. How it wore him down. How he coped.

"Life magic devours?" I said. "I thought that was Death magic's trick."

"Life magic infiltrates, overtakes, possesses. Makes everything grow: plants, people." A long pause. "Diseases, sickness." He tipped his head, licked his lips as if remembering the taste of each of those things. "Everything I touch I change. Everything that I touch I force to change."

"You know there's a price for letting magic use you like that."

He nodded once. His eyes were too sober for how much whiskey he'd been drinking. "My life. My . . ." He looked at a loss for words. So I gave them to him.

"Your humanity," I said.

I didn't think he'd ever believed me when I said that before. But this time he did.

"When I let go. When I relax, when I just let go and breathe . . ." He stopped talking. Just stared at me.

"It takes over," I said.

"I become the monster. The magic. I become the hunger. And I don't want to stop."

"Ain't life grand?" I threw back the remainder of my shot.

"I've made some bad choices," he said. "I've done some horrible things. When I just breathe . . ." He licked his lips. "I've extended . . . suffering. Hospitals are bad. Nursing homes, worse."

"Good," I said.

That startled him, but I wasn't done.

"No, as a matter of fact: thank God. Perfect Terric was really getting on my nerves. It's good to know you can fuck up like the rest of us lowly humans."

"Is that what we are? Human?"

"Until the day the monster kills us," I said. "Or we kill it."

He smiled a little. "Careful. That almost sounded like optimism."

"It's the whiskey talking."

His phone rang again. He didn't look at it. Fingers dug harder at the tabletop.

A car horn blared. Paused. Blared again.

"That your friend?" I asked.

Terric took a deep breath, pulled his hands away from the table, then worked on putting his shoes and humanity back on. "Yes."

He stood, pulled out his wallet and threw some twenties on the table. "Thanks. For this. I'd like to see you at the office again tomorrow. Think you can do that?"

"When have I ever let you down?"

He raised an eyebrow. The horn blared again, taking away his reply.

"Night, Shamus."

He took a step, reassessed his balance, seemed to pull it together, then started toward the door with a steady gait.

I got up and followed.

"I'm not that drunk," he said. "You don't have to follow me."

"I'm not," I lied. "Gotta piss. Bathroom's this way."

He didn't argue, not even when instead of turning left to the bathroom, I leaned against the wall near the door. Watched him step out. Waited a minute. Opened the door.

Terric ducked into a Jeep.

The man in the driver's seat, who I assumed was Jeremy, looked familiar. Short hair, narrow face, and when he shifted so I could see him better, I knew where I'd crossed paths with him before. He was the guy leaving the scene at the alley this morning who pointed at me like he was holding a gun.

What a douche.

Looked like he was reading Terric the riot act.

I was suddenly falling in hate with the guy.

Terric paused in pulling the seat belt over his chest, the door still open. Since his body was turned away from me, I had no clue what he said. But I saw Jeremy's face change. He shut up. His eyes narrowed. And his heart beat harder. Anger.

Then he looked up at me. Saw I was watching them.

His anger screwed down to tight, red fury.

Oh, that man did not like me. Poor bastard.

I crossed my arms over my chest and made a kissing motion.

He bit off one cussword and looked away.

Yes, I was enjoying this.

"Think I should stop that now?" I asked Eleanor, who had spent most of the last couple hours sitting with different people at the pub and eavesdropping.

She nodded.

Terric shut the car door and the Jeep rolled down the street.

"Too late," I said. "You should really speak up when you have an opinion."

Eleanor stuck her fingers into the side of my neck. Ice picks chilled all the way down my spine. "Jesus, woman. A little humor would be nice."

I rubbed at my neck and stepped back into the pub.

As soon as I was in the main room, I was once again reminded that when I am around Terric, the need to devour and consume life is lessened. Yin/yang, Soul Complements, life/death, and all that. We canceled each other out some when we were in the same general proximity.

Now that he was gone, a tight ball of rage knotted like a fist in the middle of my chest. Death magic was hungry.

Maybe it was time to settle the bill and get the hell away from this place. Away from all these lovely living people.

While we'd been talking, day had stumbled into night. The pub was filled to the walls. I made my way between people standing and yelling to be heard over the noise of the place, and paused by the table.

A woman was lounging in Terric's seat, arm over the back of the chair, ankle resting on her knee. Knockout pretty. Blue eyes like clear mountain skies, and a soft, full mouth. Her hair spilled down to her shoulders in waves, framing the porcelain white of her skin. Slender build in a tight T-shirt and jeans. My heart, which had been missing for years, kicked over and began beating for the first time.

It wasn't a come-hither gaze she was holding me with—just an even stare with a glimmer of mischief—but it might as well have been.

I didn't know her, but I recognized her. Last time I'd seen her, she had a sniper's rifle in her hands.

"Buy you a drink?" she asked.

I could say no, but there was fresh shot of whiskey already next to my three empty shot glasses. She had a drink too, an Old-Fashioned. All the money Terric had left behind was right where he'd tossed it.

Eleanor was shaking her head and doing some kind of football signal for missed goal.

But there was something about this woman that made me want to say yes for a change. I tugged the chair away from the table and sat.

"So. Is this your first time in Portland?" I asked.

She smiled a bit. "Why? Does it show?"

"Not at all. Visiting friends? Enemies?"

"I'm still undecided on that. My name's Dessa."

"I'm Shamus."

"I know."

I grinned. "Wondered if we were going to dance around that or not. Are you going to tell me why you want me dead?"

She caught her breath. Then leaned forward just a bit. "Did I say I wanted you dead, Mr. Flynn?"

"No. But that rifle on the rooftop? Kind of a giveaway."

She took a drink to cover her surprise. Huh. So she didn't think I'd spotted her. I guess I had the slacker/loser/oblivious-of-the-world act down pretty tight.

"You're still breathing, though, aren't you?"

"Apparently," I said. "Why is that, exactly?"

"I don't want you dead yet."

"Comforting. What do you want?"

"A little time."

A young couple were making their way through the crowd toward the door. The woman was carrying a baby. Just before she got to our table, she sidestepped a man taking off his coat, and a little stuffed toy tumbled to the floor.

Dessa glanced over, spotted the lost toy, saw the woman and baby moving on. She glanced at me, then at the woman's retreating back.

These kinds of situations were always telling. A woman on the prowl would ignore the whole thing. A woman on a job to get information would ignore it too.

And Dessa . . .

"Hold on." She stepped out and picked up the toy—a purple turtle—then caught up with the couple and handed it to the thankful mother. She even took a minute to smile at the baby before noticing I was watching her, and walking back my way.

Looked like my assassin had a heart.

"Do you always rescue things in need?" I asked as she sat back down.

She shrugged. "Only when I find them lost and alone in bars."

Touché.

"So you wanted time," I said.

"Yes. I want to make you a deal."

"What kind of deal?"

"You help me, I help you."

"Go on."

"I'm looking for a man. A magic user. I want you to help me find him. And kill him."

Matter-of-fact. Clear. To the point. But her tone had gone too careful. Too even. Hiding her heartbeat, the race of adrenaline. She didn't just want the man dead, she wanted revenge.

"What did he do to you?"

"He killed my brother."

I let that settle between us. "I'm not an assassin," I said.

"You could be."

"I could be a lot of things. Have you tried the right side of the law?"

"Do you think there is a right side?" She paused for a minute, stirring the ice in her drink.

I just wanted to watch her eyes, her mouth, the way she pushed her hair back so the side of her neck was bare. Thoughts I hadn't had in a long time stretched out in me.

"I've been . . . involved in that side of the law," she said. "I've even worked for that side of the law. And I know my brother's killer won't ever be put in jail."

"Why?"

"He has protection. Government protection."

"What are they protecting him from? You?"

She smiled again, and I glanced away so I wouldn't be caught by the warmth of it. "No."

"Look," I said. "I'm flattered. But there just isn't anything in this for me. I'm not seeing why I should get involved."

"I'll help you with your problem." She took another drink and waited.

"And what, exactly," I said, leaning forward so that our hands nearly brushed, "do you think my problem is?"

She swallowed and had to look away before she could

hold my gaze again. "I have information about the government and Soul Complements. Names of the people involved. Information that can keep you alive."

"You assume I want to stay alive. Maybe you've got me wrong."

The corner of her mouth pulled up and she tipped her head so that a curl of hair slid gently across her cheek and neck. Red against white, like blood on snow.

I clenched my fingers so I didn't reach up and draw her hair back into place.

"If death is what you want," she said, "I can give you that too. It will be fast. It will be clean, and it will be glorious."

She had my full, unbroken attention.

She was not kidding. Her iceberg blue eyes were as steady as if she were looking at me through a sniper's scope, finger on the trigger. No emotion. Just the sweet promise of death.

Would it be wrong of me to think that at that moment, she was the sexiest woman I'd ever seen?

Here's the thing. I knew what my future would be. No matter how I cut it, death, my death, was always the card on top. I'd always figured Zayvion would be the one to pull the trigger. But I hated what it would do to him and Allie. They'd carry the guilt of my death for the rest of their life. Because they are like that.

But here, now, this woman—this gorgeous and, yes, kind woman—was a solution I hadn't considered. I could make a deal with her, and she could make my death look like an accident. No one would carry the guilt. Not Zay, not Allie, not Terric, not my mum. No one would have to know the truth.

"Glorious, eh?" I asked.

"Unforgettable."

"How about accidental?"

"It can be arranged."

"So you're offering my life—or my death—if I help you find a guy and kill him."

"That's the deal."

Tempting. Dangerously so.

I leaned back, lacing my fingers together just behind the shot she'd bought me that I still hadn't touched.

"Why can't you kill him? I'll buy that you might need help finding someone. It's less likely you think I'm the one who can track him down—plenty of better trackers in this town. But what I'm really having a hard time believing is that you need help killing. Anyone."

"He's different."

"How?"

She shook her head. "You agree to help, I tell you. You don't, then I'm gone."

I thought it over. Several things made this seem like a good idea. One: she was hot and had stirred feelings, and a need, I hadn't had in a long, long time. Two: she had information that might keep Terric, Zay, Allie, and the rest of the Soul Complements safe. Which meant it was possible she either worked for the government or worked against them. Three: did I mention she was hot? Four: that kill-you thing she offered was a pretty sweet way to deal with my ultimate dilemma—my problem, as she called it.

It would, however, be insane to commit to a revenge that I didn't give a damn about.

It would not, on the other hand, be the most insane thing I'd ever done.

"No," I said.

It surprised her and she didn't bother to cover it up. "Are you sure?"

"Yes. Yes, I am."

She pulled her hair back with both hands and let it cascade back into place. "We would have made a hell of a team," she said.

"Undoubtedly."

"Was it the glorious death that turned you off?"

"No. I thought that was a nice touch."

She smiled. "Well, then. To happy endings." She held up her drink and I picked up the shot.

Touched the edge of my glass to hers. "To endings, happy or otherwise."

She nodded, then took a long drink.

I slammed back the whiskey, enjoying every moment of the burn. I only wished it were enough to put out the fire she'd started in me.

A slightly sweet aftertaste coated my throat. I wondered which brand she'd ordered.

"Now that business is out of the way, care to stay for a couple drinks?" I asked.

"Maybe. What do you have in mind?"

"I thought I'd unpack my boyish charms and try my hand at seducing you."

And the smile she gave me.

It lit up her face. She was, I realized, the kind of woman who knew how to laugh. Who was probably gentle to small animals, and kind to old people. Behind her mask, she was vibrant. Alive.

I wanted that.

"First," she said, "don't tell a woman you're going to try to seduce her."

"Oh, I don't think that's fair. Relationships are much more fun when . . ." The pub spun to the left and I braced my hand on the table edge so I didn't slap it with my face.

"That's not right," I mumbled.

Dessa leaned forward. "Second, don't accept drinks from strange women."

"What?"

"Well, look at that," she said. "Your boyish charms are working. I'm just all wobbly in the knees and so are you. Why don't you come home with me, kitten?"

"Kitten?"

And before I could make any damn sense of that, she was next to me, then standing with me. Her arm was surprisingly strong around my waist, and I wanted like mad to pull her into me. But the pub was coming in and out of focus as I blinked, and the only thing that convinced me I was walking was that the place was moving past me.

"Spiked my drink," I said.

Now we were standing outside.

"Yes, I did."

"Naughty girl."

She sighed. We were moving again. Around the corner. "I am sorry about this. You could have just agreed. It would have been easier."

"You knew I wouldn't. Otherwise why spike the shot?"

"I wasn't sure I could be convincing enough. One thing you need to know about me, Shamus Flynn? I never give up."

I would have told her the one thing she should know about me is I never do things the easy way, but the world was a blender of light and darkness. I didn't know what she'd dropped in my drink, but it was not a drug or magic I was familiar with.

That worried me.

Could I use magic to get myself out of this? Sure, if I could concentrate long enough to trace the glyph of a spell.

So: no.

Could I just drain down her life?

Strangely, and really, most frighteningly of all, I couldn't even think straight enough to do that. That drink had pushed magic—even Death magic—way out of my reach.

"Here we are," she said. "You can just relax. Lie down. Let me take care of everything."

"I don't even know your last name," I mumbled. I thought she was easing me into the back of her car. I was pretty sure I heard a car door open.

But I'd gotten that wrong too.

She'd popped the trunk. And gave me a shove down into it.

"You have got to be kidding me," I laughed as the world spun and shook.

"No. I am completely serious about this. Deadly, even."

She leaned above me, her lips slightly open as she adjusted something near my head. And all I could think of was I should kiss that woman.

What can I say? I like a woman who can surprise me. She'd certainly done that.

Too bad I couldn't move.

"You should be comfortable," she was saying. "And don't even think about using magic. It won't work."

Too late. I was already thinking about it. But that was about all I was doing. Because the lumpiness I was lying on wasn't the spare tire and crowbar. It was Void stones. As a matter of fact, the entire trunk was lined with them, completely canceling my ability to draw on magic.

The woman knew how to plan ahead. I wondered if she'd lined the top of the trunk too.

"I'd tell you to get some sleep," she said. "But this is going to be a bumpy ride, so just try not to get a concussion."

As the trunk slammed shut, I noted that yes indeed. The inside of the lid was lined with Void stones too.

Damn. I really should have kissed her.

Chapter 8

Here's where I act the hero and do something smart, like call someone. Or do something brave, like kick out the trunk. Or come up with a sneaky plan, like find the biggest Void stone so I could brain the bitch.

Instead I got nauseated and unconscious. In that order.

I came to no longer in the trunk. I had no memory of walking or of her dragging me. But somehow she had managed to get me into a motel room and strap me down to a chair.

This was so not how I had imagined spending the night with her. Well, not the first night, anyway.

She was pacing. It was the *thump, thump* of her flat bootheels on the carpet that had brought me awake.

Thump, thump, pause.

"You are a very bad girl," I said. It came out a little ragged. Whatever she'd poisoned me with had done some damage to my throat on the way down.

"You do make me want to do bad things to you." Her fingers drew across my shoulders and even though I was still clothed, I felt it like a lick of heat that made me shudder with need.

No fair. Focus, Flynn. She doesn't mean *those* kinds of bad things.

"Aren't you the sweetest?" I said. "How about you give a guy back some feeling in his hands?"

She finally walked around from behind me.

She was wearing a red satin bra and panties. And her combat boots.

And nothing else.

Well, a smile.

Holy shit. Maybe she did mean those kinds of bad things. Please let her mean those bad things.

She turned so I could get a good look at her ass too. Lordy. Someone spent time in the gym. Or chasing after her brother's killer. I hear revenge is a great full-body workout.

She turned back to me. With guns in her hands.

"There's some mixed signals," I said.

"This," she said, "is to get your attention. How am I doing so far?" She bent at the waist so I got a good eyeful of her guns.

She pressed her hands on her hips. Had a Glock in each hand.

I wasn't sure which guns I was supposed to be looking at.

I gave her my best Flynn smile. "I like where this is going."

She straightened and I made an effort to pull my gaze up from her panties, her flat stomach, the birthmark just over her hipbone, the curve of breasts, and all the way up to those merciless blues. Got lost in the blues for a moment or two.

"Good," she said. "Because I'm just getting started. Are you fully awake, Shamus?"

"How about you untie me so we can find out?"

She shook her head, walked across the room to a crappy table there, with an even crappier chair. Wood. Scuffed legs, no padding. Probably matched the one I was sitting on.

She lifted it, walked toward me.

"I'm going to try this one more time," she said. "Talking you into seeing things my way."

She turned the chair so that the back of it was toward me.

"I asked nice last time. This time I'm not going to ask so very nicely." She spread her legs and straddled the chair.

Mercy.

Everything went white noise for a moment or two while I did what I could to put out the fire in my groin.

Don't think of her mouth. Don't think of her breasts. Don't think of her thighs.

". . . heard stories about the great Shamus Flynn," she was saying.

"All true," I interrupted. I had no idea what she was talking about.

"Good," she said. "Because I heard you killed Jingo Jingo, one of the strongest Death magic users around at the fight in St. Johns. And you single-handedly devoured six professional magic users—drained them down so there weren't even bodies to bury. Then you took on two dead Soul Complements who tried to end the world. You came out of all of that still standing and were made into the head of the magic users in Portland."

Okay, now she was getting specific. These were things that were only known to the Authority. Maybe she'd dug through some top secret files the FBI or CIA had set up after the apocalypse to try to make sense of the whole ancient organization of secret magic users that had been operating under their noses since before they had noses.

But what she most certainly had not done was get access to this information in any easy or legal manner.

"Who do you work for again?" I asked.

"Now, now," she said. "That wouldn't be any fun. First you tell me a little something I want to know. Then I'll tell you something you want."

Her hand slipped up her thigh, stopping just short of her hip. She licked her bottom lip and smiled.

She was so playing me.

I loved it.

However, the rope she'd tied me up with was weighted

down with Void stones. While that would make it harder for me to use magic, I could still get out of the ropes if I wanted to. But I didn't want to—yet.

"Who killed your brother?" I asked.

She raised one eyebrow and leaned forward into the back of the chair. Jesus, I wanted to be that chair.

"Tell me if you're as deadly as they say you are, Shame. Prove to me all those rumors are true. Better yet . . . show me."

Really? That's what she wanted to know about me? If I could kill people?

Fine.

I relaxed my hold against the darkness inside me. Let my hunger stretch out and breathe. Brought the monster front and center.

I tipped my head just a bit. Caught her gaze. And held it until her smile dropped away. Held it until she shifted her grip on the Glocks. Held it until she instinctively turned the guns on me, stood up, and stepped back.

"What I am," I said, "is much, much worse than anything anyone has ever told you, love."

In the next several heartbeats I learned that Dessa knew fear. And I learned how she handled it: heartbeat elevated, hands steady on the guns. Taking the time to make a decision.

Who wouldn't shoot the monster if they had it tied up in front of them?

I braced for the bullet I knew was coming my way.

Instead she pushed the chair to one side. Knelt in front of me, then pressed up between my legs, her guns on the floor.

Oh. God.

"I think you're lying." And then she kissed me. Kissed me with all her body.

Every inch of me flared at that touch, burning hot and hard.

I let her kiss me, her mouth soft and hungry. And then I kissed her back, coaxing her mouth open, until she relented and let me taste her fully.

Slow. Deep. I savored the taste of her mouth—alcohol, and the sweet of oranges. Felt the low groan in her throat. She exhaled and her body melted into mine.

My hands were still tied. Her hands slid up my chest to the edge of my jaw. Her fingers drew across the stubble of my beard and then back, to knot behind my head and tug at my hair. She dragged my face closer, her fist in my hair.

My turn to groan.

We kissed, hot, wet. I couldn't think. Didn't want to.

Yes. God, yes.

The hunger inside me was not Death. Had nothing to do with magic. I wanted to taste every inch of her. Wanted to kiss her until she shuddered in my arms.

I tugged on the ropes. The chair creaked.

Dessa suddenly pulled back and rocked up onto her feet, eyes wide, lips plump and wet, her lipstick smudged.

Lord.

Her fingers flew to her neck, then her arms, brushing over them as if assuring herself she was still whole.

I wasn't the only one wondering if I'd survived that contact. I wasn't the only one breathing a little harder.

Her pale skin was scorched red across her chest and cheeks, hot with arousal. If my hands were free, she wouldn't be standing alone right now. She'd be in my arms, in that bed.

"You could have killed me just then," she said with a catch in her breath.

It took me a minute to reply. Finally, "You're the one with the gun." It came out slow, low, and I watched her pupils dilate in response.

"But you could have killed me," she said softly. "Drunk down my life."

There was no reason to deny it. "Yes."

She licked her bottom lip, and I blinked slowly, unable to look away.

"I need you, Shamus. You are the man I've been looking for."

There was something about the way she said it that made me think she wasn't talking about sex.

"How about you untie me, then?"

She drew her fingers through her hair, pulling the stray locks of it away from her face. Her heartbeat was still elevated. She swallowed and took a few more steps away from me as if space would cool the heat between us. "First," she said, "I want you to name your price."

"For?"

"Helping me find my brother's killer. I can't . . . do anything else with my life until that happens, Shame." She studied my lips with a soft longing as she said it, then stared into my eyes. Her cool blues darkened with need. "Just help me find him, and if I can convince you that he deserves to die, help me kill him."

"And then?"

"You can name your price. Tell me what you want."

"I don't kill people for sex."

Yet.

She shook her head. "I didn't mean it like that. It's just . . . I didn't realize what you are . . ." She licked her lips and stared at my mouth again, then my eyes. "How very good you are. You tell me what you want in exchange, and I'll do it."

Jesus, I was going to explode.

Eleanor drifted into my line of sight. I had completely forgotten about her. She floated up behind Dessa and put her hand on her shoulder.

"Don't," I warned her.

Dessa frowned, and a roll of goose pimples pricked across her skin. Eleanor's touch was grave-cold.

"Don't?" Dessa asked.

Before I could answer her, Eleanor was floating between us. Ghosts can occupy the same space as people, so even though you couldn't have fit a first grader between Dessa and me, Eleanor hovered there just fine.

Eleanor lowered her hand toward my crotch and raised one eyebrow.

"No. *No*," I said. "Do not touch me."

Dessa took another step away, obviously reassessing my level of crazy.

Eleanor did not pull away. She cupped my junk like a doctor. Then wiggled her fingers around a bit more just to make sure she had covered all the ground.

Her ice-cold touch ended all my happy-sex thoughts, and not in the good way.

Bitch.

"You weren't complaining just a minute ago," Dessa said.

"It's . . . Jesus." I scowled at Eleanor. Took a deep breath and tried again.

"It's not you. Listen, love. I'm all for the sex-as-bribery thing. A fan of it, really. But if we're going to trust each other enough to actually do anything about this killer of yours—not that I'm agreeing to help, let's just assume I'm entertaining the idea—you have to untie me and tell me the details of what I might—*might*—be agreeing to."

She hesitated. I didn't blame her. But what she wasn't seeing was that my head was finally, for the first time since before the bar, completely clear.

Maybe it was from the ghost clutching my junk. More likely whatever she'd slipped in my drink had worn off.

I could break out of these ropes and suck all the binding bits out of the wooden chair and free myself, Void stones or no Void stones. But it was my turn to see if she really wanted to negotiate. Really wanted to trust me.

"Set me free and we can bribe each other like adults," I said with a smile.

Her eyes flashed, then settled into a deep smolder.

She walked slowly around me. "Do you think I don't know how dangerous you are?" She paused at my back. I wondered if she was reaching for her guns. Wondered if I'd have a bullet in my head.

"Do you think I'm going to trust you enough to just let you go?"

"Yes," I said. "Yes, I do."

She was silent for a second or two. Then she bent down and her voice was warm against my ear, sending a fever across my skin. "You're *very* good, Shamus."

A hard, sharp jerk at my wrists. The rope cut free and fell away. I pulled my hands apart and rolled my shoulders.

"What about my feet?" I asked, hoping for another chance at her, on her knees in front of me, and me, with my hands free this time.

"You can handle that, can't you?" She dragged her fingers up the back of my neck then tugged on my hair.

I arched my head back, eyes closed, neck bare. Wanting her touch. She let go.

Damn.

I bent and took some time untying the ropes around my ankles, fingers thick and numb.

Then I stood.

I'm not going to lie. I was sore and bruised. I didn't know how long I'd been crammed in that trunk, nor if she'd gone through the trouble to beat me with a tire iron before tying me up. Or I could just be hurting from whatever it was she'd dosed my drink with.

Still, it wasn't the worst date I'd ever had.

"So, what exactly did you poison me with?" I turned.

She was shrugging into her shirt—a button-down that was not buttoned.

She looked over her shoulder, and her lips curved at one corner. "Just a little something I have and you want."

"Mmm," I said, not paying a lot of attention to her answer.

She must have picked up on that. She bent and, holding my gaze, took her time pulling her jeans up her long, smooth legs and over her hips before she tugged on the zipper.

I swallowed to get my tongue working again. "So we're going to bargain and blackmail over every last detail? Is that any way to build a relationship?"

"Look at it from my perspective," she said. "Having the upper hand with you is the only way you and I can have a relationship. Plus, it's a lot more interesting that way, don't you think?"

I could lie. I didn't.

"Yes," I said, rubbing at my wrists and the ache there. "Much more interesting. I don't suppose you'd like to kiss on it to seal the deal?"

She started buttoning her shirt. "We have a deal?"

"We do if you tell me who killed your brother. And before you refuse, listen to me, love. There are certain people in this world I will not kill. Will not. No matter what manner of horror they have committed."

That seemed to speak to her. She nodded.

"I don't know his name," she said. "But he was a member of the Authority. Dangerous then. More dangerous now. I have information that says he might be in the Portland area."

"Why? Do you know what he's doing here?"

"No. My guess is he's planning to kill more people."

"Or he's visiting his dear old gram for all you know. So far, I'm not seeing a lot to go on. Do you know why he killed your brother?"

"My brother was . . . mixed up with the Authority. I didn't know it then. He never . . . said anything to me."

"There's only one way to keep a secret organization secret," I said.

"I didn't want to believe it. Didn't even find out about it until I pulled his files. He worked for the group in Seattle."

"Do you know what style of magic he used?"

It used to be a big hush-hush that there were more styles of using magic than Life, which doctors tended to use, or Faith, that teachers liked to use. We'd pretty safely kept Death and Blood magic out of the public notice, although there were just enough Blood spells leaked to the public to keep the druggies and thrill seekers happy.

"He was a Closer. I don't know what that means."

"Well, that means you have a possible motive for revenge. Closers were magic users who took people's memories away. Magically," I added. "So the secrets of the secret organization could remain secret."

"Jesus," she said.

It was still strange to me that people were so surprised by that. I'd been born and raised in the Authority. Since before I could talk I'd known the price for stepping too far out of line—and getting caught—was having your memories wiped.

"He must have known something," she said.

"Or he was part of Closing someone's memories and they decided they didn't like it much."

"Enough to kill?"

I slipped my fingers in my jacket pocket, digging for cigarettes. Found them, lit up without asking her opinion on it. Sat on the edge of the bug-infested bed. She really had chosen a shit hole of a motel. I wondered why.

"Closers could take memories away," I said. "Change lives. Make a person forget those he loves: spouse, children, siblings, parents. Give a person an entirely new past. A new identity. Make it so he could never use magic again." I took a drag on the cigarette, exhaled. "So, yes. I'd say someone could be angry enough at a Closer they'd want him dead."

She grappled with that for a bit, which stalled her in buttoning her shirt and jeans. I did not mind the view.

"How did he kill him?" I asked.

"What?" she said. Okay, she was a little more shaken by her brother's past as a Closer than I'd expected.

"How did your brother die?"

She seemed to pull herself together. She shook her head. "I don't want to say. Not yet. But I can show you."

The cigarette had almost burned down, so I took the last drag to kill it. Looked around for an ashtray, didn't see one. I flicked it on the carpet with the other cigarette burns and wiped my boot over it.

"It would be a start. But I'm not saying I'll hunt anyone down for you."

"He was a good man," she said. "Had a wife and a baby girl."

"I'm sorry for their loss. And yours. But I make no promises here."

She had kicked off her boots to pull on her jeans. Her top three shirt buttons were still undone, showing just the edge of her bra and breast.

For a second, I wondered what was wrong with me. The old Shame would have promised her anything, fucked her in this dirty hotel, then left her with nothing but a pile of lies.

Was it possible I'd contracted a conscience from all the hell I'd been through? Picked up a terrible case of morality and a Zayvion-like sense of right and wrong?

Who was I kidding? I'd always had a moral code. I never used a girl who wasn't consciously using me right back. And I never promised someone something this important, something their heart was riding on, and broke my word.

Okay, maybe it wasn't all that moral, but it was a code.

"There are other people I can approach to do this," she said.

"I know."

"I have information that could mean the difference between people in this town staying alive or not."

"I know."

"I have information on the missing girl who was found dead up in Forest Park."

"So do the police."

She shook her head. "They don't know what I know." She paused, studied my face. "You don't care, do you?"

She was wrong. I cared. A lot. Especially if anything happened to harm Zay and Allie. And yes, even if anything happened to Terric.

"I'm not promising to care. Not even about your brother's killer." It was blunt. Honest. "But I want to see how he was killed. And I want to hear about the missing girl."

She didn't look at all surprised. Still, she considered me for a long moment.

"Not here," she said as she tied up her boots. "Let's do lunch instead. Also, I think you should pay for the room."

"How about I don't file kidnapping charges instead?"

She glanced up. Smiled. "You know I could kill you from a rooftop if you approach the police."

"Oooh. I like it when you talk dirty."

She stood. Stepped up close to me.

I thought maybe I ought to kiss her. Maybe I ought to talk her into seeing things my way, Shamus-style.

"You still haven't given my boyish charms a chance," I said.

"To seduce me?" she asked.

"To make you never want to be with any other man as long as you live."

She laughed, truly laughed. It was a musical sort of thing that filled the silent places in me.

"You think *very* highly of yourself, don't you?"

"Not at all. I am painfully humble."

She closed the distance between us. Close enough I could smell her perfume, a very light vanilla scent that made me want to lean in closer and taste it on her skin.

"And what if I took you up on it?" she asked, tipping her head up to meet my eyes. She was breathing deep and slow. Waiting. Wanting.

"You would not be disappointed," I said softly. I lifted my hand and gently pushed her hair away from her face.

A key turning the bolt on the door clicked. We both looked that way.

She pivoted, a gun suddenly in her hand, but I knew who was on the other side. Knew the heartbeat.

I grabbed her arm and pulled her up against me, turning to foul her shot.

"No," I said. Just as the door opened to show the man standing there.

Davy Silvers.

"Sorry to interrupt. Shame, I need to talk to you."

Davy looked like he was barely old enough to drink, although he'd shown me his license once that said he was twenty-three. Blond, sort of an easygoing-skater-kid look, complete with a turquoise beaded necklace. Most people had no idea he was the head of the entire network of Hounds in Portland. And since Hounds used to be the best at tracking illegal spells back to the caster, he liked the anonymity.

The reason I knew his heartbeat? He was the only man I knew who had been more screwed over by magic than Terric and me.

He'd made it through the apocalypse, but not before he'd been infected by poisoned magic, and then had been kept alive by Eli "the Cutter" Collins. Collins was brilliant, as most sociopaths are, and was a hell of a magic user. Eli had also been kicked out of the Authority for the horrors he'd done with magic. So even though Eli had literally carved spells into Davy's skin to keep Davy alive, I wasn't sad when I'd heard Collins had left Portland for good.

"Friend of mine," I said to Dessa.

She scoped Davy out like she was filling in a missing person report. Then she lowered the gun.

"Outside okay with you?" Davy asked.

"Sure," I said. "Outside should be fine."

Davy didn't shut the door, just leaned there with it propped open, looking like he wasn't paying very close attention to every detail of the situation.

"So," I said to Dessa, who stepped out of my arms. "This was fun. Thanks for the drink. Try not to kill anybody I wouldn't kill."

I started toward Davy.

"I'll see you real soon, Flynn," she said.

Yes, it was a reminder of our lunch date. And also a threat. I would have been disappointed by anything less.

Chapter 9

Davy had a beat-down old pickup that had been left to him by a good friend. Allie once told me it was the truck Martin Pike used to drive. Pike had been a hell of a Hound, and a mentor to Davy.

I put on my sunglasses, even though it was still dark out, then made straight for the truck, glancing around to try to get my bearings. Lots of tall fir trees, some pine sprinkled in. The buzz of a busy road tickled the edge of my hearing, but none of these things were distinct enough to stand out from any other corner of the northwest.

"Where the hell?" I asked.

And that's when it hit me. I was in St. Helens, northwest of Portland, somewhere off Highway 30. A dead zone. Back when magic was broken, but strong, there were only a few places off-grid that were naturally magicless. This was one of them.

"She really knows how to cover her bases," I said.

"Get in," Davy said as he walked around to the driver's side of the truck. He didn't give me hell for being drugged, trunked, and tied up by some strange woman, which is how I knew whatever he had come to tell me was not good news.

"Who's hurt?" I asked.

He opened the door, got in.

I swung up into the passenger's seat.

Davy started the engine and refused to say anything until we had tires on asphalt. Pretty soon the Highway 30 signs flashed by at the side of the road, white in the darkness.

"It's Joshua Romero," Davy said. "He's dead."

I leaned my head back against the headrest and took each emotion as it came: anger, sorrow, anger, loss, anger, acceptance and anger.

Joshua was a nice guy out of Seattle, a Closer who'd thrown his lot in with us Portlanders when we were trying to convince the Authority we weren't crazy, while simultaneously saving the damn world.

"How?" I asked, dragging through my memories for him mentioning health issues.

"Murder."

"The hell. How?"

"Magic."

Okay. Maybe this wasn't my call anymore, since I hadn't really been the head guy in charge of anything magic related for more than a year, but there was too damn much murdering by magic going on lately. Especially since killing someone with magic simply should not be in ninety-nine percent of the population's reach anyway.

"Do you, does anyone know who?" I asked. "Or when? Or how *exactly*? As in what kind of magic? Tell me they had Hounds on the scene. Tell me the police up there didn't just think Hounding and tracking back a spell is some kind of Ouija board voodoo trick."

"I don't know yet. I just got the call."

"How long has Terric had you tailing me?" I asked.

He glanced at me. "I'm not following you for Terric."

"Who, then? Allie? Zayvion? Please tell me it isn't my mother."

"Shame. Joshua is dead. Can we put you and your problems on the back burner for a minute?"

Like I said, he wasn't as young as he looked.

"Gladly. Where did it happen?"

"He was found in his car. In a parking garage on Burnside."

"Whoa, hold on. He was in Portland?"

"Yes. And it looked like he'd gotten in his car and dropped dead behind the wheel before he ever had the chance to turn the key."

"Where's his family?"

"They were in Seattle. They've been taken in. They're nowhere anyone can find them now."

I nodded. So the Authority was still doing its part in trying to protect magic users and families of magic users. But Joshua wasn't a Soul Complement to his wife—they didn't use magic together and couldn't break it to make it powerful.

So why was he targeted?

"What was Joshua doing?" Here's where being out of touch was working against me. I didn't even know if Joshua was still working a magic-related job, or if he'd washed his hands of it all and finally opened that restaurant he'd always dreamed of.

"I don't know all the details, but he was still involved in magic. Rehab, I think. Finally put his counseling degree to use."

"Rehabbing magic users?"

"Helping place people who used to use magic, or were harmed by magic, into magic-free or low-magic jobs. Most of those people still live here in Portland since this is where magic went bad. You know how it is for us all. To have that kind of power fade away. Hard adjustment."

"Last time I was paying attention, it took a hell of a lot of work, and a hell of a lot of people, like a hundred or more, to pull on enough magic to do anything harmful to someone," I said.

"That hasn't changed."

I was silent. So was he. We were close to Portland now, traveling on well-lit roads.

Davy had probably already come to the conclusion I'd been trying very hard to ignore. The only person strong enough to use magic to kill someone with it was a Breaker. A Soul Complement.

"We're looking for two people, aren't we?" I said.

Davy nodded.

"Balls."

"At least it will be a short list," Davy said.

That was the upside of Soul Complements being rare.

"Unless there's a pair out there we don't know about," I said.

He nodded. "That's what we were thinking."

From the tone, I knew Davy wasn't telling me everything. "We? Who are you working for, Davy, my boy? Police? Overseer? Perhaps a little freelancing with government black ops?"

"Right now? The Overseer. He has a Hound on every known Soul Complement."

"And how long have you really been following me? Come on now, tell Uncle Shame."

That got a quick smile out of him and he looked my way. "About a week. Do you know that you talk to yourself a lot?"

"Yes."

"What's that all about?"

"It's an Irish thing."

"It sounds more like a crazy-guy thing. I mean, it's practically full conversations. Arguments. You go on and on, Shame."

"It's a pity we'll never get to the bottom of this mystery," I said.

Davy smiled. "Never say never to a Hound. Also never say mystery, come to think of it."

"How about drop it? Or where are we going?"

"Or how about you tell me about your date back there?"

"Nothing to say, mate," I said.

"Nothing? You staggered out of the bar like you'd

drained half their stock, but I only saw you go through two beers and four shots over six hours. With lunch."

"So?"

"That's not enough to get you drunk."

"So?"

"So either you were faking it or she dropped something in your drink."

"By the way, do you know who she is?" I asked.

"I know she had a rifle trained on you. On more than one occasion."

"Jesus, Silvers. You didn't want to tell a man he was in some sniper's crosshairs?"

"Like you didn't know. I'm curious as to why you haven't told Terric about her."

"Who says I haven't?"

He gave me a look, then turned his gaze back to the road.

"I've seen that man he's dating," he said a little more quietly.

Didn't have to fill in the blanks. I knew he was talking about Terric's bruiser.

"Dash mentioned he didn't approve of the situation," I said. "You have any information on Jeremy I should know about?"

"He's tied into an old family of Blood magic users. Used to deal spell-laced drugs. They have connections in the region. Some say Black Crane. Powerful people who made a lot of money while magic was hot."

"And now that it's cold?"

"They still have connections. Power. Deals in place."

"Do they have anything on Terric?"

Davy didn't say anything for a minute. Slowed for a light, then turned left. "Not that we can find."

So he had been checking in on Jeremy. Nice of him. "There's that 'we' again. Who asked you to check in on Terric's love life?"

"Allie and Zay. Plus, Terric's my friend too, you know? I keep an eye on my friends. And he's been . . . different since he's been with Jeremy."

I didn't say anything so he just kept on talking.

"You want to know what I think, Shame?"

"I really don't."

"I think Terric wouldn't be trying to keep Jeremy alive if you were around. I think he'd instead use that Life magic to damp down the Death magic that's killing you."

"Killed," I said. "Not killing. Other than the whole breathing thing, I'm not much alive, mate."

"Sure," he said. "You're as dead as I am. Magic changed us. Made us into . . . something else. You don't see me whining about it."

"You know what you don't see me doing?" I said. "Being a prick."

"Or admitting I'm right and you don't like it."

"There must be someone else's business you can dick around in," I muttered.

"Oh, there is. Plenty of people's. None quite as fun as yours."

"I'm so pleased you find me amusing. Also, you do realize that Terric put Jeremy's cancer into remission? That means something to him. To both of them."

"I know. It means something to Jeremy's doctors too. And his family. As a matter of fact, some members of his family, powerful people, are taking very close notice of what Terric can do with magic."

And there it was. The angle I hadn't seen. If Jeremy's powerful family saw Terric as a way to hold off illness, cure diseases, or hell, put a new kick into the drug-of-the-week they were cooking up, then Terric was suddenly a valuable commodity. Someone worth controlling.

Maybe even someone worth hurting.

"Does this have anything to do with the government hunting down Soul Complements?" I asked.

"That's . . . news. Want to fill me in?"

"Aren't you working for the Overseer?"

"Working, yes. It's not like he invites me into his bedroom to talk over his day."

"I probably shouldn't," I said. So I did anyway. "The Overseer called a meeting. Hell, I guess it was this morning. What day is it?"

"Friday, but only by a few hours."

"Okay, so yesterday late morning the Overseer fired Terric and me, put Clyde Turner in our place, and told all the Soul Complements in the room that the government had declared it Breaker season and was most likely hunting us down."

"All the Soul Complements? How many were there?"

"Me and Ter, Zay and Allie, Doug and Nancy, and two other couples I don't know."

"What did they look like?"

I did a quick recap of the cougar and the younger man, and of the hipster pair.

"The cougar is Simone Latchly, and the man with her—he's older than me, Shame—is Brian Welling. They're out of San Diego. The other couple is from Arizona. Anthony Pardes and Holly Doyle. You should know that. You were Head of the Authority."

"I left the details to my underlings."

"Nice try. I know what you did your first year. I was there with you, remember?"

What I'd done was worked my ass off to keep the normal people in the world from killing every Authority member they found out about. There was a lot of anger, mistrust, and blatant hate in the first year of everyone getting their memories back.

If you looked at it right, I'd saved a lot of lives that first year. Well, Terric and I had.

Healing magic had proved that secrets, grudges, hurt feelings, and lawsuits do not die easily.

I just shrugged and rubbed my thumb over the edge of the ring on my finger. We were well out of the dead zone. Magic pooled naturally and flowed through the networks and pipelines far belowground.

Easy to access as it ever was.

My hunger, which must have been snuffed out by being around Terric, then poisoned, covered in Void stones, and dragged to a nonmagical zone, was gnawing on me again.

I needed to consume. Now.

Davy was, strangely, one of the only people who didn't make me want to drain him. He was right about magic changing him. I could sense it in his heartbeat too. He still carried a trace of the tainted magic that had almost killed him. A lot of magic poured through his body, in his blood and bones. It didn't give him the power to break magic, like Terric and me. It was simply keeping him alive and, therefore, not easily consumable.

Davy was not quite a real boy.

Eleanor was in the back of the truck, immune to wind or cold or rain.

I didn't have the concentration to draw on the vegetation rolling past at seventy-five miles an hour. But the truck engine was burning. Working hard. Changing mass into energy. Fire, heat. I could work with that.

"Listen," I said. "It's been a long and weird night. I'm going to catch some z's. I assume you're taking me back to Portland, and maybe to Clyde or whoever is on top of the information coming in on Joshua's death?"

"Something like that," he said.

"Right. Wake me when we get there."

I closed my eyes and very carefully drew on a thin burn from the engine. Not so much to kill it, but enough that Davy's gas mileage was going to go to hell.

I didn't really sleep, but I did my best to be still, to drink the heat and fire and destruction off the truck, and leave Davy and every living thing around me alone.

I'd gotten good at pushing the world away. At making people and anything even remotely resembling life, anything that I might care about, something that existed at a far distance from me.

Worked on doing that now. Closed out the world. Closed out the motion, the sounds. Made all the edges soft and far, far away.

And when I had finally done that, finally settled into that dark, padded place where me and my insanity could sit down for tea, all I saw was Dessa's face, her laughter breathing over me so close it dug in like a sweet, sharp dream.

Chapter 10

Where we did not go: to the police. To the office. To the Overseer.

Where we did go: to the morgue.

And yes. Terric was there, waiting for us. He looked clean, showered, clothed in dark jeans and a tight black T-shirt. Like his night hadn't been full of ropes, guns, and trunk rides.

Or, you know . . . maybe it had been.

"Davy, Shame." Terric held out a cup of coffee for each of us.

I took mine but hesitated before drinking it. "If you spiked this, I'll make your life miserable."

"It's coffee with five sugars and an ungodly amount of cream," he said.

I took a sip. Man was speaking the truth. It was sweet, creamy, unpoisoned heaven.

"Why so twitchy?" he asked.

"Been running bad odds on my likelihood of being poisoned lately."

"So she did slip you a roofie," Davy said.

"I didn't say that."

"Who?" Terric asked. "What 'she' slipped you a roofie? When? At the bar?"

I could tell he was getting worked up. Not because of his

tone or heartbeat, but his control of Life magic was slipping, sort of covering him in a glowing white light.

It occurred to me that having a Life magic user like Terric lose control in the middle of a morgue might be option C for how to kick off the zombie uprising.

"Just a misunderstanding with a beautiful redhead," I said. "No worries. Davy was watching my back."

"Really?" Terric turned to Davy. "How long have you been doing that?"

Davy gave a loose shrug. "Not long."

"Davy," Terric began in his boss voice.

"Hey!" I said. "Isn't there a dead body we should be looking at? I mean, come on, Terric. Put your issues on the back burner for a minute. This isn't always about you. Have you no decency?"

Terric turned toward me so Davy was behind him. Davy shook his head at me and rolled his eyes.

"Joshua's here, isn't he?" I asked.

That seemed to bring Terric back to the business at hand. "Yes. Davy, you don't have to come in if you don't want to."

"I want to," he said.

So we all followed Terric down the gray hall to a door at the left. Then through the doors and into a room with a metal wall of twelve closed drawers, each big enough to hold a human. Paperwork hung from a few of the drawers, and when I took a second to glance at the rest of the room I noted medical equipment, sinks, lights, and movable tables.

All as clean as could be.

Well, except for the harder-to-reach corners and tiles where vague proof of the day's business lingered.

You'd think I'd feel right at home here. All this death. All those dead bodies cooling on the shelf.

I didn't. It gave me the goddamn creeps.

Terric strolled over to the metal drawers and tugged on the one to the far left, bottom. No paperwork there. As a matter of fact, I noted he pulled out a set of keys and unlocked it before tugging it open.

"Keys? Don't those belong to Clyde Turner now?" I asked.

"I haven't had time to turn everything over to him yet," Terric said. "Was going to finish that up today."

He pulled the drawer open.

Thankfully, Joshua was draped with a sheet, leaving only his head uncovered.

Still, it wasn't easy to look down on a man who I'd last seen laughing at a birthday party.

Terric was calm, steady. He handled death a hell of a lot better than I did.

Bastard.

"They initially said it looked like a heart attack," he said. "So that's what I'm letting out to the media and police. For now. There are some marks I want you to see, Shame. And, Davy?" He glanced up at Davy, his hand on the edge of the sheet. "Are you sure you want to stay?"

"Even more now that you've asked me twice," Davy said.

Terric drew the sheet down to reveal Joshua's bare chest and stomach.

Carved into his skin with a thin, artistic hand were spells. Pain. Binding. Death.

"Jesus Christ," Davy breathed.

I glanced up, met Terric's gaze. Even though I couldn't hear his thoughts, right then, right there, he and I had an agreement: kill the son of a bitch who had done this.

"Shame," Terric said, maybe more for Davy than me, "do you recognize this signature?"

See, here's the thing. Every magic user has to draw glyphs, or symbols, that in turn magic fills and acts upon. And just like handwriting, every magic user has a unique signature. The way I cast Light doesn't look exactly the same way Terric casts Light.

Hounds, like Davy, are trained in knowing every magic user's signature. They spend a lot of time keeping up on such things, and there were databases where each magic user had to register his or her signature.

But I didn't need a database to know who had killed Joshua.

"Eli Collins," I said.

Davy's heart kicked up into fight-or-flight mode, the kind of sweat-terror you fall into when realizing the nightmare didn't go away when you turned on the lights.

"Davy," Terric said in a tone that pushed Davy's heartbeat down a notch. "Do you agree?"

Davy nodded. "That's his work. I'd swear on it."

The door opened.

We all turned, Davy with his hand on his hip—was he carrying a gun now?—Terric with his left hand casting a spell, and me with my right hand already through a spell, only the cracking red static across my rings holding the magic from filling it.

"I didn't mean to startle you," Dessa said as she sauntered in without batting an eye at any of the near deaths we were aiming her way.

"Shame," she said, "want to introduce me to your friends here?"

"No."

She stopped about halfway across the room. "Look, I'm unarmed. Well, I have these guns." She reached inside her jacket and Davy pulled a gun.

"Don't," he said.

"I'm going to put them on the counter here, so you don't have to worry about it," she said.

"Let her," Terric said.

"Fine," Davy said. "Slowly."

She reached into her jacket, pulled her guns, slowly, one by one, and placed them on the counter.

"Step away from it." Davy sounded like he'd done this more than once. Over the past three years of Hounding for the police, I assumed he had.

She stepped away and even kept her hands out to the side. "So, were they killed by magic?" she asked.

"I'm sorry," I said. "Why the hell are you here?"

"You know why." She took a couple steps closer. "Also, we forgot to set our lunch date."

Terric lowered his hand, then, to me, "Shame."

I sighed and let go of the spell. I shook my hand and a loud crack of electricity lashed out to the floor in a red arc, the pull on magic interrupted like a fuse shorting out.

Dessa's eyes went a little wide and she paused before coming any closer. I noted Davy did not put away his gun.

"Her name is Dessa," I said. "She never told me who she works for. If I had to guess?" I gave her the up-down, gauging her with sober eyes. "I'd say government."

"Very good," she said. "Dessa Leeds," she said to Terric. "And I know you're Terric Conley, and you're Davy Silvers. What I don't know is who the dead person is."

"Why should you?" Terric asked.

"She shouldn't," I said.

"I'll make it worth your while, Mr. Conley," she said.

"Ha! Barking up the wrong tree, sister," I said.

"How?" he asked.

"I have information," she said, "about the movement against Soul Complements."

Terric weighed her comment and, as I expected he would, decided the information and possible safety of others was worth the risk. "I won't give you his name," Terric said.

"That's fine," she said. "I just want to see his injuries."

Terric nodded.

I sighed again. So not the way I would have let this go down. I missed being in charge.

Terric was on the far side of the drawer, I stood near the head of it, and Davy was on the other side, closest to Dessa.

She walked over, and paused nearest me.

I folded my arms over my chest and watched her while

she studied Joshua's wounds. Okay, I'm not a sentimental guy—not really. But I've always seen pain as a very personal kind of thing. Tell someone you're hurting, and you've just told them how you are vulnerable.

So I did not like letting Dessa, no matter how nice she was, stare at my friend's dead body. Stare at the wounds that had proved his final weakness.

I expected her to keep her feelings to herself, but the expression on her face was clear and honest: sorrow.

"These marks," she said. "They're from a blade—a knife—aren't they?"

"Yes," Terric said. I didn't know if he was watching me or watching her, because I refused to take my eyes off her.

She shook her head, as if she didn't want to deal with what was right in front of her. "And magic. They're spells, aren't they? The only one I recognize is Binding there." She pointed to a Celtic-knot-looking design carved between the Death and Pain symbols.

"They're spells," Terric said.

"And they killed him?" She finally looked up. Not at me, at Terric.

Terric's body language shifted. He was measuring her just the same as I had. And he'd come to the same conclusion. She knew something about this. Something that was causing her sadness.

"My brother was found like this," she said. "Dead. With spells carved into his chest. Just like these."

"You never said that," I said.

"I was going to show you, remember?"

"Who's your brother?" Davy asked.

"He was a Closer," I said.

Davy nodded. We'd had so many threats against Closers over the years, the death rate was in a much higher percentage than other magic users.

"His name was Thomas Leeds," she said. "He worked in Seattle."

Terric frowned, searching his memory. "I think I met Tommy once, briefly. I'm sorry for your loss."

Then he pulled the sheet up to Joshua's chin and slid his body back into that endless cold.

"What can you tell us about your brother's killer?" he asked.

"Not a lot," she said. "He used to be a part of the Authority. That's all I know, other than he may be in this area."

Since they'd found Joshua's body in a parking garage downtown, yeah, I'd say Eli was in the area.

"And about the government looking for Soul Complements?" he asked.

"I'll tell you what I know if you help me find who did this." She pointed toward the drawer.

"I am not in a position to guarantee you anything along those lines," he said.

Funny, that's pretty much exactly what I'd told her. I tilted a told-you-so look her way.

"Well, I'm going to be looking for the killer. Which means I'll probably be getting in your way. I might even take my story to the police, or to the media. Blow the whole secret about magic being used to kill people right out of the water. I'm sure the citizens of Portland would be thrilled to find out all their fears about magic, and the mysterious Authority, are true."

"Blackmail, darling?" I said. "Really? How will that help your hunt? I don't think having cops and reporters crawling over every move is going to give you time to find anything except a good lawyer."

"Either I'm in on finding the man who killed my brother and your friend there, or I'm going to make sure that we're all out." An ultimatum. Gutsy move.

I opened my mouth to tell her she was out of luck.

"Then you're in," Terric said.

I kept my surprise to myself. "Wonderful," I muttered.

"Good," she said, looking surprised at his decision too. "Good. Where do we start?"

"We'll need to see if there are records on your brother we can pull," Terric said. "Did you drive here?"

"Yes."

"You can follow us downtown to the office." He locked the drawer, then started toward the door, pausing only to take her guns and shove them in his pockets.

"Those are my guns," she said.

"Not while we're working together, they aren't," he said without looking back.

Have I mentioned there are moments when I really, really like that guy?

"They're not my only guns," she said.

"Then you can give me the rest at the office," Terric said.

Davy just shook his head. "You have no idea what you're getting into, Leeds."

"Don't I?" she asked as she followed Terric. "All right. How about you fill me in?"

"I think you'll find out soon enough."

He followed behind her. I noticed Davy did not put his gun away.

Me? I paused next to the door. Let them all get a distance down the hall. Then I said a prayer for Joshua. Hell, said a prayer for the rest of us while I was at it.

I had a bad feeling we'd need all the help we could get.

Chapter 11

Davy was gone before any of the rest of us, slipping down the street and rumbling away in that big old truck. I figured he was going to report Joshua and Dessa and everything else to the Overseer.

We had maybe fifteen minutes tops before Clyde Turner found out and locked us out of the records, and any- and everything else he thought we shouldn't be digging around in.

I swung into the passenger seat of Terric's car.

"Fifteen minutes?" I said.

"Until?" he asked.

"The Overseer tells Clyde to lock us out of this case."

"Clyde might say no."

We were headed to the office. I noted it was still dark out, and checked the dashboard clock. Four in the morning. Jesus, I hated going to work this early. Or at least, I assumed I did. I didn't think I'd ever gone into work this early.

" . . . for me would you?"

"What?"

"Dash. Call him. Tell him to meet us down there."

"At the office," I said, taking Terric's cell phone.

"Yes. Don't you ever listen to me?"

"Every word."

I dialed. Dash, that overachiever, answered before the first ring was done.

"Spade," he said.

"Hey, Dash, this is Shame. Terric wants you to meet us at the office as soon as possible."

"Trouble?"

"You could say that."

"I'll be there in five." He hung up.

"Be there in five," I said. "Where does that kid live?"

"Loft space just a few streets down. So, she poisoned you?"

"Well, yes. I let her poison me."

"Uh-huh. Then what happened?"

"Nothing. Nothing happened."

"Shame, I just told her she could be a part of this hunt. I want to know everything that happened, everything you know about her. I'm giving you three minutes to cover it."

"Why three?"

"Because if I guessed wrong and she's not what I think she is, I'm going to turn right and head straight to the police. When she follows us, I'll knock her out and lock her up."

"Brutal. Effective. Very double-crossy of you, Terric. Why are you suddenly playing by the dark side of the rule book?"

"Joshua is dead."

He let that sit for a second or two. "He's not going to be the last friend of ours we bury if we don't stop Collins."

So I filled him in. Every. Last. Detail.

He didn't laugh. The only time he spoke was to clarify things like what kind of car she was driving, what other cars I saw parked next to the motel, and what kinds of guns she was carrying.

"Are you going out to lunch with her?"

"If she has something on the missing people around town, don't you think I should?"

"She could be lying."

"Sure."

"Do you think we can trust her?" he asked.

"You're asking me to judge someone's trustworthiness?"

"Yes. Your gut feeling on her." He glanced at me. "*Honest* gut feeling."

I dragged my fingers through my hair, rings rubbing and snapping as I did so.

"She makes me want to trust her. I think . . . I'd guess that before her brother's death she might have been a lot of fun to be around. She's got . . . spunk. She's calm under pressure, is trying to do the right thing. Plus, gorgeous. Her brother's death isn't a lie. She's grieving. She wants his killer to pay—not just to die, but to pay—for killing her brother."

"And she wants . . . us. Our information so she can take care of the killer and move on with her life."

"She wants you," Terric said. He waited. Waited for me to answer that.

"Who wouldn't? This?" I pointed to my face and body. "Irresistible."

The muscle at his jaw tightened and his eyes narrowed. "Is that all she wants from you?"

I took a deep breath and scrubbed my hand through my hair again, trying to smooth it this time. "She wants what I am. What I can give her: Death. A horrible, painful death for the man who killed her brother."

"Not exactly marriage material," he noted.

"I'm not planning on marrying the girl."

"Good."

What kind of tone was that?

"Terric," I said with a wide smile. "Are you jealous?"

"No."

"Aw, c'mon, now, mate. You're jealous I have a girlfriend. It bothers you that I like the look of her. The idea of being with her. And I would have done a hell of a lot more than kiss her if Eleano—"

I stopped. I didn't talk about Eleanor. Hadn't for years. Certainly not to Terric. I couldn't believe I'd almost started talking about her now. Why remind him that I'd killed a perfectly nice person because I was weak and had lost control of the monster within me?

"If what?" Terric asked.

"Nothing."

He didn't push it. And yes, I was grateful for that.

He changed the subject instead. "So you trust her?"

"To a point. She has a goal. Right now it's the same as ours. Or similar, anyway. I want the information she has. I think we can trust her to be truthful about what she knows. You know, until we can't."

He nodded. "So we don't lock her up, until we have to."

"This is nice," I noted. "Just like old times. Think Davy's ratted us out to Clyde yet?"

"He'll give us an hour. He wants Collins dead more than any of us. And the Overseer tends to make cut-and-dry decisions. He might want to lock Collins up and excuse the Authority of any other involvement in the case. But if we investigate, we'll let Davy come along while we take Collins down. The Overseer would never let a Hound into Authority business. Especially not a Hound with plenty of reasons for vengeance."

I nodded. Pulled out cigarettes and lighter. Rolled down the window. Lit up. Knew Terric was really worried about all this when he didn't even tell me not to smoke in his car.

I finished off three cigarettes, only getting five puffs in total by the time we pulled up to the office. This was becoming an expensive habit.

Terric parked along the side street and Dessa's car rolled up just a few spaces down. Okay, the good thing about being downtown this early: plenty of parking spaces.

We got out, waited for her, headed to the doors.

"What kind of food do you like?" Dessa asked as we stepped into the elevator.

"For?"

"Lunch."

"I'm flexible."

Terric snorted and stepped into the waiting elevator.

He leaned against one side of the elevator, I leaned against the other, and she stood at the back wall. Eleanor kept her hands to herself.

"I've heard there are some great vegan places," she said, "or sushi?"

"You like vegan, right, Shame?" Terric said.

"Pizza," I said, giving Terric a shut-up look. "Let's do pizza."

"All right." She leaned her shoulders back, more relaxed now that it was settled. "When?"

"Why not this afternoon?"

"Good."

The doors opened.

Dash was there, waiting by the elevator. "Shame, Terric. . . ." His voice fell off as he saw Dessa step out behind us. "Um . . . hello. Have we met?"

"Dash, this is Dessa," I said. "She's some kind of government assassin or something."

"Leeds," she said, offering Dash her hand to shake. "Dessa Leeds. Ex-government or something."

"Nice to meet you," he said. Then, "Terric. Clyde is here."

Terric paused just slightly in his stride down the hall. Enough time that I caught up with him.

"Want me to handle it?" I asked as we walked, shoulder to shoulder, down to the main office.

"Absolutely no, I do not," he said.

"I heard yes." I reached the door just a step ahead of him and pushed it open.

"Well, if it isn't Mr. Clyde Turner," I said cheerily. "What the hell are you doing down here so early?"

What Clyde was doing was sitting at one of the empty desks to one side of the room, writing on a legal pad.

He'd taken off his Giants hat, but was still wearing a flannel shirt, T-shirt, and jeans. A thermos and cup of coffee rested near his elbow.

He looked up, and took in the party coming his way. "Shame. What are you up to?"

Funny how I was always the one suspected of trouble.

"I need a word with you," I said. "Maybe in my office?"

By this time Terric had caught up with me. "We both need a word with you. In *my* office."

"Wouldn't miss it for the world." He stood. "You two boys working together again?" he asked as he lumbered between desks and down the short hall to Terric's office on the right. Terric unlocked the door so we could go in.

Terric took his place behind the desk, and I motioned for Clyde to head in before me. I shut the door behind us. Then I pulled on magic and cast a Mute spell while I drew down the blinds on the big glass windows.

I trusted Dash to be able to hold his own with Dessa out there, but I didn't want her hearing us or reading our lips.

"That's a nice piece of magic there, Shamus," Clyde said. "What's going on?"

He settled in a chair against the wall across from Terric's desk, and I leaned against the door, my arms crossed over my chest.

"We think Eli Collins is killing people," I said.

"Collins the Cutter?" he asked. "You think he's back in Portland?"

"There have been a string of murders here lately," Terric said. "Which might be connected to him. There has been an even longer string of missing persons. Have you been briefed on them?"

"Detective Stotts mentioned the case when I stopped in yesterday after the meeting. Thought I'd check with you on anything else you know that he doesn't."

"I've been keeping him up to date on everything," Terric said. "Except for what we just found out. Joshua Romero was found dead in his car down on Burnside today."

Clyde exhaled and sat back.

"Did Joshua and Eli have history?" he asked.

Terric shook his head. "I don't know. Other than the battles here a few years back, I don't know if they ever crossed paths."

"How did he die?" Clyde asked.

"Magic," I said.

"Like the bodies that keep showing up in Forest Park?"

"There's been more than one?" I asked.

Terric nodded to me. Then to Clyde. "Not quite. Joshua was cut—glyphs were cut into his skin. Death, Pain, and Binding."

"And you think Collins did this?"

"He's done it before—cut spells into people," I said. "Davy Silvers."

"I know about Davy." Clyde rubbed at the bridge of his nose, then crossed his arms over his chest. "Why didn't you go to the police if you think it's connected to the other deaths?"

"Because if it is Eli, then we have another problem on our hands," Terric said.

"Go on."

"He's killing with magic," I said. "Unless he's come up with some kind of technology to increase magic's power, then the only way one man can be strong enough to kill someone with magic is . . ."

"If he's found his Soul Complement," Terric finished.

Clyde's eyebrows ticked up. "Damn."

He took some time to think that through, while I exchanged meaningful glances with Terric. Was he going to tell Clyde we needed the files and some time to track Eli without every person in the Authority and on the police force knowing what we were doing, or was I?

"I wasn't involved in Closing Eli all those years ago," Clyde said. "Victor took care of that, I think. But I've briefly looked over his file. Especially after he was a part of the fight to rejoin magic you were all involved in. As I recall, he was instrumental in *saving* Soul Complements then."

"That was then," I said. "Allie was calling the shots and he listened to her, devil only knows why. As soon as he got the Soul Complements to safety, he disappeared."

"Tell me what you have planned," he said.

"It's not much of a plan yet," Terric started.

"Well, you should know that Ter here agreed to let an ex-government assassin in on this case."

"The redhead out there?"

"*We* agreed," Terric said. "And we don't know that she's an assassin, just that she's ex-government."

"With a sniper rifle," I said.

Terric sighed. "She said her brother was killed by wounds similar to Joshua's. She has a personal stake in finding the killer, and seems pretty intent on dating Shame."

"It's not a date," I said. "It's pizza."

"She poisoned you."

"Just a little."

"Isn't that what your kind call foreplay?" he asked.

"My *kind*?"

"So she's a liability," Clyde interrupted.

"She's someone who has information we can use," I said. "On the Breaker hunt."

Clyde held my gaze, then shifted his look to Terric.

"She could be useful," Terric admitted. What did you know? He actually agreed with me. "And I don't think we'd have any problem handling her."

"When was the last time you two used magic together?" Clyde asked.

"It's been a while," Terric said.

Which was good, because frankly, I couldn't remember the last time he and I had actually used magic together, as in hand in hand at the same time to break it and make it do really dangerous things.

That little scuffle in the alley with the ox, Hamilton, didn't count. I'd been angry, and while Terric's proximity meant I could draw stronger spells, just like the Mute spell that was currently keeping this conversation from being overheard, we had not broken magic in a long, long time.

"I'd like to keep it that way," Clyde said. "The Overseer is recommending Soul Complements get the hell out of Dodge. I agree. And if you are stubborn enough to actually stay in the area—yes, I'm looking at you, Flynn—then you'd better not pull on magic. And neither of you should break it."

Terric frowned, and opened his mouth, but Clyde continued. "Because breaking it sets off sensors we think the government has developed. Sensors that will lead them to the people breaking magic."

"That's new," Terric noted.

He nodded. "I've had some enlightening conversations with the Overseer the last couple days. Breaking magic will only paint an even larger target on your heads."

"We weren't telling you we were going to break magic," I said. "We're telling you—"

"Asking you," Terric corrected.

"Fine," I said, "asking you to give us a day or two to hunt for Collins."

"Before we get the police or anyone else in the Authority involved," Terric said.

Clyde shook his head. "No."

"Come again?" I said.

"No," he repeated.

The rings on my right hand crackled with red. I shut my mouth on what I hoped was a smile. "No?"

Terric sighed. "You don't want us hunting Eli?"

Clyde kept his attention on me, even though he was answering Terric. "I don't want you hunting Eli. I don't want Davy involved either, in case you're wondering. And I don't want some unknown woman anywhere near our business. We work *with* the law, gentlemen. We are not vigilantes. We do not pursue personal agendas or revenge. Our job is to take care of Authority business as smoothly and discreetly as possible. We have never used Breakers as assassins. We aren't going to start that now."

"We didn't say we were going to kill Eli," I said.

"I heard you. But I *know* you, Shame. This isn't your call anymore. Neither of you is the Head of the Authority. I am. If you want to remain on the payroll in some other capacity, then you're going to have to get used to my orders and follow them."

"Why are you always looking at me?"

"Because I know which of you won't play by the rules."

I gave him my best smile. "I like rules. They make that cracking sound when they break."

"Shame," Terric said. "He's right. This isn't our call. It's his. Is there anything you need from us?"

"Your keys. Dash has already given me access to the files and everything else." He paused a minute.

I was not paying attention to him. Because I was angry, and angry only led to hungry, and most days, like say when Clyde was not telling me what I could and couldn't do, I liked him.

". . . to see you both check in here if you're staying. We'll need to come up with protection plans," he was saying. "You remember there's a meeting in a few hours with the Overseer, right?"

"We'll be there," Terric promised, as if I weren't standing in the room. "I'll make sure of it."

Clyde pushed up onto his feet. "You and I square, Flynn?"

"Not really." Like I said, he and I did not bullshit each other.

"You know what I don't get about you?" he said.

"How I get all the chicks?"

"How after years of doing jack-all, you finally decide that today, and this one thing, is something you're going to apply yourself to. The one damn thing I have to tell you not to do."

"I could come up with other damn things you wouldn't want me to do."

"I'd rather you put your energy into staying alive."

"Yeah. Well, that's not really my thing."

"When you decide what your thing is?" He stepped toward the door and fixed me with a look. "Warn me, okay?"

"Now, where's the fun in that?" I asked.

I dropped the Mute spell with a slash of my hand, and black light snapped across my rings.

Clyde shook his head and walked out the door.

"Shame," Terric said before I could take a step. "You and I have a meeting this morning."

"I heard. I'm not going anywhere until then."

He nodded. "And lunch. With Dessa."

"Don't need you to be my secretary, Ter."

He was still sitting behind his desk, fingers resting lightly on the surface. "Good. I'll be out in a minute." He swiveled his chair so he could stare out at the city.

Dawn was rubbing the black off the sky. Looked like it wasn't going to rain for a change.

I left him to his moping and joined the others in the main room.

Dessa and Dash seemed to have hit it off pretty well, laughing over something—I think a recent movie.

I wondered how much information she's gotten out of him. Knowing Dash, zero.

She was drinking a cup of coffee, and looking . . . well, comfortable.

When she saw me coming and gave me that smile? Something inside me went warm and my heart tapped a hard beat.

What was wrong with me? It's not like I'd never seen a beautiful woman before. But her smile. That smile. For me. It was undiscovered country and I wanted that. Wanted to make her smile.

Those thoughts set off alarms in my head. The warm

feeling in my chest felt a lot like happiness. Maybe even hope. Two things that had never worked out well for me.

Things that might be best ignored.

"You two seem to have gotten chummy," I said.

Dash leaned against one of the empty desks. I wondered, not for the first time, why we had so damn many desks that no one ever sat at.

"Good coffee, good company," Dash said. "So, what's the word?"

I shook my head. "We're not going to pursue this."

Dash nodded and took a drink of his coffee, keeping an eye on Dessa. He had excellent instincts.

"What does that mean?" she asked.

I sat on the edge of an empty desk and stuck my hands in my jacket pockets. "I don't know how much research you've done on the Authority, but you must know that we have rules, structure, policies. We work inside the law. Yes, we kept Joshua's death quiet for a few hours, but we're getting the police involved. We're turning the investigation of his death—and who killed him—over to them."

Dash stood. "I'll start making calls." He strolled off to his office, stopping to talk with Clyde, who was on his cell phone near the far window.

"Really?" she said. "This is how you're going to play it?"

"Isn't a game, darling. We've had our see of things, and we'll be turning all information over to the police. You're welcome to come along if you'd like."

She stood. Left her coffee behind. Stepped up in my space.

My body responded to her: heartbeat, blood, breath. Pounding. Needful.

I didn't let it show. But I wanted to. Wanted to smile, and draw her in, and kiss her again until her clothes fell off.

"If you're lying to me," she said.

"I'm not."

She studied my face, the corners of her mouth pulling just slightly downward. Searching for my tell.

"This isn't my poker face," I said. "This is my truth face. We're off this case. Now, if you want to make everyone's life a little easier, you could go talk to Mr. Turner over there and tell him what you know about . . . everything."

She placed her hand on my knee. Heat scorched across my body. And I held my breath on a groan.

Keep it cool, Shamus. Keep it cool.

"You're going to take orders from him?"

"Today I am."

"What about tomorrow?"

"Tomorrow looks good too."

For a second, her mask slipped, and the woman who was grieving for the brother she loved was standing there, with hope breaking in her eyes. "So you're telling me no. Again."

"That's the way it has to be."

She glanced over my shoulder. Terric was still in his office watching the sun rise on the end of his career. Dash and Clyde had closed themselves in Dash's smaller office.

No help there.

"Shame," she began. "You could give me a list of names, and I'll take it from there. I can stay out of the way. Out of your way, out of the way of the police investigation. Please. You won't even see me."

There she was again, the woman behind the mask. The one who was willing to do anything to see that her brother's killer was taken down. The one who rescued purple turtles for babies.

"Who says I don't want to see you?" I said softly.

"Do you?"

What was I thinking? The best thing I could do for her— the best thing I could do for anyone—was keep them far away from me and my hunger.

"Well, we do have a lunch date," I said, trying to keep it light.

"Yes," she said. "We do."

"I'm not going to give you any information, though," I said.

"I understand that. I'm sure we'll find something else to talk about."

"Good. Oh, and, Dessa, if I were you, I'd give up on the revenge business."

She shook her head and lifted her hand away from my knee. "No," she said quietly, "you wouldn't."

I gave her half a smile before she turned to walk away. She was absolutely right. When it came to revenge, there was nothing on this earth that could stop me.

Chapter 12

Dessa said good-bye to Dash, got the address of the pizza place, and was gone.

"Maybe you should invest in a bulletproof vest," Dash said as he picked up the stray coffee cups and returned them to the coffee station.

"Wouldn't do me any good," I said. "I don't think she'd aim at my heart."

"Bulletproof jockstrap?"

I grinned. "Helmet. I think if I really crossed her, she'd take me down with one clean shot."

He chuckled and walked off tugging at the cuffs of his shirt. The windows were bright enough, there was no use denying day had arrived. The pulse of the city was pumping.

I sat at one of the empty desks and tried to push the spike of hunger away. Nothing here to consume, Flynn. No one deserved that kind of death.

I rolled my fingers, grinding the rings between them, the metallic scrape becoming a rhythm to cover the song of the living. I closed my eyes and tried to lose myself to it.

Dash set something down beside me with a clunk.

I opened my eyes.

"I hate this plant," he said.

Then he turned his back and walked toward the half-filled boxes by my old desk and started packing again.

I glanced down at the plant. A fern, I think. Did a check on the room: Eleanor wandering between desks, Terric and Clyde standing between the offices, talking quietly, Dash packing crap out of my desk.

No one was watching me.

I took a breath. Control would be good. Focused on the fern. This, just this one plant, was all the life I could have. So I was going to savor every damn frond.

I dragged the fingertip of my left hand gently along one arching branch of the thing, drawing out the life slowly, leaf by leaf, all the way to the arrow-sharp end, draining it, killing it. Reducing it to fragile brown bones.

I licked my lips, and my finger trembled just a bit as I moved on to the next branch. Repeated the process. Then again. And again. Slow as I could. Like a ritual. Like this would be the last life I'd ever taste. Like it could fill the endless hungry hole inside me.

Didn't work. Nothing stopped the hunger.

Still, it was something. An offering to the monster. Enough to keep me in the clear for a few more minutes.

Which, really, was as good as it was going to get.

". . . or are you going to walk?" Terric was asking as he strode across the room.

I glanced up, then around. Yep, he was talking to me.

About that time he noticed the dead plant next to me. His expression shifted from annoyed to something else.

"I'll drive," he said a little more gently. "Dash, I'm sorry to leave you with the packing. I'll try to be back this afternoon."

Dash gave Terric a smile. "The last thing you need to worry about right now is paperwork," he said. "I got this. Good luck at the meeting."

"See you boys soon," Clyde said.

"Shame?" Terric pointed toward the door. "Let's go."

So we went. Hallway, elevator, street with people headed to work, headed to breakfast, headed home, and finally, his car.

I ducked in, my heart pounding too hard.

"Are you . . ."

"I'm hungry," I said.

"Do you want—"

"No. Don't. Just don't talk to me for the drive."

Terric started the car. That was the last of the world I paid attention to other than Eleanor's cold hand resting against the back of my neck, which did some little good to cool the fire burning in me.

I closed my eyes behind my sunglasses and pushed the life around me away, far away.

If I could disappear in my head for a year, it wouldn't be long enough.

Came to with the scent of bacon filling my senses.

Opened my eyes. I was still sitting in the passenger's side of the car. The engine was not running. The car was parked. Eleanor was nowhere to be seen.

"Morning," Zayvion said. He was sitting in the driver's side of the car with a plate piled high with bacon. A fresh cup of coffee steamed in the cup holder.

"This is . . . odd," I said.

"Eat," he said. "You're not going into that inn until you do."

He shoved the plate of bacon at me, and I took it because, hey, free bacon. "Why?" I asked after I folded and ate three slices at once.

"You tuned out on the way over here. Terric said you needed food. There's coffee." He pointed.

I reached over, took the coffee, drank. Lots of sugar, lots of cream. Just how I liked it. Come to think of it, the bacon was just how I liked it too.

"I was just resting my eyes," I said.

"Bullshit," Zay said. His brown eyes were flecked with gold. So he was a little angry. Or ready to call on magic. Maybe ready to shut me down.

He was a good man.

"Do I look that dangerous, mate?"

He took a minute before he answered, then, "Yes. Terric said you haven't been eating. And you're having trouble controlling magic."

"And you believed him?"

"Is he wrong?"

I gulped down coffee, set the cup on my knee. "He worries too much. And is upset about losing his job."

"That's not what I asked you," Zay said. "Are you listening to me, Shame?"

"Of course."

He gave me a look. I stopped, put the bacon down, wiped my fingers on my jeans, and turned toward him, pressing my shoulder against the door. "You have all the attention I have left, Jones. What?"

"Allie's pregnant."

Holy. Shit.

I opened my mouth. Nothing came out. Shut it. Tried again. "Hell yes! Congratulations, mate! That's . . . It's yours, right?"

He punched my arm. Hard.

"Ow!"

"Of course it's mine," he said.

"I'm . . . without words. Damn. This is great news. Happy news. Mr. Jones is going to be a papa. How's that sitting with you?"

Some of the anger and tension drained out of him, replaced by a kind of nervousness I hadn't seen since we were teens. "I'm thrilled?" He nodded, and exhaled. "A little terrified at times."

"And Allie? How's she taking it?"

He smiled. That head-over-heels-in-love look that hadn't faded in all these years shone up the place. "She's amazing. Calm. Happy. Beautiful."

"So what does this happy news have to do with bacon?"

"She's in the inn. My pregnant wife is in there, Shame. And I need you to be in control when you're around her.

We're taking precautions until she gets through her first trimester with the baby. She and I aren't using magic. Not together. Not at all, so far. The doctors . . . There isn't any information on how breaking magic will affect an unborn baby. So we're being careful. Very careful. And I need to know you won't hurt her."

I could get mad at that. My best friend didn't trust me. But he was right to be worried about this. He was right to keep his baby and Allie safe from me.

"So?" Zay said. "How are you doing with Death magic? Really."

"It pulls pretty hard." I picked up my coffee cup but didn't drink. "I can stay ahead of the hunger. I can stay ahead of the push to use it . . . let it use me. So far I haven't done anything . . . certifiably evil. Food helps. Small destructions are good. The rings help." I lifted my hand to show him them.

"Are you in control right now?"

"Yes." I was not lying. I wouldn't lie about this. Zay knew it.

"Good. Finish eating. The Overseer is waiting."

I shoved the rest of the bacon in my mouth and took another drink of coffee. It was almost cold now. I'd been draining the heat from it while it was in my hand.

I drank it down cold, then nodded. "I'm good."

He took one last hard look at me. I must have passed muster, because he opened the door and got out of the car.

I left the plate and cup in the car, mostly because I knew it would bother Terric, and pushed my sunglasses closer to my eyes. Looked around.

Huh. We were in the parking lot of my mother's restaurant and inn. There weren't any cars here that I didn't recognize, which meant we were having a private meeting. Zay stopped next to me, a mountain of heat and life.

Man burned like a torch. More so now because he was tied to Allie, to her life, and to the new life inside her.

It was beautiful, really. Rare to see. And I was determined not to let that fall apart because of me.

We walked across the gravel to the door. I paused before opening it.

"How do I look?" I asked him.

He knew what I was asking. Was I throwing death vibes? Was I leaking Death magic?

Zay put a hand on my shoulder. Heavy. Wide. Hot.

I didn't pull on the life in him. Not a single drop of all that gorgeous, rich life. His life.

He waited a second, then nodded. "You're good, Shame."

"Good? Come on, now. You know I am the best, Z." I gave him a grin.

One eyebrow rose. "You're all right."

"The lies coming out of your mouth." I pushed on the door. "I do not know how she puts up with you."

"It's a little thing called love," Zayvion said so quietly I almost didn't hear him. "Can't run from it, can't deny it."

"Sure I can."

"Now who's lying?" he said.

We were in the main room. Warm. Smelled of breakfast food, bread, and pies or something sweet being baked for the afternoon crowd, with just a note of sausage or bacon.

The tables that lined windows and filled the high-ceiling and wood-beamed dining area were covered in dark green cloths, and centered with flowers. Chairs were wooden, floor was the original from when the old place had been a train station.

Sitting at one of the larger tables was the Overseer, Terric, Allie, and Victor.

"Morning, everyone," I called out cheerily. "How goes the plotting and planning?"

"Good morning, Shamus," Victor said.

Victor was old enough to be my father. I thought of him as my uncle, really. Gray haired, he wore heavy glasses that let him mostly get around on his own since he'd lost nearly all of his eyesight from the magical showdown before the apocalypse.

He had on a suit jacket, shirt, no tie. Looked like he was drinking tea. At his left was Terric, who gave Zay a look, then turned to watch me. Next to him was Allie, and she was beaming.

I didn't know how I had missed it at the meeting just yesterday morning. But the woman glowed—literally. The life and, yes, magic, inside her was luminescent.

I gave her a big smile. "Al, you little vixen, you. What's the good news, love?"

She pushed away from the table and walked right on over to me. Unafraid, that woman. She never disappointed. "Did Zay tell you?"

"He did. You're going to be a mum, eh?"

She nodded, and the smile lit her eyes. "I am. How do you feel about being an uncle?"

"Over the moon."

"Good," Zayvion said. "How do you feel about being a godfather?"

That, I did not expect. "What? Are you joking?"

"No," Allie said. "We are not. Would you be our child's godfather, Shame?"

"Yes," I said. "Of course. If you want me to be."

And then Allie put her arms around me and gave me a hug.

Lord.

I clamped a fist around my hunger and put my arms around her like she was made of eggshells. I was determined I'd drink the life out of the building and every tree for an acre around before I so much as touched the life in her.

My heart slowed to a low, dragging beat. A beat I controlled.

Zay, just behind Allie's shoulder, watched me. That look told me he'd take me down before I hurt her.

Good man.

She let go of me. Was still smiling as Zay stepped up and put his arm over her shoulder.

"We should celebrate," I said, letting go of my control enough that my heart stuttered through a beat or two before it got its rhythm back. "Whiskey all around!"

"It's six o'clock in the morning," Terric said. "How about we have coffee and pie?"

"Spoilsport," I said.

"What kind of pie?" Allie asked.

"For you and that godbaby of mine," I said, "any pie you want."

"I'll see what they have," Zay said.

And then he walked off to the kitchen, leaving Allie behind with us.

Correction: leaving Allie behind with me.

He hadn't given me a higher compliment in years. It stilled me.

I would not let him down.

Allie and I walked over to the table and she took her place beside Terric, an empty chair on her other side for Zayvion, then Victor and the Overseer.

Eleanor floated over to her favorite perch in the dining room—the bar at the far end.

I sat off to one side of the table, putting as many chairs as I could between me and the living.

"Small group," I noted.

"We've already spoken to the other Soul Complements," the Overseer started. "So now it's just the four of you."

Zay came back from the kitchen with two pies in his hands. Set those on the table. Cherry and apple. Not a bad score.

He applied a knife to the apple pie.

"And what have the others decided?" Terric asked.

The Overseer shook his head. "I'd rather not say. If something happens, I don't want any of you to have information that might harm the others."

"So why have all of us here now?" I asked. "Do you expect me to cover my ears and hum while Zay and Allie talk to you?"

"Shame," Victor said, "please. Show some respect."

"All right: respectfully," I said. "You do know we can hear each other?"

"Victor and I agreed it would be best," the Overseer said. "Since you've all decided to stay."

I turned my gaze to Allie. "Really?"

"This is our home," she said. "And our home ground. If something comes our way, we know the place and people better than anywhere or anyone in the world. I'd rather fight or hide here."

I didn't have to ask Zayvion what he thought about that decision. His heartbeat was steady but hard, just a little too much adrenaline pushing through his veins. He didn't disagree but he knew they were in for trouble. Fight. Flight. Maybe both.

And they had a baby to protect.

Hell.

Terric and I had already made our decision to stay put. Now there was even more reason to do so.

"Are you staying at your place?" I asked. "There's room here at the inn if you want."

"Thanks," Allie said. "But we're staying home. We're close to the well of magic out there." She nodded. "So we can access that pretty quickly if we need to."

I didn't ask her if they were accessing it because it was a powerful deposit of magic or because there was something about the St. Johns well that seemed to make healing with magic even easier. If they were hurt, being near that well might be the best for them. The best for Allie.

Zay was still busy serving pie, by looking at a person at the table, pointing the knife at one pie, then the other, and when the person nodded, cutting a generous slice and sliding it over to him.

The Overseer and Terric both took cherry; Victor and Allie had apple; Zay didn't serve himself a slice. When he looked at me, I pointed at the apple and he just pushed the rest of the pie my way.

I didn't bother with a plate. Picked up my fork and had at it, watching the others.

The Overseer sipped his coffee and sat back. He was more tired than he was letting on, and I noticed a slight tremble in his hand.

"So, what aren't you telling us?" I asked around a mouthful. The new chef kicked ass when it came to desserts. Well, she kicked ass when it came to any of the food we were serving, though I'd go to my grave saying my mum made the best bread known to mankind.

The Overseer considered me, picked up his coffee, and took another drink.

"I could ask you the same question, Mr. Flynn, Mr. Conley, but time is short. Why didn't you contact me about the Closer's death?"

Zay had been walking around the table to sit next to Allie. He paused, pivoting just a bit so he faced Victor.

"Who?" he asked quietly.

"Joshua," Terric answered. "We found Joshua Romero a few hours ago. In a parking garage. Dead."

Allie put her fork on her plate. "Oh no," she said. She pressed her fingers over her eyes, holding them there for a minute, then dropping her hands into her lap. When she looked up, she wasn't crying yet. I could tell that would come later. Instead she had that take-no-prisoners glint in her eye.

That glint always got us in trouble.

Okay: more trouble than usual.

"How?" she asked.

The Overseer glanced at me. Zay took his seat but did not eat the pie. He was looking at me too.

"You do realize I'm not in charge anymore," I said.

"Fine," Allie said. "Terric, do you know how he died?"

"Eli Collins," I said. Allie held her breath and Zay's eyes pooled with gold. Since Collins was also an ex-boyfriend of Allie's, and a man who had worked on experimental magic and technology integrations with her very dead, very disturbed father, I understood their reactions. Plus, any memories we'd tried to take away from him had been returned when magic was healed.

"Are you sure?" she asked.

I had a mouthful of pie, so I nodded.

Terric took over. "There are glyphs carved into Joshua. Death, Pain, Binding. It looked like Eli's signature."

"I want to see him," Allie said.

"Allie," Zay started.

"Don't need to, love," I said. "It was Eli's hand. Swear on it."

"Will this change your decision?" the Overseer asked.

I didn't know if he was asking me or them, but I answered, "Not a bit."

Terric shook his head. "We're staying."

Victor was tapping his finger softly on the edge of the table. He might have lost most of his sight, but he had not lost his ability to read people. I figured he had Terric and me pegged. He probably even knew we weren't planning to wait around for Eli to find us.

Take the fire to the fire, as, really, no one says.

"And you?" the Overseer asked Allie and Zay.

"No," they said simultaneously.

"We're staying here," Zay finished.

Since I was across the table, I think I was the only one who saw Allie's lips moving ever so slightly with the words Zayvion was saying.

They were probably thinking the same thoughts. Speaking to each other in their minds. Stuck together brain to brain with superelastic Soul Complement glue.

It was creepy.

But they were my friends. My creepy, creepy friends.

"I advise otherwise," the Overseer said. "I believe you both, well, all of you, would be much safer out of the area. Perhaps out of the United States."

None of us said anything. I ate another couple bites of pie, then sat back and drank coffee.

Victor's frown had gone from thoughtful to disappointed. I guess he'd hoped the Overseer could talk sense into Allie and Zay at least. He should know better than that. I'd never seen them do anything but stand their ground.

"Well, that's settled, then," Victor said. "Mr. Moretti, I think we've heard their final decision on this matter."

The Overseer pushed away from the table and stood, his fingers resting on the back of his chair. "I wish you'd reconsider, Zayvion and Allison. You have made a very dangerous choice in staying."

Zay was already on his feet, his hand reaching down to help Allie up.

A wave of hunger rolled through me, seeing them there, heartbeats joined, alive and burning. I wrapped my hand around my coffee cup and sucked the heat out of it.

Control it, Flynn. Zay's counting on you.

"Thank you for your concern," Allie said. "But this is our home. We aren't going to leave it."

Said the woman who had stood on the front line of the apocalypse and kicked its ass.

"I admire your courage," the Overseer said. "And I wish you strength. If I can help, please contact me."

"We will, sir," Zayvion said. "Thank you."

The Overseer started toward the door, and Victor followed a little more slowly.

I wanted to talk to Victor. See if he knew how Dessa fit into all this, but my control was damn near exhausted. And Terric was right there, just a few seats away.

Staring at me.

Being around him usually dampened my need to feed. But it wasn't enough to be in the same room with him right now. What I wanted was life. Allie's life, Zayvion's life. Terric's life.

Terric waited. He knew what I wanted. Knew he could give it to me.

Knew I knew it too. And was waiting for me to ask.

If I asked and triggered the monster in him, one of us would end up dead.

Besides, I'd had enough of walking among the living for the day.

"So that was fun," I said as soon as the door closed behind Victor and the Overseer. "The four of us, holding out while our doom sets us in its sights. Just like old times. Unlike old times, I plan to be drunk for as much of this as possible. Who's up for a bottle or two?"

Terric just shook his head and pushed away from the table. "Has either of you talked to Davy lately?"

Allie answered, "Not for a few days. Why? Is he okay?"

"I saw him last night. We saw him," Terric said. "And he saw Joshua's body. He knows it's Eli behind his death."

Zay took in a deep breath and did that stare-into-space thing for a second. Used to be he could sort of reach out and feel where people were in the city. Back when he was Guardian of the gates. Back when there was enough magic in the world to open and close magical gates. Back when magic was broken, but a hell of a lot easier to deal with. Except, you know, everyone was pretty damn good at using it to kill one another.

Maybe now he was just trying to decide how to talk Allie into going away somewhere safe.

"How did Davy take it?" Allie asked.

Terric shrugged, then rubbed at one shoulder as if it had a kink there. "Pretty sure he wants to be a part of taking Eli down."

Zay nodded and so did Allie.

"I want to see the glyphs," Allie said. "Where is the . . . where is Joshua?"

Terric stood, dug his phone out of his pocket. "I took a couple pictures." He thumbed through the selection, which appeared to be password protected, then handed the phone to Allie.

Zay nodded just slightly in thanks and Terric nodded back.

Allie frowned and adjusted the picture so she could see it the way she wanted.

Let them be all sleuthy. I found a decent bourbon, filled a glass. Took a long, hard swallow.

Burned all the way down.

Eleanor was perched on the edge of the bar, swinging her feet. I was pretty sure she hadn't taken her eyes off Zayvion since we'd walked in here.

"He's taken, love," I said quietly to her. "Plus, he prefers his women breathing."

She rolled her eyes and very carefully and slowly mouthed the words *fuck you*.

I shook my head. "I like them breathing too."

She jumped down off the bar. Then she pushed through it and slapped me across the back of the head. I winced and chuckled into the glass.

"Well," I said as I refilled the tumbler. "Since you three seem to have some catching up to do, I am going to my room. Call me if you need me. Hold on." I lifted one finger and navigated out from behind the bar, tumbler and bottle in one hand. "Better yet, don't call me unless you absolutely must."

Zay folded his arms across his chest and gave me and my bottle a very disapproving glare as I walked out of the room. Allie just looked sad at my lack of . . . well, probably lack of everything.

That hurt.

I didn't let it show. "Good night, all. See you on the morn."

"Shame," Terric said. "It's morn right now. It's not even noon. And you have a date in a couple hours."

"A date?" Allie asked. "Who?"

"Just a girl I met in a bar," I said.

"Ex-government," Terric said. "I'd guess CIA or FBI."

"I don't think so," I interrupted. "She wouldn't be asking us for information if she was in the intelligence community."

"There are things we've kept out of the government's hands for years," he said. "Even the CIA and FBI don't have the records we have."

"True."

"That's both interesting and worrisome," Allie said, "but not as interesting as you wanting to date her. How long have you known her?"

"A few hours."

"Hours?"

"Yes. Which is why I'll leave you creatures of the light to your day, and get some sleep while I can." I strolled down the hall, Eleanor not far behind me. Listened to Zay and Allie and Terric. Talking. Talking about me. I tried to ignore their whispers. Shame wasn't the same. Was worse than they'd ever seen. On the edge of losing control. Of becoming the monster.

They didn't know how right they were.

Closed myself in my room. Kicked off my boots, while finishing off the tumbler in deep gulps. Trying to drown the hunger, the need. It helped, but not enough.

Pulled off my coat, my shirt. Sat on the edge of my bed, hands and heart shaking.

I was hungry. Hungry to kill.

Eleanor stood across the room, her hands in her ghostly pockets. I lifted the bottle toward her in a toast. Then drank from it. Trying to burn away my need. Trying to dull my sorrow for Joshua. He was a good man. A decent guy. Husband. Father.

Dead.

We'd lost him. To Collins the Cutter. To that heartless bastard.

When I found Eli—and I would—I was going to make him pay for every cut in Joshua's flesh. For every moment of life he'd stolen from him.

I tipped the bottle up, drank. And drank.

Eleanor finally drifted over. Sat on the edge of my bed next to me. Pointed at the book that had fallen out of my coat pocket and onto the floor.

"Ah, now. I promised, didn't I?"

She nodded.

I pushed off the bed. Scooped up the book. Got myself sitting again, with my back against the headboard.

I patted the blankets next to me. "Come on. I'm not going to read it to you."

She tipped her head, and for just a second, she gave me that hopeful glance. The one women tend to give men they think can be saved.

I blinked, slowly, the alcohol taking some of the hard, hungry edges off the world. And waited for her.

She finally drifted up, sat down next to me, her back against the headboard, knees curled up beneath her. She rested her hand on my shoulder and propped her chin there too so she could look down at the book I held. I opened it.

We had a system, Eleanor and I. I'd drink. Hold up the book with one hand so she could see both pages. She'd tap me on the shoulder, and I'd turn the page. Drink again.

We did this until the bottle was gone.

Because the bottle was always gone before the pages were done.

Chapter 13

I'd be lying if I said I was completely sober by lunchtime. But just like the cigarettes that burned down too quickly in my hands, the edge-dulling effect of the bottle I'd drunk was fading fast.

Zay and Allie and Terric had left the inn so the staff could open it up for the lunch and dinner crowd. I decided a cab was my best bet. I didn't want to deal with the bus or light rail crowded with beating hearts.

The pizza place was over on Mississippi Avenue, a two-story green-on-green stucco building with a clay tile awning stretched over white-framed windows and doors. I strolled in and helped myself to a booth by the window.

Eleanor drifted between wooden tables and patrons, then paused to study the pizzas lined up along the counter behind glass.

I glanced out the window and watched Dessa walk across the street. She'd pulled her hair back in a clip that allowed most of it to fall down around her shoulders, and had put on a gray formfitting dress that showed a kick of orange at each step where the skirt hit her knees. She wasn't wearing a jacket, or carrying a purse big enough for a handgun.

She was poised, confident, strong. And beautiful.

Eleanor floated back over toward me and put her hand on my shoulder, pointing a finger out the window.

"I see her," I said.

Dessa stepped into the room and strolled right over to me. She'd probably staked out the place and had watched me walk in.

"Didn't think you'd come," she said as she took the bench opposite me.

"Why not?" I asked.

"You don't seem like the kind of man who likes to be inconvenienced."

"Who says this is an inconvenience?"

She stopped, studied me. "Do you ever take those sunglasses off?"

"Only when there's something worth seeing." I reached up, pulled them off, and gave her a smile.

She blushed just a bit, which was cute. "I see you brought your charm."

"What did you bring, Dessa?"

"I do have information you want."

"That's true," I said. "Should we pretend to like each other over pizza and a beer?"

"What if I already like you, Shame Flynn?"

My turn to pause. "Naw, you just like what I can do." I leaned forward a bit. "How I can kill."

"That's why I found you," she said, her gaze holding mine. "That's not why I'm on a date with you."

"Mmm," I said. "Then how about I buy us a beer?"

"Let's make it two."

We ordered pizza and a couple pints. Talking took a backseat while we made a dent in our slices. She'd gone for a mix of veggies and meat, while I'd opted for the full-on carnivore. She ate her pizza the right way—with her fingers.

"Dating me, yeah, sure, I can understand the draw," I said after I'd demolished my lunch. "How could you resist tall, dark, and dangerous?"

She raised an eyebrow. "Tall?"

"Hush. What I don't understand is why you want to give me any information at all."

She shrugged and wiped her mouth on a napkin. "My brother was a part of your organization. He was the most honest, caring man I knew. He wouldn't have gotten involved with the Authority if he didn't agree with what it stood for."

"That's a lot of blind faith you have there."

"Just faith. I know you people have done illegal things. But from what I can tell, he believed the Authority was dedicated to doing the right thing, even if that meant making some hard choices."

I nodded. "That was the idea. But like all ideas, once people are added to the mix, there are bound to be problems."

"Problems like the man who killed my brother."

I took a drink of my beer. I wasn't going to give her information on Eli, didn't want her in the way of whatever he was planning on doing to people. "Did you grow up in the area?"

"My dad was in the army. I grew up everywhere."

"And when you got out on your own, where did you settled down?"

"San Francisco."

"What did you do there?"

"Officially?" She smiled. "I was a national account manager for a bioscience division of a tech company."

"Unofficially?"

She sipped her beer. "I spied on people."

"CIA? FBI?"

"I wasn't offered details," she said. "Just money in exchange for being reliable and discreet."

"Is that what you're doing now? Gathering intel?"

"Not for them. I said I was ex-government. I meant that. The only intel I want is who killed my brother." She held up her hand. "I know. You're not going to give it to me. But I said I had a few things to tell you, and I'm going to."

"Why?"

"We started off on the wrong foot," she said. Her eyes slid away to the window and the people moving about out there, then back to me. "I misjudged you."

"Are you sure about that?"

"I thought you didn't care about anything. I thought you'd like the deal, the hunt, the payoff."

"Maybe I do."

"Maybe. But it's not what you care about."

"It's fascinating how you think you know me and we've barely met."

"You've seen me naked."

"Not quite."

"You care about Terric, Dash, and Clyde," she went on. "You care about Zayvion Jones and Allison Beckstrom and Cody Miller."

I was surprised she'd brought up Cody, not that she was wrong. He and I had run together, gotten into a lot of trouble when we were younger, before he'd had his brain broken by the last set of Soul Complements who'd wanted to take over the world. He'd ultimately been the one who had held magic together long enough for it to join. He was the one who had healed it. And, yes, he was my friend.

"You care about the missing people who have been showing up dead in Forest Park," she said.

At my raised eyebrows, she shrugged. "Just because I'm not working for the government doesn't mean I don't know how to gather information. You are a target, you know."

"Yeah, sure. Plenty of people want me dead."

"People, yes. But so does the Black Crane Syndicate."

It was my turn to drink beer and look out the window for a bit. "What do they want me dead for?"

"They want Terric Conley. They know you're the only person standing in the way of them owning him."

"Owning?"

"I don't have the details, but they are grooming him for something that involves magic and their drug trade. There's a man who is part of the power in the organization. Jeremy Wilson. He's promised he can deliver a new mix of magic and drugs. He's promised product that will send half the world begging at their feet."

I didn't say anything. Couldn't hear over the hard anger that scorched hot and unreasonable across my brain. Dash was right. Jeremy was using Terric. For more than just a clean bill of health.

"And what?" I said, like I was exhaling a hard stream of smoke. "Do you want me to pay you for this information?"

She shook her head. "Nothing. I'm just doing . . . something I think my brother would approve of. I might not be positive that the Authority has always done the right thing, but I know some things about the Black Crane. Drugs, magic, human trafficking, blackmail, backdoor deals. I know what they are. And if they're coming for you, for people who my brother believed in, then I want you to have a fighting chance against them."

"This means something to me," I said. "You telling me this—if it's true."

"It's true."

"I don't leave a debt unpaid."

"Reconsider telling me who killed my brother."

"No."

She held still, didn't even breathe, her hands clasped together in front of her on the table. "It was worth a shot, right?"

"I would have done the same," I agreed.

"All right." She tipped back her beer and set the glass on the table. "How about you buy me a beer, and we'll call it even?"

"That easy?"

"I still want information," she said. "But I don't have to get it from you. Tonight."

So I bought her a beer.

She might be a player, willing to bribe or bludgeon her way to what she wanted, but she was sincere about this, about giving me information because she thought it was the right thing to do, even if I didn't give her what she wanted in return.

Looked like I'd misjudged her too.

Somehow day burned down to evening. We finally moved away from our table and back toward the lounge and bar. We spent a couple hours listening to live music, drinking, and talking over other things—not the Authority, crime syndicates, or dead loved ones. Just movies, politics, and embarrassing high school memories.

Everything felt normal with her, easy with her. Like this was a life I could live. Wasn't that a surprise?

When the band turned to reggae music, we both groaned.

"Don't like reggae?" I asked.

"I do not," she laughed. "It's getting late. I should be heading home."

I threw some money on the table to settle our bill, then walked with her out of the place. The cold night air stole away the remaining warmth of the club as we lingered outside the door on the sidewalk.

"Do you need a ride?" she asked.

"So you were spying on me before you walked in. I wondered."

She paused, her hand in her purse, and grinned up at me. The color was a little high across her cheeks, and the whiskey gingers she'd been drinking put a soft glitter in her eyes. "I have no idea what you're talking about."

"Now, now, darlin'," I said. "Let's not ruin a good night with bad lies."

"So good lies are okay?"

"Sometimes those can be the best."

"Are you sure about the ride?" she asked. "It isn't out of my way."

"I think I'll find my own way home tonight."

"All right," she said. "Good." She took a step to the corner, then turned back toward me. "This was nice, Shame. Maybe we can do it again sometime."

"Maybe we can," I said. "But we probably shouldn't."

"Well, then," she said. "I guess this is good-bye. Good-bye, Shamus Flynn."

"Good-bye, Dessa Leeds."

She gave me one more smile, then crossed the street and strode down the alleyway opposite before I could change my mind.

I started walking and did not look back. Waved down a cab three or four blocks later, and closed my eyes, trying not to think of Dessa, or what might have been between us.

It wasn't long before the cab pulled up to the inn.

The inn was winding down for the night, the cleaning staff turning down lights and setting the locks. I crossed through the dining area and down the hall, then up the stairs toward my room. Halfway up the stairs, I heard the front door open and shut.

I wondered who was returning to the inn so late.

By the time I reached my room, I heard footsteps thunking up the stairs behind me.

Just because I am a curious bastard, I took my time unlocking my door, waiting to see who had arrived behind me.

The footsteps paused. Something scratched and skittered.

An animal?

I glanced over at the stairs.

Dessa slipped up the last few steps, a duffel bag slung over her shoulder, large purse over the other, and a square, cloth-covered wire cage in one hand. She stopped. Waited for me to say something.

"Miss me already?" I asked.

"I don't know what you mean."

"I mean, you appear to be stalking me."

"No," she said, "I'm renting a room."

"Next to mine."

"Is it?" she asked with an air of innocence that fooled no one. "They said it was the only room that was open."

"Really."

"You aren't worried about me being here, are you, Shame? Afraid of a little girl next door?"

I smiled, leaned against the hall, and pointed at the cage she was carrying. "What's in the cage?"

"It's not a cage, it's a hatbox."

"With a cloth over it."

"I have shy hats."

"Come on, now. Let's have a see."

She shook her head. "My curtains don't rise just because some man expects them to. Ruins the mystery."

The hatbox scratched and skittered again.

"Bird? Gerbil? Lizard? Am I close?"

"Fedora, cloche, baseball. Hats." She walked down to the door on the left, flicked her keys forward into her fingers. She unlocked the door and leaned into the room.

This was an old inn and the doors were narrow. She had to slide in sideways, which meant the cloth over the cage lifted and I saw a tiny, furry black-and-white face, with close-set ears.

A ferret. She was smuggling a ferret into the inn.

"There's a no-pet rule, you know," I said.

"Oh?" she asked, unconcerned.

"Yes. So make sure your hats don't go for a stroll in the middle of the night."

She was in the room now, and had placed the cage on the floor. "I assure you, my hats are very well behaved." She shut the door, and I heard the slide and click of the locks setting.

Ferrets. I shook my head. Not what I'd expect out of an ex-government spy. But then, Dessa was proving to be a lot more than just a woman on a mission of revenge.

I smiled, stepped into my room, and closed the door behind me.

Chapter 14

You know those soft, lazy kinds of mornings where you wake up, realize you are in a comfortable bed, buried beneath your favorite blanket, warm, relaxed, and don't have a worry in the world?

This was not like that.

A spear of ice slid into my chest, shocking me awake faster than a lightning bolt. I opened my eyes.

It was dark. Eleanor was sitting on my hips. Her eyes wide, panicked. Her hands had disappeared up to her wrists in my chest.

Jesus. I mean, I'd always assumed she'd try to kill me someday, but two things: it wasn't working, and it hurt.

"What?" I yelped. She was really agitated, and therefore, much more solid. I could feel the weight of her across my hips, like a vise of winter.

She shook her head and hurriedly twisted. I grunted as she pulled one, then the other hand out of my rib cage. She pointed over her shoulder. Toward the door.

No, not toward the door. Toward the man who stood there.

About six foot, built a little on the slim side, wearing dark slacks and a button-down shirt that was undone at the cuffs and away from his neck. His dusty brown hair stuck up, like he hadn't brushed it in a day or two, and his round wire-rimmed glasses caught the faint moonlight seeping in through the window.

It'd been a while since I'd seen him. About three years. Back before magic had been healed. Back before we knew if we were going to survive the apocalypse. He'd looked like a slightly crazy mad scientist magic user back then.

Hadn't changed much.

"Eli Collins," I said as I sat and put both my feet on the floor. "Really nice of you to stop by, my friend. I've been looking for you."

He hesitated there in the shadow for a moment, like a fly on the edge of a spider's web.

I waited, listening to his heartbeat. Elevated, but not fear. More like anticipation.

"Shamus." He took a step into the room. Moonlight slipped across him like an airport scanner. "You're alone?"

What did he expect, that I'd have Terric stashed in my closet? "Sure," I said. "I'm alone."

"Good," he said. "Very good."

He lifted his hand and in it was a gun.

Eleanor flew at him, flew through him. I raised my hand, the rings across my fist crackling with red light.

But I was too slow.

Bullets are faster than magic.

So are tranq guns.

The gun in his hand popped. The dart hit me right in the chest.

The sun exploded there and wrapped me in fire. I clenched my teeth and moaned against the pain.

Holy fuck, that hurt.

The drug and magic crawled through my veins, knotted my muscles, and locked me down hard.

I couldn't even blink.

Even the monster inside me was still. Knocked out cold. This wasn't good. This wasn't good at all.

Collins tipped his wrist, checked his watch, then looked

back at me and pressed a button that beeped. Counting down the minutes?

"I don't have any time to waste," he said as he walked over to me. "No time for you to argue, or try to kill me. They'll pull me back into my cell in two minutes. Two minutes of freedom." He spread his arms and smiled.

He glanced around, found a chair, set it close enough I could see his eyes and the wildness within them, even in the dark. Then leaned forward, his arms across his knees.

"Did you get my message, Shame? Did you see it? On Joshua? My handiwork? Did Davy see it? I hope that he did. I couldn't have made it more obvious."

I moved my tongue, opened my mouth. "Fuck. You." Huh. Well, at least I could talk, though magic, and any other movement, was out of the question.

"So you saw him? What I did to him? How I killed him? Good." He checked his watch again. He was amped up, distracted. Not exactly what I liked to see in a psychopath.

"I am not on your side, on the side of the Authority," he clarified. "I do not care what the tattered remains of that powerless organization does. Nor am I on the side of the forces that are rising against the Authority. I am a prisoner." Here he paused, and swallowed as if just saying that word would bring the bars of his cage slamming shut around him.

"Prisoner," he repeated. "They have me locked down, except when they let me go for two minutes. Such a short time to do my work. To make my mark. To kill the way I like killing. You see the problem before you: you know they are looking for Breakers. Soul Complements," he said a little softer, as if those words meant something to him now.

Then, "They want the weapon, Shame. They want you. They want the magic only you can tap. No matter that there are ways, other ways to tap magic. Things you haven't seen. Things I have shown them are possible."

He waved his hand as if he'd argued this before.

"Costly. But effective. Ways I have shown them they can

tap in to the power of magic." He seemed to catch himself. "Not that I will tell you. Even that—magic—is not the real problem. Do you know what the real problem is?" he asked.

"Just say it, freak," I managed. Talking hurt. My head was pounding spikes of pain through my brain with each hard heartbeat.

"The problem is a woman. You have met her. Dessa Leeds. She knows. Knows where I am. Knows what my chains are made of. They have her, Shame."

"Dessa?" He used to make sense. But now . . . maybe the madness had finally taken its toll.

"No, not Dessa. My soul. They have my soul." He pulled his glasses off and rubbed his eyes. Sniffed hard, then wiped under each eye before replacing his glasses. "You have to save her. You're the only thing they can't fight, Shame. Death. And you crave it, don't you? You like killing just as much as I do. Find me and my prison. Save my soul. I've tried. Tried everything. You." Here he shook his head. "You're all I have left. If you stop them, all this will be over."

"And if I don't?" I asked.

"Then people will die. People you care about. Oh, don't look so surprised. It isn't personal. I am doing what I must to survive, though I will enjoy it."

He smiled. "I have orders to kill the people standing in their way. You're standing in their way, Shame. You and . . . others I would love to see dead. And if you don't find her, I will do more than just kill your friends. I will destroy everything you've ever touched. Everyone you've ever touched. It won't matter that you carry Death magic. I'm the one with my finger on the trigger of the gun. And I will make your every breath a study in pain and misery."

He glanced at his watch again. "You don't have much time. Maybe a day. Maybe less. And you'll have to be sharp, Shame. You will have to be much, *much* better than this . . . pitiful wreck you've become if you are going to save her. To stop me."

His watch beeped once and he jumped just slightly. "Out of time. And so are you." He tugged a needle out of his shirt pocket, bit the plastic cover off it, then leaned forward and stabbed me in the neck.

Oh, I was so going to kill the slimy little fucker for this.

"This is just the start of what they have to control magic users. To control people changed by magic. Enjoy the ride."

Maybe I'd convince Terric to bring him back to life so I could kill him twice.

The room swirled like water down a toilet bowl. I watched Eli. Watched something that looked like a hole in space—a gate—open up behind him with a hard snap of electricity. Watched as he stood and was yanked backward by men in lab coats and face masks I could not see through.

Then the gate was gone. Eli was gone. And so was my mind.

Chapter 15

Flashes of images: the parking lot in darkness. Trees. Under-brush rustling with animals that fell deathly still as I passed.

Flashes of sensation: gravel cutting my feet, wind on my bare chest and back, blood on my fingers, my lips.

Flashes of sounds: forest, the river, cars. Eventually, my own breathing. Too loud. And then: voices.

First too many voices. A bar, a club, laughter, anger, lust. The rhythmic pound of music. Heat I could consume. Life I wanted and could have. If I stepped over the threshold.

Then only one life, sweet and burning in front of me: Dessa.

"Shame," she said through my pain, around the finger-painted slide of colors and agony that made up the world. "You can't go in there. You're safe. Safe with me."

The world pushed past me. Life roaring by like a thundering wave. Maybe she was still there. I didn't know.

A scream of colors slashed me to the bone. Then everything went black.

"Don't move."

Was that Dessa? It sounded like her. I could smell her perfume, a burst of vanilla and sweet spices. Could feel her strong, beating heart. A singular, pure note.

"You're going to be okay," she said.

Felt the soft release of her hand lifted from my hip. The

hushed chirp of a cell phone dialing. Footsteps retreated. And then the engine of a car rolled to life.

I was alone. Alone with my pain.

"Hey, Shame."

Darkness parted. Light poured over me. Terric's voice. Terric's light.

I wanted to tell him I thought I might be really screwed up this time. That he should get far, far away from me. I wanted to tell him there was a reason for the state I was in. That someone, someone whose name I could not remember, had done something to me. But my thoughts dissolved as I tried to stack them into order and form.

This was not good.

Fear slipped between each breath I struggled to take. Fear that if I was losing my mind, the monster in me would devour every living thing. Even him.

"I got you now," Terric's words said, falling like soft snow around me. "You're going to be all right."

His hands touched me—one on my arm, one on my chest. I shuddered as that light pushed away the darkness and pain, holding the worst of it away.

"Just breathe," he said. "I've got you."

So I closed my eyes, or I hoped I did. And breathed.

Maybe we moved, maybe we stood there. Maybe this was all a dream. Terric's words drifted around me, soothing, cooling. In them was comfort and peace.

There was no fighting it. I didn't want to.

I breathed his words. His light wrapped me in gentle arms. And all the world disappeared.

I gasped, opened my eyes. Tried to push up onto my feet.

A hand appeared out of nowhere and pressed against my chest so hard my shoulder blades sank into the cushions at my back.

Cushions?

"Stay down," Terric said.

"Where the hell?" I blinked, swallowed. Whatever drugs Eli had used on me left the taste of vomit in my mouth. I felt like I'd been run through a meat tenderizer. Twice.

"You're at my house," Terric said. "In my living room. It's the middle of the night—"

"Two o'clock in the morning," another man's voice said.

"—and," Terric continued, "you've been hurt. Do you understand me, Shame?"

I blinked again. The room slipped in and out of focus. Finally cleared.

Terric sat next to me in a padded chair. His hand gripped my upper arm, applying a slight pressure so I remained seated.

He wore a gray tank top and dark blue pajama bottoms. Barefoot, hair a little messy like he'd just gotten out of bed.

Middle of the night. Of course he'd been in bed. I was all about the smart right now, wasn't I?

I tried my brain out on the rest of the room. It'd been a while since I'd been over to his house. Instead of the fine photography he usually had on display, the walls were covered in bold, ugly abstracts and a huge TV screen swallowed up the corner by the window where he used to keep his favorite reading chair. Even so, I was indeed sitting on his couch in his living room.

Standing behind him was the man I'd seen in the car with him: buzz-cut light brown hair, narrow face, and brown eyes set too wide. Jeremy.

Jeremy scowled at me, his arms crossed. He had on a black T-shirt, flannel over that, and jeans. Couldn't see his feet, but I'd guess his shoes were on.

I could not guess whether he had just arrived or was headed out the door.

From the look on his face, I knew he and I were not friends. Not by a long shot.

No, we were enemies.

So Dessa and Dash had been right about him.

"Shame?" Terric said again. "Can you understand me?"

"Yes," I said. Talking took more effort than it should. I didn't think the drugs had done the last of their work on me.

"What happened?" he asked.

Jeremy scoffed. "You have to ask? He's wasted."

"Jeremy," Terric said quietly, "I wasn't talking to you."

"He's a waste, Terric. You want to do something for him, dump his ass in rehab."

"He's staying here," Terric said.

"Fuck that. Aren't you done with this piece of crap? After everything he's done to you?"

"Jeremy," Terric snarled. "Get out."

Lots of anger in that Jeremy. I was following along, but the conversation was going by so quickly that by the time I pulled together a comment, they had moved on.

"You can't just pretend this is normal, Terric. You can't ignore what he is. Look at him. He's a junkie piece of crap, baby. Win some, lose some. You lost him a long time ago. Let it go."

Terric stood, and I tipped my head back to see what he was going to do.

He was looking down at me.

I gave him a smile. I'd seen that anger before.

Thought about putting together some words to warn ol' Jeremy that he was about to get his ass handed to him on a platter, but figured he'd catch on soon enough.

Terric turned so he blocked my view of Jeremy. "Leave. Now." Two words. Words that Jeremy really ought to listen to.

I actually hoped Jeremy would push it. It had been a while since I'd seen Terric punch someone in the face.

"Please, Terric." Jeremy leaned toward him, the chair Terric had been sitting in between them. "He has you where he wants you. He's preying on your sympathy. You have to be strong, remember? We talked about this. All he wants is to use you—"

"Out."

"—use your magic for whatever rush can score—"

"Jeremy." Terric pointed to the door. "Leave now before I do something to end this. End us."

I could cut the tension with a knife. If, you know, I could actually lift my hand. Or make a fist tight enough to hold a knife.

Also, if I had a knife.

Jeremy looked past Terric to glare at me.

I winked at him.

Oh-ho, that did not go over well.

He used a few choice four-letter words and stormed across the room. A door slammed shut. Aw. I hurt his feelings.

Terric was still standing with his back toward me.

He shifted his shoulders just a bit, as if taking the weight of the damage that might have just been done to their relationship.

I was, once again, not a lot of help in his love life.

He turned to me. The anger wasn't gone, but it was under control. Set aside for now. "Are you okay?" he asked quietly.

"Super," I managed.

"Are you thirsty? Do you hurt?"

"Yes." I answered both questions, even though I knew he could tell I was still in pain. Just one of the many joys of being tied to another person's soul: he hurt, you hurt.

He sat back down in the chair with a sigh and handed me the glass of water from the side table.

It took me two tries to get my hand around the glass. Those were some long odds I'd actually get any of the water in my mouth.

"Here." He hadn't let go of the glass yet. So he stood, sat next to me, and pressed the glass back in my hand.

Then he lifted my hand with the glass to my mouth. Helping me drink.

It was embarrassing. But I needed that water. And needed the help. I gulped as much of it as I could before I had to breathe again.

Terric tipped the glass away, waited for me to stop gasping, then helped me drink the rest.

"What happened?" he asked as he placed the glass on the coffee table in front of the couch.

"Eli," I said.

Terric froze. "Where?"

"My room. Shot me with a tranq." I swallowed, trying to get my brains in order. "Jesus, hate this." Pointed at my head.

"Eli was in your room," Terric repeated. "And he shot you with a tranq gun? Did he say anything?"

"Lots. The usual crazy." I was out of air. Worked on filling my lungs. "He cut up Joshua just to get our . . . attention. Just to fuck with us." I was shaking now, a tremble I couldn't seem to get under control.

Terric made a blanket appear from somewhere nearby, draped it over my legs and up to my neck.

"What else?" he asked.

"Said he wanted me—us—to save him. Find him. Save her." Stopped for breathing again. This was getting old.

"Find who?" Terric shifted off the couch and knelt on the floor in front of me, then settled there cross-legged.

"What are you doing?" I asked, suddenly alarmed.

"Your feet are a bloody mess," he said. "You showed up on my doorstep with no shirt, no shoes, and looked like you'd walked all the way from the inn to here, barefoot."

"Did I?"

"You may as well have. Dessa called. She found you at a bar downtown. Brought you here. I'm going to heal your feet."

"Wait. Don't."

He wrapped his hand around my left ankle. I didn't think I could pull away if I tried.

I tried anyway.

Nope.

"Just tell me what else he said."

A soft warmth spread out over my foot, which was a far cry better than the pounding ache I'd been unsuccessfully ignoring.

"Anytime now, Flynn," he said.

Huh. I must have drifted. He set my left foot down carefully, then picked up my right foot by the ankle.

"Said Dessa knows where he is. Knows what's going on. Said he's a prisoner. Going to kill everyone. In two days if we don't find him. Stop him. Save her."

"Her who?"

Terric put my right foot down, and that lack of pain made me realize how damn exhausted I was. "His soul."

"Fuck," Terric breathed. "So he does have a Soul Complement. And they're using her against him?"

"I think so," I said. "Or that just might be what he wants us to think." I wouldn't put it past Eli Collins to manipulate and use his Soul Complement for whatever dark scheme or experiment he was involved in. "Or maybe he's telling the truth and someone is using her against him."

Terric didn't say anything for a bit. Just sat there, crosslegged, with one hand absently on my bloody bare foot. "Did he say who he's going to kill?"

I nodded, which sent the room swinging. Not doing that again. "Anyone who stands in their way. All of us. You. Me."

Terric took a deep breath, let it out.

"So Jeremy is unhappy," I said.

"He was being an ass. He doesn't like you," Terric added. "And he is the least of my problems right now."

"Am I the most?" I asked, trying to pull together a smile. I wasn't sure if both sides of my mouth were working.

He looked up at me. "Always." He shook his head, as if trying to figure me out. "What the hell were you thinking, walking half a city barefoot?"

"I don't remember. Any of it." A hard image of blood on my lips flashed through my mind. "Might have hurt people."

"I already thought of that. Sent people to see if you did any damage. Did he look sane?"

"Collins?"

"Yes."

"Not really. Desperate and crazy."

"Not a winning combination," he said.

"Maybe for him," I said. If you believed the records on the man, Collins had done a lot of brilliant things while being stark raving mad.

Terric stood. Walked away. By the time I began to wonder where he'd gone, he was walking back, bare feet quiet in the thick carpet.

"Whatever he shot you up with isn't out of your system yet," he said. "You want a doctor?"

"Doctors don't work on me."

"You're not inhuman, Shame."

I didn't say anything. This was an old argument.

He must not have expected me to say yes to the doctor anyway. He had a pillow in one hand and another blanket in the other. "Then you should get some sleep," he said. "I'll take care of . . . whatever needs to be done until morning. You've got four hours."

"Find Dessa," I started.

"I will." He set the pillow on one side of me. "Lie down."

I worked on getting my legs to move. Lifted one with the help of my hands. Then the next. Didn't have the energy to do anything else.

Just sat there staring at my feet stretched out on the couch in front of me.

Terric bent, putting his mouth near my ear. "Don't argue and make this harder," he said. He slid one hand and arm behind my back, and the other under my knees.

I was about to be manhandled. It was as physically close to him as I'd been in years.

I shut my mouth and stared at the ceiling, trying not to say anything, trying not to think anything while he half lifted, half slid me into a prone position.

I couldn't have done it on my own. Not right away, anyway. He didn't say any more about it. Didn't mention how weak and wrecked I was.

Just straightened, retrieved the blanket, spread it out over me. I shivered from the pocket of cold air followed by the warmth of the blanket settling around me.

"I'll put some water on the table," he said. "If you need the bathroom, try to wait until morning. I don't think your feet can take the walk, and there's enough of your blood on my carpet I have to clean up already."

His voice was fading. Walking away, I thought. Couldn't see him. My eyes were closed.

"Ter?" I whispered.

"I'm here." Close. Sitting in the chair again. I thought I smelled tea.

"Thank you," I said. "I . . . I'm sorry."

"Don't," he said. "Whatever you're apologizing about, I won't accept it until you can tell me in the morning light, looking me straight in the eye."

"You are a picky bastard," I mumbled.

"Yes," he said, "I am."

And then darkness and warmth swallowed me whole and dragged me down.

Chapter 16

"Wake up, Shame," Terric said. "Time for food."

What the hell was Terric doing in my room? I opened my eyes.

Correction: what the hell was I doing in Terric's house?

"French toast, sausage," he continued. "Think you can eat?"

I lifted a hand, rubbed my face. My arm was sore; the side of my neck felt swollen, bruised. And when I breathed in too deep, something in my chest scraped my bones.

So, not the worst I'd ever woken up feeling.

"Food," I repeated. "My mouth tastes like ass."

"Spare toothbrush in the bathroom. Be careful on your feet."

That brought it all back to me. Or at least the clear images. Half of what I remembered was pain, blurry flashes, and a muddle of sensations and sounds.

"So he drugged me," I said.

Terric had showered. His hair was still a little damp, combed back, and dripping just a bit on the shoulders of his white T-shirt. He also wore jeans and boots, one ankle propped on his other knee. He was drinking tea from what I knew was very expensive china.

He lifted his cup toward the tray of food on the coffee table. French toast, coffee, sausage, and apple butter.

"Not going to feed you. Unless you want me to."

"No," I said. "I don't."

I bent, groaned as I pulled the tray over to me, setting it across my legs. Didn't spill a drop.

If Terric was talking, only the walls were listening. I didn't hear a thing while I consumed every bite, lick, and morsel of breakfast.

I felt like I hadn't eaten for months. And after I'd plowed through the food, I felt a lot better.

"Did you spike it with . . ." I wiggled my fingers over my empty plate.

"No. You walked for miles last night, Shame. Anyone would be hungry. Also, I am a hell of a cook."

"Yeah, you are."

I scraped the last bit of tart and sweet apple butter off the plate with my fork, licked the tines clean, then set the tray back on the table. Noticed the coffee carafe, cream and sugar there.

Refilled my cup. Sat back and took a drink.

"Did you find Dessa?" I asked.

"Not yet. The Hounds are looking."

"Try the inn."

"Why?"

"She's renting a room. Did you tell Clyde about this?"

"Just that Collins contacted you last night and said we have a day or less before more people die."

I thought that through. "So you didn't tell him he wanted us to find his Soul Complement? It's not like you to lie, Terric. That's my shtick."

Terric drank his tea with that quiet grace that reminded me of elegant people in old movies. "He could have gone to anyone," he said. "Why did Eli go to you, Shame?"

"Fuck all if I know."

"Maybe he still thinks we're the head of the Authority?" Terric said.

"Everyone knows *you* were the head of the Authority.

But no. He made it clear he doesn't think the Authority has any power."

"If I tell Clyde Eli wanted us to find his Soul Complement, Clyde's going to want that handled through proper channels. What do you suppose that is?"

I rubbed my fingers across my scalp. God, I was filthy. "I don't know. Call the cops? Start an investigation?"

"We're already investigating Eli. The police already know he's a suspect in Joshua's death. They're already looking for him. The Authority knows he's behind Joshua's death. We're looking for him."

"So . . . what? The police would question me, I guess."

"Detective Stotts would lock you up," Terric said. "For your own safety. Maybe as bait for Eli, but mostly to keep you safe. Plus, you wouldn't be out barefoot on the streets destroying swaths of innocent horticulture from one end of Portland to the other."

I cringed. "I killed plants?"

"Trees, bushes, grass, greenhouses. Took out a neighborhood garden off of Lombard."

I waited. Waited for him to tell me how many people I'd killed.

"None," he said over the rim of his cup, guessing correctly what I was thinking.

"There was blood on my mouth. In my mouth."

"I think a few raccoons and possums met their maker."

"Are you sure? There were people, a lot of people." The memory was chaotic, but I knew it wasn't a dream. "A bar?"

"No missing persons reports, no unusual injury reports at the hospitals. No unknown causes of death. Not bad for being half out of your mind."

I closed my eyes. Realized my heart had been beating. Hard. With fear. Worry. Terric wouldn't lie to me. Not about this. Not about the monster inside me.

I sat there for a bit, until my heartbeat quieted.

"So if we're not telling Clyde that Eli tried to kill me so I would agree to help him, what's next?" I asked.

"You," he said, "are going to take a shower because you reek. I have some clothes I think will fit."

"Jeremy's clothes?" I asked, my eyes still closed.

"No." Tight. Didn't want to talk about it.

So, of course, I did. "Other than thinking I'm a waste of skin, is there some specific reason he hates me? We haven't met before last night, have we?"

"You haven't met," Terric said quietly.

"He seems to know a lot about me."

A pause. Then, "He thinks he does. I've ... said a few things."

"Bad things?"

"You make it hard to say good things, Shame."

"True."

Silence again.

"You know his family is involved in Blood magic," I said.

"Used to be involved," he said. "Blood magic isn't what it used to be."

"It's not nothing," I said. "With the right spell carved in blood, added to the right drug, you can still get results. People pay big money for those customized highs."

"You're telling me he's a drug dealer."

"I'm telling you he's a part of the drug syndicate, Terric. The Black Crane. And the only thing he wants from you is your magic."

Terric didn't say anything for a minute.

"Where are you getting your information?" he asked far too calmly.

"I know people."

"You don't know him, Shame. He's not like that."

"He jumped pretty quickly to accuse *me* of using you."

"And that makes him a part of a drug cartel?" he snapped. Then, with a lowered voice, "Shame. I don't need two jealous men on my hands."

So much for him listening to me. That was fine. I hadn't expected him to. He cared about Jeremy, I knew that. I could take care of Jeremy on my own. And really, maybe it was better Terric didn't know about it.

I smiled. My eyes were still closed.

"What?" he said.

"Jealousy is for people who know they can't hold on to what they want."

"My statement stands," he said.

I opened my eyes, rolled my head so I could see him. "No. I can't lose you, Terric. Not if I tried. Which is pretty much my default mode, come to think of it."

He narrowed his eyes. "Why is that, Shame? Why do you insist, still, after all these years, to close me out?"

I sat up, put a little weight on my feet. Nothing popped, split, or bled. So I stood. Managed it well enough. Took a step toward the bathroom. And another.

Ouch.

"You're not even going to talk about it?" he asked.

I paused, put one hand out on the wall to keep my balance. "Talking doesn't seem to be our thing."

"It needs to become our thing. We're a part of each other's lives. Whether you want to acknowledge that or not."

I turned so I could see him.

"Lives?" I shook my head. "Deaths. That's what we're a part of, Terric. Each other's deaths. When we're together, one of us always gets hurt. The more we are together, the more we hurt each other."

He watched me for a moment. "Tell that to your healing feet."

"Jesus." I pushed away from the wall and made my way to the bathroom. "You're impossible," I said too quietly for him to hear.

He answered me anyway. "No. I'm right."

Found the bathroom. It was depressingly clean and color-coordinated. Started the shower, stripped, and stepped in the water. Saw something bright out of the corner of my eye. Eleanor, sitting on the sink.

"Hey," I said. "Thanks for waking me."

She floated up so she could peek over the top of the shower door and down at me. I didn't care that she would see me naked. We'd been together for so long, she'd seen me do many worse things than bathe.

She pointed at her neck about the same spot where Eli stabbed me with the needle.

"It hurts," I said. "Feels like someone sewed a golf ball under my skin."

She pointed at her chest.

"That hurts too."

Shook her head, disappeared, then faded through the shower door so she was standing in the shower with me. The water rushed through her, but didn't stir her hair, or dampen her glowing skin. She pointed at my heart, and pressed just the tip of her finger there.

"My heart?"

She drew the letter *T*, her cold touch leaving goose pimples across my wet skin.

"Don't," I said, pushing her hand away, even though my hand just passed right through her. "He's the last thing I want to talk about."

She stepped back and eased through the door. I scrubbed my head, face, and body. Tipped my feet so I could see how bad off the soles were. Bruised black and purple-red, lots of long cuts from heel to toe that were scabbed and not weeping, thanks to Terric. What had I done? Walked across glass?

I washed the cuts as gently as I could, then rinsed and got out.

Pulled a towel that was folded on the edge of the sink and rubbed my head.

Good. God. It was the softest towel I'd ever touched. I shut out everything but that sensation—soft cotton drifting across my skin—whisking the water away.

If it was wrong to have carnal feelings for a towel, I didn't want to be right.

Terric had an eye for luxury. Lived his life like it was worth doing right.

Maybe he had something there. We were all going to die. Might as well savor whatever time we had.

Maybe it was the towel, maybe it was thoughts about mortality, but I found myself thinking about Dessa and smiling. Terric said she'd dropped me off. So she'd been following me.

Who knew I'd have the hots for a ferret-smuggling stalker girl with an overactive desire for revenge?

If she'd dropped me off, then that meant she'd approached me when I was out of my mind and devouring all the life around me.

Correction: stalker girl with an overactive desire for revenge and a hell of a lot of guts.

She'd been with me when I was dangerously uncontrolled. I could have killed her. And yet I hadn't. Or at least I thought she was okay.

She also hadn't come inside with me so we could ask her what Eli said she knew: namely where the hell he, or his Soul Complement, was being held prisoner.

If Dessa was making it a point to keep an eye on me, she should be nearby. It seemed strange that Terric hadn't found her yet. Maybe she had a lead on Eli and was following it.

Great. She might be walking right into a situation that would get her killed.

I looked around for the clothes he said might fit me. Spotted a folded gray T-shirt, a heavy brown sweater, and faded blue jeans. A belt was set out next to the jeans. Not exactly my colors, which were, by the way, black, but better than being naked.

I shook out the pants, put them on. A little long, but not by much, too loose at the waist. Belt took care of that. I shouldered into the T-shirt, fit me fine, then the sweater.

Everything smelled like Terric. The colors looked like Terric.

I toweled off the mirror. Got a good look at myself while brushing back my hair.

Dark green eyes a little bloodshot. Needed a shave. The bones of my cheeks and jaw were squared and prominent. However, even in the bulky chocolate brown sweater, I looked like I could kick ass and take names.

Not my colors. But not bad.

I looked around for socks. Nothing. Then I pissed and left the bathroom.

Terric was on the phone. Pacing. Couldn't tell who he was talking to.

I started looking for my shoes. Remembered I'd come over barefoot. Crap.

Terric stopped pacing. Glanced over at me. One look at me and he paused a second in his good-bye, which made me grin.

Damn straight I was worth looking at.

He pocketed his phone. "I know it's only brown, but damn, it's been a long time since I've seen you in a color, Shame. You should wear colors more often."

"I do wear colors: black, coal, ebony."

He smiled. "Sit. I want to look at your feet."

"This foot obsession you've got going?" I said. "Unhealthy."

I sat in the nearest chair and propped both my feet up on the coffee table. Realized something that had been nagging me. "Your place smells like cigarette smoke."

"Does it?"

I took a deep breath. "A bit."

"Hm."

"Why? Did you take up smoking?"

"No. Jeremy smokes." He sat on the couch, bent a bit so he could see the bottom of my feet. It really was sort of weird having someone stare with such interest at my heels and arches. "I've told him not to, but." He shrugged, then put his hand on my ankle, firmly.

"That's—" I started.

"Don't," he said.

So I didn't. But if I had finished the thought it would have run along the line that Terric hated when his things smelled like smoke. And after that it would have gone down the path that his house didn't look like he lived here anymore.

The things that always made it feel distinctly his, things like his photography, his collection of hardbound books, and the wall that used to display the pictures of all of his many—and I do mean many—brothers and sisters and aunts and uncles and nieces and nephews and cousins, were gone. Wiped away. Replaced with the abstract art. Changed.

Jeremy had made Terric change for him. Or maybe Terric had done it willingly.

I was no expert on relationships. Still, this total takeover didn't seem . . . healthy.

I had plenty of energy to pull my feet away from Terric's grasp this time. But I didn't. The magic that Terric called upon was like sliding my feet into warm, soothing oil. And since I was in possession of most of my gray matter this morning, I paid very close attention to what he was doing and how he was doing it.

Mankind had wanted to use magic for healing for years on end. And while magic can help speed up the healing process, or support the body while it naturally heals, or ease the pain brought on by magical damage, I'd never seen anyone straight-out heal with magic.

Doctors used magic, yes. To assist and support surgeries and other medical procedures.

But that's not what Terric was doing.

Terric had his eyes closed and was whispering slightly. Not a spell, more like a mantra. Sounded like Latin and maybe a little French. I didn't know either well enough to take a guess at what he was using to keep his concentration sharp, but I knew that's what he was doing.

Also? My feet were glowing. Not the bright green-edged white that Terric usually called upon. This was the soft yellow of candlelight.

"No word on Dessa?" I said.

Terric didn't answer. Kept his concentration on the healing.

"That's strange, right? She's following me. Which means she should be close by."

Terric just kept whispering those words, guiding magic to knit my cuts and ease my bruises.

I was starting to feel good. Much better than I should feel after a night like last night.

Was this hurting Terric? One way to find out.

"Ter," I said, "open your eyes."

He did. Still whispering. That was a blank, empty look. Not feverish, not like he was thinking over some kind of complex calculations. Just inhuman, alien. Life magic was staring back at me, hungry and hollow.

There wasn't a scrap of Terric in those eyes.

I pulled both feet out of his grasp, stood, walked halfway across the room. "Stop it," I said.

He didn't seem to hear me, just frowned and stood, then came marching toward me. That glow in his eyes turned into a hard, hungry glint.

I knew the face of the monster in his bones. It was the twin to mine.

His fingers curled into claws as he spread one hand toward the floor, and the other toward my heart.

The bushes outside the house suddenly leaped against the windows, lashing and twisting and growing so fast they completely blocked the morning light.

Heat shot up my legs from my feet. My skin pricked like electricity was riding my nerves. And I felt my body *change*. Change into something the magic in Terric wanted it to be.

Oh, hell no.

"Terric, if you don't snap out of this I will shove Death magic down your throat."

I figured he could hear me, but I didn't know how much power Life magic had over him.

"No? Fine." I pulled on Death magic and let it whip toward the Life magic he was bleeding out.

The connection was electric. Literally. Dark and light magic clashed and exploded, the force of impact canceling both magics. The backwash rushed over me in a wave that should be agony, but was pure pleasure.

Soul Complements and magic. Heady stuff. If we continued using magic together like this, soon we'd be taking up residence in each other's brains. Then it was a real possibility we'd slide on over to insanity together—use magic to shape the world, shape the people around us, in any way we desired.

I'd fought Soul Complements who had used magic in that way—monsters who had brought the apocalypse to my city and nearly destroyed it. I'd kill us both before letting us become that.

I slipped off two of my Void stone rings and stepped up to him. I grabbed his hand—which finally got his full attention—and dropped the rings into his palm, closing his fingers over the rings.

"You got this," I said. "You can control it. Just take it down a tick, mate."

I stepped back, not wanting to risk our connection becoming any stronger for fear I'd be lost in it. He locked his hand around mine and didn't let go. "Just. Stay," he panted. "Give me a minute."

I stayed and gave him a minute.

He whispered something over and over. Maybe a spell, maybe a litany to focus his will.

At about the thirty-second mark, the rings in his palm that were scraping against the rings on my knuckles went hot. Then very cold.

The vegetation outside stopped writhing.

He dropped my hand. Ran fingers over his face, then hair. Finally held out the rings to me.

"Are you sure?" I asked.

He nodded, still not looking at me. "I'll get my necklace." His voice was a little rough.

Terric left the room. I slid my rings back into place like a man counting prayer beads.

"And some shoes for me!" I called out after him. "Or at least socks."

It took a few minutes, but I figured he needed them.

So did I. I hadn't gotten out of that unscathed. He had done something—no, the clash of our magics had done something—so that I could feel him. Usually I sensed his heartbeat. Now I could feel how he was breathing, and weirdly, I got an echo of what he was feeling—anger, sorrow, hunger.

Soul Complements.

I didn't like it.

When he came back, he was wearing the Void stone necklace over his T-shirt, his expression calm, his eyes just his eyes again. He was also holding up a pair of socks and the ugliest footwear I'd ever seen.

"What the hell is that?" I asked.

"UGGs."

"No."

"They're comfortable."

"No."

"They're all I have in the house that will fit you." He jiggled them a little, like I was some sort of cat who could be tempted by string.

"No."

"Shame, you can't walk around barefoot all day."

"If my only alternative are those boots, I can. Why do you even have those ugly things? Aren't your people supposed to be fashion forward?"

"My people?" he asked with a dangerous arc of his eyebrow.

"Graphic designers," I said.

"You wear the boots, or you walk to the car barefoot."

"Do you have real shoes in the car?"

"No. But if you stow the attitude and the mouth, I'll take you to a store and you can buy a pair."

"Take me to my place and I won't have to buy anything."

"That was Victor on the phone. He wants to talk to us. Immediately."

"Did he say what it was about?"

"No." He jiggled the boots again.

I strode over to him and grabbed them out of his hands. "If you give me one single word of shit about this . . ."

"Silent as a saint," he said.

I shoved my feet into the boots, which were, damn it all, comfortable.

"Not. One. Word." I stomped off to the door, ignoring Terric's grin.

Chapter 17

Not a shoe store. Terric parked at a local Fred Meyer, a one-stop-shopping department store between his place and Victor's. I shuffled in, past the pumpkins in huge boxes outside the door, past the produce section with a colorful display of fruits and gourds. There was also a scarecrow, which might explain why Eleanor was suddenly drifting so sullenly beside me.

She didn't like Halloween, which, when you thought about it, was ironic. A ghost who didn't like the celebration of dead things. I figured it was because on that first Halloween, she and I had both held some hope that she might cross into death because they say the veil between the living world and death is the thinnest then.

I'd even taken her out to the graveyard with the Death magic well beneath it.

Other than me getting rained on, and her getting depressed, nothing had happened. Ever since, she'd been sad on Halloween.

I took the most direct route to the shoe section, kicked off the UGGs, and bought the first decent pair of work boots I could find. Nothing fancy, but if someone needed a tree cut down, I could probably handle it. I snapped the tags, shoved the UGG boots into the box, then started toward the checkout on the other end of the store.

Eleanor had drifted maximum distance from me. She was studying an end shelf filled with Halloween trinkets and decorations.

I took a couple steps, expecting her to follow. She stood there, bent just a bit, her long, ghostly hair covering her face as she stared at something in the shelf.

I walked around behind her, looked over her shoulder.

Jack-o'-lanterns, witches, ghosts with smiling faces, and a Frankenstein stein cluttered the shelf. But behind all the cheerful candy-colored decorations was a single statue. Made out of metal that had been treated to a green patina, it was the figure of a cloaked and cowled man, head tipped down, face hidden in the shadows. He held a scythe by the handle, the curved blade at his feet, as if he were too weary to lift it again. And spread wide across his back were angel wings.

The angel of death, grieving.

"You like it?" I asked her, not caring about the woman who looked up at me and hurried away.

Eleanor just shrugged one shoulder. But she did not look away from it.

I picked it up. Was impressed at the weight and craftsmanship.

"Let's go," I said softly.

Eleanor looked from me, to the statue, then back to me. She gave me a small smile.

I bought the boots, the statue, and a pack of cigarettes. Made my way toward the front of the store. Passed in front of a stockroom door and noted a guy walking out of it.

Walked past him before I heard the click.

I turned.

Did not expect the Taser in that man's right hand, nor the gun in his left. I also didn't expect the other two guys who strode out of the sporting goods and household paint aisles.

I called on magic, just as the guy with the guns raised them both and pulled a trigger.

Heads or tails. Would I be shot or electrocuted? Heads said bullets.

Before I could raise my hand for a spell, before I could lash out and drain their lives down, someone flipped a switch and a million volts of electricity blew through me.

Huh. It was tails: electrocution.

I came to being dragged away from bright lights and basketballs, and into the stale, cold stockroom.

Maybe another door went by. Then the two guys who had my arms over their shoulders dropped me into a chair.

I decided not to let them know I was conscious.

They stepped away and a new set of boots came closer.

"I know you're awake, Shamus," Jeremy said. "Don't make me shoot you to prove it to my men."

I opened my eyes, tipped my head back. He wasn't holding a gun, but the four other guys around me were.

Bullets are faster than magic. Even my magic.

"Some reason why you don't want to face me alone, Jeremy?" I asked. "That's an awful lot of firepower for a junkie piece of crap like me, don't you think?"

He was a good five feet away from me, and didn't come any nearer. "You have two options here." He started like I hadn't even been talking. "You either leave town, leave Terric, and leave me the hell alone, or we will kill you."

I rolled a shoulder and wondered if that blast of electricity and the drugs Eli had shot me up with were going to get in the way of me killing this prick.

"Really?" I said. "Is this how you Black Crane lads take care of your problems? Threats in department stores? Does anyone ever fall for that?"

Jeremy's eyes narrowed. "I could kill you before you took another breath."

"What's stopping you?" I asked. Really, I was curious.

From the fear that slipped across his eyes, I suddenly knew what it was. He wasn't sure I'd die. After all, I carried

Death magic in my bones and that hadn't killed me. He probably thought a bullet or two wouldn't work either.

He'd be wrong.

I hoped.

"Let's get this straight," he said. "I am giving you one chance to get out of my sight, and out of our territory."

"I don't think Terric would like that," I said.

"Terric isn't your concern."

"Well, you're wrong about that, mate. Terric *is* my concern. As a matter of fact"—I pushed up onto my feet to the accompaniment of his boys racking the slides and lifting their weapons toward my head—"you have suddenly made *yourself* my concern. This is not a good move on your part."

I didn't wait for him to threaten me again. I didn't wait for him to snap his fingers so his minions would blow my brains out.

I let the monster free. Death magic lashed out, dark whips hooking tightly into each gunman, cutting down to bone, piercing organs. The rush of drawing on their lives rocked through me in a wave of adrenaline and orgasmic need.

In that split second, four men collapsed to the floor, unconscious, while Jeremy was reaching for the inside of his jacket.

"You pull a gun, and I will kill you," I said. No more nice. The monster in me was lapping down those men's lives, even while Eleanor was standing in front of me yelling at me to stop. I wasn't listening. I wanted more. I wanted Jeremy.

Jeremy smiled. Just half of his mouth cut upward to gave a quick flash of teeth. He wasn't a stranger to death. Didn't look afraid of me now. "What would Terric say if you killed me?"

"'My boyfriend? Again?'"

Okay, that was worth it. He blinked. All that smugness drained away.

"Here's how this goes," I said, strolling over to him. "You are going to go back to your bosses, and tell them that if the Black Crane crosses my path, or the path of any one of my friends, I will take it as a personal insult, and I will kill every single person involved in the organization. Every last person. You will tell them that Terric is no longer their toy. They, and you, are no longer allowed anywhere near him. You will tell them that I am watching and that I would be delighted—" I licked my lips and one of the men on the floor screamed and writhed. "—to remove them all, permanently, from this world."

"You think you have the power here?" His voice shook a little, but he managed some scorn. "Go home to your bottle, Shamus. You're nothing."

I nodded, thought about just how easy it would be to kill him, how easy it would be to kill whatever was left of those men on the floor.

Eleanor stood in front of me and pushed her hand on my chest.

No, *in* my chest. Until her icy fingers wrapped around my heart.

Ow.

She shook her head and then pointed at the unconscious gunmen. Alive. Maybe alive. I didn't care.

But looking away from Jeremy gave him the time to pull his gun.

Well, that was stupid of me. Stupid of him too, come to think of it.

"You're a dead man, Shamus."

I laughed. He didn't know how true that was.

The fear rolling off him was palpable. He was sweating so hard I didn't know how he kept hold of the gun.

I reached out with magic.

His finger twitched. Bullets are fast. The silencer smothered the explosion.

Pain blew through my upper arm, as his shot went wide.

Jesus.

Eleanor was already on him, both hands around his gun hand. He stiffened from her icy touch, his eyes wide as his hand went numb.

I tore the gun from his useless hand, pulled the clip, and threw it across the warehouse. The pain in my left arm was excruciating, but I fed it to the Death magic inside me, pain from dying cells, torn nerves, ripped muscle, broken skin feeding my hunger.

A wash of pleasure rippled through me. It was wonderful. Also, nauseating.

"Wrong decision," I said to Jeremy.

Eleanor let go of his hand and advanced on me, angry. She mouthed, *No*, then *Terric* and *Now*.

Crap. I had no idea how long I'd been gone. I didn't want Terric to find me here, killing his boyfriend. He had said Victor wanted us right away. He must be looking for me by now.

Plus, I was bleeding.

"So," I said, "this was fun. You trying to kill me. But if you ever get in my way again, you'll be dead. I promise you that, mate."

I turned, started walking, and threw his gun in a trash can. "Do tell your bosses what I said."

"Fuck you."

I lashed out with magic and slapped his heart. Hard.

Heard him groan, then retch. Served the bastard right. I hoped he was having a seizure.

I pushed through the doors, then stuck one hand over my arm to stop the bleeding. It wasn't as bad as I expected. I think Death magic had cauterized it.

I took a little more care watching the people around me and finally headed outside again.

Just in case there were more gunmen watching me, I paused outside the front of the store and pulled the statue out of the bag I'd somehow kept ahold of, trying to look casual. There was a lot of blood drying on my hand.

No gunmen I could see. I scanned for signs of Dessa. If she was following me, she had gotten good at staying out of my line of sight.

Eleanor touched the back of my hand and pointed at the car. She hadn't seen any other gunmen either.

I lit a cigarette and crossed the parking lot. Eleanor stayed at a distance from me. She was still angry about me almost killing those men. I didn't know what to do about that.

I ducked into Terric's car. Chucked the UGGs in the backseat, then twisted and carefully propped the statue in the seat for Eleanor. "I'm sorry," I said to her.

She sat next to the statue and shook her head, her eyes sad. She didn't like it when I lost control.

"Then don't smoke in my car," Terric said.

"You made me wear those things." I turned back around and rolled down the window so I could exhale smoke. "You have to deal with the terrible, terrible trauma they caused me."

"For God's sake, Shame. UGG trauma?"

"Look at my hands. They're shaking." I held my hand out and rocked it slowly back and forth.

"You have blood on your hand."

"And on your sweater. Sorry about that."

"What happened? Are you bleeding?"

"Just a nick. My arm. Besides, aren't we late?"

"What. Happened."

"I ran into Jeremy."

"And?"

"We had a discussion."

"About?"

"He's part of the Black Crane, Terric, what do you think we talked about?"

"You don't know that for sure."

"Yes. I do. And you could know it too if you ran his record."

"I don't run records on my boyfriends."

"I think he was counting on that."

"What about your arm?"

"He shot me."

"What the hell?"

"Bad aim, though, I think it grazed." I rolled up the sleeve to look. Okay, so not just a graze. A thumb-sized angry red hole marked my upper biceps. When I twisted my arm to look at the back of it, I discovered the exit wound was twice as large.

"Crap," I said.

"Put out the cigarette."

I sighed. Threw it out the window. "Happy?"

"Thrilled." He pulled a lever to open the trunk, got out of the car, rummaged around back there, then got in the car, slamming the door shut behind him.

He had a red first aid bag.

"I don't want you healing me," I said.

"I'm not. I'm going to clean and bandage that so you stop bleeding on my interior."

He set about doing so with the efficiency of an emergency room doctor. It hurt. I didn't tell him, because I figured he already knew.

"What did you do to him?" he asked.

"Nothing."

Quieter: "What did he do to you?"

"Threatened me. Shot me. Tased me. You know, the usual."

"Tased you too?" He glanced up.

"Black Crane, Terric. Drugs and magic. He's the drugs, you're the magic. He wanted to make that clear to me."

"He said that? Exactly that?"

"He did not say exactly that. He did say he wanted me out of his territory and away from you."

"Shame—"

"Forget it," I said. "He might be someone you care about,

but one: he shot me and two: he's using you. For himself, and for the Black Crane. So he and I have decided to agree to disagree."

"Which means what? You're both going to kill each other?"

I waited until he'd stuck a thick cotton pad on both wounds, then wrapped my arm in gauze he pulled tight. Didn't answer him. Because yeah, that was pretty much what we'd agreed upon.

"Have you seen Dessa?" I said to change the subject. "Or Davy?"

"No," he finally said, dropping the conversation. I hadn't expected that. Maybe he was having second thoughts about the man. He threw everything back into the bag and tossed it in the backseat. Then he started the car.

"Davy hasn't reported in to anyone," he said as he navigated out of the parking lot.

That was odd. Davy had said there was at least one Hound on each of us Soul Complements. I should have seen someone following us, and thought it would be him.

"Did she say anything when she dropped me on your doorstep?" I asked.

"Dessa?" He shook his head. "Just that she'd found you wasted and wandering and was leaving you at my door. Said you were my problem now."

"Now?"

"That was my reaction," he said. "Eli said she knows where he or his Soul Complement is?"

"Yep."

"Doesn't line up with her story."

"I know."

"If you had to put money on it, who's lying?" he asked.

I thought about that for a second or two. Eli I had some history with. Dessa I'd barely met, but I was more inclined to trust her over Eli. "Could be both. Dessa knows more than she's telling us. Or Eli might think she knows something her brother knew before Eli killed him."

"Someone needs to teach him rule one of negotiation: don't kill the people who can give you the information you need," Terric said.

"He said he kills whoever they tell him to kill."

"And you believe that?"

"I believe that's one of the reasons he does it. I also believe he's enjoying it. Joshua was a Closer. Eli's had a vendetta against Closers ever since Victor Closed him and took all his memories and ability to use magic away years ago."

"So you think he's going to hit Closers?"

"I'd say it's on *his* list. Don't know if it falls in with the plans of the people who have him captured."

"*If* people have him captured," Terric added.

Yeah, I'd thought of that too. I lit another cigarette, got three drags off it. Then dug around in his very clean glove compartment, looking for sunglasses.

Even though there were heavy clouds today and it was only half past seven in the morning, the light was too damn bright for me. Apparently Tasers and poison were hard on my delicate constitution.

Terric pressed a button on the ceiling and a pocket opened.

"Thanks." I pulled the sunglasses out of the pocket and put them on. Didn't care if I looked ridiculous, just as long as my eyes were covered.

I hunkered down in the seat. I missed my coat.

"If you're cold, I have a coat in the back."

"Does it match the boots?"

"Maybe."

"Pass."

Victor used to live in a very nice home beneath the Japanese Gardens. A home that was built back in the early nineteen hundreds to guard the Faith well beneath it.

We'd pretty much demolished the place trying to survive the apocalypse, and while I'd been told it had been repaired and rebuilt, Victor had moved into a modest one-level home with a couple of acres and a small creek behind it.

He said it was easier on him because of his bad eyesight. I think he just hadn't ever gotten over his house being blown to bits by magic.

In some ways, he hadn't gotten over how much the world had changed now that magic was healed and reduced to a fraction of its strength.

Well, unless you were a Breaker.

Terric pulled up into the drive. We both got out.

"Want the statue?" I asked Eleanor.

"What?" Terric said as he walked to the front door.

"Nothing."

He shot a look back at me, then kept walking.

I nodded toward the car. Eleanor shook her head.

So we strolled up the path. Terric was already walking inside the house and I slipped in after him.

"Thank you both for coming." Victor wore a sweater with a shirt collar beneath it, and jeans, and of course, his heavy glasses. He shut the door behind us and turned the lock. "Let's sit in the living room."

I chose an overstuffed chair, sat there feeling a little bit like the pupil I once was, and tried to keep my hands and hungers to myself. Terric settled on the couch near me, which both helped and, for some reason, annoyed me.

Victor walked with that slow, old man pace he'd settled into since he'd lost almost all of his sight.

"To begin with," he said, "I didn't know Eli Collins was involved until yesterday when Joshua's body was found. I want you both to know that."

"Victor," I said. "A confession? My, how the tables have turned."

"It is not a confession. I am simply clarifying why I haven't told you this before," he said. "We know who Eli's Soul Complement is."

He stopped at a rolltop desk in the corner and retrieved a file folder. That, he handed to Terric.

"Who?" I asked.

Terric scanned the file, then looked up. "Brandy Scott." He tipped the file so I could see the picture clipped there. Short dark hair, almond eyes, shy smile with a dimple. She didn't look old enough to drive.

"How old is she?" I asked.

"That picture is from a while ago," Victor said. "She's fifteen in it. She's thirty-five now."

"Mental institution?" Terric said.

"That," Victor said, "is what I needed to tell you. We've known Eli had a Soul Complement. Have known it for many years. They were even tested. But Brandy wasn't stable. We did everything we could, medicine, magic, counseling. But she never recovered from the test to see if she and Eli were a match. Over the years her condition has grown worse. The last report we have from her doctors is that she has grown less and less responsive."

"You took her from him, didn't you?" I said, putting it all together. "When you Closed Eli's memories away, you made him forget her."

Terric glanced up at Victor over the file. Waiting.

It was, if you thought about it too long, a horrifying thing to do. Like cutting a person in half straight down the middle.

Victor had been standing behind the chair that matched mine. His fingers squeezed the top of the upholstery; then he let go and walked around, sat and exhaled tiredly.

"Mr. Collins . . . Eli is brilliant." He nodded. "We have the tests that prove it. But he is also unstable and dangerous."

"A sociopath," Terric said.

"Yes," Victor said. "Soul Complements can make magic break its own rules. We've always known that. Even when magic was strong, Brandy and Eli were a danger then. To themselves. To the Authority. To mankind."

"So you kept them apart?" I didn't know why it was bothering me so much. I mean yeah, I had stayed as far away from Terric as I could these last few years. And a few years before that. But that was my choice. No one had made me forget him. No one had forbade me to be with him.

It was my choice.

Eli and Brandy hadn't had a choice.

"It was decided, by more people than just me, that it would be best for them to never know about each other," Victor said.

"So you Closed Eli," Terric said, "took the memories of Brandy away from him. And then you took the memory of how to use magic away from him too?"

"Yes." He was quiet a moment, maybe thinking over those times, those decisions.

I'd always wondered if Victor followed rules, or made rules to follow. Too many times in the past he'd leaned a decision one way or another to make sure things in the Authority turned out the way he approved of. The way he thought was right, despite what the Authority stood for.

"Yes," he said, "I did. I made him forget Brandy. I took away his ability to use magic."

"Not that he didn't relearn it," Terric said.

"And when Eli demanded you Unclose him back when Davy Silvers's life hung in the balance," I said, "you didn't give him the memories of Brandy back, did you?"

"No."

A pause while I, at least, swallowed the fact that my teacher, my friend Victor, had been playing God with someone's life. With their soul.

"It was my decision not to let him know about her. I still believe it was the correct thing to do. She is broken. There is no future for them together."

"I had no idea you have a crystal ball," I said. "How very convenient you know what they can and can't be."

The rings snapped with tiny sparks of red.

Yes, I was angry. Even though I hated Eli, I hated even more that Victor had made decisions that only Eli and Brandy should have made.

"Would you rather I have let two very unstable people have full access to a magic more powerful than ninety-nine percent of magic users in the world could access? It is not unthinkable that they could have destroyed the world."

I knew he wasn't being overly dramatic. Soul Complements could be walking time bombs. Soul Complements, in fact, had almost ended the world just three years ago.

"But to just cut them off from each other? There had to have been other options."

"There were not."

"Have you considered that by not having Brandy it drove Eli to extremes? That all this—all the crap he's doing—is because of what you did to him? Joshua might still be—"

"Shame," Terric said gently. "Don't."

I just glared at Victor.

He nodded. "Yes," he whispered. "I have thought of it many times. Especially over the last three years."

I'm sure he had. One of the side effects of surviving the apocalypse was that Cody Miller had healed magic with the intension of making everything better. That healing had made magic soft, and it had given memories back to everyone in the world who had had their memories taken away by Closers.

Closers like Victor.

So Eli had remembered Brandy and the part Victor and the Authority had played in keeping her separate from him.

"Damn," Terric said softly. "He's known for three years that she's his match? And that she was locked away?"

Victor nodded.

"When did he find her?" I asked.

"Our sources say it was two years ago. She doesn't have family, was a ward of the state. They were trying a new medication. It seemed to be helping. She was more responsive. Aware."

"Then?" Terric asked.

"Then the war." Victor spread his hands. "The end of magic being separated into dark and light. The end of our power. And the beginning of the new world where the Authority is no longer secret, where memories are no longer hidden, where those of us who fought to keep the world, and all its people safe, are ignored. Unwelcome. Silenced."

"You're not unwelcome," Terric said. "The Authority still needs you. Needs what you can teach."

"Faith magic?" Victor smiled sadly. "The things I would teach are nothing more than a history lesson now. Those spells, Closing people, guarding gates, fighting to keep dangerous uses for magic secret and safe? Unnecessary."

"All right," I said, "fine. Things might not have worked out the way you wanted them to. We've all shed our tears. But we're still breathing, and we all have a problem: Eli. How do we find him? How do we stop him?"

"I don't know the answer to either of those questions, I'm afraid," he said.

"Do you know about a woman named Dessa?" I asked.

He frowned. "The name isn't familiar to me."

"Dessa Leeds?"

His gray eyebrows pushed wrinkles up his forehead. "Leeds? Do you mean Thomas Leeds?"

"That's her brother," I said. "Dessa's brother. You know him?"

"He was a Closer. Out of Seattle. He was working for us. What do you know about him?"

I leaned back. Studied him. "Nothing, really. I do know that you're holding out on me, though."

"Shame," Terric said.

"Come on, Ter. The old man's got a secret he doesn't want to share."

"Old man?" Victor drew himself up and gave me a stern glare. "You know I'm in contact with your mother, don't you, Shamus?"

I grinned at his indignant tone. For all that I was angry

about his decisions with Eli and Brandy, Victor was one of my teachers. I'd grown up with him being a stern, proper sort of uncle. Plus, he'd taught me some of the dirtiest tricks you could do with magic. He was family, and that bond couldn't be broken. Not even over dangerously poor decisions.

"Go ahead," I said. "Tell her I'm being disrespectful to one of my teachers. It won't be the first time she hears it. Oh, and while you're at it, ask her why you don't have the balls to tell us the whole truth."

Terric leaned back on the couch and threw his hands up. "Jesus, Shame. Did that Taser fry your brain?"

I just watched Victor. In the past, needling him couldn't make the old man change his mind. I didn't think it would work this time, but figured it wouldn't hurt to try. People who are upset or angry tend to say all sorts of interesting things they would never say in a calm state of mind.

"We've known the government was becoming . . . interested in the members of the Authority," he said quietly. "Certain members. Our Closers, our Soul Complements, and those of us in higher positions. But we didn't know why. We needed someone on the inside. Someone who had a contact."

"Thomas?" I asked.

"Yes. Thomas thought he could use his relationship with his sister—I do believe her name was Dessa—to get closer to the matter."

So Dessa did work for the government. "Which department was he infiltrating?" I asked.

"He worked his way into a government-sponsored research and development facility. On the surface, it is a testing lab for biotechnology. Everything from increasing crop yields to deterring invasive species. But beneath that facade, Thomas found evidence of other tests. Human tests."

"Medical tests on humans are far from rare, Victor," I said. "What made these different?"

"The tests weren't for medical advancement. They were searching for ways to weaponize people."

"What?" Terric said.

Took the word right out of my mouth.

"Now that magic is a known resource, the government is very interested in what people can do with it. How it can be used as a protection. As a weapon."

It made sense. Any government would want to know how magic could be used, and by whom.

"Okay," I said. "How do Eli and Brandy fit into this?"

"Brandy disappeared a year and a half ago," Victor said. "The official report is that she died from a stroke caused by side effects of the medication she was on. But we know she was taken. Stolen out of the institution. By the government. By this research lab."

Terric opened the file again. Thumbed through it. "Thomas was looking for her, wasn't he?"

"Yes."

"And Eli?" he asked.

"We'd lost trace of him at the same time. I don't know if he was taken, if he went looking for her, or if he was behind her kidnapping. Our . . . resources aren't what they used to be. But our goal, that has remained the same. To keep the innocent safe from magic and the things people would do with it. Brandy is an innocent in this. But we believe she was taken by men who would use her as a weapon."

"Tell me you know where the research facility is."

"From the information Thomas was able to gather, it has branches across the country. We suspect one of them is here in the Northwest. And if they are trying to tap magic, it will need to be near a well."

"There are a lot of wells. One under almost every city," Terric said.

"And five under Portland," Victor said.

"Eli opened a gate," I said.

That got his attention.

"He— What?"

"He was in my bedroom, and after about two minutes, a gate opened behind him and he was pulled back through it."

"He used magic?" Victor asked. "Broke magic to open the gate?"

I thought about it. "No. I can usually feel when magic breaks." From the corner of my eye I saw Terric nod.

"There was magic involved. But there was also technology."

"Eli spent too long working under Beckstrom Senior," Terric said.

"I think you mean worshipping," I said. "Spent too much time worshipping Allie's father and all that experimental tech the Beckstrom fortune funded."

"If they have gate technology," Victor said, "then none of us are safe."

"Which means we need to find Eli," I said. "You didn't happen to shoot him with a tracking chip over the years, did you?"

"Unfortunately, no," Victor said. "I wish we'd thought of it."

"Have you followed up on everyone connected to Brandy and Eli?" Terric asked. "Her doctors, caregivers? Eli's contacts, where he's lived, worked?"

"Yes," Victor said. "We hit a dead end about eight months ago. That was also when we fell out of contact with Thomas." He paused, then, "We think Thomas was killed."

"He was," I said. "Dessa said he was killed by Eli. Said he had marks in him like Joshua."

"Was she sure?" Victor asked softly.

"She saw Joshua," I said. "Saw the glyphs carved into him. She thinks it was made by the same magic user."

Victor took off his glasses and closed his eyes. For a moment, I saw the weight of years change him. He had been in the Authority for longer than I had been alive. He'd seen all manners of horrors committed by both the right and the wrong people having too much power.

And now this.

"You have to stop him." Victor replaced his glasses and opened his eyes. There was the iron strength of resolve in his words. "Eli Collins should have been killed years ago. We thought then that it was a mercy to just take his memories away. To give him a chance to build a normal life. But he turned to darkness. To killing. To murder. Joshua should not have had to pay the price for our mistakes. I want you to stop him. At any cost."

"We should let the Overseer know," Terric said.

"No. Not this," Victor said. "It has never been the way of the Authority to kill unnecessarily. It is not the way we want to go forward in this new world of magic. But this is an old wound. An old ill that must be ended. Before more innocent people die. I do not want to be hampered by the Overseer's decisions.

"Eli must be stopped. He will kill each Closer involved with his closing, and then he will kill more. Anyone who ever spoke against him or stood for the laws of the Authority. Anyone who ever stood aside, knowing what had been taken from him. If he finds his Soul Complement . . ." Victor paused, swallowed. "Her broken mind will drive him deeper into darkness. And if they break magic together, and use it to shape the world to their desire . . ."

He didn't have to tell us what would happen. Having that much power drove people insane. Even people with good intentions were lured by the madness in magic, the temptation of simply making and unmaking the world. And people with bad intentions did things like start the apocalypse.

"Do not show him mercy, Terric," Victor said, "for he will refuse it. Stop him before he removes every Soul Complement and every magic user in the Authority."

Terric opened his mouth, but I spoke up over him. "The

only way to stop him will be to kill him," I said. "You understand that, don't you, Victor?"

"Yes, I do."

"At any cost?" I asked.

"Yes."

"I'll do it."

Terric sighed heavily. Here's the thing: Death and me pretty much saw eye-to-eye. I knew one of these days someone would have to take me down when I lost control of magic. And Eli wasn't just a poor magic user caught by an evil government. Yes, he'd been used by the Authority and others. But even if he had once been a good man, that was over.

He liked killing. Craved it. If the world bowed at his feet, he would want violence, destruction.

I understood those kinds of dark desires. I had no problem ending it for him.

Victor looked between Terric and me. Finally settled on me. "Thank you, Shamus. I know your burden isn't easy. Death magic—"

"Don't," I said.

"Shame," he said firmly. "Let me finish. I know the changes magic has made in you and in Terric have been painful. I know you struggle for control."

"Hey, now," I started, but he just leveled a gaze at me. What could I say? It was the truth. And he knew it.

Victor was not a stupid man. He had known me my entire life. It didn't take eyes to see how close I walked the edge of disaster every day.

"Your father was a good man, Shame," he said. "A dear friend of mine."

I hunched my shoulders unconsciously. I didn't like it when people brought up my father. He and I had gotten on as most fathers and rebellious slacker sons do. Really, he was a lot more patient than I would have been. I missed him, but I'd had enough time to know he was gone from my life for good.

That wasn't what bothered me. No, what haunted me was the thing Jingo Jingo had said before I killed that sick bastard. That my father had fallen on his knees and begged Jingo Jingo to end me. To end the monster he knew I would become.

A Death magic user.

Only I hadn't just become a Death magic user—I'd become a vessel that carried Death magic in my body and soul.

If my dad were alive, I figured he'd want me dead. Before I gave in to the monster inside me.

"This is something that I've wanted to tell you for a long time," Victor said. "Jingo was lying. Your father didn't beg him to keep you from using Death magic. Your father warned Jingo that if he grew too hungry, if *he* ever lost control, it would be you, his son, who would stop him. Your father saw the strength in you. Saw how you, of all magic users we had ever seen, have the ability to use Death magic without succumbing to its allure.

"He was proud of you, Shamus. As am I."

Not what I was expecting to hear. And for once in my life, I didn't know what to say.

Chapter 18

Victor gave us all the information he had on Thomas Leeds, which wasn't much, but it was more than the files Terric and I could access. Actually it was a lot more than the files Clyde and Dash could access too. I found that very interesting, and Terric found it very annoying.

"We were the head of the Authority," Terric said, slowing for traffic in the afternoon downpour. "We should have had access to every file on every person we wanted."

"Victor doesn't play by the rules," I said. "He'll probably always see a reason to keep the secret organization secret. Or at least as secret as he can. Very old-school skullduggery. I like him for holding to the old, distrustful, cynical standards."

"You would."

I grinned and folded my arms, carefully, over my chest. The run through the rain to the car had gotten both of us pretty wet, but Terric had on a coat. Even though I was still wearing the sweater, I wished I had my black peacoat instead.

"Stop by the inn," I said. "I want a coat."

"I have a coat in the trunk."

"I want *my* coat."

"We are not stopping this investigation so you can get your comfy clothes."

"Investigation? Is that what you're calling it?"

"What do you want me to call it?"

"A manhunt," I said. "That's what it is."

"We're going to the office," Terric said.

"Why?"

"I want to tell Clyde what Victor told us, in person. Or at least most of it, so he has the heads-up."

"Why?"

"If I were running the Authority, I'd be furious that I didn't have this kind of information. Also, I want to find out if they've seen Davy."

"Fine," I said. Mostly because I was pretty sure I'd left an old coat there.

"Why the statue?" Terric asked.

"What?"

"Why did you buy a statue of the Grim Reaper with wings?"

"Caught my eye."

"I've seen your apartment, Shame. Art never catches your eye."

I didn't say anything. Didn't care what he thought. This conversation was done.

He glanced in the rearview mirror, at where the statue was carefully propped up so that Eleanor could sit next to it.

Don't remember her, I thought. *Don't ask about her.*

Unlike Zay and Allie, we couldn't read each other's minds. But we'd known each other a long time. My bluff didn't hold.

"It's Eleanor, isn't it?" he asked quietly.

I stared out the window.

"She's still . . . connected to you," he said. "I'd forgotten. I'm sorry, Shame. I'd forgotten."

"Don't want your pity. Don't want to talk about it."

"Is she still angry? Can you hear her? Talk to her?"

I dug in my pocket, pulled out a cigarette, lit it, smoked. Didn't open the window.

He rolled his eyes at my petty disobedience. "She wanted the statue, didn't she?" he asked. "Why?"

I glanced over at him, lifted the cigarette to my mouth, inhaled, tipped the sunglasses down so he could see my eyes. When he looked over at me, I said, "Leave it the hell alone."

"Maybe I could help you with her. Maybe we could—"

"No," I said. "We did what we could. We tried what could be tried. Now I deal with it my way, and you don't ever speak of it again."

He glanced in the rearview again. "Later," he said. "We'll talk about it later." Then he turned his attention to where it might actually do some good—looking for parking.

Found a spot a block away from the office, which was about as good as we were going to get at this hour. I was not looking forward to the walk in the rain, but I was looking forward to getting out of the car and the silence that was filled with Terric's promise to not let the Eleanor situation go.

Pushed the door open before the engine was off, clomped across the sidewalk and under the awning. We were in front of a bank. It was an uphill walk to the office. Not as many people out right now, which made it easier on my hunger. I lit another cig, then put my boots to work.

Terric was still in the car. Even though I wasn't looking at him, I could sense him, his heartbeat, his mood. Being around him so much lately only made me more aware of him. Right now he was angry, but more than that, I sensed sorrow.

Who knew what he was sad about? Could be any number of things: the loss of his job, Joshua's death, Eleanor's not-death, Jeremy . . . or me. Or maybe it was just that he didn't like the idea I was going to take care of Eli the best way I knew how—by killing him.

I felt more than heard him get out of the car. Felt more than heard his footsteps in the rain, jogging to catch up with me. Then he was beside me, matching my stride.

"Just because you don't think a conversation needs to happen doesn't mean it isn't going to."

"I said drop it, mate."

"Drop it. Drop the fact that you have a ghost—an undead soul tied to you, trapped, haunting you every second of the day? No wonder you're so damn morose."

"Drop it just like I dropped you not wanting to believe that Jeremy is a lying bastard."

"This isn't about me—it's about you," he said. "We can save her, Shame. The answer to every problem isn't always killing or ignoring every damn thing."

I stopped, turned to him. "What if I don't want an answer, Terric? What if I like killing things? What if I look for every opportunity to kill?"

"Don't say that."

"What? Don't tell you the truth?" I lowered my voice. "You are a piece of work, Conley. You say you want to talk, but you don't want to listen, do you? I am not you. I am not a good guy. I destroy things. I *like* it. I like killing. I like that Eleanor is shackled to me. Because it reminds me of the power I have. Power you should not underestimate."

I pulled my hand into a fist and arcs of red electricity licked across my rings.

Terric squared off from me, the Void stone necklace at his chest burning with white-green light.

And he smiled. The son of a bitch smiled.

"You don't frighten me, Flynn. Your magic doesn't frighten me. And neither do your lies."

I lifted my fist.

He lifted his hand.

I never even had a chance to draw on magic.

Pain, hot and twisting, shuddered through my head and down my spine.

Had lightning just nailed me to the ground?

Terric hissed, and I knew he felt the same pain.

I hadn't cast anything. Hadn't hit him.

He hadn't cast anything. Hadn't hit me.

"What the hell?" I breathed.

Terric's gaze met mine, his blue eyes wide in the falling rain.

And I knew it, knew the reason for the pain at the exact moment he did.

"They broke it," Terric said. "Someone broke magic."

"Zay," I said, swallowing back the burnt scent of mint and rose. "Jesus. Zay's hurt. Or Allie. One of them."

We ran to the car. Terric outpaced me, but only by a step or two. In the car, doors slammed, engine. Terric tore through the city, heading northeast. Heading to St. Johns. Heading to Zayvion and Allie.

He tossed me his phone. I caught it without looking, dialed Clyde.

"This is Clyde Turner," he answered.

"It's Shame. Someone broke magic. We think it's Zay and Allie. We think they've been hit."

"Hit by magic?"

"We don't know. We're going out there now." I hung up. Terric probably would have told him to call the cops, or the cavalry or whoever it was we had to answer to these days, but I did not give a single damn about procedure.

Terric and I were enough to deal with whatever was going down.

His phone rang. Dash. I thumbed it on speaker and answered, "Shame."

"The police are on their way," he said. "Do you need anything else? Anyone else?"

"We got it," I said.

"Were there any reports?" Terric asked. "Has anyone else called this in?"

"No," Dash said. "Just you two."

"Let us know if you hear anything," Terric said.

"I will. Be careful." Dash hung up. I did too.

Terric pulled up to Zay and Allie's place, double-parking

on the gravel lane that ran between their three-story farm-house and the empty lot in front of the river. They had a front door. We didn't use it.

We jogged past their low stone fence, the leafless rose-bushes, and the hedge of dormant daisies. Past the garden Allie was so proud of, which held three decent-sized pump-kins and some random gourds and flowers the Hounds had thought would be funny to plant when she wasn't looking, up the weathered wooden steps of the porch, to the kitchen side door.

I tried the door handle. It was unlocked.

Got exactly one step into the room.

A fist came out of nowhere and hit me in the head like a bull at full charge.

Holy shit.

I stumbled into Terric, who didn't bother catching me on my way down to the floor. He was halfway through a spell.

"Stop." Allie's voice. Allie. I blinked upward. At a very angry Zayvion Jones, who was glowering down over me, his eyes molten gold.

"Jesus, Zay," I said. "We came here to help you."

"Zay," Allie said calmly. "It's Shame and Terric. Let them in."

I didn't think Zay was listening in the language we were speaking.

"Zayvion," Terric said. "It's all right. We got this. The po-lice are on their way. Tell us what happened."

For no apparent reason, he listened to that.

Zay closed his eyes, opened them again. Still gold, but this time there was sanity mixed in with the anger. "We were attacked."

"Fuck," I said, picking myself up off the floor. I wiped the blood off my nose and almost howled. "Also, you broke my nose. Asshole."

"Are you all right?" Allie said.

"I'm fine." I looked at Zay and he finally moved that

mountain of muscle over to one side so I could walk the rest of the way into the room.

They had the old-fashioned farm kitchen thing to go with the rest of the old-fashioned farmhouse. I walked to the oversized sink and found a washcloth hanging from the facet. Used that to mop up the blood running out of my face. Then turned to get a look at the situation.

Allie was sitting at their kitchen table. She had been crying. Zay was still in guard mode. Terric was trying to talk him down toward something resembling reason. Wasn't getting anywhere.

"For crap's sake." I pinched my nose with the cloth, crossed over to Zayvion, grabbed his wrist, then led him over to Allie, who held her hand up for him. "She's fine and she's right here."

Their fingers touched and I pulled my hand quickly away from the connection between them—an almost physical sense of heat.

"What happened?" Terric asked again. "Allie, we felt magic break. Did you break it?"

She nodded. Her eyes were wet. "I don't know why I'm crying. This is so . . ." She wiped at her eyes with her free hand and sniffed, then took a deep breath. "I'm fine. I'm not hurt. I'm just angry."

"Want to tell Mr. Jones to stand down and make with the talking?" I asked.

She looked up at Zay. Maybe for the first time realized how furious he still was. "Zayvion, I'm fine. The baby's fine too."

Right. Baby. No wonder why Zay had gone feral.

"Tell us what happened, Z," I said as I leaned back against the counter, rag over my nose. "Tell us why you broke magic."

Maybe it was the angle of light from where I was standing, but that's when I noticed Zayvion's black T-shirt was dark with blood. He was injured.

"Zay, mate," I said. "You're bleeding."

Terric was looking out the door, but at that, turned and shut it. "Sit down, Zay."

Zay sat in the chair next to Allie, and Terric lifted his shirt to see the damage.

"Who did this?"

"Collins," Allie said. "It was Eli Collins."

Chapter 19

"Everything you can tell us," I said. "Quickly. Zay. Step it up, man. Use words."

Terric was at the sink now, getting a clean cloth wet so we could clear some of the blood off Zay's chest to see if there was a serious wound beneath it all.

"We were at the table," Zay said in that very, very calm tone he had that really meant he was very, very angry. "We both heard something crack. He was standing inside our kitchen. Smiling."

Zay jerked as Terric pressed the cloth on his stomach. "Did he shoot you?"

"No," Allie said. "He had a knife. He didn't want to kill Zayvion."

Zay picked up where Allie left off. "He wanted to hurt me and make me watch while he killed Allie. Said he was going to carve the life out of her."

The baby.

Fuck.

"So you broke magic," I said.

"We broke magic," they said simultaneously.

"Did you kill the bastard?" I asked.

"No," Zay said. "He had something like a gate."

"Yeah, I've seen it. Tech, I think."

"You've seen it?" Allie asked. "You've seen Eli? When?"

"Last night. He left me a message. Said that people are going to die if I don't find him and save him. Oh, and he's the one who's going to do the killing."

"Why would he warn you that he's going to kill people?" The shock of what had just happened appeared to be wearing off and Allie was back on her game.

The distant wail of sirens filled the air. Maybe the police, maybe an ambulance. Maybe coming here.

"He said he's being held captive and being used to kill people. People like Joshua. He said they're holding his soul. His Soul Complement."

"He's lying," Zay said.

"No," Terric said. "Victor told us. They've known who his Soul Complement is for years. She had been in a mental institution all this time until she disappeared a short while ago. Victor took away Collins's memory of her."

"Shit." He exhaled. "How long?"

"She's fifteen in the file photo," I said. "Thirty-five now. And Eli says they might have her."

"What do they want with him?" Allie asked.

"Their very own Soul Complement pair weapon? I'll give you one guess. But the thing we ought to worry about, boys and girls, is that he's a Breaker. Even though she's damaged and he's bat-shit crazy, if they work together, they can break magic and make it do whatever they want it to do."

"What isn't adding up for me," Terric said, "is why Eli came here with a knife. He's not shy about guns. He's not shy about taking his one shot and making it count."

That was true. Eli liked death, destruction, and bloody mayhem and didn't mind getting his hands dirty. "So he didn't want to kill Zay. Probably didn't want to kill Allie. Or at least not quickly. Did he have anything else with him?"

"A needle."

I nodded. "Right. Had that with me too. But no tranq gun?"

Zay frowned. "No."

I looked over at Terric. "Maybe this was a diversion. Maybe this was just to scare us. Force Allie and Zay to run. Or force them to stay. It feels like a chess move, more than an attack."

"The hole in my chest says otherwise," Zay said.

The sirens were getting closer.

"Are you staying?" I asked.

Allie and Zay looked at each other. Maybe read each other's thoughts.

Allie nodded. "We're staying. We'll set up Hounds to keep an eye on the house."

"He has the tech to show up anywhere he wants," I said. "Hounds wouldn't react fast enough."

"We'll set up guards," Zay said. "Trip spells. Traps."

"You'd have to break magic for anything to be strong enough to stop him," Terric said. "And with the baby . . ."

"The baby will be fine," Allie said.

I didn't care how brave and steady her words were. She was white as a sheet. This had scared the hell out of her. She was afraid the baby would be damaged if they broke magic and used it. Was probably already worried the baby had been damaged.

"We'll do it," I said.

No one hurt my friends. No one.

Zay looked at me, raised one eyebrow. "Who?"

"Terric and me. We'll break magic, set the traps and trips, make it so that if he techs into the place again, he's knocked out cold. Shouldn't be too hard."

Silence in the room. I thought Terric had gone completely mute.

"When was the last time you two broke magic?" Allie asked.

"I do not like the tone of your voice, young lady," I said. "We're . . . capable. We can do it."

Zay was staring at me like I was an unsolvable puzzle.

He took a breath and looked over at Terric instead. "What do you think?"

"Really, Jones?" I asked. "First you punch me in my beautiful face. Then you kick me right in my tender ego. I don't need Terric's permission to make a plan. A good plan."

"We can do it," Terric said with a smoothness that probably hid the fear I could feel in the fast beat of his heart. He didn't want to break magic with me.

Or maybe he really desperately did.

Didn't matter. Didn't care. We were doing it. Discussion done.

"Let's get it done before the police arrive. We'll pull from the crystal well," I said, tugging my rings off, one by one. "Three levels of spells. By the time he's able to break through all three protections—if he can break through them—Zay and Allie will either be out of the house, ready to defend themselves with magic—"

"Or have guns in our hands," Zay finished.

"Right," I said. "That works too." I started pacing, suddenly full of too much restless energy. "Three spells: Block, Hold, Sleep. Or maybe not Sleep. We could do Pain, or Freeze, or something more permanent."

Yes, I was talking a mile a minute. I was nervous. It had been a long, long time since we'd broken magic. I had an overwhelming need to control this event.

"Shame," Terric said. I think he'd been talking to Zay and Allie while I paced. I think they'd decided on things without me. Also, Zay had a new towel he was pressing against the puncture wound.

So, I'd lost some time.

"Let's take this outside. Allie needs to be at some distance from us when we break magic to protect the baby. And since the police are almost here, we don't have a lot of time."

"The police can wait. I'm not going to cast a crappy spell because they're in the way."

"It will be fine," he said.

"Of course it's fine. Of course it will be fine. Fine is the way it's always going to be."

Okay, now I was rambling.

Terric walked over to the door. Opened it. Pointed outside. Like I was some kind of dog who needed to pee. "Outside."

Zay was already on his feet. He didn't move like he was in much pain, but then, he had been through worse than a knife in the gut. He wrapped his arm around Allie protectively and she leaned into him as they walked out of the kitchen.

It was odd to see Allie so shaken by this. She was one of the bravest women I knew. And I would lay good money that she hadn't flinched in the face of danger. Hadn't been afraid to fight Eli. But now that the danger was past, she had time to think of how the situation could have turned out, had time to realize her life could have been very different in the matter of seconds. She could have been babyless, Zayless. They were realities she did not want to come true.

And neither did I. I dug in my pocket with shaking fingers as I walked back down the porch stairs.

"No time for cigarettes," Terric said.

I left them in my pocket. My hands weren't steady enough to light them anyway. It was almost frightening how much I wanted to do magic with Terric, to break it and make it into the glorious, dangerous force it used to be.

And on the other hand it was the absolute last thing I wanted to do.

"How long?" I asked.

"Until the police get here?" he asked. "I think about a minute. If we're going to do this, we need to do it fast."

Terric was calm, relaxed. Looked like he was talking about cataloging receipts, not breaking magic open like a ripe melon and letting all the fruity goodness spill out into the world.

"Somewhere where they won't interrupt us," I said. "The car?"

"Not enough space," he said. "How about down by the river?"

"River works for me." We walked through the undeveloped lot, stepping over a low chain fence there and ignoring the sign that insisted we were trespassing. The rain had let off a bit, but it was a gray enough day that I couldn't see the river, even though I could hear it—the lapping of water, the distant metal and engine sounds of boats and cranes. I knew we'd run into the refinery before we hit the sand or the river, but was happy when Terric stopped, after having walked only a few feet across the lot.

"You don't have to do this, Shame. We don't have to do this," he said.

"Yes," I said, "we do."

"Then let's do it." Terric turned toward me. "Three spells. Hold, Block, and Pain."

I was surprised he'd picked Pain, not Sleep. "Seems more like what I'd want to cast. Are you sure, Mr. Goody-goody?"

"I don't like Eli either," Terric said. "And I am pissed he hurt Allie and Zay."

"Good," I said. "Nice to see you here on the dark side. We do have more fun, you know."

Terric shook his head once. "Work, not bullshit. Tap the well, let's get this done."

Well, well. Look at who had gone all bossy.

Still, he was right. I reached out with that part of my head that was always aware of magic, of how it whispered in the back of my thoughts, how it tempted and begged.

Then I tapped in to the well not too far from here and felt magic cover me like an electric heat over my entire body. Pure magic, not just the Death magic that lurked inside me.

It was glorious.

Terric tapped the well too. I didn't know what he was

feeling, didn't care. I was having a hard time not being swallowed by the sensation of drawing on magic. God, I loved it. Missed it. Craved it.

I pulled magic to me in huge greedy handfuls, holding it tight. I'd have to carve a spell, have to make the glyph for magic to fill and bring us whatever outcome we wanted, but right now all I wanted was to stand there with magic burning across my skin.

I might have moaned. Normally, that would be embarrassing. But right now I didn't think Terric was paying any attention to what I was doing or what I was feeling either. He was dealing with his own experience of drawing on raw magic—drawing on it knowing that we were going to break it, make it stronger. Make it into what it used to be.

Make it into the thing we loved.

"Hold," Terric breathed.

Took me a second to realize he was talking about the spell. Right. We were supposed to be casting spells.

I did what I could to focus my attention on the spell, on casting it with him. Best I managed was mirroring his movements. Terric drew the spell, I drew it facing him, opposite to him, but frankly magic had me so distracted that, if he hadn't been leading the charge, I would have given up and fallen into other, much more pleasurable spells.

"Shame," he said, out loud I thought. Not in my mind. I hoped. "Focus, for fuck's sake."

That got a smile out of me. Fine. Focus. I could do that. Enough that I did not do a shabby job completing the glyph for Hold.

"Ready?" Terric asked. He was breathing in rhythm with me, his heart in rhythm with mine.

It felt right. It steadied the hunger inside me. Pushed it away, and filled me with ease. Made me feel whole again. Real again.

"Always."

Our eyes locked.

We broke magic.

It was like running a knife along the soft, ripe skin of a fruit and feeling it split beneath my fingers. But instead of digging down into the fruity middle, we tore the seal on magic open and released the power. A hell of a lot of power. An explosion of power that had been waiting for us to set it free.

Magic poured into the glyphs traced in the air in front of us. Hung there and burned like fire.

"Hold," Terric said. "To stop those who would break this sanctuary."

One thing I had to admit, Terric knew how to set a spell so it stuck.

I waited until the glyphs were burning a hot cherry red before I passed my hand across it, sending it out to wrap the house. It would be visible for a moment or two. We'd done our best to cast a Fade into the spell so it wouldn't be seen with the naked eye.

Ever since magic had been healed, it had also become much more visible. So the smart magic users now made sure they included something to hide the spells they cast.

The spell wrapped the house from roof to foundation, glowing red for a moment, then fading away beneath the gray of the day.

The sirens were getting closer.

"Block is next," Terric said, his voice a little husky.

Glad I wasn't the only one enjoying this.

I got my fingers busy and drew the negative image of the spell as he drew the positive. We both pulled on more magic, poured it into the glyphs, which glowed a deep blue this time.

"Block," Terric said. "To protect those within this sanctuary."

He didn't really have to say anything out loud for the spells to work, but he had studied for a long time beneath Victor and Faith magic. Some of the history of those kinds of spells involves prayer, intonation, mantras. I guess old habits are hard to break.

I waved my hand across the spell and sent it spinning to the house, where it immediately sank into the walls.

"Last is Pain," Terric said, beginning the spell.

"Let me."

He nodded and wiped his fingers through the beginnings of the glyph, clearing the air.

I carved the glyph for pain in the air between us, making sure it would wrap and hold and bite and paralyze. I carved it so that if Eli tripped it, he'd be lucky to be breathing by the time the spell ran its course. Terric mirrored my movements, no comment on the viciousness of the spell I was shaping.

The police arrived. We were behind a screen of brush. With the fog closing in, I didn't think they'd immediately notice the black spell smoldering between us.

And because Terric had done it, as soon as the spell was formed and filled with magic, I spoke too.

"Pain," I said. "To bring our enemy to his fucking knees."

"Amen," Terric said. He wiped his hand across it and pushed it toward the house, where it fell like a hard hail of dark rain, soaking it through.

That, the cops saw. But I didn't think they knew where it had come from. Until I glanced out at the road, and noticed Detective Stotts looking our way.

Chapter 20

"Act natural," Terric said.

"Seriously? Natural? Like we're just two guys who happened to have dressed out of the same closet, standing in the rain and fog on an abandoned lot casting magic the likes of which hasn't been seen for three years? That kind of natural?"

"It's just Paul," he said. "He knows we're on the side of the good guys."

"Speak for yourself."

"Terric, Shame," Detective Stotts called out. "Can I have a word with you?"

"I say we run for it," I said.

"You have zero survival instinct, Flynn." Terric started toward Stotts and I followed.

"What are you two doing out here?" Detective Stotts asked.

"Skipping rocks," I said.

He turned to Terric. Why did people always ignore me?

"Terric?" he asked.

"We came out to see Allie and Zay."

"So you know they were attacked?"

"We're the ones who told Clyde Turner."

"You know I'd prefer it if crimes were reported to the police first."

"It was a matter of seconds between me knowing they were hurt, to Clyde knowing, to you," he said.

"Those seconds count," Stotts said. "I'd like to have them so that my people, our guns, and the *law* can get here in time to keep things contained."

"We weren't even sure that they had been attacked," Terric said calmly.

"Then why did you tell Mr. Turner they were?"

"What we told Clyde was that Zay and Allie cast magic," Terric said. Then, a little quieter, "They broke it."

Paul Stotts was the boyfriend of Allie's best friend, Nola. No, wait. Husband. They'd tied the knot a couple years back. And Paul had stood by us through the worst of the apocalypse. He knew things about magic and magic users that no one knew back in the day.

He knew things today about magic we still try to keep quiet—namely that Soul Complements can break it.

"Why did they do that?" he asked.

"That's what we wanted to know. Especially since Allie is . . ." Terric paused. "Has Allie talked to Nola?"

"Are you kidding? She's planning the baby shower."

"Right. Since Allie is pregnant, they didn't want to break magic," Terric continued. "So when we felt it break . . ."

"You can feel it when magic breaks?"

Terric shrugged. "We did this time. We assumed they wouldn't have broken it if they weren't in trouble."

Stotts nodded, then glanced over at the house. "I'll need a statement."

"You know we can't admit to breaking on record," Terric said.

"I'll want something from you, even if it's just you had a bad feeling and followed up on your hunch."

An ambulance rolled up, and the EMTs got out and walked up to the kitchen.

Good thing we'd triggered the spells to only react if Eli tripped them.

"Zayvion's been stabbed," Stotts said.

"We know," Terric said.

"I don't suppose you know anything else about this, do you?"

"No," Terric said.

Yes, that surprised me. I thought he liked telling the truth and following procedure.

Stotts finally looked back at me. "Shame, do you know anything else about this?"

"Nope. Not a thing."

"All right." He glanced up as one of his officers walked our way. "I want to see you both in the station later today."

"We'll be there," Terric said so smoothly, even I had a hard time telling if it was a lie.

Stotts moved up the path toward the house and Terric went the other way to the car.

I glanced back at the house. A movement along the rooftop drew my eye.

There was a gargoyle on the roof. Namely, Stone.

Well, he was really an animate—which is a construction of stone and gears powered by magic. He'd been made by Cody Miller, who had once been an incredible artist and magic user.

Even though magic shouldn't be strong enough to keep Stone going, he was still as mostly alive as ever. He'd been Allie's loyal companion for years now, was a good-natured doofus who liked to stack household items.

In a fight he was a deadly, ferocious brute.

He folded his wings and four-footed it to the chimney, sitting with his hands wrapped over his toes. He peered down at the police moving around, then looked out at me.

I held up a hand. "Look after Allie," I said in a normal voice I knew he'd hear. He tipped his head, both ears rising into sharp points, and showed a little teeth.

He must have been with Cody when the attack happened. I was glad he was here now. I suddenly felt a lot better knowing a ton of fanged, clawed, winged living rock was going to be there with Allie and Zay.

I turned and caught up with Terric and walked along beside him. "I see what you did there with the detective, you little liar."

"Shut up, Shame."

He got in the car and I got in after him. Eleanor slipped into the backseat.

"You lied to a police officer," I said with mock disappointment. "Aren't you worried they're going to take your hero card away?"

"If he knew what we knew, he'd stop us from doing what we're going to do," he said.

"Kill Eli?"

"Kill Eli."

"Let's drink to that. Swing by and get me a coffee, won't you?"

"Coffee, not booze?"

"When they open a drive-through bar, I'll be the first in line. Until then, coffee."

What could I say? I was in a good mood. Breaking magic had taken care of my hunger, and made me feel lazy and satisfied, like finally scratching an itch I couldn't reach. Watching Terric lie to the cops was the candy sprinkles on top of today's donut.

Terric stopped at a coffee shop, ordered an Americano for himself and a double caramel latte for me.

Score.

"Do you think we should have stayed with Zay and Allie?" I asked after I'd drained half the cup.

"We talked with them about that. Don't you remember?"

"No." It was probably when I'd been pacing and not paying attention to them. I pushed at my cheekbone gently and flipped the visor down for the mirror. The bruise had spread down to my jaw and was making it a little difficult to see out of one eye. Zayvion Jones knew how to land a hit.

". . . offered," Terric was saying. "Zayvion refused. He said they'd call Stotts and make sure there were EMTs coming to look at his wound. He said he'd rather stay at the house with Allie, since he had planned on casting protections on it."

"Protections we cast." I flicked the visor back up. My face hurt, but I didn't think anything other than the nose was broken.

"Yes. He'll call if anything happens, but if you and I do our job—"

"Kill Eli?" I just loved how that rolled off the tongue. Felt like I could say it all day.

"No, find Dessa, who might know where Eli is."

"Then kill Eli?"

"Maybe, yes. Stop him for sure. Find Brandy and release her, or use her as a bargaining chip against Eli."

"That's . . . calculated."

"That's practical." He took a drink. "If we do our job, then Eli will be in no position to attack Allie or Zay or anyone else."

"Because he'll be dead. Come on, Ter. You know that's how this is going down. We're going to take Eli out. And by 'out' I mean mulch him into grave filler."

Terric's phone rang. It was in his cup holder, so I pulled it out. "Dash," I said. I thumbed on the speaker. "This is Shame."

"Shame," Dash said. "Can I speak with Terric?"

"I'm listening," Terric said. "What's going on?"

"We have a lead on Eli. Davy just called in—"

"From where?" Terric asked.

"Don't know. He rigged a blocker on his phone so I couldn't track it."

"Okay," Terric said. "Are you at the office?"

"Yes."

"We're on the way over now. Let's finish this conversation there."

"I'll put the coffee on," he said.

I hung the phone up. "Don't want to talk to him?"

"Don't want a phone record if we've been bugged."

"Do you think you've been bugged?"

"No, I'm sure I haven't been. I don't know about the lines at the office, though. If they know where Eli is, I want to hear it in person."

I finished off the last of my coffee, sat back, and let the man behind the wheel take us to the office.

By the time we found parking, the rain had stopped. We got out. Everything was wet and when the higher clouds broke, the fog torched up with sunlight.

Eleanor drifted beside me of course. On the drive over here, I caught her staring at the statue. I almost brought the statue in with us, just in case Terric and I didn't leave in the same car after this, but she shook her head.

So we stormed across the street, Terric and me step in step. People moved aside. I supposed we made quite a pair.

We walked into the building, took the elevator up to the office.

It had only been a few hours since I was down here getting the riot act read to me by Clyde. Funny what a difference a few hours made.

The haphazard tower of empty boxes was now a squat pyramid of neatly taped, labeled, and stacked boxes. Probably contained the few things I'd left behind and were otherwise filled with Terric's possessions.

The framed picture of Paris he had taken back before college that used to hang in his office was propped against the pyramid.

I guess Clyde was moving in.

"Terric, Shame." Dashiell paused halfway across the room and looked me up and down. "Those are good colors on you, Shame. But what happened to your face?"

"I ran into Zay's fist."

"So . . . wait. What's that now?"

"Nothing to worry about," I said. I strode off to the small storage closet just outside the bathroom. Mop, cleaning supplies, extra toilet paper. And up there on the top shelf next to a box of caulking tubes was a jacket.

My jacket.

One of them, anyway.

I pulled it down, turned my head, and shook the dust off it. Black, lightweight, shorter than the peacoat. Really not much more than a hoodie, but hell, it was my hoodie.

I shrugged into it. Realized that even with the bulky sweater, the hoodie still fit.

I was seriously tired of things reminding me of how thin I was. Maybe I should start working out.

Ha!

I strolled back into the main room where Dash and Terric were standing and Clyde leaned against a desk. They all had coffee in their hands.

Detour to the coffeepot. I made myself a cup, stole a truly sorry-looking bear claw sitting alone in a bakery box, and noted I'd left the baseball bat those thugs had threatened me with propped up by my desk. That was leaving with me. And so was the gun I figured was still in my drawer.

I walked over to my desk. Pulled the drawer and stuffed the gun in my pocket.

". . . EMTs are taking care of him," Terric said. "We'll be giving Stotts our statements later today if we have time."

"And what are you going to tell him?" Clyde asked.

"That we were planning on stopping by anyway," Terric said. "And had a hunch that something was wrong, so we let you know in transit."

He nodded. "Not the best we've ever come up with, but it should do. And you, Shame? Where do you stand on all this?"

"On the side of better donuts," I said, turning toward them. "Where the hell did you buy this greasy sponge?"

"They weren't for you," Clyde said.

"Thank God for that," I said. I shoved the last of it in my mouth and chewed. "Awful."

"Where do you stand on this, Shame?"

"Whatever Terric just said, I'm probably against it, but am too lazy to do anything about it. So, what do we know about Eli?"

"We got a call from Davy," Dash said. "He thinks Eli is working out of one of the hospitals in the area."

"As a doctor?" The implications of that made my skin crawl. "Ew."

"He didn't say," Dash said. "But he found this." He walked over and handed me a printout of names.

"It's a printout of names," I said.

"Right," Clyde said. "The first twenty-five on that list have hit the missing persons reports. Three of them have shown up dead in Forest Park."

"Davy thinks Eli is . . . smuggling people out to Forest Park and killing them?" I guessed.

"He thinks it's connected," Clyde said. "Said there's security footage of him being in the waiting room while one of the people on the list was there too."

"Doctors see lots of people. Lots of patients in waiting rooms," I said.

"You know what all those people on that list of names have in common, Flynn?" Clyde asked.

"They're on this list?" I held up the paper.

"They were all hospitalized for tainted magic poisoning three years ago during the battle to heal magic."

I looked at the paper. Tried to follow the logic of how that linked up with Eli. "Uh . . . buy a vowel?"

"Davy thinks Eli's using those people who carried tainted magic as experiments," Clyde said. "That he's been picking them out, running tests on them, and then killing them and dumping their bodies."

"Two things," I said. "One: Davy does not trust Eli, has good reason not to. Two: Davy considers Eli a monster who likes to carve magic into people to screw with them just like he screwed with Davy. And two-part-two: Collins the Cutter is not that sloppy. If Eli wanted to do tests on someone and not get caught, we'd never find the bodies."

Terric nodded. "So do you think he wants us to know he's killing these people? To . . . lead us to him?"

"Are any of the victims altered in any way?" I asked.

"You mean with glyphs?" Dash asked.

"Or any other way."

"Not that we found," Clyde answered.

"Well, there were the tattoos," Dash said.

"What?" I asked.

"Tattoos. Each of them had a tattoo somewhere on his or her body."

"What kind of tattoos?" Terric asked. "Roses, hearts, serpents?"

"Glyphs."

Clyde hooked his thumbs in his pockets. "Lots of people have tattoos of spells now. Especially since magic has changed. There's a bullcrap myth that if you get a tattoo of a certain kind of spell, that spell will be stronger when you cast it."

"I'm guessing there's a lot of fertility inks out there," I said. He nodded.

"Do you have a list of them, Dash?" Terric asked.

"Fertility spells?" Dash asked, a little startled.

I laughed. "The look on your face! Priceless!"

"No," Terric said, giving me a scorching glance, "the tattoos on the missing people."

"That, I have," Dash said. "Shut up, Shame. I didn't get a lot of sleep last night." Then, to Terric, "Give me a sec."

"Thanks," Terric said.

Dash smiled like the sun had just decided to shine on him.

I watched Dash walk off and considered Terric. He had no idea. Zero clue that Mr. Dashiell Spade liked him.

So dense. I wondered if I should give Terric a hint about his secret admirer.

"If it is Eli," Terric said, back to business before I had a chance to put my thoughts together, "why did he choose those twenty-five out of all those people on the list?"

Clyde shrugged. "Convenience and availability?"

"Naw," I said. "Eli doesn't mind doing things the hard way if it means he gets it his way. There's a reason he picked these specific people. What do we have? Fifteen men, ten women?"

"Yes," Terric said.

"Do you have files on these people?" I asked. "Photos, medical history, addresses?"

"Yes." Dash walked back into the room. "We do." He placed twenty-five files, folded open, across the desk closest to Terric.

"Perfect," Terric said as he leaned down to look at the files. "I don't know what I'd do without you, Dashiell."

Dash smiled, and shot me a warning look.

I just blinked innocently.

"Which are still alive?" Terric asked.

Dash pulled away three folders. I noted, with a twinge of anger, one was the ten-year-old girl.

"And what are the tattoos?" Terric asked.

Dash pointed a finger at files with each word his spoke. "Refresh. Enhance. Light. Light. Ground. Impact. Combust. Refresh."

"Strange collection of spells," I said. "I can understand Enhance and Refresh. But Ground and Light? Who uses light spells so much they want that tattooed on their body? Ground isn't even needed anymore. Magic doesn't ever get so out of control that it needs to be Grounded."

"Some people just get a tat because they like the look of it," Dash said. "Even when they don't know what it means."

"Okay," I said, "so that's one explanation. But if Eli is a part of this, a part of the tattoos, then they are in no way random."

"Can you put the people in the order of when they went missing?" Terric asked.

"Yep." Dash moved the files, lining them up in order.

"And the tattoos?" he asked.

"Light, Ground, Light, Refresh, Enhance, Impact. Combust, Refresh."

"That's a better setup," Clyde said. "Cast Light, maybe it doesn't work, so Ground to keep magic stable, then cast Light again. Maybe it fades too quickly, so you'd need Refresh, then Enhance to make it more focused and then Impact. Combust? Light doesn't lend to that, Fire does, but okay. And Refresh to keep that strong. Not sure what that can be used for other than knocking the crap out of something or someone."

"These are tattoos," Dash said. "Not actual spells. It could be coincidence. You could be seeing order where there really isn't any."

"When did they get the tattoos?" Terric asked.

Dash thumbed through the files. "Um . . . other than this older man, Walter, all of the tattoos were fresh ink."

"How fresh?" I asked.

Dash looked back a couple pages in the file. "On the dead? Coroner said very fresh. Maybe a few weeks or a month at the most."

"So there's a chance they were tattooed in preparation for being taken," Clyde said.

Terric nodded. "They've each been missing for more than a few months, but they weren't all kidnapped on the same day. They were kidnapped weeks, sometimes months apart."

"Clyde's theory is starting to look promising," I said.

"But they're tattoos," Dash insisted. "Magic won't fill a tattoo. It fills a glyph."

"We don't think Eli is using magic like normal people," I said.

"How else can he use magic?"

"He can break it," Terric said. "He has a Soul Complement. She's been in a mental institution. Went missing from there. We think he knows where she is. And we know he wants us to rescue her before he kills again."

Clyde went silent, rolling through just exactly what that all meant.

Exactly what it all meant was that Eli was a weapon now. Potentially just as powerful as Terric and me, or any other matched set.

"So, where is she?" Dash asked.

"We don't know," I said.

"And we don't know where Eli is, other than his possible connection to a hospital," Dash said.

"Yes," I said. "But he has technology—probably triggered by magic—that lets him open up holes in space and walk into any room he wants to."

"Which is how he got to Allie and Zay," Clyde said.

"Yes."

Clyde took off his baseball hat and rubbed his fingers through his thick black hair. "That, boys," he said gravely, "is a situation."

Chapter 21

We ordered in lunch. Terric and Clyde eventually went into the closed-off office to talk about responsible Authority things. Which was what Terric and I had planned.

That left me and Dash to dig into old Authority files on Thomas Leeds. I was hoping something in there would give me a little inside information on Dessa.

Not a lot on Thomas I could use. An old photo of him, looked like it was taken in a sports bar with friends. I didn't see much of the family resemblance, except maybe around the eyes and forehead. Otherwise, he looked like a guy you'd expect to be running a small but useful business of some sort, who spent his weekends watching football.

All of the addresses on his file were in the Seattle area, the phone was disconnected, and when it came down to the list of family and friends, the file had been wiped.

Thanks, Victor.

Bored, I went outside to smoke and pace. Hadn't even gotten a puff off my cigarette before I heard a voice behind me.

"Four sugars, four creams?" Dessa said.

I grinned, turned.

She had on jeans, a white collared blouse, and a short black jacket. No purse, shoes she could run in without breaking bones. She also had a cup of coffee in each hand.

"Dessa," I said. "How did you know it was time for my coffee break?"

"I bugged the office." She smiled, held the coffee out for me.

"That kind of behavior will get you in trouble," I said.

"Bugging your office?"

"Ex-office and no, telling me about it. And I prefer six sugars and six creams, thank you." I took the cup.

"I know." She reached into her pocket and handed me extra sugars and cream.

"Why are you here?" I popped the cup lid, stuck a thumbnail in the creams, poured, and tore sugar packets with my teeth. Didn't bother to stir. I liked a sweet kick at the end.

"You make it sound like I want something."

"Because you do."

She took a drink of her own coffee. "Yes, I do."

"Good," I said. "Let's hear it."

"I want you to take me to whoever is in charge of the Authority."

"So they can tell you who killed your brother."

"Am I that predictable?"

"Not at all. As a matter of fact, I think you already know who killed your brother. And you know why he did it."

Everything about her stilled, tensed. If she had a gun smuggled somewhere on her body, all signals pointed to her pulling it.

"Who told you that?" Her voice had gone from playful to dead serious.

"Do you know a woman named Brandy Scott?"

Her brows tucked down, folding a line between them. "The name sounds familiar. But I'm not placing it. Should I know her?"

"Thomas's killer thinks you should."

"You talked to his killer?" That drunk 'em and trunk 'em look flashed in her eyes.

"We heard from him."

"You know giving me a name—Brandy Scott—is enough to lead me to him."

"Might be if you can find the connection. That's not how I want this to play out."

"How you want it? You had your chance, Shame. I asked you to help me, remember? You said you didn't want to get involved. So I don't see why you should have a say in what I do or don't do with this information."

"Wouldn't dream of having a say. I want to make you a deal. You help me find Brandy Scott and I will cut you in on all the info we have on the killer."

She hesitated. It was a tempting offer. "I'm supposed to believe you'll do that?"

"I'm not a man who makes a habit of lying."

"Yes, you are."

"Okay. Yes, fine. But this is the truth."

She drank coffee, thought about it. Then, with regret, "You're still holding all the cards, Shame. And I know you don't really want me involved and you'll find a way to go around me. Sorry. I need to do this on my own."

I don't know why, but I hadn't expected that. "Really? We had pizza together. I thought we had a certain something."

She pressed her lips together and nodded. "We did. We do. It's why I've changed my mind. I started this alone. I think it needs to stay that way. Then whatever we have . . . or don't have, we can figure that out on its own terms."

"Dessa." I reached over and touched her arm, but I could see that she had made up her mind. I pulled my hand away. "Be careful."

"I'll let you know how things turn out."

"Unless we find her first."

That got a smile out of her. "I suppose that could happen. Did you look into that thing with Jeremy Wilson yet?"

"We spoke."

"Is he dead?"

"Not yet."

"But what I said about him was correct? That he's a part of the Black Crane and using Terric?"

"Yes." I knew the point she was making. She'd held up her end of the deal, and she wanted me to hold up mine.

"So, please don't follow me," she said. "Please don't come after me. Good luck, Shame." She turned and walked down the street, dropping her barely touched coffee in the nearest garbage bin.

Eleanor had been leaning against the building. I glanced over at her and she shook her head. She mouthed, *Stupid*.

"She'd have found out anyway," I said. "She bugged the office. I'm sure she's bugged my room by now too. This way I'll know what lead she's following and I can follow her. I'm going to put a Hound on her."

Eleanor rolled her fingers outward and shrugged in an obvious "why?" pose.

"I don't want her hurt in the cross fire."

She cupped her fingers together to make a heart shape, and raised one eyebrow. I turned my back on her.

"Not listening."

I pulled out Terric's phone I'd nicked and called Zayvion.

"Hello?" Allie's voice, not Zay.

"Hey, Al. Where's the man?"

"Sleeping. Are you okay?"

"I'm fine. I just wanted to check in on you two. What did the doctor say?"

"That he's lucky the knife missed his lung. It's going to hurt for a while, and they gave him antibiotics, but he's going to be fine."

The relief in her voice was an almost tangible thing.

"And you? Honest, now, love. How are you?"

"Shaken. I'm okay now, but when he came in the door, Shame . . ." She paused.

I lit another cigarette, ignored Eleanor, who had come around to stick her tongue out at me.

"When he came in the door," she went on, "I froze. I've never frozen in my life. All I could think was I was going to lose the baby."

"You did fine. Just fine. And the baby's okay, right?"

"Yes," she said quietly.

"So it's all good. Just like it should be. Is Stone there with you?"

"He showed up after the police left. He's next to me right now. Hasn't left my side. And Nola's here too. With her shotgun."

I had to grin at that. You could take the girl out of the country, but you couldn't take the country out of the girl.

"So you don't need anything?" I asked. "Anything I can bring you?"

"No. We're good. I'm good. Thanks, Shame. For being here earlier. When we needed you."

"Wouldn't be anywhere else. Say, Allie, did you know Thomas Leeds?"

"I don't think so. Was he a Hound?"

"No. Closer. I don't suppose you knew a Dessa Leeds?"

"My memory's pretty sketchy, but neither of those names rings any bells. Why? What do you want them for?"

"They're tied to Eli. I'm looking for someone to follow Dessa. You got any spare Hounds I could borrow?"

"I don't really do that anymore. You could talk to Davy."

"Can't find Davy."

"Then check in with Sunny. She'll know where he is."

"I thought Sunny was in Florida or something. Visiting family?"

"Maybe," she said. "I don't remember Davy mentioning anything, but I haven't seen him since last week."

"Maybe I'll stop by the Den, see who's running things while she's gone and he's wherever he is."

"That's a good idea. And, Shame, I'm really sorry you

lost your job. And that you had to . . . that you and Terric had to break magic for us. Because we couldn't. Because I couldn't."

"Allie, those are not your worries. It is what it is. And it worked out fine. We used magic together and I didn't have a single moment of wanting to snog him."

That got a short laugh out of her. "He wouldn't have argued."

"He would have had a coronary."

Terric stepped out of the building. Spotted me. "Speaking of, I've got to go now. I'll try to come by soon. Stay in touch."

"Be careful, Shame."

"What, and ruin my streak?"

I thumbed the phone off and held it out for Terric.

"You really have to get your own phone," he said, taking it from me.

We started toward the car.

"I have a phone. It's at the inn. In my room. With my clothes. And my coat. And my boots. All of which I'd love to have, but you won't take me there."

"Fine," he said. "I'll take you there. Did you and Dash find anything?"

"Not a clue. Checked on Al and Zay. He's fine, she's fine. She doesn't know anything about Thomas or Dessa."

"What about going to a bar?" he suggested. "Dessa picked you up at a bar last night. Picked you up the night before, come to think of it. You might run into her there."

"Not without my coat. My *good* coat."

"Two-year-olds have more patience than you." He slid into the driver's seat.

"That's because two-year-olds have coats," I said, getting in the other side. "Also, I saw Dessa. She doesn't know who Brandy Scott is, but now she's looking for her."

"Alone?"

"I offered her our side of the sandbox. She said no."

He shook his head and drove. "We'll need to track her."

"I'm already on it."

We pulled up to the inn a few minutes later. The drive had made me realize how damn tired I was. I didn't know if it was from breaking magic with Terric, Zay practically snapping my neck, or just the last couple days of way more activity than what I'm used to, but right now sleep sounded better than a bottle of booze.

"You want me to wait while you get your coat?" Terric asked.

I yawned hugely. "No. I'm going to catch an hour of sleep."

"If you go out looking—"

"I'll call you." I got out, opened the back door, took the statue and the baseball bat I'd nicked from the office. Started walking.

Stepped into the inn, and waited until Terric pulled away. Then I stepped back out again, walked around to the back of the building, and got in my car. Keys were in the glove box. So was my phone.

Dialed Sunny. She had been a hell of a Blood magic user, studied under my mum for a couple years. Fell in lust with Davy Silvers, and sort of moved in with him. She and he managed the Hounds in the area, making sure security, info, and tracking jobs were fulfilled, that the Hounds stayed clean, and that paychecks got cut.

"What do you want, Shame?" Sunny answered.

"Nice to hear from you too, Sunny. You back in town yet?"

"Just got in a couple hours ago. Is there a reason you've suddenly crawled out from under your rock?"

"Ouch. Also, yes. I need a Hound to follow a woman by the name of Dessa Leeds. She came into town a couple days ago. Ex–government spy of some sort. Packs heat. I don't want anyone to engage or get in her way, but she's looking for someone I'm looking for, and I want to know if she finds her."

"Who do I bill?"

"Me."

She laughed. "Right. Who do I really bill? Terric?"

"Sunny. This is my thing. It's not the Authority's thing, it's not Terric's thing. Bill me."

"If you don't pay—"

"I will."

"I know where you live, Flynn."

"I know. Just call me if you find out anything."

"I'll call if you keep your phone on."

"Promise."

I could hear her sigh. "Anything else?" she asked.

"Have you seen Davy since you got back?"

"No. He said he's on a job."

"Who's shadowing him?"

I heard the clicking of a computer mouse, as she looked up the job records.

"I don't know." She sounded concerned. "Do you know something about this?"

"Eli Collins is in the area. Davy knows it. There's a chance he's trying to hunt Eli on his own. When you find Davy—as I am certain you will—tie him down somewhere and keep him out of this, okay?"

"I will," she said. "Shame?"

"What?"

"It's nice to have you back."

We both thumbed off our phones since that was about as much mutual affection as either of us could handle.

I sat there for a second thinking out my next move. I really was tired, but it wasn't my most pressing problem.

That was how to deal with Jeremy before he harmed Terric.

I needed Jeremy out of the picture. But he was just a cog in the machine that wanted to use Terric. It made more sense to take out the mainspring of the operation. Which meant it was time for me to deliver a personal message to the Black Crane.

I'd been out of the loop on the criminal activity in the city for more than a year. I had no idea where the Black Crane was headquartered now, and it wasn't really something I wanted to ask the police or the Hounds.

I needed someone who knew the dark side of the city and wouldn't rat me out to the law, or anyone else, for that matter.

I knew just the man. I dialed. Waited. He picked up on the fourth ring.

"Cody Miller."

"Cody, this is Shame. I need a favor."

Back in the day, Cody and I had been young, reckless men. His terrible gambling skills had nearly gotten him killed, but his amazing ability with art and magic put him under Allie's dad's employ for a while, where he'd made wondrous things like Stone, the gargoyle. He had also been the best damn forger of magical signatures in the States—maybe in the world. That caught the attention of all sorts of unsavory folk and he eventually managed to get in the way of people, living and dead, who wanted to rule the Authority and magic.

To make sure he wouldn't ruin their plans, he'd been Closed, several times. Finally his mind had broken. For several years, he'd been nothing but a childlike shell of a man. But when our last-ditch effort to save the world included trying to join light and dark magic, he had volunteered to be the Focal—the vessel in which magic would be joined again.

It should have killed him. Instead it mended his mind and destroyed his ability to use magic. Joining magic had changed him in good and strange ways, just like the rest of us. Just like the world.

"A favor? You owe me, Shame. I should be collecting from you."

"What's stopping you, mate?"

"Well, you don't have a job."

"Employment is overrated. This will be worth saying yes."

"What are you up to?"

"I need to go make a point clear to some people."

"People."

"Black Crane."

Silence, while he rolled that over. "Why?"

"It's personal."

"I'm going to need more than that if I'm getting into this with you."

"So that's a yes?"

"No, it's a why."

"They think Terric is their own personal bucket of magic they can dip into any time they want to."

"Please tell me that's not a euphemism."

I couldn't help it, I laughed. "They are using him for the magic he can access, jackass. Life magic. And they want me to stay out of their way."

"So you're going to get in their way."

"What can I say? I have a contrary nature."

"They kill people, Shame. They make people disappear."

"I know. And they think they own Terric." I didn't say any more. Didn't have to. Cody could take the next logical step. As soon as Terric decided to turn on them, to leave Jeremy, or to refuse to do what they wanted, they'd kill him. I wasn't going to let that happen.

"You know I can't use magic," he said evenly.

"Not what I need you for."

"Why do you need me?"

"I want what you know about who's running the syndicate. I want your contacts. That's all."

"Come by. I'll have what you need."

"Thanks."

He hung up. I checked the gun in my pocket. I'd never really used it much, but it was a great attention getter when people lost focus. Yes, it was loaded.

I started the car and took the shortest route to Cody's place over on the east side of town. He'd taken the art scene by storm over the last three years and had made enough off it he'd never have to work again. He might not be able to use magic, but there was something about his art that drew a person to it, and made that person willing to empty out bank accounts for it.

Instead of living big, he had bought a quirky little place on southeast Thirteenth Street, not too far from pubs and coffee shops.

And he'd apparently painted it several shades of purple, blue, and yellow since I'd last been by.

I parked the car in front of the place and Eleanor drifted into the backseat of the car.

Cody was already walking down the porch and past the rosebushes. He was yellow haired, tan, muscled, quick to laugh, and, if I remembered correctly, just a little older than me. He had on several layers of shirts and jackets in browns, oranges, and blue, a dark green scarf tossed over his shoulders that should have looked messy, but somehow came across as fashionable, and was carrying a bowling ball bag.

He opened the passenger door, and ducked down as he got in. "You'll want to head back over the river. West."

"I need an address, I don't need a passenger," I said.

"You need both." Cody slid the seat belt over his shoulder and snapped it in place. "And I want to see you." He turned toward me. "I want to see what you're about to do. With magic. With death." Those blue eyes were just this side of madness, and when he smiled, I realized magic might have done more than just change him.

"Cody," I asked before I put the car in gear, "are you sane?"

"Oh no. But then, neither are you. That's what makes this so fun."

I slowly removed each of my Void stone rings and dropped them into my cup holder. Then I drove west, because damn it, he was right.

Chapter 22

"That's it?" I asked.

Cody tipped his head to better see around the slight bend in the road where I'd parked. We were in the southwest hills on a narrow one-lane that snaked up along the hillside between cliff-clinging houses with grand views of the city and Mount Hood. We were so close to downtown it seemed like I could spit and hit it, but the way the neighborhood was built to soak up the wide horizon, the city felt like a world away.

The address had led us to an immaculately landscaped spread with a multileveled house that showed some beige and cedar between the expanses of windows. Decks, probably a pool. Rich, without standing out among the other rich.

Houses on both sides had bikes tucked up against porches or doors, or a couple kid toys. Families lived here.

"That's it," Cody said. "Head man goes by Phillip Soto. Second is Rene Schuller. I have other names if you want them."

"I don't. You should stay here."

"Right."

I glanced over at him, surprised he'd agreed so quickly.

He raised one eyebrow. "I *should* but we both know I won't. Are you taking the gun or the baseball bat?"

"The gun. For show."

"How are you going to play this?"

"No playing. I'm going to walk in there and start killing people until they understand my point of view."

"That's . . . direct."

"Things have changed, Cody. I don't follow Authority rules now." I drove down the hill a bit and parked the car in the driveway. Then I opened the car door, and he did too, climbing out with his bowling ball bag.

"That doesn't sound very different than how things used to be," he said.

"It's different."

Afternoon sunlight slipped yellow and heatless through the scattered clouds. It would be dark in a couple hours. I didn't need the dark to get the job done.

I strode across the tasteful beige driveway to the tasteful beige stairway, up one flight to the glass-on-glass double-wide doorway framed in yet more glass. A balcony wrapped at that level around the wall of glass windows to my right, and a second balcony and wall of windows wrapped the same way on the next story up.

For people who lived on the wrong side of the law, they sure had picked a house that was nearly transparent.

Cody was behind me, not too close, and taking his time to enjoy the architectural details. Eleanor had already slipped into the house ahead of me.

I kicked the door.

Glass did not shatter, but a Break spell took care of the hinges and the whole thing fell inward.

Quick rundown: everything about the place was glass and chrome. A black marble bar curved a crescent to my left, red stools edging the outer arc, the floor was brown marble and a deeply textured beige carpet, and the three men in the room were all reaching for their guns.

I killed them before they even had their weapons in their hands. Lashed out with magic dark and fast, and stopped their hearts.

Cody, behind me, let out a little "huh" sound when the three gunmen collapsed to the floor. I didn't wait to see if he was going to remove himself from the situation, or stick close.

He chose to stick close.

Around the bar, past a glass-tiled alcove holding wine bottles hung by chrome hooks, was a staircase. Just planks of glass going up, cabled wire and metal creating an open banister.

Either I'd been loud or, more likely, the place was wired and I'd been spotted on the security monitors. I could count the hearts pumping up on the next floor—four.

I pulled my gun and strode up to the second level. Short hall that likely ended in bedrooms, the rest of the space opened up in a huge vaulted ceiling level made even larger by the wall of windows overlooking another balcony and the wide green spread of downtown Portland broken through by tall buildings.

Rich wooden floor anchored the room and a stone fireplace stretched off to the left. Two gold couches did nothing to take up the space, and even the mini grand piano seemed dwarfed by the sky and city.

The four heartbeats belonged to four men, three who were standing, and one who was sitting at the gold couch to my right. No one had a gun in their hand, which surprised me. Maybe I hadn't been spotted.

No, they wouldn't be that careless.

I lifted my gun to get their attention.

"Have a seat," I said to the men standing around. "This won't take long."

The three glanced at the man sitting on the couch. Black hair, soul patch, fake tan, he wore a jacket that was obviously designer and sat with his arms across the back of the couch.

"Mr. Shamus Flynn," he said, a slight smile narrowing his eyes. "What brings you to my home?"

"I have a message I'm not sure has been made clear to you, Mr. Soto," I said, guessing correctly who he was. "I don't care how big a network the Black Crane has developed over the last three years. Don't care how powerful or rich you think you are. This is still my town. And there are people within it who are off-limits to you and your goons."

"Of course," he said. "We respect the Authority has certain concerns for its people. Boundaries we respect."

"I'm not talking about the Authority. This is just about me. You've pissed *me* off. You're using people I care about. I'm here to make you understand that if you don't back off and leave my friends and Terric Conley alone, I will destroy your little pop shop and kill your members one by one."

"Mr. Flynn, please," Soto said. "We are all reasonable men here. Surely we can discuss this without resorting to threats. It is a crude way to do business."

"I want your word you will leave Terric Conley alone."

"I don't think you understand the situation properly," he began.

He didn't finish. Because I killed him.

Drank down his life without even twitching my fingers.

His eyes rolled into the back of his head, his heart stopped. He slumped forward and the remaining three men bolted off the couches, reaching for their guns.

"Keep your hands off your weapons," I said.

"I'd do as he says," Cody said behind me.

I didn't look back, but the men in the room all glanced at him, then held their hands out to the side.

"Let me make myself clear," I said. "I am not here to discuss the situation. I am not here to do business. I am here for an unbreakable guarantee that Terric Conley will be cut free from everything and anyone involved with the Black Crane. Who's going to give me that guarantee?"

"I will see that Mr. Conley is removed from our attention," one of the men said. He was taller than me, probably in his early fifties, with light brown hair going gray and receding at the temples. His eyes were heavy-lidded, and his mouth at the bottom of his long, narrow face was thick-lipped.

"My name is Rene Schuller. I have a position in this organization that can ensure my desires are acted upon."

"And your desire is?" I prompted.

He smiled, even though neither of us was buying it. "To make you happy, Mr. Flynn."

"Good. Make me happy, Mr. Schuller, and I won't go out of my way to kill you."

I could feel their pulses as if they were my own, three thrumming beats that would be so easy to slow, slow, slow until they were gone.

Instead I turned my back and walked across the room toward the stairs. Cody stood to the right of the staircase, holding a sawed-off shotgun at his hip. So that's what he carried in the bag.

"Don't bother," I said to Cody loud enough they'd hear. "I could kill them before they squeezed a trigger."

I paced down the steps and Cody followed behind. Passed the bar and dead bodies, then got into the car.

"You've become a little more blunt, I see," Cody said as he got into the passenger's seat.

"I tried subtle. It chafed." I started the car but didn't back out of the driveway yet.

I drew on the magic deep beneath the city and cast a spell. It was a spell that required quick, scribbling strokes, winding into a tightly coiled center.

A few seconds later, Scatter hung in the air between me and the windshield. I cast it with a push of both hands, and it rolled into the big house. If they had surveillance cameras, they were now fried, the information that might have been stored there scattered and irretrievable.

"In the old days you'd have done that first," he said. "You're getting sloppy, Shame."

"I'm not sloppy," I said, finally putting the car in gear

and getting the hell out of there. "If I'd screwed with their cameras before we walked in, they would have known someone was coming and would have been waiting for us. This way, no one got hurt."

"Except the four men you killed."

"Yeah, well. They were in my way."

"That was probably a little over the line, don't you think?"

"What line?" I glanced over at him. He stared calmly ahead, maybe at the city, maybe at whatever else it was that man saw.

"The law's line, to begin with. After that, justice. You didn't know those people, Shame. They might not have been guilty of the crimes you accused them of, crimes you killed them for."

"Cry me a river, Miller," I said. "Everyone in that house was guilty of crimes, whether we know about them or not."

"And you are now guilty of murder."

I let that sit for a minute or two. "Those aren't the first men I've killed in my life. I grew up in the Authority, remember? Ran with the Closers, was a star pupil of Death magic. There are casualties in any war."

"Is that what this is? A war?"

"Not yet. Right now it's just my life."

"So pretty much the same thing?"

"Yeah, pretty much the same," I agreed.

"How long have you been fighting the magic inside you?" he asked.

"None of your business, crazy guy."

That got a smile out of him. "I think it is, but fine. We can talk about something else. When did you suddenly become Terric's guardian angel?"

"Never, because I'm not."

"You just killed four people for him."

"I killed four guys to get them off my back. The Black Crane didn't use to be anything but a couple of punk drug dealers, and now they think they can run this town? They came after me with a baseball bat. They jumped me with a Taser. They might even be behind the missing people cases the police can't crack."

"And yet you never brought any of that up," he said. "You just told them to leave Terric alone."

"I said more than that."

"Not much more."

I drove for a while, heading back toward his house. He was right.

"I know I am," he said.

"What?"

"Right."

"Lay off the mind-reading trick, mate. I'm not impressed."

"Who says it's a trick? It's been a long time since you and I sat down and talked, Shame. You don't know what I'm capable of."

"Let me guess: reading minds?"

"No. Hearts."

"What does that even mean?"

"It means I know you've tried to stay away from Terric. But you're drawn to him. The magic in you and the magic in him can't be separated. You hate it. And you want it. Want to use magic as it should be used—with someone who perfectly matches your power. So much so, you'll kill people if they get in your way."

"Not even close."

He was totally close.

"Well, it's good to see some things haven't changed about you, Shame."

"Oh?"

"You still lie like a rug."

"I will also still pull over this car and make you walk your own ass home if you don't shut up," I said.

Cody grinned. "Just like old times."

Chapter 23

I dropped Cody off at his place, then drove around the area, just to make sure no one had followed us and that he wasn't in danger. Waited until sundown but didn't see anything out of the ordinary.

Cody couldn't use magic anymore, but I knew he could take care of himself.

Satisfied he would be okay, I headed home.

The inn was up and running full speed tonight. Plenty of diners and people at the bar. We'd started with live music a few months ago, and it looked like tonight the old piano was getting a workout.

It was, in some ways, a clash from my childhood growing up in the apartment above the other side of the inn. Back then it was home. And while it could have been very busy and alive with customers, there were late-night meetings of the Authority members, and, down in the basement around the well of magic hidden there, all sorts of tests and magic events had gone on.

Now the well was still hidden, but it didn't matter. People could tap in to it and magic wouldn't do anything dangerous. So the whole "here's our happy home, which also happens to be sitting on a time bomb" atmosphere of the place was gone.

Honestly? I missed it.

I wove through tables, winked at the pretty blond waitress, who was definitely jailbait, and then headed up to the room I'd been in since Mum had kicked me out of the house proper.

Up a flight of stairs, dragged the bat behind me down the hall.

I paused outside my door. My Shamus senses were tingling.

Something was wrong with the door. For one thing, it was unlocked and wide open. Sure, I'd left the place drugged out of my brain, but someone would have shut it.

Interesting.

I tucked Eleanor's statue under my arm and lifted the baseball bat, resting it above my shoulder.

Walked into the room.

Room looked like my room. Couch covered in clothes and a few books I hadn't reshelved. Small kitchen area clean because who in their right mind would cook when they had an entire restaurant at their feet? Bedroom door cracked open.

That wasn't right.

Eleanor whisked past me and through the door into the bedroom. She came out and shook her head. Mouthed a word I couldn't quite make out.

What? I mouthed.

She said the word again. Rolled her eyes. Walked up to me and held out one finger. I took one hand off the bat and turned my palm up for her.

In icy strokes, she spelled out: D-E-S-S-A.

And if it was Dessa in there, she probably already knew I was in the room.

"I know you're in the room," she said. "Why don't you come on in?"

"Do you have a weapon?"

"Oh, sure. But I promise to keep my hands off my guns this time. That is, if you play nice."

I didn't put down the bat. But I did leave the statue on

the side table before pushing the bedroom door open the rest of the way.

Dessa was sitting on the edge of my bed. Fully clothed, which was, I'll admit, a little disappointing. The bed was made, and after I pulled my gaze off her to the room, I noticed she had folded my clothes, set them on the two chairs in the room, and had thrown away all the food wrappers and beer bottles.

"I didn't peg you as the domestic type," I said.

"I didn't think you were into sports." She pointed at the bat.

I grinned, rested the bat next to the door. "So . . . you clean?"

She shrugged and looked down at her hands for a moment before looking back up at me. "I've thought about what I said today. When I told you I wanted to do this alone. I've changed my mind."

"You're making nice so I'll let you in on finding your brother's killer, aren't you?"

"You already told me you'd do that. This is just me making nice."

"A little pleasure before business?" I asked.

"A little pleasure." She held my gaze. "Maybe we don't need business right now."

Huh. I nodded.

"Why did you drop me off at Terric's last night?" I asked.

"He's your friend, right?"

"Sometimes."

"He's more than that too. Life magic?"

"Yes."

"Was I wrong to do it?"

"No. But I wish you would have stayed. I've spent half the day looking for you. Worrying."

"And here I was, in your bedroom all along."

"And here you are. So. What's this really all about?" I waved my hand at my semiclean room.

"I told you. An apology."

"Because . . . ?"

She quirked a smile and tipped her head to one side. "Can you seriously not just take me at face value? Must you question everything I do?"

"It's a failing, my terrible, terrible curiosity."

"I got your attention, didn't I?"

"Is that what you wanted? My attention? Because you already had that."

Her heartbeat was steady, but strong. She licked her lips and the blush that bloomed against her pale skin gave her away. That wasn't fear she was feeling.

She wanted me. Wanted us.

Why had I not slept with her? Sure, there was the whole drugging and kidnapping and bondage, but I liked a girl who knew what she wanted and went after it.

"I want more than your attention," she said softly.

"Tell me you're not going to follow that up by pulling a gun on me." I took a step toward her. Unzipped my hoodie, tossed it on the floor.

She stood. "I said this wasn't about business."

"True." I didn't walk any closer. Waited to see what she'd do.

"Why haven't you asked me where I thought Eli was?" she asked.

"Is that your sexy talk? Because it doesn't sound like sexy talk. It sounds like business talk. I thought you didn't want to mix those."

"I could." A slight smile curved her mouth.

"Go on, then."

"Why"—her finger slipped to the first button on her blouse and she slowly pushed it through the hole. Her shirt opened a bit, revealing skin—"haven't you"—fingers pinched the second button, flicked it through the hole to show just the edge of breast and bra—"asked me about"— she ran her fingertip around the third button, the one that strained to hold the fabric together between her breasts. She didn't unbutton it—"Eli?"

"I don't care about him," I said, advancing on her. "Not right now. Not here."

My heart was pounding hard, heat firing across my body, drawing me awake, alert. She wasn't backing away, wasn't backing down. Just stood there, her hands resting on her hips, watching me. Wanting me.

"What do you want?" she whispered.

I reached out and for the first time, touched her hair— silken fire through my fingers—drawing it gently away from her face.

I stroked my thumb along the corner of her lip, up her cheek, then down to pause at the pulse point on her neck, pressing there just hard enough that I could feel the thump of her heart.

She closed her eyes at my touch, her lips parting as she inhaled.

"I want you."

"You don't even know me," she said with a hitch in her breath.

"I could." I slipped my hand to her waist, fingers angled down to her ass. "If you want me to."

She opened her eyes, looked up at me. And the hope there, the doubt there, made me hold very still. Waiting.

"I want you to."

I exhaled and my heart began beating again. "Look at that," I said softly as I leaned over her. "We agreed on something. It's a miracle."

"You should stop talking and kiss—"

She didn't have a chance to finish that. I drew her against me, all the soft heat and curves of her body. Pushed my fingers up into her hair, my rings muffled by the weight of her curls.

I lowered my head and caught her lips with mine, gentle, slow, teasing. I wanted to savor every sweet texture, every pulse beat that made her. Then I wanted to find out what would unmake her.

She kissed me back, her lips soft, her tongue asking for entrance I willingly gave, then stroking deliciously against mine. She matched my lead, taking it slow, until the hesitancy finally melted out of her muscles and she softened, her arms wrapping around my neck. She stepped into me, her hips against mine.

A pulse of need burned through my bones and made every muscle in my body hard.

I slid my hand down her back, spreading my fingers wide so I could press her closer. Her hands were busy too.

She tugged at my sweater, her hand sliding beneath it only to find my T-shirt. She made a soft moan of disappointment, and I couldn't help smiling a little.

I drew away from the wonder of her lips. "Problem, love?" I dipped my head again, kissed instead the side of her neck, the heat of my lips against her pulse causing her to gasp, the scent of her filling me with an aching hunger.

"I want . . . ," she began.

I bit her tender skin, gently, and she gasped again. Her hands clenched in my sweater, tugging, or maybe to steady herself.

"Shame. Now. I want you."

"Patience," I said. "We have time."

I pulled away, rested my hand on her hip until her eyes focused again. I leaned back, far enough so that I could pull the damn sweater off without hitting her in the face. Dropped it to the floor then muscled out of the T-shirt.

She wasn't standing idle. Her hands pressed against my stomach, and every fiber in my body clenched as she dragged warm fingers downward over my bare skin.

Good God.

Okay, maybe we didn't have as much time as I thought. Maybe I was the one who didn't want to be patient.

The T-shirt joined the sweater.

For a moment, standing there, in the low light of the room, she tensed again. Looked up at me. "What's wrong with your arm?"

I glanced at the bandage. I'd forgotten about it. "Hurt it. Not badly."

"And this?" she asked. "Is this a glyph?"

She traced the old scar on my chest—well, one of them. The scar from when Terric shoved a crystal containing magic into my mortal wound to make me live again. The crystal was gone now—blown apart when I'd died a second time, sacrificing my body and soul at the altar of Death magic so I could kill that son of a bitch Jingo Jingo.

I didn't think about the scar much anymore. Told most women it was from a knife fight, or whatever I thought they'd want to hear. Something that would make me sound strong. Heroic.

But that wasn't what I was going to tell Dessa. I was going to tell her the truth.

"It's not a glyph, but it was put there by magic. Terric, he did something with magic to save my life. This is the scar from that."

She nodded. "He's . . . more than a friend, isn't he? The look on his face when he opened his door and saw you there the other night, Shame. He loves you, doesn't he?"

"I think so," I heard myself saying. Apparently, one truth tonight wasn't going to be enough.

"But you don't love him?"

I took a deep breath. The churning mix of feelings I had for Terric came rushing to the surface as if Dessa had opened a part of me that had been long buried. I cared for him—hell, I'd die for him. That was a kind of love, wasn't it? But the love he wanted wasn't something I could give.

"I just . . ." I shook my head. "I care. He's a brother. But I'll ruin him. One day I'll be his death. Or he'll be mine. And that will ruin him too." I couldn't say any more because there were tears in my eyes.

Well, that was new. I couldn't remember the last time I'd cried. No wonder why I never told the truth.

"Lord." I choked on a laugh. "The things you make me feel, woman." I lifted my hand to wipe my eyes, feeling like a damn idiot.

But her hands stopped me, one on each wrist, pulling my hands away from my face. So she could see me.

She stood there, her gaze shifting, studying my face, studying my very vulnerable pain I knew she could see there, this weakness I had never showed anyone before.

Then she stood on tiptoe and kissed me. No more hesitation, no more slow.

I kissed her back, until her warmth replaced the sorrow inside me. Then I picked her up, laid her down upon my bed, and slowly took every stitch of clothing off her, kissing each part of her as I did so. Slid her panties gently down the silk of her skin, and ran my palms up her thighs, as I kissed the curve of her hipbone.

She unhooked her bra and drew it away, offering all of her body to me. I looked down at her, and she smiled softly.

I lowered my mouth to her breast and gently ran my tongue there, savoring the taste of her skin and the shiver of pleasure that ran through her as her nipple hardened.

Her fingers stroked through my hair; the other hand slid up to my right arm braced beside her. She slipped her fingers between mine and pulled my hand toward her.

I reluctantly shifted away and looked down at her again.

"I want all of you," she whispered. And without breaking eye contact, she removed my rings, one by one, and kissed my bare flesh there.

She was my air, my sensation, my world.

And, for the first time in a very long time, I wondered if this was what love felt like.

"Dog or cat?" she asked.

We were lying together under the covers, me on my back,

her beside me. Our bodies were pressed together, her head tucked against my chest, her fingers tracing the old scars there.

"Both," I said. "Ice cream or sorbet?"

"Sorbet all the way. Have you ever wanted kids?"

"That's the kind of question that makes strong men run, you know."

She stopped tracing my scars and looked up at me. "Want me to get your boots?"

"No, no. I got this one. Kids." I took a deep breath. "I'd never thought I'd live long enough to be a father. So. No."

"You didn't say you didn't want them."

"True."

"I think men who want kids are very, very sexy." She dipped her head. Kissed my nipple. A ripple of pleasure slid through me.

"Well, then, of course I want kids. Loads of them." It came out, strangely, not flippant. For a second or two I lay there trying to imagine myself holding a little chubby-cheeked Flynn baby with her blue eyes.

"Your turn," she said.

"Mmm. *Star Wars* or *Star Trek*?"

She giggled. "Really?"

"Civilizations have crumbled under this question. I expect you to answer me truthfully."

"*Trek*."

"What?" I said with mock horror. "You're a Trekkie? No. This will never do. We should just say our good-byes now."

"Hold on. I get to ask you another one," she said.

"All right. Make it good."

"Do you want me to tie you to the headboard and do wicked things to you, or do you want to ask me another question?" Her hand moved down my chest, my stomach, my hip.

Mercy.

"I think that's enough interrogation for one night," I said.

"Well, then," she said, "headboard it is."

Chapter 24

I was freezing. I was also lying in my bed. Naked.

Huh.

I opened my eyes. It was dark out now. My room was lit by the moonlight pushing through the blinds.

Moonlight that showed me I was not alone in my bed.

I grinned. Dessa had every damn one of my covers wrapped around her, tucked tight up to her chin. She was curled on her side, facing me.

She was asleep, and if I weren't shivering so hard my teeth were beginning to rattle, I'd probably do the gallant and manly thing and lie there watching her sleep while I compared her to flowers and sunrises in haiku. Instead I pulled on the covers.

"Wake up, woman. I'm freezing out here."

She smiled, but didn't open her eyes. "Does that mean you'll stop snoring?"

"What? Lies."

She opened those innocent blue eyes and gave me a wicked grin. "Admit it. I wrecked you."

Caught by that look, I couldn't help doing the comparing thing, while my heart tapped up a warm beat. I decided she was a sly little fox, and that her smile was sweeter and hotter than any whiskey I'd ever tried to lose myself in.

I suddenly realized I'd been looking for her for a long, long time.

"Well," I said, swallowing back the emotions that I wasn't sure how to deal with. I glanced up at the silk stockings tied to the headboard and rubbed the faint mark they'd left around my wrist. "If I concede that there was mutual wreckage going on, do I get the password for your blanket fort?"

She rolled her eyes as if considering it, then locked her gaze on me again. "Kiss me nice enough, and I'll think about it."

"That sounds like a fair enough deal." I scooted closer and leaned down like I was going to give it my all.

Instead I reached out, grabbed a handful of blanket, and pushed up onto my knees, pulling the blanket with me.

"Aha!"

She clung to the cover and squealed, pulling back. "We had a bargain!"

"No more bargains, woman," I said as she laughed. "I claim these blankets in the name of Flynn!" I threw the first blanket over my shoulder, which just made her laugh harder.

"I shall de-fleece you. Then I shall have all the blankets, and all the warmth, and you will be at my mercy!"

"Fine." She used her feet and hands to push all the blankets off her, then pulled up onto her knees. "You can have the blankets. I didn't want them anyway." She wadded them up and threw them at my face.

I didn't do much to catch them as they fell in a mess to one side. Because suddenly she was in front of me, on her knees, naked, her hair falling in tousled waves around the curve of her shoulders, the graceful arc of her neck, unafraid as she gave me a challenging smirk. Her hand was to one side, clutching the pillow in preparation of braining me.

I blinked slowly and gave her a predatory grin. "Oh, I like this *much* better." I reached out, brushed my fingers down the outside of her hip, then down the back of her leg to that particularly sensitive spot behind her knee I'd discovered.

She closed her eyes and goose bumps washed over her skin. She bit her lip and made a needful sound.

I lifted my finger and placed my palm on her hip.

She jerked back, her eyes wide.

I tipped my head. Wondered what had spooked her. If I had hurt her.

"Your hands are ice!" she accused.

"Really? You think? Maybe if someone hadn't stolen every damn blanket."

She gave me a glare that was wholly ruined by her small smile. "Hands off until you shower. Hot shower. No touching until those hands regain human temperatures."

"I am so not showering alone," I said.

"Wouldn't dream of it." She slid out of bed, just inches away from me, careful not to brush against me as she passed by. She stood, stretched her arms up over her head, and arched her back.

I lost track of breathing for a moment or two.

Then that gorgeous woman sauntered off to the bathroom, swinging her hips. She paused, and gave me the come-hither over her shoulder.

Oh, baby. I hithered.

The inn is an old structure and the showers had been put in somewhere around the nineteen twenties. And while they were the height of modern convenience then, a Realtor might categorize them as "quaint" now.

Small for one person, downright cozy for two.

Not that I was complaining. And after my skin had gone up a few degrees so that I could once again use my hands along with my boyish charms, Dessa wasn't complaining either.

We finally untangled from each other, toweled off, and got back into our clothes. I made her help me find my rings, which were in the bed, under the bed, and one, strangely, in my half-open sock drawer.

Something darted out from under the bed and burrowed under the towel I'd thrown on the floor.

"Uh, Dessa?" I said. "Your hat got loose."

"What?"

I pointed at the towel just as a tiny furred triangular head with a black mask peeked out and made an equally tiny grunt/squeak.

"Your hat," I repeated.

She took a few steps toward the towel. The ferret must have spotted her because it took off at a ridiculous Slinky-like hop-run, darting under the chair, then suddenly reappearing under the pillow on the bed.

"Jinkies! How did you get out of your cage?" She crawled across the bed and snatched the thing up midescape route, which apparently involved trying to wiggle its way into the nightstand drawer.

"Jinkies?"

"That's his name."

"You're a fan of *Scooby Doo*?"

"No. My brother was. He named him Jinkies. He was his." She crawled back off the bed one-handed, the little furry monster in her other hand, then blew her hair out of her face and walked over to me. "Shame, this is Jinkies, the ferret."

The ferret was pretty cute up close. It wriggled around in Dessa's grip, clever black eyes glittering.

"You sure it's not a weasel?"

"Ferret."

"Whatever. You have to admit it's a terrible hat."

Dessa rolled her eyes. "Give me a minute. I'll get him settled."

She padded out of the room, holding the feasel up to her face so she could coo at it.

Yes, I thought it was adorable of her.

Once she was out of the room, I realized I was ravenous. I glanced at the bedside clock. It was an hour and several minutes off, but with some quick math, I figured it was about three in the morning.

As soon as Dessa returned without Jinkies, I caught her hand and walked toward the door.

"Hungry?" I asked.

"Yes."

"Good thing I know how to break into the kitchen." We snuck hand in hand through the darkened hallway and down the stairs.

Eleanor followed along behind us, and I was grateful that she had given us as much privacy as the ties between she and me allowed.

The dining area was empty; the cleaning crew had gone home. And I knew the morning shift wouldn't be in to start the breads and pastries for at least an hour.

I stepped up to the kitchen door, took hold of the handle, lifted, and gave the door a shove with my shoulder. The old lock gave, and the kitchen was ours.

Eleanor stayed on the other side of the door.

"What is your pleasure, lass?" I asked, walking over to the refrigerator. "Anything you want, sky's the limit. Let's see, we have beef stew, hand-tossed pizza, rosemary chicken. Ah, spanakopita. I know what I'm having."

I pulled out the Greek dish, turned.

Dessa was leaning against the counter with a brownie in one hand and a half-eaten piece of cheesecake in the other.

"What?" she mumbled around the cheesecake. "You said anything, right?"

"Why am I not surprised you are an eat-dessert-first kind of gal?"

She swallowed. "No. This is my second course. I had you first." And before I could say anything, she held up the dessert. "Want to taste my cheesecake?" She blinked big, innocent eyes.

Lord, how could I say no? "Why, yes. Yes, I do." I walked over and leaned into her until she had to arch back just a bit. Then I kissed her, holding her lips with mine, stroking my tongue along hers until she exhaled contentedly.

"Good?" she asked as I pulled back a bit.

I licked my lips. "Never had better. But all it did was whet my appetite."

"Oh," she said. "So do you want to . . . ?" She pointed at the door with the brownie and wiggled her eyebrows.

"Good God, woman," I said with a laugh. "Yes, I want that. But a man needs his strength. Let me get some food in my belly." I shoved the entire spanakopita in the microwave, heated it more or less evenly, then set it on the counter and ate damn near half of it before I noticed Dessa had wandered off, because she was wandering back with two beers and a fork in her hands.

"I didn't take the expensive stuff," she said, setting a beer bottle in front of me. She'd already removed the cap.

"Last time you bought me a drink . . ."

"I only poison on a first date," she said. "Share a bite or two of your spanakopita?"

"Help yourself." I pushed the pan closer to her, and she took a bite.

"Mmm. Not as good as the cheesecake, but mmm."

I tipped back the beer took a long draw. God, could a man be happier? I suddenly understood this be-with-one-person thing. The let's-give-this-a-go thing. Coming home to her every day would be like visiting heaven. If heaven were a sweet-eyed, naughty-minded redhead.

I took a deep breath and savored the silence and bliss filling me.

It had been a long time since I'd felt so good.

Dessa picked up her beer, then sidled over to me and slipped her arm around my back. I wrapped my arm around her and kissed her temple. She took a drink of beer, then tucked her head into my shoulder.

"Shame," she said quietly against my chest.

"Hmm?"

"This is nice."

"But?"

"No. Just this is nice," she said. "Better than I expected."

I chuckled. "How badly did you underestimate me, darlin'?"

"No." She took a drink of beer, was quiet for a minute. "I underestimated myself. How . . . how I would feel about you."

"That makes two of us," I said. "I'm surprised how much I feel about me too."

She slapped my stomach.

"Ow," I chuckled.

"What about me?" she asked, shifting so she could look up at me.

I didn't want to lie to her. So I didn't.

"I've never felt this way about anyone else in my life," I said evenly.

She nodded, understanding, I thought, the rarity and truth of that statement. She let go of the breath she was holding. "To tomorrow," she said, holding up her beer.

"And all our days after that." I clinked my bottle against hers, took a drink.

A simple toast to hide a lingering promise. That maybe we'd do this together for a while, see if two lives could become one.

That's when I heard the car engine approaching, the gravel shifting beneath the tires. Someone was coming our way in a hell of a hurry.

Here's the thing about having an assassin as a girlfriend: she didn't ask me who I thought it was, didn't ask if she needed to grab her things, didn't ask what she should do. She was out of the kitchen before I was, and up the stairs for her things.

I went to the window, looked out.

It was Terric's car.

This wasn't good. This couldn't be good.

He parked as close to the door as he could without plowing into the place and left the engine running.

I strode over to the door, wishing I'd put on my boots and grabbed my coat before I'd come downstairs. Or wishing I'd told Dessa to get them for me.

I pulled the door open. "What's wrong?" I asked.

Terric was shock-pale, his hair pulled back in a band tight against his head. His eyes were bloodshot red, and his heart was pumping too fast, erratic.

"Victor," he choked out. "He's been hit."

"How bad?" I asked.

Terric just shook his head.

"Fuck. Where is he? Terric, where is he?" I reached out, dropped my hand on his shoulder. My touch seemed to help him focus. He swallowed.

"I don't know, Shame. I think his house."

I didn't ask him why he had come all the way out to the inn before going to Victor's to check on him. I didn't ask how he knew he was hurt. I'd find that out on the way over.

"Give me your keys."

He dropped them into my hand.

"Let's go," I said.

"Here are your shoes." Dessa was right behind me.

I turned. She'd put on her coat and shoes, and from the cut of her jacket, and the duffel bag in one hand, I knew she also had her guns.

But along with her things, she'd had the foresight to bring me socks, shoes, my sweater, and the baseball bat.

I loved a woman who was steady in a crisis.

"Get him in the car," I said. "I'll drive."

Dessa took Terric's hand and said something to him in a soothing tone. He went with her, and sat in the backseat of the car, which showed me how confused he was. She got into the front.

I pulled on socks and boots, pulled on my coat, and picked up the baseball bat. Then I locked and shut the door and ran to the car, Eleanor right behind me.

I slid into the driver's seat, adjusted it for my legs instead of Terric's, and got us out of the parking lot as fast as I could.

"Tell me what happened, Ter," I said. "Tell me what you know about Victor."

"I got a call. From Davy. He only got a few words out. That Victor had been hit."

"Did you call Victor?"

"Yes. He didn't answer."

I was taking the fastest route I could to Victor's house, and was going eighty-plus. This time of night at least I didn't have to worry about traffic.

"Did you call the police?"

"N-no."

"You just drove straight out to the inn?"

"Yes. You were there." He was starting to sound a little clearer. I don't know how he'd managed to drive in the state of mind he was in.

"Do you have your phone?" I asked.

He sat up a straighter and checked his coat pockets. "Jesus," he said in a shaky voice.

"Hand it to Dessa."

"I can do it," he said. "Hello," he said to Dessa, as if just noticing her in the car.

"Hey," she said back.

"Call Stotts," I said. "Dessa, do you have a phone?"

I'd left mine in the room, but she pulled hers out.

"I need you to dial this number." I told her Allie's number. She dialed.

I took the phone from her, each ring an eternity. What if Victor wasn't the only one who'd been hit?

Stotts must have answered almost immediately because Terric was already talking, and as far as I could tell, his voice was steady, and he was giving clear information.

"Jones," Zay answered.

"This is Shame," I said. "Victor's been hit. Davy got a message to Terric. We're on our way to Victor's now—"

I braced, ran a light at speed, and avoided a head-on collision with a garbage truck.

"Shame?" Zay said.

"Keep your eyes open and be ready in case anything's coming your way," I finished. "I'll call in when we know more."

"Keep it tight," he said. "Listen to Terric."

I glanced in the rearview mirror. Terric looked like he'd finally shaken off his confusion and had gotten his head straight. "I'll do that," I said.

I handed Dessa the phone, then slowed to seventy or so as I navigated the neighborhood streets.

Came up on Victor's house. The cops hadn't made it here yet. We were out of the car before the engine stopped growling.

Dessa pulled her gun. My gun was also somewhere in my room with my jacket. Neither Terric nor I carried any weapon other than the magic at our fingertips. I glanced over at him, checking to see if he was together enough for this.

"I'm clear," he said without looking at me.

I got to the front door first. It was locked. But then, if Eli had used that gate technology, he wouldn't need to open the door.

"Shoot it," I said.

Dessa stepped up, shot it without hesitation. Then she shouldered into the room, gun raised.

Damn it. I did not want her in harm's way.

And there was the drawback to having an assassin girl-friend.

"Victor!" I yelled. No answer. "Fuck."

I took off running to the living room and kitchen. Terric ran past me to the bathroom and bedroom.

Victor was an uncle to both of us—no, more than that. A father when my father died. A trusted counselor when Terric had lost his ability to use Faith magic. A steady wisdom and calm voice throughout all the pain and struggle and uncertainties of magic, the Authority, and our place in the world.

He had, in a very real way, made us the men we were.

He trusted us, demanded the best of us. He stood by us when we took on the challenge of building a world where magic was no longer a secret.

I knew the moment when Terric found him. Knew it even before I heard Terric's anguished moan. Could feel the pain and sorrow like a shot straight through Terric's heart, tearing through mine.

Victor was dead.

I knew it as I ran to Terric, knew it as I stepped through the doorway to the bedroom. Terric knelt on the floor next to the bloody, broken form of Victor.

Everything went silent. I couldn't hear Terric pleading, couldn't hear Dessa jogging our way, couldn't hear my own heartbeat. The world was smothered.

I closed my eyes, hovering there in that mad lucidity.

The monster within me stretched, opened its arms, and latched each slick tentacle around me, drawing me into it, into the nothingness where it promised blood, destruction, and vicious release. Where it promised I would never have to feel pain again. Where it promised the terror of others would fall upon me like a numbing salve.

"Shame?" Dessa's hand rested on my arm.

I opened my eyes.

And the world, the room, pounded down around me.

Terric, on the phone, blood on his hands, blood streaked through his hair where he must have pulled at it with his fingers. Dessa at my side, her gun still in her hand and aimed at me.

"Dessa," I said. "Are you . . . are you all right?"

"I'm not the one on fire." She nodded at my hand.

I lifted my right hand. The rings were glowing red, but as I watched, the burn was fading like coals dusted at the edges.

"He's sane," Terric said to Dessa as he pocketed his phone. Then, in a voice louder than that whisper, "Dessa, put the gun down. He could kill you before you pulled the trigger."

She hesitated. Finally lowered the gun.

I turned. Looked into blue eyes that were not frightened—but were very wary.

As she had every right to be.

"Did I hurt you?" I said with what gentleness I could manage.

She searched my eyes. I did not know what she saw there. Maybe Death magic. It was there, just behind my will, lapping at my control. Pressing and promising.

She held up her hand, turned it one way and the other to examine the skin. "Felt like all the skin burned off when I touched you."

"And now?"

She curled her fingers to her palm. "Everything works." She pulled her shoulders back.

"Don't touch me for a while," I said. "I'm in control, but it's not solid."

She nodded.

I finally turned my full attention to Victor.

He was on his back, in his pajama pants, his shirt cut to shreds, the edges of it burned. Blood soaked the carpet. Terric was kneeling in it.

I walked the few steps to Victor's prone body. It seemed to take three long years before I reached his side. I rested my hand on Terric's shoulder and for a second, he leaned his head against my arm.

I felt his sorrow as if it were my own. Because it was.

I wanted to scream. Instead Terric whispered a prayer. It was the words of a very old spell—Peace.

Grief knotted my throat and clenched my gut. I didn't have time for grief. I couldn't have time.

So I pushed it away, fed it to the monster within me. Any pain would sate it, even my own.

Terric lifted his head away from me and stood as I knelt, trading places, his hand falling now on my shoulder. Perhaps it seemed an odd thing, the way we moved in tandem without thought, but it was natural as breathing to me.

"The marks," Terric said.

I moved the edge of Victor's shirt away, uncovered the shredded mess that was his torso. He had been carved, and carved, and carved again.

Spells: Pain, Refresh, Fire, Refresh, Crush, Break, Sever. Refresh, and Refresh again. Every dark agony cut into him in a continuous circuit of unending torture.

The bastard hadn't even had the fucking decency to carve Death into his skin. He had carved Life instead. He had squeezed every last ounce of pain out of Victor.

And in the blood around his body was another spell. But from the ragged streak trailing off to one side, it was clear that the spell had been interrupted before it was finished.

"Eli," Terric and I said at the same time.

It wasn't a name anymore.

It was the shape of the thing we were going kill.

Chapter 25

I paced. Smoked. Just outside his room. Just over the threshold of his death.

Waiting. For Terric to finish talking. Couldn't remember who was here worth talking to. Didn't care.

Cigarette burned down. I flicked it to the fireplace as I paced past, lit the next one. Hungry. Angry.

Because there wasn't room in me for grief.

Just rage.

The floor cracked like ice under my feet. I'd drawn all that could be drawn out of the wooden floor, out of the bracers beneath them. Had drawn all of the moisture from the air. Three plants in the room: dead. The bushes outside: withered.

Six people in the house, only one was dead: Victor. But there would be more if I stayed longer.

Rings on my fingers hissed and snapped as I turned and followed my anger back to the other side of the room.

This house was my cage. And I was an animal who wanted out. But I'd stay here until Terric told me differently.

Because I'd promised Zay I would listen to him.

I didn't know if Terric called Zay or not. Hadn't been paying attention to the bedroom's blood-covered walls, hadn't listened while the police came in and Terric told me to stay in the living room and kill no one. Had no idea where Dessa was.

Better that I didn't.

I was anger. Anger that keened for the hunt. Eli had said he'd give us a day, maybe less.

Eli had lied. He was never going to give us time.

Terric was walking my way, I could feel it before I saw him.

Strode into the room. Still had a streak of dried blood in his white hair, blood on his jeans, his shirt. Victor's blood.

His eyes were as hard and steady as his stride.

Didn't stop, didn't pause. Walked right up to me. Stuck one hand against my shoulder, and grabbed the back of my neck with the other.

"I need you to come back, Shame," he growled. "If you can't fight the magic in you, I will."

The rings on my fingers hissed with magic. The stone on his chest caught white fire.

Life and Death pushed between us like two magnets repelling each other while being shoved together.

Then Life slipped like a clean knife to clash with Death in the middle of my head.

It hurt.

And with pain came clarity.

". . . are you clear on that, Shamus?" he was saying.

"I got the last half," I said.

"We are going to let the police take care of this. You and I are going home together so I can keep an eye on you."

Oh, that was not going to fly. Terric's fingers dug into the back of my head, and I realized he wasn't telling *me* this. He was saying it for someone else.

"Jesus," I said. "Fine. But you are not my fucking boss, Conley."

His expression washed in relief. He must have thought that I wouldn't catch on to his lie and help him tell it. Or maybe he didn't think I'd return to a semblance of sanity.

Right now I'd do fucking anything to get out of this house. Because I had a man to kill.

We had a man to kill.

Terric let go and stepped back, his body language falling into that corporate clean-cut, responsible, trustworthy falsity. Sure, sometimes Terric was all of those things. But right now I knew he wanted Eli just as dead as I did.

"I'll keep him for the night," Terric said. "Please let me know if you get any leads on this."

"I will," Detective Stotts said, not unkindly. "We upped the drive-bys on Allie and Zay's house too. Do you want us to send a unit past your place every hour or so?"

"No," Terric said smoothly. "If anything happens, we'll break magic and Hold him."

"Are you sure you can do that?" Stotts looked over at me.

I just gave him a slow blink.

"I can control him," Terric said, meaning me, not Eli. "I promise you."

Stotts nodded, but didn't look away from me. "If you have any trouble at all, call me. We can lock him up and put him under so far he won't even know what his name is."

I couldn't help it, I smiled.

I could never forget my name because it was stamped in the face of every person I saw: Death.

Stotts's gaze finally skittered away. With a nod to Terric, he walked back to the other beating hearts in the room.

"Let's go, Shame," Terric said.

He walked toward the door. I followed, the floor snapping like old glass beneath my boots.

Then we were outside. His car was there. And so was another pulse beat—Dessa.

"I'm going with you," she said.

"This isn't any of your business," Terric said.

"We're hunting Eli, aren't we?" I said, my voice a little too low.

Terric didn't say anything, just shot me a look.

"She wants him just as dead as we do. She comes."

Terric didn't argue. Not with so many police here, not with the ambulance and EMTs pushing the gurney and body bag.

Jesus.

Terric shoved me firmly toward the passenger seat and Dessa got in the back. Eleanor clung to the corner by the window.

Terric drove. I didn't know where. Probably his house in case any of the police had a Hound on us. I was out of cigarettes, and in no place to be carefully siphoning the heat off the engine. I crossed my arms and tried to push the world away, tried to push Terric away, Dessa away. Tried to push the whole damn living city of Portland over the edge of my awareness. But there was too much within my reach to consume, to hurt, to kill.

Far too much to ignore.

Terric's hand landed on my upper arm, squeezed. He fed Life magic into me in a steady stream. I didn't want it, didn't want the edge of my anger to dull. Thought about doing the same to him. Let him try to keep up with the death I poured into him.

I glanced at his face. Stone cold, flat, and expressionless as he drove. The single tear track he hadn't wiped away was the only thing that betrayed his grief.

So I kept my hands to myself, let him pour Life magic to sate the hunger in me, and the hunger in him.

By the time we got to his house, I was no less angry, but I was a hell of a lot more in control.

I pulled my arm out of his grasp, and he put his hand back on the wheel, saying nothing.

"Are we going in?" I asked.

"Yes." Terric got out. I followed, Dessa next to me.

Up the steps to his door, then in his house.

Jeremy was not here. I could tell because I didn't sense his heartbeat.

Once I was inside, I paused at the door, tipped my head

down with my hand still on the doorknob, and listened to the world outside.

Not for the sound of cars. For the beat of a heart.

I wanted to know if Stotts or Clyde had put a Hound on us, and I wanted to know where that Hound might be.

It took about five minutes. Then I felt it. A heartbeat about two houses down. Close enough, probably in a car where, she, I guessed, could watch us. And farther off, a second beat.

Hounds never traveled alone. Sure, only one of them would work a job, but there was always a shadow, always another Hound watching after the first.

"Two," I said as I walked into Terric's living room.

"Two what?" Dessa asked.

I looked at Terric. Didn't have to explain. "Allie said Sunny is running things since Davy is AWOL."

"She's looking for Davy," he said. "I'll call Dash."

Terric got busy doing that, telling Dash that he needed to call off the Hounds. We'd done this just a few other times when we had first taken over the Authority. While I liked the eyes and ears of a Hound, there were times when we didn't want even our closest allies knowing what we were doing.

Times like tonight.

So we'd set up an agreement with the Hounds. We'd only call them off if it was of utmost importance. The respite lasted exactly twenty-four hours, and we'd never hunt one of their own.

Yes, we had a list of who the Hounds considered part of the pack. Allie and Zay fell on that list. So did my mum, and ironically, both Terric and I.

Eli was nowhere on that list.

Terric hung up. I paced, waiting for the heartbeats to go away.

Took less than a minute. Both Hounds cleared out.

"Tell me why she's with us, Shame," Terric said. Not angry, no, not at all. He had become very precise, as if all his thoughts and movements were razor sharp, heartlessly cold, deadly. Man was in a killing mood.

"She knows where Eli is."

"I think I know," she corrected.

"And we're lovers," I added.

Dessa raised her eyebrows and stared at me. Terric took a moment to study her. She might not think it was important that Terric know what I felt for her, things I knew he was getting right now through our connection, but if she was going into a fight with us, I wanted Terric to know that she was important to me, and was to be protected.

"Understood," he said. "Show me what you have in the duffel."

Now she stared at him. "Why?"

"I'm not going to take anything. I just want you to have enough of the right things with you to make a difference. Sooner would be better. We need to be moving."

She looked back at me.

"If we know what you have, we know how to cover you. Simple as that."

She lifted the duffel, put it on top of his coffee table, and pulled it open.

Terric looked into the bag and so did I.

Quick inventory: two Glocks, a couple throwing knives, a hunting knife, the rifle, and a sawed-off shotgun.

"Looks like you've got it covered," he said. "Might want to put the Void stone on, in case there's magic."

She reached in, pulled out a beaded necklace with a silver-dollar-sized Void stone hanging in the center of it, and drew it over her head.

"So, where is he?" I asked her.

"I said I might know," she said. "There's a warehouse down on Macadam."

"Why do you think he's there?" Terric asked.

"I got a tip from a friend."

"Who?" Terric asked.

"A Hound. She can be trusted."

"How long ago did you get this tip?"

"Yesterday morning."

"It's a start," I said.

Terric nodded. "I found this in Victor's hand." He reached in his pocket and handed me an unused hypodermic needle. There was a label on it with a glyph for Clarity crossed out by a glyph for Chaos.

I held it up to the light. Looked like the liquid had flecks of dust in it. Whatever was in that needle was what had sent me barefoot across Portland, mindlessly destroying things. Victor had just put one of Eli's weapons into our hands.

"Are we taking the time to analyze it now?" I asked.

"No," Terric said. "But we will."

I handed it back to him. "And not with the police?"

"We don't need the police," Terric said. Then, "I'm going to get into something clean. You two need anything?"

"We're good," I said.

He left the room and I turned to Dessa. "I'm suddenly wanting to talk you out of this. Any chance you'll listen?"

She had pulled a footstool up to the coffee table and was going over her weapons.

"You know how you said Terric is like a brother to you?" she said.

I waited.

"Well, my brother *was* my brother. We were close. And I am going to kill Eli for him."

"Right," I said slowly. "Something I've been meaning to ask you. Why did you come back to me after you had the lead?"

"Because I knew you'd killed other powerful men." She looked up at me, snapping the last piece of the rifle in place. "With magic."

"So," I said, "you knew you could kill him with bullets . . ."

"But I got nothing when it comes to magic. And people like you and Terric—"

"Breakers," I said.

"—'Breakers,'" she agreed, "can kill him with magic."

"Was that the only reason you came back?"

She considered me a second. Then stood and kissed me. When she finally pulled away, she tipped her eyes up to meet my gaze. "No. Last night was real. Wasn't a part of the rest of this. However this goes down, that stays the same."

"People might get hurt," I said. "I might be the one hurting them."

"I know."

Terric was out of his room, new jeans, new black T-shirt under a black peacoat. He handed me a gun. Had one of his own.

Dessa's eyes widened up.

"Sometimes the direct kill is the best," I said. I shrugged out of the sweater, leaving me in just a gray T-shirt. I didn't need a coat. I had my hate to keep me warm.

Terric strode to the door and I followed him, Dessa at my side. Back to the car.

I'd barely noticed Eleanor, drifting with me, finally caught the glow of her out of the corner of my eyes. She looked like she'd been crying, though I'm not sure how that could be for a ghost. I didn't think she had liquid in her.

Still, the way she moved, the bend of her head. Everything about her was sorrow.

She'd known Victor too. Had spent some time training in magic with my mum and him. "You see something I don't," I said to her. "Tell me."

Eleanor noticed I was noticing her and nodded. She pressed her hand over her heart. I didn't know if she was indicating her promise, or saying it was broken.

"I will," Dessa said.

"I know," I said to Eleanor.

Terric didn't say anything. Didn't have to. He knew who I was really talking to.

Here's the thing. I've spent a good amount of time doing my best to put distance between Terric and me, for both our survival.

But right now that wasn't my goal: survival. My goal was to take Eli down. And if I knew exactly what Terric was doing, if not exactly what he was thinking, it made it easier to get things done. No hesitation. No slack. So the closer together he and I were right now, the better it was.

He drove. I sat in the passenger seat, Dessa behind us.

Terric didn't break any speed limits getting to the warehouse, so as not to attract the cops, but he pushed a few lights. From the color of the sky, we still had about an hour before the sun rose.

Good. I did my best work in the dark.

"This it?" Terric asked.

The warehouse didn't look abandoned. It was being retrofitted into offices or maybe apartments, construction equipment surrounding it.

"This is where she said he was," Dessa said.

"Did you come by here and look for him earlier?" I asked. "Before you came to my place tonight?"

"No," she said. "I wanted to talk you into coming with me. That didn't go quite how I planned it."

"Outcome was the same," I said, opening the door.

"Outcome was better," she said softly.

I could almost feel my heart again, captured in her voice. Terric was through the gap in the chain-link fencing. Dessa and I caught up with him.

There was some logic in splitting up to cover all exits, but on a retrofit building, there would be more exits than we could cover.

So I listened for heartbeats.

Felt Terric's probably beating in time with mine. Felt Dessa's. There were more in the buildings around us. A few in the only car that passed by. But in the warehouse, there was only one.

"He's in there," I said for Dessa's sake.

We pulled our guns. I could use magic one-handed. I intended to do so.

Terric and I pushed through the door, walked step in step, guns raised.

The inside was gutted. Framework where walls once were, and maybe where walls were going to be. Plastic draped from the ceiling, rubble on the floor.

Noted it all absently. I was headed for that heartbeat. Eli's heartbeat.

Corner room. To the left. There was a door here, hung half-shut. Terric kicked it open. He and I pushed into the room, arms straight, guns locked on the heartbeat.

But the huddle of clothes in the corner was not Eli. It was a girl, well, a young woman, and she was unconscious.

We lowered our guns and Terric crossed the room to her. "She the only one you feel, Shame?"

I listened, let the monster stretch out to feel lives it could consume.

"Yes. Do you know her?"

He had turned her face and was checking her pulse. The blood from her head was making it hard to see her features clearly, but she seemed faintly familiar to me.

"It's Gillian," Dessa said, rushing forward to her. "She's my Hound. Holy shit. Is she okay?"

Terric ran his fingers quickly over her head, checked her neck, and finally pressed two fingers on her chest, just below her collarbone. He closed his eyes and I could see the yellow-white magic responding to his touch. Healing magic poured into her as he whispered a prayer.

Dessa inhaled a hard breath.

"He's healing her," I said. "She told you Eli would be here?"

She nodded. "Who would do this? She's just a kid."

"Stay here." I strode through the building looking for any sign of Eli—what he'd been doing here, which way he'd left. Wished I'd brought a flashlight.

Screw it. I drew a light spell, filled it with magic. It wrapped around my left hand with scrolls of white that rolled upward like licking flames. It lit up a twenty-foot space around me.

"That's . . . wow," Dessa said behind me. So much for her staying with Terric.

I turned on my heel. "I asked you to stay with Terric."

"He told me to go with you."

"Jesus." I made quick work of the place, figuring the light was going to be pretty easy to spot this time of night through the broken windows. I did not want a nosy neighbor calling the cops.

And then I saw the sign I was looking for. Next to a door that faced south, a glyph was drawn. It was the glyph for Direction, one of the finding spells. It was definitely Eli's handiwork.

Right there in the dirt was something else: a turquoise bead. I bent, picked up the bead. I knew where I'd seen it before. It was from Davy's necklace.

Chapter 26

Terric was on the phone with Dash when I walked into the room. ". . . wait. No, just a Hound, or you. That's best."

He flicked the phone off. "What did you find?"

"Sign that says Eli's south of here. Direction glyph. Also this." I walked over to him, dropped the bead in his hand.

He frowned.

"It's from Davy's necklace. Broken."

"Davy was here. So was Eli," Dessa said. "Great. But where did they go?"

"I don't think Davy left willingly," I said.

"Why?" Terric asked.

"His truck is out back."

Terric swore. "He shouldn't be hunting Eli alone in the first place."

"Who's coming for Gillian?" I asked.

"Dash. He's close, and it won't involve the Hounds. He'll take her to the emergency room, then call the Den. Go search Davy's truck in case he had a chance to leave something there for us."

I didn't even bitch at him for ordering me around. I crossed the structure then jogged out across the lot that was still mostly paved. The fact that the truck was parked so close and in the open bothered me. Davy wasn't that reckless. So either he had thought there was no one inside, or he had come here, not looking for Eli, but looking for Gillian instead.

"What are you thinking?" Dessa asked. I remembered she was with me, glanced over at her.

Had her gun in her hand and was keeping an eye on the buildings around us.

I tried the door on the truck. Locked.

"It's not like Davy to drive into a situation and park in the open. Makes me think he didn't know what he was walking into. And that's even less like him."

"Conclusion?" she asked as I checked to see if the other door of his truck was unlocked.

"Maybe a trap. Coming to find Gillian, an injured Hound, and got ambushed."

"I don't think he was looking for Gillian," she said, handing me a slim-jim from her duffel.

"Because?"

"Gillian was following Davy."

"Is that what you hired her for?"

"Yes, but I told her not to engage."

The lock popped and I pulled the heavy door open. "After the morgue, right? You saw how much Davy hated Eli, knew he'd go after him alone."

"I had a hunch."

"Wish you would have shared it," I said, climbing into the cab.

"I didn't know you as well back then," she said, getting into the cab from the other side after I unlocked the door. "Or I would have done it differently."

There were a couple gas receipts, insurance, registration, and random papers but nothing else that indicated Davy had left clues in his vehicle for us to find.

A car rolled up on the other side of the chain-link. Killed the engine.

Dash got out. He was wearing a dark leather jacket, dark jeans, and boots. And the vibe he gave off had nothing to do with the office. He looked like a man who could handle himself in a fight.

I suddenly wondered if he had combat training. Something I'd never asked him about, though I should have.

"Where's Gillian?" he asked, coming up on me and Dessa.

"This way." I took him in the building.

He and Terric managed to get Gillian awake and aware enough, she spoke, guessed the right number of fingers, and understood Dash was going to take her to the hospital. Even did some moving of her feet so we didn't have to carry her.

After we got her settled in the back of Dash's car, Terric paced back toward the warehouse.

"Listen," I said to Dash. "I've kicked a few hives. I want you to be careful."

"Which hives?" Dash asked.

"Black Crane."

"Define 'kick.'"

"There's been a change in leadership, 'cause the other guy's dead."

He nodded. He knew what that meant. "Jeremy?"

"Haven't gotten my hands on him yet. But I will. Don't tangle with him. Promise me."

"I promise."

"Be careful," I said.

He nodded. "Take care of him."

Dash left and I strode over to Terric.

"Show me the glyph," he said.

I took him to the south door.

"It's Eli's work," Terric said. "But why didn't he complete it?"

I looked closer. He was right.

"Maybe the better question is, who do you think he put this here for?" Dessa asked.

"Me," I said the same time Terric said, "Shame."

Which meant he'd left it undone so I could finish it.

I didn't know that I liked his calling card. Yes, it was a Directional glyph. I figured it was a trap, but we wouldn't know for sure until I triggered it.

"Might want to step back," I said.

I stuck out my finger, drew over the glyph to get the flow of his signature, then closed the arc at the end of the spell.

The spell flashed, and in the afterburn I could see an address.

"Shit!" Terric yelled.

The air cracked. Just outside the door stood a man. Not Eli. This was an older man.

I'd seen him. I knew his face. He was the old man in the missing person report. The one with the tattoo for Impact.

He stared at us with blank eyes as if he didn't see us, or the world around him. Then he raised his hands, thumbs crossed, fingers spread.

And said one word.

An explosion hit, throwing us across the room, and bringing the building crashing down around us.

Chapter 27

Concrete, wood, metal roared down around us, slammed into us.

Terric and I were on our feet, hands raised, standing back to back. I pulled Dessa up against me.

"Hold on," I said.

I reached down below the building's foundations to the magic flowing there as Terric did the same.

We didn't just draw on magic, we ripped it out of the ground. Forced it to sever, to scream and break.

I didn't have to talk to Terric about what we were doing. We each knew what the other was thinking, knew what we had to do: Shield.

We cut that protection into the air with wide strokes and left a burning, dripping trail of magic behind. Shield snapped into a barrier around us, like an unbreakable bubble.

Just in time. The ceiling beams shoveled down, bounced off the Shield, and fell to either side.

Terric was chanting.

I was concentrating on pulling on enough magic to feed the spell and keep it strong.

The other thing about magic—doesn't matter how powerful you are. If you lose your concentration, you lose the spell.

We could try walking, but if we stumbled, the Shield would break and we'd be crushed. So we waited.

Turns out it doesn't take long for half a building to collapse.

Felt like an eternity.

We didn't wait for the dust to clear. We pushed and climbed our way out of the rubble, before the other half of the building came tumbling down too.

Made it out by the car.

There was no one around us. Yet.

"That man did that?" Dessa asked. "One man?" She was a little louder than necessary, maybe a little panicked. I didn't blame her.

"Yes," Terric said, striding as quickly as he could around scattered debris to the car. "Go," I said, grabbing Dessa's arm and following Terric.

"H-how?" she asked. "He said one word and blew up a building."

"I was there," I said. "I don't know how he did it."

"Can you find him? Did you see where he went?" Dessa got into the car and so did I, in a hurry to get away from the very loud falling-building noises that had undoubtedly woken everyone in a square mile.

Terric peeled out fast, took a side street, slowed, and crept along a normal speed until we were a good mile away. Then he put on the speed. Heading south.

"Shame?" Dessa said. "Can you find that man?"

"No," I said. "I've got nothing to go on. If he's around, he's just another heartbeat in the crowd. But Eli planted an address in the afterburn of the Direction glyph I triggered. Did you see it?"

"I was shielding my eyes," she said.

"Terric?"

"I saw it. The hospital."

The address burned in that spell pointed straight at OHSU, a medical complex and teaching hospital built beneath, on top of, and into a hillside south of downtown.

"Hospital?" Dessa asked. "Why?"

"Davy has a theory," I said. "That Eli was using the labs, or operating out of the hospital."

"Again, why? What does he need a hospital for?"

"People," Terric said.

"Test subjects," I clarified.

"Testing what?"

I could tell from Terric's body language that he didn't want me to say anything. But as far as I was concerned, she was in this just as deep as we were. Wanted him dead. Would do bad things to make sure that happened.

"Testing people," I said. "People who were poisoned by tainted magic three years ago."

"Tainted magic? Is that even a thing?"

"It was," Terric said.

"How do you taint magic?"

"It helps if you decide you want to change magic into a weapon," I said. "It helps if you are Breakers who are crazy and come back from the dead."

"Like you and Terric."

Damn. I hadn't drawn those parallels. From the look Terric shot me, he hadn't thought of us that way either: Breakers who had come back from the dead. But she was right.

"No," Terric said. "We aren't nearly evil enough to poison magic. To destroy the world for our pleasure."

She was silent. I could see her reflection in the rearview mirror. She had that reality-upside-down look on her face like when I'd told her her brother had gone around stealing people's memories with magic.

She caught my gaze. I waited. Would she see the man in me or the monster? I gave her a soft smile.

"All right," she said. "Do you know why? Not why Breakers tainted magic. Do you know what results Eli is looking for in the tests?"

"Maybe men who can blow up buildings with a single syllable," I said.

"Jesus," she whispered. Then she nodded. "Okay, what's the plan?"

Neither Terric nor I said anything.

"At least give me an idea of what weapons he has at his disposal."

"If that man is any indication, magic," Terric said. "As strong as Shame and me. Maybe technology that enhances magic, which would make it stronger. We don't know anything else."

"Do you know anything else?" I asked her.

"No."

"Dessa," I said, catching her gaze in the rearview mirror again. "Do you know anything that will help us?"

Come on, baby. Don't leave us in the cold.

"I know what my brother told me. But that's all second-hand information. I can't prove anything."

"Don't care," Terric said. "Tell us."

"Thomas said that there was a man under observation. He was . . . creating new technology for defense abroad and for Homeland Security. But it was biotech. Thomas said that man was the most powerful man he'd seen use magic. And the most ruthless. Next to you, Shame."

"Did he tell you about us? About Breakers?" Terric asked.

"Yes."

So that might have been our leak into the government. Thomas, or maybe her.

"And you told your superiors?" Terric went on, pressing the point.

"It was my job to pass on information." She tipped her chin up.

Jesus, she knew she was the reason her brother had been killed. No wonder she wanted Eli dead.

"Did they send you to bring in Shame and me?" Terric asked. "Was that a part of your job too?"

"No," she said. "I left. As soon as I found out about

Thomas. I gathered as much information as I could without triggering any traces, covered my trail, and I left. I made it look like I was going to South Dakota to visit family, and then into Canada to see friends. I don't think they followed me. I don't think I led them to you." That last wavered with doubt. She was worried. Worried she'd get us killed.

"They already knew where we were," I said calmly. "They've known since before we broke magic yesterday for Zay and Allie. And that building, Gillian's injuries—nothing but a trap."

"To kill you?" she asked.

"If Eli's involved," I said, "it wasn't meant to kill us. It was meant to test us."

"Which means the address will be another trap," Terric said.

"He wanted us to find Brandy," I said. "Maybe he's leading us to her."

"Maybe she's the trap," Terric said.

"Who is Brandy?" Dessa asked.

"She's the other half of Eli, the person that makes him a Breaker," I said.

"Like Terric and you."

"Yeah, like Terric and me."

"And you're going to save her?" she asked. "If she's half of what Eli is, how do you know she isn't behind all this?"

"She's insane," Terric said quietly.

"Lots of powerful people are," she said.

True.

We were silent as Terric took the turn to the hills.

"We kill Eli," Terric said. "That's what we do."

The monster in me pushed. One death would be good, Eli's death. But two deaths would be better.

"We kill Eli," I said, "after we make him hurt."

"After we make him hurt," Terric agreed.

Dessa just turned and looked out the window. But I saw her nod. This was, I realized, going as she wanted it to. For a bare moment I wondered if she was playing us. If she was part of the government testing us to see what we could do together. If she had been sent out to bring us in at any price.

Maybe the cautious man would hold on to that idea and test it. But I knew her. She was here for revenge, a very personal revenge. She was not under orders.

"What are we looking for?" she asked. "A car? A sign?"

"Eli." Terric pulled over on the shoulder. "Track?" he asked me.

"Yes."

We'd already broken magic. If there were guns waiting for a signal, they were probably pointed at our heads. Didn't care. They could bring all the world's weapons at us.

I intended to see Eli breathe his last breath.

We traced Track, the ragged edges of the spell flicking like questing limbs that snapped out as if the entire glyph were floating on water. Pulled on magic. Filled the spell until it hummed a hot orange. Set it free with a push.

It lifted and passed through the windshield of the car, leaving a thin thread of the spell connected to the dash as it pulled ahead of the hood like a dog tugging a leash.

Terric followed it, the spell bobbing or leaning left or right, but never out of our sight. One of the advantages to Track was it would find a route that feet or wheels could follow, not just drift off over treetops or rivers like some of the other less specific Direction spells.

The spell led us up the hill and then shot left, hard.

Terric slowed.

"Is there a road over there?" I asked.

"Looks like a maintenance road."

Track continued to pull that way. So we went that way. Up a steep hill and then twisting down it, trees and underbrush close enough they slapped the concrete dust off the car.

The road ended at a wide warehouse built into the hill, only the first couple feet of it visible before it was swallowed by darkness, stone, and foliage.

A set of three windows two stories up were dark, and in the car's headlights, I could make out a triple-wide door.

"Storage?" Dessa asked.

"Maybe equipment repair," Terric said.

The Track spell had drifted down and was now perched at the front of the car like a many-legged glowing hood ornament. It wasn't doing anything because it didn't need to track Eli anymore. It had found him.

"He's in there," I said.

"What are we going—" Dessa's words were cut short. The warehouse door was opening, yawning up in one big slab to reveal the dimly lit interior.

I squinted to see through the darkness. The headlights weren't doing much more than throwing shadows into shadows.

Then a man walked forward to the edge of the open doorway, strode into the headlights, and stared straight at us, shaking his head in disappointment.

Eli Collins.

Chapter 28

"Get out of the car, Terric, Shame, and it's Dessa, isn't it?" Eli said distractedly. "There are guns aimed at you that could blow you apart before you blink."

Terric and I opened our doors and stepped out. I brought the baseball bat with me. Yes, I still had the gun too. Dessa got out a moment after us, probably loading the weapons on her body.

Eleanor drifted at a distance from me, which was just short of the warehouse. She was bound to me and couldn't move into the warehouse to look around unless I moved toward Eli.

"I gave you time," Eli said. "A full day! And I gave you clues. So many clues. But have you found her? No! You have failed me. You have failed us all. She'll die because of you, Shame."

Dessa stepped to one side of me, pulled her gun, and fired several rounds at Eli.

He didn't even flinch. The bullets hit the air about three feet in front of him, slowed, stopped, and fell to the ground.

"Just put it away, Ms. Leeds," he said. "This isn't a place for childish toys."

"You killed Victor," Terric said.

"What?" Eli looked genuinely surprised. "Of course I did. Did you think I would miss my chance to pay him back for the living hell he made of my life? Twenty years he toyed with me. And I had less than two minutes with him. Not enough time to kill him the way I wanted. Not nearly enough time to do to him what he deserved. It hardly seems fair."

"He was our teacher," Terric went on. "He was our family."

"It's nothing personal," Eli said. "It's. Just. Business." He smiled and spread his hands. "But our business isn't finished, gentlemen. Is it? This business between you and me. You still *owe* me."

I lifted the bat over my shoulder. "You know what, Eli?" I strode toward him, the ground beneath my feet turning from grass to dust, the brush on either side of the road withering, cracking, falling, as I passed. "I'm here to pay."

I drank all the living things down. Filling up with life. Feeding my anger. My rage.

So I could use it to beat him to a bloody pulp.

Trees groaned and went ash white in the night. Ferns, vine maple, and brush blackened and died.

Eli's eyes narrowed. "I'm not afraid of you, Shamus."

"It's mutual." I was almost in front of the protective barrier now. "Tell me if you change your mind when I'm breaking you."

Eli didn't move.

Terric was at my side, Dessa behind us, her gun still out, scanning the shadows.

"You think you can hit me with a bat?" Eli said. "Did you not see the bullets that couldn't penetrate that wall?"

The barrier was powered by tech, not magic.

Too bad for him.

I swung for the bastard's head.

Damn straight he jumped back.

The barrier snapped to life and poured insane amounts of wattage across the open space.

Electricity was energy. Energy was life. I absorbed it. Hot

enough it blistered the inside of my mouth. Electricity snapped and arced across my arms and down my back.

I yanked the bat away, turned my head to spit blood. I pulled off my rings and let them drop into the ground. Then I smiled at Eli.

No rings to block my reach to magic. No rings to block my power.

I swung again. Hard.

The barrier sparked, flared, and shattered.

Eli ran.

Emergency lights caught to life inside the structure.

It was a huge, three-story warehouse with arched metal ceiling and steel beams splayed out to the metal walls. Concrete floor, repair stalls to the left separated by more steel beams. The rest of the place was broken up by industrial shelves filled with boxes and things that might belong to a hospital or a machine shop.

The whole place looked like a military silo tipped on its side and nailed into the hill.

I put one foot inside and I knew why Eli had chosen this warehouse. The structure was built like a bunker. There was nothing alive in it, and thick metal and stone made it much more difficult for me to draw on the environment—life and magic—outside the structure.

It didn't make it impossible.

I reached out for Eli's life. Ran into some kind of Diversion he'd cast. I could untangle that spell given time.

Or I could beat him to death with my bat.

I preferred the second option.

Terric, Dessa, and I ran, our boots striking in matched rhythm across the warehouse to the hall at the end where Eli had disappeared. Eleanor flew in front of me and pointed up to the catwalks at the edges of the building.

Eli had said there were guns trained on us. He had not lied.

A barrage of bullets rained down.

Terric drew magic up from the floor in a blinding white arc. I called magic up in crackling black flames.

We didn't draw spells. We didn't have to.

We could break magic and make it do anything we wanted it to do.

Stop bullets? Yes.

Stop hearts? Yes.

There were eight shooters. Before we made it to the other side of the warehouse, there were eight dead shooters.

Stop Eli?

That was the question, wasn't it? Because he could make magic do what he wanted it to do too.

Even with the spells he'd cast and the magic he'd broken to protect himself, I could feel his heartbeat. Eli was running for his life.

It would be the last thing he ever did.

The hall was wide enough to drive a truck through. Pipes and wires snaked above our head, down the walls. The floor was metal grating. I heard the thrum of machines and rush of water somewhere far below.

That, I could reach. That, I could use.

"He's slowing," I said.

"How far ahead?" Dessa asked.

"Not far," Terric answered.

Eleanor flashed into the walls, flew out, flashed through them again. Searching for Eli.

The hall ended at a massive metal wall and hatch, bolted together like something made to handle deep-sea pressure.

Eleanor darted toward it, struck the wall, and pulled back, screaming in pain.

Holy shit.

I hadn't heard her voice in years.

"Don't!" I said as Terric jogged to the door. "Something's set here. A trap."

He didn't ask me how I knew.

"Do you see something?" Dessa asked.

I cleared my mind. Drew Sight. It was magic that surrounded the door. But no spell I'd ever seen before. It wasn't formed in a shape, a glyph, an order of some sort. It was just a pulsing blob of magic.

"What?" Dessa asked.

Terric drew a spell: Reveal. Different from Sight, it should show the true form of any physical object.

"What the hell is it?" he asked me.

"I don't know. It made Eleanor scream."

"Eleanor?" Dessa glanced around us as if expecting another person to be hiding in the shadows.

"What hurts her?" Terric asked.

"I have no idea." I looked over at Eleanor. She stood at a distance from the door, her arms crossed over her chest. She was frightened and angry.

"Do you know what it is?" I asked her.

She shook her head.

"Who?" Dessa asked, but Terric was already talking.

"Three heartbeats on the other side of that door."

"I noticed."

"Is Eli one of them?" Dessa asked.

"Yes," Terric and I said together.

"That's enough for me." She strode to the hatch, her hand out.

I stood in her way. "No."

"Move, Shame."

"No."

She reached for her gun. "I'm not going to let him get away."

I wrapped my arm around her waist, pulled her against me, and kissed her. She kissed me back, but her hand didn't leave her gun.

I pulled away, looked down into those hard blues. "We do this smart, and we do this together," I said, staring into her grief and pain and anger. "Because we are all making it out of this alive. Do you understand me?"

"Except Eli," she said. "Eli dies."

"That's right," I said. "Eli dies."

Terric began a spell, probably Cancel to clear the door so we could go through.

"He's the only one who dies today," I said.

Terric reached out with magic. I let go of Dessa and turned to him.

He wasn't casting Cancel. He was casting Explosion.

Shit.

I grabbed Dessa's arm and tugged her back down the hall, even as I was supporting the spell Terric was casting. We carved a quick Shield spell into the air to block the explosion and Terric stepped back to join us.

Then we broke magic and sent the spells flying.

The door blew apart with a huge roar, smoke and molten metal shooting toward us and into the room beyond.

We waited a heartbeat, two. Dropped the Shield and strode through the smoke and rubble into the room.

"We didn't think you would come this far," a man's voice said. "We hoped you might, but never thought you could." I didn't recognize the voice. It carried a soft burr, like the speaker was practiced at standing on a stage and reading Shakespeare. "But we underestimated both of you, didn't we, Mr. Conley and Mr. Flynn?"

The room was a quarter the size of the warehouse, but would still take a jog to get across. It was lit to obscure the walls, ceiling, and the lumps of machinery it contained. I thought it might have originally been used as a generator room.

Eli stood about a third of the way across the room. He had something metal in his hand that looked like a controller of some sort. Chained to the wall at the far end of the room was Davy. He was naked and unconscious, held down by the neck, wrists, ankles.

The glyphs carved into his chest, down his stomach, and over his arms pumped with a sluggish light—magic—

pushing and pooling there. I didn't know what they were using Davy for. But I knew they were using him.

Above the room, on a walkway with metal railings that overlooked the space, stood the man who had greeted us.

His long gray coat covered most of his body, but his shoes shone, and a smudge of white at his neck told me he wore a white shirt and jacket. His features were obscured by the shadows and the fedora-like hat he wore.

"We don't care what you're doing here, Krogher," Dessa said as she lifted her gun and aimed it at him. "All we want is Eli."

"Why, Ms. Leeds," the man—Krogher—said. "How disappointing to see you here. Apparently I've wasted my efforts trying to track you down in Canada."

"You know him?" Terric asked.

"He was my boss."

"You were useful to me, Ms. Leeds. But then you ran," Krogher said. "This is the only mercy I will show you. If you put the gun down, stand aside, and let me take care of the business at hand, you will walk from here alive."

"Give me Eli," she said. "And we'll walk out of here and leave you alive."

Krogher chuckled. "It amuses me that you think you can bargain with me."

"Well, it was worth a shot," she said.

She took aim and fired six shots at Eli.

And all hell broke loose.

Eli blocked the bullets with another one of those electric barriers. Then the room filled with magic, hot as acid. Eli adjusted the controller in his hand. Davy gave a strangled yell.

No bullets on us this time. They'd tried that, and it hadn't worked.

This time it was fire.

Terric and I ran. For Eli. We could save Davy by killing Eli. We could get the hell out of here when Eli was dead.

The man above us was using magic to call up the very real fire that burned over the metal walls and stone floor. Fire made by magic.

"How?" I said, or maybe thought, as Terric and I carved Cancel spells, absorbed and diverted the fire, the heat, the magic, like we had choreographed this dance and knew every move.

"Eli," Terric replied, or maybe thought. "And them."

I ducked a fireball roaring toward my head, glanced up. There were five people standing at equal distance across the catwalk. These were not men in business suits. These were regular people, all of them in sweatpants and loose shirts—hospital issue.

All of them staring blankly, hands pushed palm out, thumbs crossed.

Holy fuck. The last guy I'd seen stand like that had blown up a building. As a matter of fact, he was up there too, assuming the position.

"What the hell are they?" Dessa yelled. "Breakers?"

"No," I yelled back. "They're using magic. Stay back."

Dessa apparently did not know what those words meant. She pushed her way through the fire, running for Eli.

"God. Damn. It. Woman!"

I drew in the magic, a god-awful lot of it, twisted it, felt Terric's hand behind mine supporting the weight and chaos of it as we heaved it back at the people standing on the catwalk.

"Very good, Shamus," Eli somehow said so close to me I thought he was next to my ear. "But not good enough."

Davy moaned again, a gut-wrenching sound.

Time slowed.

This wasn't a trick of my mind or adrenaline that made it seem like time was slowed.

All the world around Terric and me *was* slowed. Even Dessa.

But not Eli. And not Terric and me.

"You lift one finger, take one step, and all bets are off," Eli said hurriedly. I noted he was sweating. Whatever he had done with the controller, with Davy, took a toll on him too.

"Krogher has Brandy bound. Trapped. I cannot touch her without killing her. Save her and I will give Davy a quick death. Refuse and his death will be long and agonizing."

Brandy had to be close enough he could draw on her to break magic. But I didn't see her or feel her heartbeat.

Just because the world was slowed didn't mean it was at a standstill. Dessa was pulling another gun on Eli. The people upstairs had recovered from the backlash I'd thrown at them. At this speed, I could see that it was Krogher who controlled them, and he did so with some kind of device in his palm.

Probably something Eli had invented. The people were like individual generators of magic. Like matching bombs just waiting for Krogher to tap their power.

Strong as Soul Complements.

Maybe stronger.

Weapons.

"Fuck you, Eli," I said. "You got no card in this game."

I reached out for the spells he was supporting to protect himself and drank the magic out of them.

Davy screamed.

"Shame!" Terric said. "Don't. He's tied to Davy. You're killing him too."

I glanced over at Davy. Terric was right. Davy was weakly thrashing, the magic burning into him, blood streaming out of the glyphs and pouring down his body.

I broke my connection to Eli's magic. "As you see," Eli said, "I do have a card to play, Shame. The last card."

He pressed a button and ribbons of razor-sharp magic shot out from the thing in his hand, aiming straight for Dessa's heart.

Chapter 29

Time was not slow anymore. It was suddenly, *brutally* fast.

Dessa yelled as the magic slammed into her, throwing her across the floor.

Terric and I lifted our guns. Terric aimed at Eli's head. I aimed at that damn thing in his hands.

We unloaded the clips.

He had a choice of which part of himself to Shield. Chose his head. The controller fell to the floor.

And the blank-eyed monstrosities from above hit us with another spell.

Impact.

It blasted through the room like a sonic wave. Threw me off my feet. An entire ocean of magic pounded and roared through the room.

Crushing us.

I couldn't breathe. Tasted blood.

Tumbled, hit my back, shoulder, head, into something metal, felt my spine crack. Felt Terric's pain too: arm, shoulder, neck. Could not tell where he was, or hell, where I was.

Ran out of air.

Drowning. Drowning in magic.

"Dessa!" I yelled. I didn't hear her. Couldn't see her.

Then Terric was there, standing above me. A goddamn angel with alien eyes. He did something with Life magic that made my ears ring with an ungodly chorus of sound. My head spiked with pain.

And then I could breathe, I could think. I stood. A little woozy, but kept my feet. It felt like they'd aimed the entire ocean of magic at me.

"They did," he said in that flat, creepy tone that was not Terric, not human, and somehow louder than my own voice.

"Where's Dessa?" I yelled.

"They're taking Davy. Using him." He might have just pushed the brunt of that Impact off us, but there was no Terric in those eyes. Just raw magic.

Get a grip, Flynn.

I stuck my hand on Terric's chest, drew off the Life magic burning through him until he stopped glowing and some sanity came back into his eyes.

Situation: the room was filled with a snarling maelstrom of magic that burned across the ceiling, walls, floor, picking up metal, debris, and glass and spinning it through the room like a caged tornado.

The people above us, including Krogher, were gone. That wasn't good.

The air cracked again and three holes in space materialized on the far side of the room. Gates.

Eli turned and limped toward one, holding his arm against his side and breathing hard. I hoped to hell one or a dozen of our bullets had hit him.

The second hole in space appeared right next to Davy. Men in black suits and black sunglasses stepped out of it and were quickly unchaining Davy and dragging him through that hole.

And the third . . . well, in the third stood a woman.

Terric turned to stare at her, his eyes gone alien again.

She wore a plain cotton nightgown. Looked like the room behind her was a hospital. She even held an IV bag in her hand. Her hair was dark and cut boy-short. She was about Eli's age.

I'd seen her picture. I knew who she was. Brandy Scott. Eli's Soul Complement. She looked lost. Confused.

"Brandy!" Eli yelled. "Save her, Shame! You must save her!"

He took what looked like an impossibly painful step toward her, one hand stretched out, but there were already men in black coming for him.

I had been standing there, getting a grip on the situation for two seconds, max.

Something cold punched my face. Eleanor floated in front of me, panicked. She pointed to my right. *Dessa,* she mouthed.

I turned away from Terric, who was already marching toward those gates, and looked for Dessa.

Dessa lay on the floor, holding her hand to the gaping hole in her chest. A hole put there by magic. A hole that was steadily growing larger. Eating away at her.

There are moments when you know your life is forever changed. You hold your breath and for that heartbeat wish it wasn't true. You make promises. You offer sacrifices. You lie to yourself.

But you know your world will never be the same again. You know you are lost and will never find your way back home. You know you will never be who you were just a heartbeat ago. This was my moment.

The moment my world broke.

The entire damn room was blowing up around us. Eli was getting away.

I didn't care.

I crossed to Dessa, knelt. Pulled her into my arms.

There was blood. Too damn much blood. Covering her. Covering me.

Her eyes searched mine. "Shame," she said. "Kill him for me."

"Shush, now," I said. "You know I'll do more than that. I will make his remaining breaths eternities of agony."

Her eyes were sad, filled with thick shadows of fear. She managed a smile.

I yelled for Terric. He could heal her. Like he'd healed me. He could make the hole in her go away.

"Look at that," she whispered as if she hadn't heard me screaming. "Your boyish charms are showing."

"Did they work?" I asked, smoothing her blood-soaked hair away from her face.

Don't die, baby. Hold on. Just hold on for me.

Where the hell was Terric?

"Yes," she said. "But then, they always have."

I shouldn't be touching her. The Death magic I held was only going to make her wounds worse. I shifted slightly, thinking I could ease her down to the floor.

She screamed in pain.

"God*damn* it, Terric!" I yelled again, holding still, holding her in my arms.

Her breathing had gone shallow and ragged.

"Dessa," I said. "It's going to be all right." The hole in her chest was growing, leaving nothing behind. No flesh. No blood. No Dessa. She was dissolving in my arms, like sand falling through my fingers.

"Just," she said. "Kiss me, Shame."

I lowered my head and pressed my lips gently to hers. Kissed her even though my body was shaking. Kissed her even though tears mixed with our blood. Kissed her for the last time.

I could feel her heart straining. I knew how little life she had left.

"I think I could have loved . . ." she mumbled against my mouth.

And then she exhaled. Her heart stilled.

I pulled back.

A flash of light devoured her body, the sudden, intense heat burning my hands, arms, face, chest, and legs. I yelled.

But Dessa was gone. No bones, no blood. Not even dust left behind. My arms were empty. Blistered.

I was alone.

"I told you!" Eli yelled. "I told you I'd kill everyone you love!"

I heard Terric snarl and call on magic.

Even though the storm of magic in the room tore at me, there was a stronger storm inside me.

I could keep her. I could keep her forever.

Her soul stood in front of me, a beautiful, ghostly image. She looked surprised and thoughtful but not sad.

"Please, Dessa," I whispered. "Don't go. Stay with me, love. Forever."

Eleanor stood a short distance behind her. She was shaking her head and saying no. She didn't approve of what I was about to do. I knew she wouldn't. But I couldn't let go of Dessa. I'd only just found her.

With mind and magic, I reached out for Dessa's soul.

This I could do. Bind her to me forever. I'd done it once before.

Terric yelled again.

His pain shot through me like a hammer shattering glass. I tipped my head back and yelled at the agony that was not my own.

Instinct pushed me to my feet.

Fury made me turn.

Terric stumbled backward, clutching his gut. Blood flowed there. Three bullets. Not made of metal, made of Void stones. I could feel each one digging toward his spine, tearing him apart. Tearing apart his magic and his life.

Done. I was done with this. Done losing the people I loved.

Fuck Eli.

Fuck them all.

I threw my hands out to each side. And called on Death magic.

It leaped to my command, rushing into me, consuming me. Until I was no longer just Shame. No. Until I was no longer Shame at all.

I was darkness. Power. Death incarnate. And I was going to tear apart the world.

The room rumbled, metal girders screaming as I drank life out of the walls, out of the floor, out of the cliffside, stones, forest, and soil around us.

The hospital was so near. So full of life teetering on the edge of death. I could have that. Drink down those lives.

So I did. One, twenty, forty delicious sweet deaths burst through me with carnal pleasure. I laughed. It wasn't all the people in the building—it was only a start.

Eli Collins was at the gate. The men in black were dragging him through.

That was all I could see. He was all I wanted.

So easy to destroy him. But I wanted time. An eternity to make him suffer.

I reached out for the men around him. Their hearts, their brains.

Magic whipped out, caught them, heart and brain. And squeezed.

The men screamed. I drank their lives, then consumed their bodies, flesh, muscle, and bone until there was nothing but dust left. Then I licked that up too.

But I hadn't touched Eli, who still carried his protective spell and the torture controller. Eli, the Breaker.

I strode toward him. Lashed at him with so much magic the hill shook.

Before the magic hit, before I could break that protective spell, the gate he'd been standing in slammed shut. The hole in space was gone.

Taking Eli with it. Before I could hook him, before I could crush him, before I could kill him.

Leaving nothing but the wall of the warehouse where he had just stood.

I tore at the building, tore at the building with fury. Hatred. Rage.

"Shame," Terric called to me from a far, far distance.

I wanted more to kill. I was not nearly done destroying. I wanted Eli.

Then Terric staggered to stand in front of me. Blood on his face, bullets in his chest, where his hand was clamped, the glow of yellow-white healing unable to stop the bleeding. His other hand was extended to one side, holding a spell there.

A bruise covered his temple to neck, but his blue eyes were so very, very sane.

"It's over," he said quietly, his words resonating in my blood, in my bones, in the core of me where something more than death used to dwell. "Come back to me."

He put his hand against my heart. Where my heart should be.

Unafraid. Touching me should be his death.

But he was Terric.

He was my brother.

I would be his death someday.

Today was not that day.

"Let it go," he said, still there, resonating deep inside me, coaxing out the shredded remains of me that was not death. "We will kill him. I swear. But I need you clear, Shamus. Come back to me. Please." He swallowed, and I could taste his sorrow, his fear. "God, I can't lose you."

It wasn't magic that made me let go of the death I clung to.

It was his words.

It was Terric.

I tipped my head down, fingers splayed to the floor. But I could not force myself to let go of magic.

Terric wrapped his hand around my wrist. Life magic burned strong in that grip.

I released the Death magic. It blasted into the metal

floor, melting it, pouring out of me like a rush of blood and fire from my veins.

It took time. A lot of time before I noticed the room had no magic raging through it.

It took even more time before I noticed Davy was gone. The gate he had been dragged through was closed.

We had failed to kill Eli.

We had failed to save Davy.

And Dessa. . . .

I looked over at where she had been, hoping. That she was all right. That Terric had reached her soon enough to heal her. That her spirit had lingered behind for me.

But she was gone. Not even the ghost of her remained.

I was unable to move. Unable to think. The world took on soft edges and retreated so far away I couldn't feel the floor beneath my feet, couldn't feel my body, couldn't feel my breath.

"Are you all right?" Terric asked.

"Yes," I said, the words dust in my mouth. "I am fine."

"I need you to help me get Brandy to safety. Shame, are you listening to me?"

He reached out this time and put his hand on my arm. It took me a minute, but I finally realized he was steadying himself with that grip. Leaning on me.

Because he was very, very injured.

The world came slamming back into me.

Edges, pain, heat, odors, heartbeats crashed down.

"There you are," Terric said, his voice no longer soft and close, but rough and worn as if he'd been screaming this whole time. "We need to get out of here. I can't. I can't do this without you."

His left hand pressed tightly against his stomach. Holding back the bleeding there. He was also supporting a second spell. I had seen him cast it, but I didn't know what it was.

"You're shot. Jesus, Terric, you've been shot."

He nodded. "I can keep my insides stable with magic. Think I have about half an hour left before I pass out, and that might be a problem. But hey—the hospital's right up the hill. If it's still standing."

He took a breath, a little too much rattle in it. Licked his lips. "Listen to me, Shame. Don't drift off. We need to get back to the car. All of us. I need your help with her, because I can't keep this up forever."

He turned his head. I looked that way.

The "her" was Brandy Scott, surrounded by an Illusion spell. She stood just a few feet away from us, rocking softly back and forth. She still had her IV bag but didn't seem to notice it in her hand.

"What. The. Hell?" Too much had happened. I couldn't put all the events in the right order in my head. "Jesus Christ, Terric. Did you save Brandy? Did you fucking do what Eli told you to do? You could have saved Davy. You could have killed Eli."

"I . . . wasn't in my right mind." The hurt from admitting that crossed his eyes. "All that mattered was calculating the correct outcome. Taking her was the correct outcome. I wanted to save Davy, but the magic . . . it took everything to hold it, manage it through the pain."

I knew what he was saying. The monster in him had taken over. Life magic had chosen who to save, no matter what he wanted. Heartless. Cruel. Inhuman. He had saved Brandy and not Davy. Not our friend.

"How?" I asked.

"I cast an Illusion to hide her. To replicate her where they expected her to be. They'll know she's missing in the next half hour too, if I pass out. Or when the spell fades. She's our bargaining chip, Shame. She's how we're going to find Eli. She's how we're going to kill him."

I stood there. Couldn't get my brain clear enough to know whether I should yell at him or hug him. That was a staggering amount of magical finesse and strength under any circumstance. But with Void stone bullets digging through his gut, and the rest of the magical bombardment, it had taken incomprehensible skill. I didn't know anyone in the world other than Terric who could have pulled it off.

"I can't touch her," I said flatly. "I'll kill her between one heartbeat and the next."

"All right," he said. "I'll lead her, but if I pass out . . ."

"No guarantees I'll catch her, and not hurt her. I . . . can't."

I waited as Terric said calm things to Brandy. He put his hand softly on her arm and took a step.

She followed along without question.

Chapter 30

The room looked like a goddamn war zone. I crossed it. Out the blown hatch, and down the hall. I knew the way, but Eleanor was in front of me, making it very clear which way I should go, which was probably for the best.

The warehouse was how we had left it. Except for the eight dead gunmen. They were gone. Krogher, or whoever was behind this operation, had done the work to erase their tracks.

The car was also where we left it.

There didn't appear to be any traps set on it. Which meant either they didn't care that we had escaped or they didn't think that we would.

Terric got Brandy into the backseat and eased in next to her. I stood there for a little too long, trying to decide if I could do this. If I could face living.

"Shame. Please," Terric said.

I got into the driver's seat, glanced in the rearview mirror. Terric's eyes were closed. He was pale, bloody, burned, and sickly green around the edges. His head rested on the back of the seat, but he was in a lot of pain.

"You still with me, Ter?" I asked.

"Always," he said. "Doctor might be nice, though."

I heard sirens. Fire trucks, I thought. Coming our way.

So I drove up to the main complex that I had not destroyed. Parked in the garage. Got out of the car. I didn't know how I was going to take him in there. Should I bring Brandy? She looked like she'd just escaped from the place. But I couldn't leave her out here alone either.

I opened Terric's door. "Do you still have your phone?"

"Inside coat pocket."

His voice was less than a whisper and he didn't even open his eyes. I reached in his pocket and pulled out the phone.

It still had a charge. I thumbed it on, called Dash.

"Spade," he said.

"It's Shame. I need someone here. Discreetly. And now."

"Where are you?"

"Main parking garage at OHSU. Now," I said again. "Terric's hurt."

I hung up.

"Hey," Terric said quietly.

I crouched down so I was on eye level with him. "What?"

"We don't have to go in."

"You have bullets in your gut. Void stone bullets. We go in."

"Void . . . ? No wonder if hurts like a fucker. Don't think I'm gonna . . ." He moved his lips, but no words came out. ". . . dizzy."

No. He was not going to pass out.

I reached for him. Put my hand over his hand, my fingers between his fingers, his blood welling slick and hot as he relaxed his hand, letting me keep the pressure on the wound.

"Damn, I'm tired," he sighed.

I didn't know what would happen if he passed out. I didn't know if something was already permanently damaged in him. And I couldn't heal him, couldn't sustain him like he could sustain himself.

I was death. The very thing we were trying to avoid here.

But we were tied, he and I. Maybe by more than magic.

"You're going to be fine," I said, giving him my words as he had given me his—a lifeline. "I called Dash. He sounded worried. Probably about you. You know he has a massive crush on you, right?"

Terric opened his eyes. Bloodshot, glassy. Not tracking all that well. He'd probably be shocked if he had the energy for it. "The hell."

"It's true," I said, glad something had made him stir. "You move between boyfriends so fast he hasn't even had a chance to ask you out."

"I." He blinked. "Huh."

And that was all he had time to say. Because a car pulled into a parking spot near us.

I twisted on the toe of my boot, keeping the pressure on his gut, and looked over my shoulder to see who Dash had sent.

Zayvion and Allie got out of the car, both looking un-scathed, ready to kick ass, and worried as hell.

They shouldn't be here. Shouldn't be outside the protections we'd left on their house.

But I had never in my whole damn life been so glad to see them.

"Shame," Zay said, taking in the scene with one glance. "You need to go in with Terric. I'll stay out here with her."

"Brandy," I said. "Scott."

Zay nodded. "I know."

Of course he knew. He had been a Closer, Victor's star pupil. He had probably been there when Victor Closed Eli.

I wondered if he knew Victor was dead. Gone.

"Is Terric conscious?" Allie asked.

"He is," Terric whispered.

So I helped Terric out of the car, got his arm over my shoulder. Allie made a move to put arm around him too to help him walk.

"You shouldn't," I warned. "I'm not safe."

"You're a mess," she agreed. "But I'll be fine."

I didn't have it in me to argue with her, so I just did my best to keep from touching her. I focused on getting Terric into the building and down the hall. We found an empty wheelchair and navigated him into that, and then I wheeled him to admittance, Eleanor somewhere at the edge of my vision.

I was glad Allie came along. When they asked me what had happened to us, I came up blank. What should I say? We'd been in the middle of a magical firefight and had had our asses handed to us?

Allie decided on an easier story: shooting in the park, didn't see the guy. Didn't see the car he drove off in. I didn't know how she was going to explain our other burns and contusions since I was slowly realizing a good share of the blood and pain was also mine. But she had that covered too. Car accident on the way over here.

Apparently I'd called her in shock after I'd driven the car into a ditch trying to get Terric to the hospital and she'd shown up to help me get Terric and me treated.

They bought the story, probably because she put a little of her family's natural Influence behind it to make it stick.

Terric was immediately taken away for surgery. I snarled about it. I think I told them I would be in the room with him while they cut him open whether they liked it or not. And if they harmed him I'd do unspeakable things.

Allie took care of that too.

In the form of flagging down a burly nurse who looked like he could break me with one hand.

Turned out, he was very good at giving fast and painless shots.

Turned out, those shots were even better at taking the world away.

I woke up to an annoying alarm clock beeping. Which was weird since I never used an alarm clock. Opened my eyes.

This was so not my room.

"You're in the hospital," Zayvion said from beside me.

I rolled my head, which hurt, and squinted at him. "Why am I in bed? Terric was the one who was hurt."

"You were both hurt," he said, switching off the screen he'd been working on and leaning all that muscle of his forward in the chair. "You have six fractures, soft tissue damage, and some organ bruising. He was shot."

"Where is he?"

He twisted a bit, pointed. There was another bed in the room. Terric lay in it, hooked up to tubes and wires. He was breathing evenly and on his own, though he had an oxygen tube taped below his nose. I could tell he was sleeping, and currently not in pain.

"What did the doctors say?"

"It was a . . . difficult surgery. Void stones." He shook his head. "Dr. Fisher was called in. He made it through fine. Better than the doctors expected. He's recovering faster than they expected too. You've been here for twenty-four hours. And we're calling that barren mess you left behind down the hill a bit a gas explosion. Triggered a landslide. Half the hospital's been evacuated."

But I wasn't thinking about the damage I'd done to the land. "Zay, Brandy. Terric had an Illusion on her."

"We know. We took care of everything." He put his wide hand on my arm and squeezed it, his expression sympathetic. "Dash filled us in on a few things, but we don't know what happened up there."

So I told him. It took me some time to get it all out. I couldn't seem to say Dessa's name without being swallowed by pain.

The nurse came in before I'd finished—same guy who looked like he should have gone into pro wrestling instead of health care. Turned out, his name was Carlos. He gave us both a cheerful greeting and went about checking the machines, meds, and everything else, while singing softly. Had a hell of a voice.

When he was gone, I went over the last of the events.

Zay rubbed at the back of his neck. "Fuck," he said.

"Yeah."

That was pretty much how I'd sum up the situation. Some government jackwad named Krogher had control of both Eli and Davy and a crew of magic-wielding people modified by Eli so that they were magic-holding drones that had kicked our Breaker asses.

"We know what Eli wanted," Zay said quietly, "and we know he lured you into a trap. But our information said they wanted to use Breakers, to capture them, not to kill them." He paused a second, staring at the wall like there was a window there.

"They were testing you. First the electrical barrier, then guns, fire, magic. They wanted to see what Breakers could do. They wanted to see what the modified magic users could do against you."

Zayvion is a man who can hold his own in a fight, and he's got that don't-fuck-with-me presence that makes people avoid him in dark alleys. In light alleys too, come to think of it. But he is also a very smart man.

"We played into their hands," I said. "Fuck. Me."

"I'll talk to Clyde," he said, "call a meeting to get everyone up to speed. We'll turn this to our advantage. We learned a hell of a lot about their strengths and weaknesses too. Plus, we made other . . . gains."

He meant Brandy. Eli's Soul Complement.

Zay stood, stretched like a big cat that had been cooped up in a cage too long. "I'll be back later. You should get some sleep, okay?"

"Zay?" I said.

"Mmm?"

"He could have died. He almost died."

He knew I was talking about Terric. Zay walked up to the side of my bed, paused, looked over at Terric, then back at me.

"He could have died," Zay said. "But you wouldn't let him, Shame. You're Death magic. You have a lot of say over the matters of his soul."

"Dessa died." It came out hard, flat, angry.

"Terric's your soul, Shame. Soul." Zay was quiet a minute. "You'll never lose him like that."

I stared up at him, wondering if that was true. And in his eyes was absolute confidence in me. "I think you might overestimate my abilities, Z."

He gave me half a grin. "I never have. But you, despite your big mouth, have always underestimated yourself."

"Morning," Dash said quietly from the doorway. "How are they today?"

"Awake," Zay said. "At least Shame is."

"Is he talking?" Dash asked with a lot of worry in his tone.

"Yes," Zay said, giving me a look. "Mostly bullshit."

"So, normal, is what you're saying," Dash said.

"Fuck you both," I said as Zay left and Dash settled in to take a stint of watching over us.

It was nice to be loved.

Chapter 31

I walked down the street with two coffees in my hand. Sunglasses, beanie, fingerless gloves, and heavy coat. November had arrived with ice in the wind. Not that I felt it.

I hadn't slept much in over a week since we'd fought Eli and Krogher's blank-eyed, magic-wielding drones. Every time I closed my eyes, I saw Dessa. Every silence was filled with her voice.

She wasn't haunting me. Not like Eleanor. But her absence was a shadow across my soul.

I'd fallen for her too hard to stand up again easily or quickly. She'd left me bruised on the inside. Touched me in places I didn't even know I had. Places where only pain remained.

I walked up the stairs to Terric's place. Rang the bell with my elbow. Waited.

Heard his footsteps. A little stronger than when I'd visited yesterday. And while the doctors were stunned with the rate of his recovery, I knew without magic to support him, he might not have made it through the surgery at all.

The door opened.

"Morning, Shame," he said, stepping aside to let me in.

He was dressed, showered, his hair left to fall with the male-model perfection that he achieved with annoying ease. But the dark circles under his eyes against the sallow pale of his skin gave away his injuries.

I handed him his coffee as I walked in past him with this new morning ritual I'd fallen into. "Morning. Brought you coffee."

I headed to the living room. Stopped on the threshold to it. There was a fist-sized hole in the wall by the fireplace.

"There's a fist-sized hole in the wall by the fireplace," I said.

He walked up behind me, sighed. "Jeremy stopped by last night." He moved by me, over to the couch where he preferred to sit.

I worked on reminding myself why I hadn't killed Jeremy yet.

"You still like him?" I asked, covering some of the anger with a gulp of coffee.

He pushed a couple books to one side so he could sit, and placed his coffee next to the lamp and the bottle of antibiotics and painkillers. Then he looked up at me. Gave me that stare that all of my friends seemed to use around me now. Like he was seeing a new person. Someone he wasn't quite comfortable with.

"He's funny," Terric said carefully. "We have the same taste in movies. He's good in bed."

I just raised one eyebrow. "Don't need the details."

"No," he said. "I don't like him like that anymore. He came by last night to tell me he was in trouble again. That he had promised people I would do things for them. Life magic. I told him I wasn't a currency he could bargain with. Things got heated."

"Did he hurt you?" I asked calmly. "Did he touch you?"

Terric paused, gave me that cautious look again. "Sit down, Shame. You worry too much."

I said nothing. Walked to the chair across from him, sat. "Did he?" I asked again.

"No. He yelled for a while, but then, so did I. He punched a hole in my wall." He shrugged, took a drink of his coffee.

"I'm sorry," I said.

"You never liked him."

"No, I didn't. Still." I took another drink of coffee. "Did you break it off with him?"

"No."

"Do you want me to do it for you?"

He paused. "No. I can do it. Just . . ."

When he didn't pick up that thought, I tried again. "Let me be there when you do."

"Shame . . ."

"That's all I'm asking."

He exhaled. Looked as tired as I felt. "I think it's a bad idea. But okay." Then: "Did you drive over?"

I nodded.

"Do you want to take your car or mine?" he asked.

"We're going to see him now?"

Eleanor stopped studying a photo on his wall, which was when I noticed all the art was removed and a few of Terric's pictures were back in their place. She drifted closer to me.

He frowned. "No. Allie and Zay invited us over. In an hour. I told you yesterday. And the day before that when I got the invitation."

I didn't remember him talking about it. "I can drop you off, but I'm not—"

"You're going." He pushed up off the couch, something he did with a fair amount of grace to cover the fact that it still hurt like a mother to move so quickly.

I knew, because I could feel his pain.

We were closer now, since the fight. I didn't know if that was a good or bad thing.

"We need to stop off at the store," he said as he picked up his coat from the back of the chair and pulled into it very carefully. "I promised I'd bring flowers."

It didn't make much sense to me why we were going, nor why we'd need flowers. But then, a lot of things just seemed . . . beyond me this last week or so. I could not muster the energy to give a single damn about any of it.

He handed me his keys, so I guessed I was driving his car.

Did so, stopping at a florist that Terric insisted had the best bouquets this time of year. I walked with him, my pace shortened for his.

By the time we'd bought a bunch of flowers of which I only recognized two—lilies and the pink ones—and had made it back to the car, the sky was filled with black clouds and it was raining hard enough to back up the gutters.

Terric was breathing heavily from the hurried pace he'd managed on the way back to the car.

"I'm going to be so glad when I can move again," he said. "Really move."

I think he talked about flowers or maybe it was salsa dancing while I drove to Allie and Zay's house. I listened, heard each word, but they all slipped away as quickly as they came, leaving no impression of their passage behind.

Then we were there. And we weren't the only ones. Cars lined the alley behind their house.

"What is this?" I said right in the middle of his discussion on the nasturtium, which could have been a flower or a dance move for all I knew.

"What is what?" he asked.

"Why are we here? What are we doing here?"

He paused, watched me. I was staring at the cars, trying to remember what he'd said we were going to do.

"It's just some of us getting together in honor of Victor," he said calmly. "It's not a meeting. It's not business. Just a low-key gathering of friends."

Frankly, I think it would have been easier if it were business.

"You don't remember me telling you about it, do you?"

"No."

"Let's go in." He opened the door. I got out too, and we walked through the pouring rain to the kitchen-side door.

Terric didn't knock, he just walked right into the house. "And here I thought we'd be early," he said, holding out the flowers for Allie.

"You are just in time. Both of you," she said, giving Terric a quick kiss on the cheek. "Shame, if you stand on my porch dripping any longer, I will pin you to my clothesline in the basement."

I didn't want to do this. Enter this houseful of caring faces, warmth, love. I wasn't what they thought I was. Not anymore.

But they were waiting for me. Waiting for me to come home to the living.

I dug down deep, down beneath the darkness, looking for the shreds of me that were still Shame. Held that up like a familiar mask.

"You have a laundry line?" I asked. "How eighteen hundreds of you, Beckstrom. What's next? Indoor plumbing?"

And for the first time, I realized the extent of my disconnect over the last week. Because everyone in the kitchen let out the breath they'd been holding, and chuckled.

It was not that funny of a joke.

But it was a start.

Chapter 32

The gathering was just what Terric said it would be. A bunch of us sitting around, talking, eating, drinking. Nola had outdone herself with the cooking and forbade us all to give her any more compliments about it since she was blushing so hard.

Detective Stotts was there too, being very nondetective. I appreciated that he didn't ask a lot of questions when certain details came up about Victor's death.

Like the fact that Terric and I had gone off looking for his killer on our own. Though from the look on his face, he'd have us down to the station soon to talk.

Allie and Zay sat in an oversized chair, curled up with each other, Stone sitting next to them like their own private guard gargoyle.

Allie had made sure there was a comfortable place on the couch for Terric. Dash sat at the other end, trying not to stare at Terric too much, which I thought was amusing.

The rest of the group included Clyde, a few of the Hounds, but not Sunny, who had been told the bad news of Davy being held captive. She was busy coordinating every Hound in a three-state area looking for him. The police were also looking for him and so were several members of the Authority.

As soon as I got my head clear, I'd be looking for him too.

Eventually Kevin Cooper, who was a longtime member of the Authority and a close friend of Victor's, showed up along with his wife and Allie's ex-stepmother, Violet Beckstrom-Cooper, who had been a more recent friend of Victor's.

They'd also brought baby Daniel, who was a little over three now. He ran through the room, headed straight for Stone, who tipped his ears up and caught Daniel in his arms. Then that big pile of rock wrapped his wings gently around him and snuffled at his neck, making rumble-gurgle noises.

Daniel squealed in delight.

Cody Miller was there too. It wasn't too long before he was standing in front of me. Looking down at me with ice blue eyes that looked too old and too mad.

"Cody," I said, holding my Shame mask firmly in place and wishing he would go stare at someone else.

"This will be interesting, I think," he said. "And I'm going to help you with it, Shame. When you're ready." He walked away.

I didn't know what the hell he was talking about. And didn't ask.

But it was my mum showing up that really made me want to crawl out of my skin.

Terric must have felt it, because he speared me with a look to keep me seated.

Mum looked great, really. Had pulled her red hair up in a loose knot that made her green eyes wider. She was fit, strong, wearing slacks and a sweater, and when she smiled, the lines around her eyes were more from happiness than pain.

She and Hayden had been staying at his place in Alaska for the last couple years, though they came down three or four times a year to check in on the inn, friends, and, I supposed, me.

"Maeve," Allie said. "It's so great you made it. When did you get in?"

"Last night," she said. "Well, early this morning. We got a little sleep before we headed over. I brought a couple pies. They're in the kitchen."

Allie stood, gave her a hug. "Wonderful."

Zay was standing too, shaking Hayden's only hand. Zay was a big man. But Hayden was a damn giant. Dark hair, trimmed beard, he'd put on a few pounds living with my mum's good cooking. He grinned at Zay, genuinely looking happy to be back.

"Shamus," my mum said.

"Hello, Mum," I said. "Have a seat?"

"Why don't you help me with the pie?"

"I can—" Nola started.

"No," Maeve said. "It will give us a chance to catch up."

I glanced over at Terric. Wanting him to make an excuse so I didn't have to talk to my mum. He just raised his eyebrows and gave me a mind-your-mother look.

Bastard.

"Shamus," Mum called from halfway across the room. "Come with me. Now."

"Better just do it, son," Hayden said in his rolling baritone. "She is not a woman who likes to be kept waiting."

He heaved his bulk down into a chair gratefully and got busy catching up with Kevin and Zayvion.

No one was even looking at me.

I wiped my fingers over the top of my lip, clearing the sweat there. I did not want to talk to my mother about what had happened. Didn't want her to see what I had become.

I didn't remember walking into the kitchen. One minute I was sitting; then I was in the doorway, unable to make my feet go any farther.

"Do you know where she keeps the serving knife?" She wasn't looking at me.

I tried and couldn't find a way to say anything.

"Shamus? Son?" She looked over at me.

Something changed in her as she studied me. She put

down the plates and crossed the room. Then tugged me in, away from the door, away from where anyone would see me.

And wrapped her arms around me.

I squeezed my eyes shut. Her familiar perfume and warmth surrounded me, comfort I had known all my life. It had been years and more since she'd held me like a frightened, broken child.

But I didn't pull away.

"Ah, my love," she said gently. "Someday your heart will mend. Someday the pain will become a part of your memories instead of your every living moment."

I realized she wasn't talking about me grieving Victor's death, though I was certainly doing that too. She was talking about Dessa.

"Wh-who told you?" I asked around the pain in my chest.

"About Dessa? Zayvion."

I pulled back from her embrace, wiped at my face to keep the tears from falling. "He's such a mother hen."

She tipped her head and smiled gently. "He told me you killed, Shamus. With magic."

"You know what I am," I said softly. "What I've become." I pulled my shoulders back, wishing I could put more space between us, but not wanting to leave her comfort.

"Yes," she said, touching my cheek with her fingers. "You are my son. A man I am proud of."

"No. Not . . . now. I am death."

There it was, the truth. She studied me, then pushed my bangs out of my eyes. "Well, then, death needs a haircut."

"Mum!" It was such a motherly thing to say.

"It is the truth," she said. "And much truer than the nonsense you're telling me. You carry Death magic, Shamus. But you are still a man in control of it. And you have handled that heavy responsibility better than ninety-nine percent of the people in this world."

"By killing people?"

"Death comes to us all, my child."

I didn't know what to say to that. It seemed like she was grossly oversimplifying the situation. But then, Mum had seen my dad killed, her friends possessed, destroyed. She'd raised a Death magic user, and had already seen what hellish thing I could become, back when I'd ripped Jingo Jingo to bloody shreds.

She was, I realized, very comfortable with the workings, and reality, of death. No wonder she was nonchalant about it.

"True," I said.

"Good." She drew her fingers along my cheek one last time and looked at me as if sizing me up for a new suit. "Now help me with the pie."

I did that, and mostly managed to handle myself in the rest of the day's conversations.

The other Soul Complements had cleared out of town. So had the Overseer, though Clyde had kept him informed on everything that was happening.

We knew who we were up against: Krogher. We didn't know his position in the government yet, nor what his plan, his final plan was for the modified magic users he had controlled.

They had taken Davy, one of our own. And we all agreed that would not stand.

And Eli . . .

Well, no one talked to me about Eli. They didn't have to. I had my own plans for him.

Because I had a promise to keep.

In the meantime, I tried to smile at the appropriate moments, nodded like I was listening, and dug deep to be the Shame they all needed me to be, not the monster they refused to believe I had become.

When Terric said he was tired, I got up, said my goodbyes to my mum and Hayden, then Allie and Zay.

Allie suddenly went domestic on us—this baby business

made her weird—and insisted she had to wrap up leftovers for us to take. I left her and Terric to their girl talk in the kitchen.

I needed silence. Rain. Darkness. I needed away from my mother, and all of my friends.

Zay walked with me out to the car.

The rain had let up, but everything was wet, cold. I lit a cigarette and leaned against the hood of Terric's car.

"How you holding up?" I asked him.

Yes, he looked surprised.

"Victor was a father to you, Zay. I know that," I said softly.

Zay nodded. There was a stiffness to his shoulders, like there was a pain he hadn't quite figured out how to breathe around.

Welcome to the club.

"I'm dealing," he said. He came over and leaned on the hood next to me.

I offered him a cigarette.

He took it. Now it was my turn to look surprised.

"Everything really okay with Allie?" I asked as I flicked my thumb over my lighter for him.

He sucked heat into the cigarette, held the smoke for a moment, exhaled with a nod. "We think so. Dr. Fisher is keeping a very close eye on her. Nothing seems out of the ordinary, not even after we broke magic."

"Good," I said, meaning it. "That's good."

We smoked for a while staring up at the house, the trees beyond it, listening to the river rushing by behind us.

"Did you love her?" he finally asked.

"I barely knew her." It had become my stock answer. A parry Terric and Dash and most other people who had asked me that very same question would not engage with.

Zay wasn't most people.

"So you loved her."

"I thought I did."

"Did she love you back?"

"I don't know. Maybe." Then, since he waited me out, "Yes."

"You're going to hunt him down, aren't you, Shame?"

I inhaled smoke, exhaled. We both knew who he was talking about: Eli.

"Yes," I said. "You won't want to get in my way, Zay."

He shook his head. "Wouldn't dream of it. But if I can be there to hold him down while you pull his lungs out of his chest, I will be."

Terric said no one knew me better than him. I thought he might be wrong about that. Zay understood. Understood pain. Understood love. Understood vengeance. Understood me.

"Call me if you need me," he went on. "Any day, anytime. And I'll be at your side." The door opened and Zay finished his cig, tossing it to the ground.

"Thanks," I said. "But you need to take care of Allie. Of both of them. Of your family."

"I take care of all my family, Shame," he said, pushing off the car and walking away with that alpha swagger of his. "My family includes you."

Terric was walking down the steps. Allie waited for Zay just inside the doorway, the light of their home framing her.

"Zay," Terric said.

"Don't let him forget we hate the bastard too," Zay said.

Terric gave me a quizzical look as Zay passed him.

I just shrugged. "Fatherhood makes him sentimental."

I heard Zayvion chuckle as he walked up the steps.

Chapter 33

I took Terric to the office because he wanted to talk to Clyde. For a guy who had been fired, he sure spent a lot of his time at his not-job. Dash promised to take him home.

We'd gotten a hit on that syringe Victor had been holding. Turns out there was only one pharmaceutical company that could manufacture the mix of chemicals it contained. And we had hopes that since Eli was using it, we could track the purchase to Eli, or the people keeping him.

More importantly, that we could track it back to where Davy was being held.

I hit a bar at noon, left before one. Ordered a beer, but only took a couple drinks off it. Eleanor sat across the table from me, still and patient, but I was restless. So I walked the streets for a while, wandering. Aimless. Then a while turned into hours, and I found myself at Victor's place.

I stood there, hands in my pockets, staring at his front door. Imagined him opening it and telling me to come in. Walked up, pulled the key I'd had made years ago without him knowing about it, unlocked the door, and stepped in.

The late-afternoon light fell through windows. His home looked like his home, felt like his home. I walked through every room except the bedroom. Couldn't bring myself to going back in there.

Thought about stealing one of his books, or knickknacks,

or something to keep as my own before whoever was in charge of his estate vultured down on the place.

Found myself at his desk in the corner of the living room. Ran my fingers over the closed rolltop. Opened it. There were two files neatly stacked there, a fountain pen—so very Victor—and his computer.

I was surprised the police hadn't confiscated all this. Figured Clyde had put the kibosh on that. After all, we didn't need an investigation. We knew who killed Victor and why. The carvings on his body had been verified as Eli's signature by several Hounds.

I flipped open the folder. Lost my breath at the picture. Blue eyes that knew you were watching her, looking at her. Red hair, pale skin. And that smile.

Dessa.

I waited until the knife stopped twisting in my heart. Blinked until the text on the page made English again.

He'd had a file on Dessa? Why hadn't he given it to me? I took it, looked at the file beneath it. That one was on her on her brother, Thomas. I took that too.

Then I closed his desk. Eleanor hovered near a bookshelf.

"Do you want something?" I asked.

She turned to me, startled I'd spoken to her. Wow, how out of it had I been?

"Pick one. We can bring it back tomorrow."

She nodded, chose a slim poetry volume. I pulled it out and pocketed it. And hell, since I was in a burglarizing mood, I picked up a small frame on his fireplace mantel. It was a picture of Zay, Terric, and me, back when we were lads, laughing, and a much younger Victor laughing right along with us.

Rare, that.

Mine now.

I left, locked the door behind me. Was not about to walk all the way home, so I caught the MAX to the bar where I'd left my car, removed the parking ticket from under my windshield wiper, threw it into the gutter, then drove home.

It was dark by the time I rolled up to the inn, but the place was open, busy. I tried to remember what day of the week it was. No luck. Went inside, ordered whatever the special of the day was, took it up to my room.

The ferret was sleeping in the little hammock strung at the top of the cage. I'd tried to take him down to the animal shelter, but at the last minute found myself setting up his cage in my room, doing research on what to feed him, and getting Eleanor's promise she'd help me keep an eye on him. He was staying with me for now.

I spent some time eating and reading over the files. When I was done with that, I showered, then brought the book Eleanor had wanted to bed and turned pages for her while I smoked and thought.

I had set the picture of Victor, Terric, Zay, and me on the table by my bed and noticed something wasn't right about the back of it.

"Hold on a sec," I said to Eleanor. I placed the book facedown on the bed about where Eleanor's legs would be if she were solid, and picked up the picture, tipping it to better see the back. There was something glued between the cardboard backing and the photo. I removed the backing. Three microthin flash drives no bigger than my thumbnail were stuck to the cardboard. Written on each was a name: Terric, Zayvion, and Shamus.

I pried mine free and took a closer look. Victor's handwriting. I pushed out of bed, went into the other room, and pulled my laptop out from underneath the bills I hadn't been paying. Took that to the couch and plugged in the flash drive.

There were two files on the drive. One labeled LIFE, the other labeled DEATH.

I hesitated, then clicked on LIFE.

The file was full of photos and some videos. I clicked on

a slide show view, and lost an hour to pictures of me, my friends, my family, my schoolmates, a few from before my father had died, but most from after. Victor had created a virtual scrapbook of my life, of all the good times, and sure, some of the bad we'd been through together.

When the pictures were done, I wiped my palms over my eyes to clear the tears there. I was going to miss him for the rest of my life.

I closed out that file and clicked on the other labeled DEATH.

I figured it would be friends and family who had passed away, or maybe a will or last message he wanted me to have.

Instead it was filled with photos from surveillance cameras, mug shots, and files. Each photo had a file behind it containing a name, discipline of magic, last-known address and occupation, a list of crimes, and a Closer's name. The documents were written by Victor, and other high-ranking members of the Authority, and they were all marked CLASSIFIED.

These were people who had raped, murdered, stolen, blackmailed, and betrayed. These were people who had used magic to do those things and more.

It was a hit list.

And Victor had left it in my hands.

I sat back and thought about that for a bit. What did he expect me to do with it?

I pushed out of the chair and retrieved the flash drives marked for Terric and Zayvion. Terric's contained one file, filled with pictures, a lot like mine, and several reviews of the art that I guess Terric had once displayed at a gallery. The second file contained some information about some of the greatest Life magic users in the history of the Authority, and an exhaustive history on Soul Complements.

Zay's file was filled with photos, a few that contained a man and woman that might have been his parents. He'd been fostered out pretty young, and as far as I knew, he'd never looked for his birth parents. I'd honestly assumed they were dead, and realistically, they might be.

The other file looked like Victor's diary from the day he joined the Authority. Read like a history book of who's who and what was what.

Neither of them had received a hit list. That he'd given only to me.

Because he knew I would do something about it.

A knock on the door made me jump.

"Mr. Flynn?" the night clerk said. "Call for you. A Mr. Conley."

"I'll be right down." I pocketed the flash drives and turned off my laptop. Pulled on a T-shirt and boots and walked down to the office.

I picked up the phone. "Are you all right?" I asked.

"You said you wanted to be here." Terric sounded tight, but calm. "I'm at my house. Jeremy's on the way."

"You invited him over?"

"No. But he's coming anyway."

I scrubbed my fingertips across my scalp, my new Void stone rings warming as they dampened the magic surging through me.

"Shame? You don't—"

"I'll be there."

I walked out into the cold without my coat, without a weapon. But when I pulled up to Terric's place, I dug through my glove box, then checked under the seat. Found my knife, flicked it open, then walked up to Terric's door.

Tried the latch. It was open. Walked in.

Heard voices in the living room.

Terric stood by the fireplace, his arms crossed over his chest. Jeremy paced opposite Terric, which put his back to me.

Terric didn't look up as I walked in. He didn't have to. He'd know if I were within a mile of him now.

". . . it him?" Jeremy was saying. "Whatever he's been saying, it's a lie."

"This has nothing to do with Shame," Terric said calmly. "This has everything to do with you and me, Jeremy. With how you've been using me."

"Bullshit."

I flipped the knife up into my fingers. Terric's eyes flicked over to me, along with a very clear "no stabbing" look.

"Do you want to get your stuff now, or do you want me to mail it to you?" Terric asked.

"Damn it, Terric. Why? We have something. I thought it was important to you. I thought *I* was important to you."

"You lied to me, Jeremy. You've always lied to me."

"You just want me out of the way so you can fuck that shithead Flynn." He had stopped pacing the edge of the room and was advancing on Terric.

Terric's shoulders tightened and his eyes narrowed. "You and I are over. Leave."

"Like hell I'm leaving. You need me."

"No," Terric said.

"He told you to go," I said. "I'd suggest you listen to him."

Jeremy stopped as if an icy wind had suddenly frozen him in his tracks. He turned to glare at me. "You called him?" he accused Terric. "You called this waste of breath to save you?"

"I don't need saving," Terric said. Then, a little quieter, "Not from you."

"Fuck you, Flynn. I know you did this. What did you tell him? What lies did you tell him about me?"

He crossed the room in five hard strides, and I waited, shaking my head. "You really should have left."

"Shame," Terric warned.

"I should have killed you!" Jeremy swung for my face. Stupid move. I ducked that and buried the knife up to the hilt between a couple ribs, then yanked it out and stepped out of his reach.

He staggered back, but had enough anger, and whatever

other substance in him, that one wound wasn't going to shut him down.

I'd gotten what I wanted, though: his blood.

He stuck his hand in his pocket, reaching for a gun.

"Stop!" Terric ordered, and a concussion of magic wreaked havoc on the air pressure and my eardrums.

Jeremy was motionless, tightly frozen from knee to neck in the paralyzing Hold spell Terric had cast. "This is out of control," he said. "Crazy. Both of you. I won't stand here and watch you kill each other."

"I didn't come here to kill him," I said. "I can do that anywhere, anytime I want. And when I do"—I looked Jeremy in the eye and smiled—"I will make sure there are no witnesses."

"Shame, you are not helping."

I dragged my fingers across the blade, catching up Jeremy's blood, which he was still leaking quite quickly. Before Terric could start arguing with me, I nicked my finger. With his blood and my blood combined, I drew a Truth spell.

The strong scent of cherries filled the room, the unmistakable mark of Blood magic being used.

Jeremy's eyes widened as the Truth spell spun out from our joined blood, locking us into the binding of Truth, shaped by my hand and will.

"Do you love Terric?" I asked.

"Shit." Terric exhaled.

Jeremy was sweating. Thing is, a Truth spell is as strong as the user's will, and I was a very determined man.

"No," he snarled through gritted teeth.

"Do you care for Terric?"

"No."

"Were you planning on using him and his magic for customized drugs for the Black Crane?"

He was shaking now, his face gone purple-red. "Yes."

"Did you ever care for him?"

"Enough," Terric said. "Shame, break it. It's enough."

I broke the Truth spell. It fell around his feet like loose ropes that soaked into the carpet and were gone.

"You piece of shit," Jeremy said.

"I'm done," Terric said. "Done with this. If you don't walk out that door right now, Jeremy, I'll call the police and have you forcibly removed."

"Police?" I said. "We don't need the police for him."

"Yes," Terric said, "we do. It is too late at night to be dragging a corpse out back and burying it. Which," he said as he finally moved away from the fireplace and walked over to stand next to me, "is what will happen if you stay."

"You think he's going to kill me?" Jeremy said.

"He wouldn't have to," Terric said.

Jeremy finally seemed to hear him. He switched tactics. "Come on, Terric," he said, pouring on the nice and sweet. "I lost my temper. You know how I get sometimes. I just love you so much I go crazy. If you fix my side, I wouldn't be hurting so bad. You and I could talk this out. Privately."

"Good-bye, Jeremy."

Jeremy looked at Terric, then turned his gaze to me. He was a little pale from blood loss, but he must have finally realized he had lost this battle.

"You know what, Conley?" he said. "You were a lousy lay."

Then he turned and walked out of the house, his hand clamped tight over the knife wound. Even managed to slam the door behind him.

We stood there for a minute, me staring at the door, Terric looking at the new bloodstains on the carpet.

"What a mess," he whispered.

"Want me to follow him?" I offered. "Make sure he gets to the ER or something?"

"No. Just. Would you stay? For a while?"

I finally looked over at him. It was like someone had smothered the fire in him. He looked exhausted, pale, and when he spoke, his voice was too soft.

"Just an hour?" he asked.

"I've got time," I said. "Maybe you should get some sleep."

"Yeah," he said, "you're right. You're probably right." He walked carefully around the blood and got halfway to his bedroom door before he stopped and came back into the living room. "I'm going to have to burn some memories before I sleep in there again." He folded down on the couch, facing the back of it.

The blanket he'd used on me was folded on a chair in the corner of the room. I picked it up and placed it over Terric, who, as far as I could tell, had already escaped into unconsciousness.

I did not sleep. Spent too much time thinking about relationships and love and how nobody got out of either unscathed.

After a couple hours, I got up, checked to make sure he was still asleep, then went outside, locking the door behind me. I checked to see if my phone was in my car. It was. I dialed Sunny.

She picked up on the first ring.

"This is Sunny."

"I need a Hound and a favor."

She sighed. "I've had zero sleep in the last two days."

"I know," I said. "How are the leads on the syringe working out?" She had been looking into finding Davy just as much as Clyde and the Authority. Maybe more.

"Nothing solid," she said. "What favor?"

"I want a Hound to find Jeremy Wilson and tell me where he is right now."

"That's a job, not a favor."

"I'll pay. The favor is I don't want anyone knowing I sent them to do this. I want the Hound to contact you, and I want you to tell me when they find him."

"Who's Jeremy Wilson to you, Shame?"

"He hurt Terric."

Out of all the people I knew, Sunny understood running against the rules, running on instinct, and doing everything possible to keep someone you loved safe. She was a Blood magic user. There was no getting out of that discipline without dealing with the darker side of the world.

"We'll forget we ever talked about this, I assume?" she asked.

"Yes."

"And you'll make finding Davy a top priority. Pay me a favor when I want it?"

"Deal."

"I'll call you back." She hung up.

I lit a cigarette and waited. It was cold out, but the sky had cleared, letting stars pierce holes in the heaven.

Took fifteen minutes, flat. Yes, the Hounds are that good.

The phone rang. "Shame."

"He's at a bar down on Third Street. You owe me."

"I owe you." I hung up.

Didn't take me long to drive down there. I found his Jeep and parked nearby, waiting for the bar to close. Got out of the car and smoked a cigarette, pacing the shadows of the building by his Jeep. Eleanor was with me. She hadn't tried to talk me out of this.

I wasn't going to let her.

Jeremy walked out of the bar. Maybe drunk, maybe not. Didn't matter. He strode across the street toward his car.

Didn't see me in the shadows.

When he reached the sidewalk, I sent magic to snake out, dark, silent. It wrapped around his heart, shot up his spine to his brain, paralyzing. His fear washed through me.

Good.

I pushed him into the shadows, forcing his feet to move to my command.

And then I released the hold on the hunger inside me. It consumed. Tore apart his body, snapped his bones, boiled his blood, and burned flesh with fire darker than shadows.

A second passed. Two.

No time to scream. No time to beg.

I drank until there was nothing but ashes falling to the ground.

I drank until his ghost hovered in front of me, frightened, confused.

I threw my cigarette into his ashes and crushed it under my boot. Stared straight into his dead eyes. "Welcome to hell."

He opened his mouth to scream, but I couldn't hear him as he faded away.

With a flick of my fingers, even his ashes were gone.

Problem solved.

Chapter 34

I went back to the inn. Found myself sitting at my desk, staring at Eleanor's angel statue.

There was one more death I needed to deal with.

Just before dawn I texted Terric and Zay. Told them I was going out of town to clear my head for a day or two. Mountains or coast, I hadn't decided yet. And if they needed to reach me, I'd have my phone on.

Then I stuffed the phone in my sock drawer, made sure the clerk would look after the ferret, and picked up Eleanor's statue since she made several gestures that she wanted me to do so.

I left.

Headed to Seattle. Lost myself to the drive and my thoughts.

Stopped for coffee once and bought a red rose from a roadside vender. Took me some time to get where I wanted to be. Finally found what I was looking for.

A graveyard where Thomas had a plot. Where Dessa had a headstone since there wasn't anything left of her to be buried.

I had still been in the hospital, sitting in Terric's room waiting for him to prove he was going to live through another day, when they'd done this.

She'd told me she had family. But the Hounds who had spied on the burial said only a minister had been there.

It make me think that was why her brother's death hit her so hard. He was all the real family she had had.

I rolled slowly through the graveyard, parked, and got out of the car. Wandered to the southwest corner. I had forgotten to bring the files with me, but I had a decent memory of the layout.

Eleanor always seemed a little wary in graveyards, though I never understood what she feared. Because, seriously, she was a ghost.

I finally found the grave. A headstone was already placed and simply read DESSA OLIVIA LEEDS, along with the dates of her birth and death.

Eleanor touched my hand, where I held the statue of death with angel wings. Then she pointed at the grave.

"Are you sure?" I whispered.

She touched my heart and nodded. So I placed the statue there, Death's weary head lowered, the scythe useless in his hands, as his wings stretched out for a sky he would never know.

Eleanor stood beside me, her arm cold around my waist.

I didn't know how long I stood there and stared. Maybe an hour. Maybe more. It rained, stopped, and rained again.

Eventually I became aware of a heartbeat that wasn't mine. Blinked and looked around. Terric stood just a short ways off. Noticed me trying to decide if he was a mirage or not. Came walking over.

Bastard had followed me up to Seattle. I wondered how many Hounds he'd had tracking me. Probably dozens. I hadn't been very observant lately.

But at least he didn't say anything, just came closer until he was beside me, looking down at her grave with me.

Everything around me was dead. The grass over her grave, the trees and bushes.

I remembered the rose in my hand, the only flower I'd

ever bought for her. I knelt, but once my knees sank into that cold, wet, dead grass, my hands started shaking. I suddenly realized it was pouring rain, merciless. And very, very cold.

I placed the rose where I thought her heart might be. But the flower had been in my care for too long. It was withered. Dead.

Just like everything I touched.

I wiped rain off my face. "I can't even keep a flower alive," I said. "Everything dies. Anyone I . . . care for is going to die. I'll make them die."

"I'm still alive," he said.

"Not forever. Not for long," I said.

"Maybe."

That admission, that it was a very real possibility for me to kill everything I laid a finger on, for me to kill him, did more for me than any attempt at comfort.

"You can still make choices," he said. "Choose to be a man."

"No," I said, the memories of drawing on Death magic, the memories of surrendering to its vengeful need filling me with a shudder of pleasure. I wanted that. The pleasure. The oblivion. "I don't think so. Not anymore."

Terric knelt in the rain next to me. Reached out and placed his fingers on the dead rose. Bent his head, like a man grieving, or praying.

I felt magic draw to him like a mist over the grass. Felt it filling the words he spoke.

The rose trembled, then washed with life again, velvet red petals, deep green stem and leaves, and roots that reached out and dug deep into the rich earth. Planting there in the newly green grass. Growing. Alive.

The bushes around us stirred as if caught in a wind, and new sprouts pushed up from the ground.

He pulled his hand back and caught me with his gaze. He was still human. Still Terric.

"We do this together," he said. "You're not alone, Shame. And, yes, we might not be men anymore," he said. "But that doesn't mean we have to be monsters. Our fate is still our own."

"Do you believe that?" I asked quietly.

"I'm trying to," he said. "Because it's all that keeps the madness away."

He stood. Held his hand down for me. I took his hand and pulled myself up onto my feet.

"Did it hurt?" I asked.

"What?"

"Admitting you're not perfect."

He scowled at me. "Shut up, Shame."

I smiled and shut up because, well, most of the time, Terric was my friend. Sometimes he was more than that. A brother.

He hung his arm over my shoulder.

We walked away from the grave. Walked away from the death we'd never be able to leave behind us, walked away from the past we could not escape.

I guessed we had decided to face the madness together, or die trying. Sounded good to me. Might even be fun.

I wrapped my arm around his shoulder too and he leaned his head against mine.

It wasn't much of a beginning.

But it was ours.

Epilogue

I had waited. Long enough that no one was following me to make sure I wasn't doing something wrong. Something destructive.

But now it was night, and darkness was exactly what I needed.

It wasn't hard to walk into the facility. I could cast Sleep without using so much magic Terric would know what I was doing.

So I did.

I could cast Scatter to interfere with the cameras.

So I did.

And then I walked through the high-security facility, counted the doors until I reached the one I wanted.

Locks are easy to pick.

Then I was inside. With her.

Brandy lay in her bed, eyes open, but not seeing this world. They kept her heavily medicated. They said it helped her remain calm.

And they needed her calm, because they needed her alive.

So we could bargain with Eli. So we could bargain with his masters.

But there was no bargaining with monsters. I should know. I was one.

I stepped over to her bed, my boots loud in the hollowness of the room.

She didn't see me. Didn't hear me.

That was fine. She wasn't who I had come here for. She was simply a way to get what I wanted.

And I wanted revenge.

I sat on the bed next to her, studied her face, her hair, her lips. She could have been pretty, if there was any sense of humanity looking out from her eyes.

But she was a shell, cored out and emptied by madness many long years ago.

I understood madness too.

I brushed her hair away from her face, then leaned so I was directly in her line of vision even though she didn't see me.

I put my hand over her mouth.

Death can be painful, or . . . sweet. I didn't need her death, not just yet. But I wanted her pain.

I reached out with Death magic, letting it cover her. I drank down an ounce of her life.

Brandy's body arched and she screamed.

"Do you feel that, Eli?" I asked, keeping eye contact with Brandy as she trembled. "Do you feel her agony?" I drank more of her life down, Death magic twisting her nerves, catching fire beneath her skin.

The monster inside me liked it.

I liked it too.

"Do you understand what I can do to her?

"Yes, of course you know," I said as fear set her heart beating faster. But this was not her fear; she was too far gone to know fear.

This was Eli's fear.

And that was the fear I wanted.

His sudden cold knowledge of what I could do to the other half of his soul shone through her empty eyes.

"You know what I can do to her, because you killed just

like this. Killed Joshua, killed Dessa, killed Victor. You killed people I loved. With no shred of remorse.

"But you did not think about who you left behind, injured."

I drew the magic away from her, and her body went limp. She was sweating hard from the absence of pain. But her eyes were still open. And they were filled with Eli's terror. With his knowledge, his attention.

"You have left me injured, Eli. A very bad mistake. I am the wrong man to hurt."

I let the monster forward, which was not hard, as it took up so much room in me now. I smiled as his terror turned to panic. Desperation.

"I am going to destroy you, Collins. I am going to make you writhe. Consider this your invitation to start running. Away from me, or toward me, it doesn't matter. Because I am going to make the remainder of your life agony." I smiled at the pleasure I would gain from that. "And then I will make you beg for death until I am tired of hearing you scream."

I placed my palm flat over Brandy's eyes.

Death comes for us all. Sometimes when we least expect it. Sometimes at our bidding.

I sent pain twisting through her again, knowing Eli felt it. Knowing how it tormented him. Knowing how helpless it made him feel. Then pulled my hand away so he could see me. So he could see exactly what I was doing.

I was surprised to see a second awareness in her eyes. For just a moment, it was Brandy looking at me. *Please,* she mouthed. *Kill me.*

I hesitated. She was begging for mercy. For relief from the tortured life she had been living. But I hadn't come here to show her mercy. Only to make Eli hurt.

Then Brandy was gone, and it was Eli looking through her eyes again. Panicked. Begging me not to kill her.

"You know where to find me," I said to him.

I placed my fingers against her chest and drew a glyph there. I stared into Eli's pleading eyes, wanting to see his pain.

Magic filled the invisible line I traced, crushing her heart. Tighter. Tighter.

Until there was no beat left. Until she was cold and dead. Until even Eli's hating eyes were gone.

Brandy's ghost stepped free of her body and threw her arms wide, head tipped back, smiling as if she had taken her first deep breath in many, many years.

I waited for her to see me. Judge me.

She touched the side of my cheek with cold, cold fingers. *Thank you*, she mouthed.

Then she was gone.

Revenge, mercy. Tonight they were the same.

I left the room. Left the building. Strode away into the darkness of night.

I flicked my fingers and canceled the Scatter spell and Sleep spell. No one would know I had been there. No one would see the glyph I had drawn. No one would remember.

Only Eli.

Everything was just how it had been only moments before.

Except everything had changed.

This was my war now.

Read on for an exciting excerpt from the
next Broken Magic novel by Devon Monk,

STONE COLD

Coming in April 2014 from Roc.

The door behind Eleanor opened, letting in the March wind, a little rain, and the man I had come here to kill.

The man was a few years older than the photo I'd seen, black hair shot through with gray, white face gone pudgy behind square bifocals. His name was Stuart, and he carried himself like someone who was irritated with his own skin: stiff movements, coat clutched closed with one hand over his stomach, a scowl hammered into his face.

Not what I'd expected a murderer to look like, but then killers came in all shapes and sizes.

He glanced around the diner. Didn't notice me. I didn't stand out in a diner that hadn't passed a health inspection in a decade. And although it would be fun, I didn't wear a sign that said "Shame Flynn. Death magic user, loyal friend, troublemaker, and the last guy you'd want to meet in a dark alley if you'd done something naughty."

He didn't notice Eleanor either, but that was understandable.

Eleanor was a ghost.

She sat across from me, long blond hair flowing with an underwater grace as she moved. Soft features, sweet smile, she was beautiful when alive, and still beautiful when dead. She noticed me noticing him. Tipped her head a bit, narrowed her eyes. "What?" she mouthed.

I couldn't actually hear her because—hello—she was dead. But I'd learned how to read her lips over the last couple years since she'd been stuck with me.

"Nothing," I lied.

She, as usual, didn't believe me.

She scanned the diner, saw the guy take the booth just off to our right, looked back at me. Shook her head.

"Not listening." I stared at my breakfast so I didn't have to see her, poked at the waffles. My fork bounced off the hardened whipped cream.

She shifted through the table like someone forging a stream and floated in front of me, half of her body stuck in the table.

"Jesus. Do you stay up at night thinking of ways to creep me out?"

"No killing," she mouthed. Or maybe it was "No kidding." I didn't say I was *good* at reading lips.

"Sorry. I made a promise. I never go back on my word."

She rolled her eyes.

"Fine. Lately," I amended. "I never go back on my word lately. And that man"—I lowered my voice because, seriously, I did not need people looking at the crazy guy who was yelling at his waffles—"has done unspeakable things to people. With magic. For years. He'll continue doing unspeakable things, with or without magic. He should have been dead a long, long time ago. I'm just taking care of business."

"Terric." She pointed at my heart, which wasn't beating all that well today. A problem I intended to take care of as soon as the ghost got off her high horse so I could kill the guy.

I lifted my knife. "We'll leave Terric out of this. Plus, he's avoiding me, not the other way around."

Not that I could ever get away from him. We were Soul Complements: Death magic, Life magic. Ever since the magical apocalypse a few years ago had made magic a gentle force, it was just us Soul Complements who could break magic and make it do the old, horrifying things.

Well, and the old, wonderful things too, but that wasn't really my department.

I was the guy who handled the darker side of things.

I'd been a damn fine Death magic user back in the day. And now? Well, now I *was* death.

While it had its perks, it didn't come without a hell of a price. I carried death, but if I didn't let it loose, didn't let the Death magic in me consume and kill, then it simply consumed and killed me.

I was never going to be an old man. Hell, I'd be lucky to live another year.

But I was damn sure going to live long enough to take out some people before my time was up. For one, that killer in the booth across from me, and for two, the psychopath Eli Collins, whom I still hadn't tracked down.

A cold slap of pain hit my shoulder and forced my attention back on my surroundings. The grease and noise of the diner fell back around me again, the heat of the air, the cool of the wind coming through the door. Eleanor had her hand up, ready to slap me again to get my attention. She didn't need to.

Another man stood just inside the door, scanning the diner.

Terric Conley was a bit taller than me, dressed better than me, and had blue eyes and good looks angels would fistfight for. His hair had been white since the day I'd tried to kill him and he'd killed me back. Altogether, he was the sort of man women fell for. Unfortunately for women, he was the sort of man who fell for men.

He was also a hell of a Life magic user, and, when we admitted such things, my friend, my partner, and my Soul Complement.

He annoyed the hell out of me.

He spotted me and started my way.

"Shame." He stopped by the table, glanced down at the untouched plate of waffles, strawberries, and whipped cream in front of me. A frown wrinkled his forehead. "Breakfast? Why are you eating breakfast here? Now?"

"What's wrong with here and now?"

"For one"—he glanced back across the diner, then at me—"this place is a dump. And you promised you'd go with me to a meeting today."

"*I* promised?"

"Okay, fine. I promised. Allie and Zayvion want you there. Us there," he corrected.

"Busy. Sorry." I sawed my way through the waffle with a wholly inadequate knife, then shoveled waffle and whipped cream into my mouth. Chewed. And chewed. And kept on chewing.

Tough didn't describe this waffle. Kevlar had more give.

"Just . . . come, Shame," he said. "Allie wants you there."

Ever since Allie had gotten pregnant, she was all sorts of unpredictable in the emotional department. I found it endlessly amusing. Terric had taken to tiptoeing around her, and Zayvion had threatened to tie my spine in knots if I riled her up. Again.

I spit the waffle into the napkin. "If I don't?"

Terric raised an eyebrow. "You need me to threaten you?"

"Might be amusing."

"I can promise you it would not be."

Had some fire behind those words. Man could deal out the hurt when he wanted to. Apparently, me not going would make him want to.

"What the hell kind of meeting is it, anyway? You and I are no longer employed by the Authority."

"We aren't the Head of the Authority. Doesn't mean we aren't a part of it."

The killer at the booth had finished his coffee and small bowl of oatmeal. He tossed cash on the table, pushed up on his feet, and, glancing at me, walked out the door.

Damn it. He knew I was tailing him.

I could kill him from here. Without even standing up. Without even laying a finger on him. I could reach out, let the Death magic inside me pop his heart, blow his brain, drain his lungs.

Just the thought of it made my heart stutter, then pause, for several beats too many.

Eleanor put one hand over her mouth and watched me with wide eyes.

It was weird to see her worried that I might die. I was, after all, the bloke who had killed her and then hogtied her to my mortal coil.

I took a couple even breaths and focused on not panicking. Terric was saying something, but I wasn't listening.

Finally, the vise of death released my heart and blood pushed a hot flood under my skin. Painful and heady.

". . . drunk?" Terric was asking.

"Yes." I had no idea what he was talking about. Hoped it was an offer.

I checked the diner again. Killer guy was long gone. Well, there went two weeks of hunting down the drain.

"Cover that for me, will you?" I asked. "I left my cash in my other coat." I stood, wavered a little from the head rush.

Eleanor nodded and then pointed at Terric. "Do it," she mouthed.

Terric sighed and threw a bill on the table.

I gave Eleanor a back-off look. "Is it about Davy?" I asked as we made our way to the door.

He glanced out at the rain and flipped his collar before taking the plunge to the sidewalk. "Weren't you listening? Never mind. Don't answer that. No. Nothing new there. We still haven't found him."

"So what is it about?"

We strode down to his car double-parked down a block or so. I could feel every heartbeat like a finger tapping a rhythm against my spine. Forty-seven lives in the office building, twelve in the coffee shop, eight in the bank.

He didn't say anything until we had ducked into the car.

"How's Eleanor?" He couldn't see her unless he drew on magic to do so, but lately he made it a point to ask about her. Which she loved.

Women.

She smiled, then made pointy motions toward him again.

"Still dead," I said.

She slapped me in the back of the head. Ow. Brain freeze.

"Also, angry."

"What about?"

"Who can tell?"

He glanced at me. Didn't buy my dismissal. I didn't care. Time to change the subject. "You going to tell me what's really wrong?"

He started the engine. "What do you mean?"

"You didn't get in until five this morning. You paced until six. It's what, nine o'clock?"

"Ten thirty."

"You've had three hours of sleep. Not like you to miss your beauty sleep."

His eyes narrowed just a bit. Uncomfortable subject. I should probably just leave it alone.

So of course, I didn't.

"Come on, now, Ter. Got a new guy working your night shift?"

He stopped at a light and watched the pedestrians without umbrellas take their time crossing the street.

"I've been . . . keeping busy. Looking into things."

"Do these things have names? Social Security numbers?"

He shook his head.

Huh. I don't know why, but I'd never thought of Terric as the kind of guy to keep secrets. He was too by-the-book, too goody-goody.

"Look at you," I said. "All mysterious and secretifying. Please tell me it's both a deep and shamefully dark secret you're hiding."

"I'm not hiding anything. Nothing you need to know."

"Those are not quite the same thing, are they?"

I glanced away and caught the blur of light from the corner of my eye. Light that surrounded him. Huh. Maybe it wasn't a new boyfriend on his mind.

Maybe it was magic.

ALSO AVAILABLE
FROM
Devon Monk

IN THE NATIONAL BESTSELLING ALLIE BECKSTROM SERIES

Magic to the Bone
Magic in the Blood
Magic in the Shadows
Magic on the Storm
Magic at the Gate
Magic on the Hunt
Magic on the Line
Magic without Mercy
Magic for a Price

"Fiendishly original and a stay-up-all-night read."
—#1 *New York Times* bestselling author
Patricia Briggs

Available wherever books are sold or at
penguin.com

facebook.com/acerocbooks